Inhuman

Eric Leland

Copyright © 2021 Eric Leland

All rights reserved.

ISBN: 978-1-7355063-0-2

For my father – U.S. Army 1967-1973

ACKNOWLEDGMENTS

A very special thank-you to Chantelle Aimée Osman, who edited this book; and who gave Jaran her magic.

And to my friends who watched this book grow—Yami Alvarez; Eric Arcand; David Astorga III; Pat Black; Brianna Canadine; Mandy Chase; Molly Cox; Joshua Dallaire; Dan Eckroth; Chuck Fridline; Jack Fuehring; Mike Fullerton; Wes Hall; Chris Heiniger; Sarah Haskins; Nathanial Howard; Mark-Anthony Jarboe; Matt Kopenhaver; Chelsey La Valley; Jadi Le; Terry Little; Jamera Massop; Trent McDonald; Jesse Moore; Ian Mitchell; Jason Nicholas; Michael Pardoe; Mike Parker; Sean Rafferty; Jennifer Starr; Gwynne Tavel; Vicky Walter; Craig Yuen—I hope you like it.

PROLOGUE

Screams in the dark. The sharp *spat* of a suppressed pistol shot echoed off the pit's curved walls.

Conway gripped his flashlight hard and peered into the dark. Hard to see.

"What's your status?" he shouted down to Sergeant Sutton.

Nothing.

Silence.

From behind came the sound of struggle. Shouts.

Conway shined his light back down the passageway to where his soldiers held the Mongol man and woman. The man—arms tied behind his back—jumped and jerked, trying to break free from the hard grasp of a big noncommissioned officer. Conway's Vietnamese interpreter stood in front of the small group and the Mongol man shouted in the interpreter's face.

"What the fuck is he saying?" Conway called.

"Keeps saying the same thing, Captain!" The interpreter yelled, straining to be heard over the shouting. "'Cut the rope!' He keeps saying 'Cut the rope!'"

Conway turned back to the pit and tapped Jones, his CIA handler, on the shoulder. "Why do you think he keeps

1

saying that?"

Jones shook his head. "No idea."

Conway rubbed the sweat from his face and again called down into the pit to his man. Again, no answer.

More shouting from behind. The woman's voice now joining the din.

With a hard calm Jones said, "Shut those people up, Captain."

Conway yelled over his shoulder. "Shut those motherfuckers up!"

The interpreter said something in Vietnamese, but they kept shouting. Now that Conway was paying attention, he caught the phrase that the Mongols kept saying: *Cat day leo*. When the interpreter couldn't quiet them, the slap echoed in the cave's passage, followed by the wet sucking groan of someone losing their wind. They were quiet after that.

Far below in the pit, the tiny star that was Sergeant Sutton's flashlight moved.

Thank God.

"Sergeant!" Conway called. "What's your status?"

The flashlight pointed up at Conway. Blinding. "Oh, Captain," Sutton yelled. "I haven't felt this good in years."

Conway and Jones looked at each other. An odd thing to say.

Into the pit, Conway called, "Glad to hear it. What the hell happened down there?"

"Just got a little frightened. You're not thinking of cutting that rope, are you?"

"Not particularly."

"Good!" Sutton called. "Mind if I come up now?"

Jones cut Conway off before he could respond. "What do you see down there?"

Sergeant Sutton's light shined down at the corpse they had discovered. "Just this poor fellow here. Those Mongol dogs didn't treat him well."

Jones scratched his face and called down, "There must be something else. This is the place. Look around some more."

Sutton's flashlight swept around the pit and lit up the gouged walls. "There's nothing else down here. May I come up now?"

Conway watched Jones think for a long beat. At last, he stood and turned away and waved a frustrated hand at Conway.

"Come on up, Sergeant." Conway called.

"Thank you, sir!"

Something about Sutton's voice sounded strange. Not scared. Not anxious to get out of that hole. He sounded…

Excited?

The rope pulled taught as Sergeant Sutton grabbed hold and started the long climb up out of the dark. As if they sensed the movement, the Mongols started screaming.

Conway didn't even have to ask the interpreter what they were saying. They had repeated the phrase about a thousand times in the hour that Recon Team Florida had been in that cave.

Turning from the pit, Conway went down the passageway toward the exit. To where the Mongol man and woman waited with the rest of Florida.

As he approached, their screams quieted. Instead of screaming for him to cut the rope, now they were pleading.

Conway shined his light on them.

"Cat day leo," they repeated. Eyes squinted and tear-filled. They were *begging*.

Footsteps echoed from behind. Sergeant Sutton. The Mongols looked behind Conway. In the light their eyes went wide. Their mouths dropped open.

"Sergeant," Conway said over his shoulder. "Do you have any idea why these people kept telling me to cut that rope?"

From behind came a tiny echoing *click*. Distinctly the sound of a 1911's safety being switched off.

With the cave walls and the suppressor so close to Conway's ear, the explosion of gas was a hurricane roar.

3

Pain popped in Conway's ears and he slapped his palms over them.

The Mongol man's head jerked and he dropped limp on the ground. The Recon man who had been holding him staggered back, clutching his chest, blood blossoming through his dark green uniform where his heart should be. His lips moved. But over the ringing and fuzz in Conway's ears, he couldn't hear what the man said. The Recon man slumped to the ground.

Conway jumped as Sergeant Sutton fired a second shot. The Mongol woman's head snapped back and she fell.

The soldier holding her jumped away in surprise and yelled something.

Conway spun. Shaking with surprise and fear and confusion, he stared at Sergeant Sutton. The afternoon light outside the cave illuminated Sutton's perverted smile. His eyes…

His eyes…

"Oh, God," Conway mumbled.

You'll know him when you see his eyes. That's what Jones had said in his mission briefing.

When the ring in Conway's ears quieted, the sound that replaced it was Sutton's soft laughter. "Thanks for not cutting that rope." Still laughing, he pointed the pistol and shot Jones in the face.

Conway didn't understand. Legs wobbling, he fell to his knees, hands still cupped over his ears.

Shouts from behind. One of his men. Conway couldn't even remember the names of the men he commanded. Only Sutton.

"Put the fucking gun down!" A voice commanded. "Put it down *now!*"

But Sutton pointed his 1911 and fired—

—and the commands ceased.

Conway stared down the suppressor's dark hole. Sutton's finger flexed on the trigger, but no sound came. Sutton turned the 1911 to examine it. The slide was locked to the rear. He looked at Conway and frowned. "Would you mind telling me how this works?"

It took Conway about two heartbeats to react. Yanking his rifle slung across his back, he aimed at Sutton. "On…" Conway stammered. "On your knees. Now!"

Slide still to the rear, Sutton pointed the empty pistol at Conway's face and pulled the trigger. When nothing happened, Sutton threw it down with a frustrated grunt. He looked down at himself, patting the various pockets of his LCE until his hand fell on the handle of the combat knife sheathed on his thick pistol belt. "Oh," Sutton said. "I prefer these anyway." He drew it, metal scraping. Shining sharp in the ambient light.

"Drop it," Conway pleaded. "Goddamnit!"

Sutton rolled his eyes. "If you're going to shoot, get it over with." He waved the blade. "Otherwise…"

"On your knees!"

"No." Sutton lunged.

Conway fired. And fired and fired. And when Sutton hit the ground Conway kept firing until his rifle went silent.

Over the iron sights, Conway watched Sergeant Sutton take his last wet, bloody breath. Watched those white eyes watching him.

And when those white eyes closed, the light in Conway's periphery dimmed with them. And darkened. Until all was black. Turning toward the exit, trying to find the light, Conway suddenly felt very dizzy. He leaned up against the wall.

He could feel the warmth of the light on his face. He walked toward it. He had to get out. But something grabbed hold of him from the inside and shoved him to the ground. He couldn't move.

Then, from somewhere—from everywhere—a voice said, *You should have cut that rope.*

CHAPTER ONE

Jaran pressed through the tall grass in the dark morning. Grandmother, following close behind along the river path, had never woken her this early for lessons. Mother and Father had not even been awake.

Starting their ascent up the hill to the training circle, Jaran asked why they couldn't have slept a bit longer. Grandmother said nothing. Only the sound of her labored breath hissing as they climbed.

"Grandmother?"

She answered with a hard shove to Jaran's back. Jaran went sprawling in the grass still wet with the early morning dew.

"Up!" Grandmother shouted.

But for the moment, Jaran couldn't move. The anger in Grandmother's voice paralyzed her.

"Move, girl."

Frightened and confused, Jaran tried to get her feet beneath her, but kept slipping in the grass. Grandmother slapped the back of Jaran's head. Jaran kicked, scrambled for something to grab. Grandmother's hands came again. Slapping and stinging.

Jaran found her feet and ran, sprinting up the hill. The steep incline burning deep in her legs. At the top, panting, she tried to figure out why her elder was so angry. But Grandmother was fast.

Fingers like stone dug into the back of Jaran's neck. She yelped and Grandmother forced her down to her knees.

"Grandmother, what have I done?"

"Look," Grandmother shouted. "Look at it!"

In the dark, Grandmother's outstretched hand was silhouetted against the soft, far away glow of the village lamps.

"Grandmother, I—"

"What do you *see*?"

Jaran's voice trembled. "Our village."

"And who lives there?"

"Our people—"

Grandmother squeezed. The blood in Jaran's neck thumped against hard fingertips. Grandmother shrieked, "What is your responsibility to your people?" She shook Jaran with every word. Every syllable. "All these years, what have I taught you?"

Frightened tears welled in Jaran's eyes. "To care for them."

A hard slap caught Jaran on the ear. "Have I *ever* taught you to harm them?"

Jaran went cold all over.

Grandmother *knew*.

How could she possibly know?

With one final shove, Grandmother released her. Standing before Jaran now, her elder looked like a demon. Some living darkness come to punish her. Two tiny flames of village light reflected in her eyes.

"Please," Jaran whispered. "Grandmother, *please* let me explain."

But Grandmother drew her arm out to the side. The sound of long, thin leather slithered in the dark. Thumped in the grass.

The dozens of raised and purple scars on Jaran's back knew that sound. Her muscles tensed. Her skin stung with phantom pain.

"Grandmother, no! Please! That boy! He was so mean to me!"

"Robe," Grandmother said. Voice flat. Like hate.

Jaran crawled to her through the damp grass. Clutched the hem of Grandmother's robes. Scrunched the coarse fabric tight in her fists. "Grand—" Jaran said. "—mother." Breath coming so quick. "Plee—*ease*! Please!"

Grandmother slapped her. Jaw going *pop*, Jaran fell in the grass.

"Robe," Grandmother said, voice filled with disgust.

Sobbing on the ground, hands held up to Grandmother as if she were a God, Jaran whimpered, "I just, I just wanted him to stop, to stop teasing..." but the rest of what she wanted to say was lost in tears.

"He won't tease you for a long time. I've seen the boy. His mother summoned me in the night, terrified her son was possessed. The boy can no longer speak." Grandmother squatted down. Her whispering breath hot on Jaran's face. As if a fire burned in her throat. "Robe. Now. Or I will tear it from you."

"He said we lie about our magic." Tears flowed hot down Jaran's cheek. Down into her ear. "He said Mother and Father aren't protecting us from anything. He said they go up the mountain all day to sleep because they're too lazy to work."

"Robe."

"I wanted to show him!" Jaran shoved herself to her knees. "I wanted him to know what we protect our people from!"

"You protect them from *nothing!*" Grandmother's hand rose. "You've shown me that I must protect them from *you*."

Shutting her eyes, Jaran put up her hands against

another slap.

It didn't come.

Jaran peaked between her fingers.

Grandmother's outline in the lamp light shuddered. "I walked in that boy's dreams." Beneath the anger there was something else in her voice. Something sad. "Did you think I would not recognize the terrible things I helped you create?"

Jaran could say nothing. The shame of being caught and the anticipation of the whip held her mouth shut.

"Those dreams cut deeper than that sword you carry, Granddaughter. They are *weapons*. You saw what we did to those soldiers. You drove some of those soldiers mad with the dreams you crafted. Some of them…" Grandmother shook her head. "You would use them against a *child?*"

Shameful tears welled in Jaran's eyes.

"We are sworn to protect those people." Grandmother looked down toward the village. "*All* people if it comes to that." She breathed in deep. "You nearly killed that boy."

The profound disappointment in Grandmother's voice stung Jaran's heart. Jaran was so angry and scared and confused. But what Grandmother said next lit some kind of angry fire in Jaran's chest. And those tears evaporated.

"What has happened to you, Jaran?"

What has happened to me*?*

The anger came so fast.

Jaran knew exactly what had happened.

She had seen.

Those nightmares she had made to force those soldiers from her home, Jaran had not pulled them from her own mind. She had used those soldiers' own memories. And in those memories she had discovered what Grandmother had kept hidden from Jaran for her entire life.

She had seen war. But not just war. There was some kind of dark evil she could not understand.

With its position on the river so close to China, the soldiers had been going to use Jaran's village to store weapons for their fighters in the south. The rice produced by the village was barely enough to support itself, but the soldiers demanded rice be sent south as well.

To not arouse suspicion, Mother and Father had agreed to do as the soldiers said. Like other outsiders, Mother and Father had hoped the soldiers would sense the evil hanging over the village and simply leave. But they didn't. When the soldiers became curious about the rock spire on the far side of the river, that was the day Mother and Father knew they must act quickly.

Mother and Father had crafted for the soldiers dreams of sadness. Their dreamers spent their waking hours wallowing in an inexplicable bereavement.

The dreams Jaran crafted had been just as powerful. But to craft her dreams she used this new horror she had discovered in their memories.

The soldiers carried faces of the dead in their memories. Jaran had used every one.

She had woven for a man a nightmare of his own memories so vivid he had woken half his comrades with his screams. Sometime in the afternoon he was found mumbling by the village docks. Clutching his rifle to his chest as if it were the only thing tethering him to his sanity. And when his superiors yelled at him to get back to work, when they tried to take his rifle, he had put the rifle in his mouth and pulled the trigger.

Night after night, and one by one, Jaran's family entered those soldiers' dreams. And night after night Jaran had to see new memories. New horrors. Forced to see what men could do to other men. To women. Children.

Every morning, two more soldiers had awoken with an affliction of terrible sadness. One woke screaming.

Unease had spread fast amongst the soldiers. But that unease turned to terror when men started killing themselves. The soldiers began to fear the sun going down. They'd begun to fear going to sleep. They feared they would be next.

The sight of his men descending into madness had frightened the commander. A villager overheard his instructions to his subordinates. The commander was a superstitious man and he believed the dreams were bad omens. After nearly two weeks of occupation in Jaran's village, and the loss of ten men, the commander had ordered his troops to pack up their equipment and leave Jaran's village.

It had been a success. Jaran's family had honored their First Oath and guarded their secret. But Jaran had paid a price for that success. The price was knowledge.

Searching through memories to craft those nightmares, the horror of war had clung to her. The things those soldiers had done to people, the things they laughed about, it all disgusted her.

Soon the foulness of those memories polluted her own dreams. Even her meditations, once so peaceful, had been perverted by the things she had seen.

Before the soldiers had come, Jaran's entire knowledge of the world had come from Grandmother's stories. The taking of the *Three Oaths*. The bravery of her ancestors as they hunted the evil Jaran's family now guarded. The old promise to stand between that evil and protect what was good in the world.

What was good...

Grandmother's stories never mentioned war.

"Jaran?" Grandmother said. "Are you listening? That boy—"

"That boy is a monster," Jaran muttered. The words felt alien leaving her mouth. As if that flame of hatred burning inside had stolen her voice and made it its own. "That boy deserves to suffer."

"*Deserves?*" Grandmother gasped. "Our duty to our people is to care for them. Guide them. Protect them from evil. We are not the ones who decide punishment."

"How can we protect them from evil if they are capable of that same evil? You lied to me, Grandmother. In your stories all men were good. What good man goes to war? What good man burns children? What good man rapes women?"

"You cannot compare the actions of men at war to boys teasing you."

"If that boy grows up to be just like those soldiers, how is he worthy of our protection?"

"Is your father not a good man? He and your mother dedicate their lives to keeping evil hidden from the world. *True* evil. If you are to join them in their duty you must learn to see the good in the world.

"Those soldiers have perverted your understanding of good and evil. If you cannot unlearn this, then you will fail to keep your oath. And if you fail, you are useless to this world."

"I will not sacrifice my life to save the souls of evil men. I would rather drag them up that mountain and feed their souls to Erlik—"

Grandmother's hand came down and cracked so hard on Jaran's face she temporarily lost her vision.

Wobbling on her knees, beyond the daze and sparkling lights, some part of her knew that this pain was not the sting of a hand. This pain was a deep, pulsing ache in her jaw. Warmth bubbled over Jaran's tongue. In the dim village light, the shine of the thick leather whip handle jutted from Grandmother's hand. Jaran tried to speak but the sound came out wrong.

"You will never speak such vileness in my presence," Grandmother said. "If your mother would have borne more children I would abandon you this very instant. But you are your mother's only child. I will not abandon my duty to our people by refusing to train you. I will make you into a shaman who cares for her people. You have been blinded by the things you saw in those dreams. I will open your eyes."

Grandmother stalked around behind Jaran. The whip slithering in the grass. In the pre-dawn chill, Jaran's bare skin prickled with the anxious anticipation of pain.

"Embrace this," Grandmother said. As she had said countless times before. As she would certainly say again before Jaran's training was complete. "May it prepare you for eternal suffering if you must honor your Third Oath."

Jaran gritted her teeth. Squeezing her eyes shut. In the black came the sound of Grandmother's whip jumping from the grass. Jaran grunted. Tried to block out the pain. Tried to focus her rage on the evil she hated so much. But the whip came again. And again. And soon she could focus on nothing but her screams.

Later, when it was done, Jaran's breath came in wet spasmodic snorts. Coolness leaked from the fiery gashes and dribbled down her back. The robes bunched around her waist soaked up her blood.

Head limp, chin buried in her chest she was stunned in the numb exhaustion after a whipping. Pain did funny things to time. She wasn't sure if the sun had just risen, or had been up for hours. Either way, her village now sat hazy and golden beneath the morning light spilling down the river valley.

Grandmother, her face shiny with sweat, pulled a cloth along her whip's length. A kind of slop collected on the cloth and when Grandmother pulled it free of the whip, brownish chunks of blood and skin plopped in the grass.

Another tremor of breath came and Jaran winced as the little slashes stretched their tiny mouths.

Grandmother rolled up her whip, tucked it away in her sack and knelt before Jaran. Rough fingers, filthy with dried and flaking blood brushed aside Jaran's sweat-soaked hair. "Breathe," Grandmother said.

Jaran was surprised she had forgotten the breathing exercise. In moments of extreme stress or pain, breathing the way Grandmother had taught her, that long and deliberate *In... In... Out...* repetition, it always seemed to help.

Jaran breathed.

And after a time, the spasms stopped.

"Good." Grandmother looked into Jaran's eyes. "Embrace comforting memories."

Another thing she had forgotten in her agony.

Jaran breathed. She didn't try to conjure the memories. Forcing them to come was not the way. She let the river of her mind flow. Her mind would know what to show her. Comforting memories would present themselves. That was the way.

In time, they came. But none of them were her memories. Not truly. These she had found in someone else's dreams. Memories of food. Memories of friends laughing.

How odd. That despite her hate for those Vietnamese soldiers who had tried to take her village, she would somehow find comfort in *these* memories. The memories of a soldier. But she supposed this particular soldier was different. In a way, he was like Jaran.

He just wanted to live.

And when Jaran had secretly walked his dreams, she believed him. And the more she walked, the more she pitied him.

For his love of cooking, the villagers called him the Soup Soldier. He had come months before the other soldiers, but for different reasons.

He had deserted the Vietnamese Army. Very thin and missing an arm below the elbow. Someone from the village had taken a boat across the river to fetch him when he had stumbled out of that great and dark jungle.

When Mother and Father had arrived home that evening he had fallen face-down before them and begged for sanctuary.

"I just want to live," the Soup Soldier had said to them. "I can work the rice paddies. I can mend fishing nets. I can cook." He had looked around at the villagers gathered there. "I can protect these people. Please just let me stay." On the dusty path between the huts, he had stripped himself of his rifle and his possessions and shoved them all toward Mother and Father, begging the whole time for refuge. The binoculars presently stowed in Jaran's satchel, they had been his. Gifted to Jaran from Mother.

Mother and Father had been reluctant at first, but he was given a place in the village. That was that. And the days had gone on.

Jaran had later overheard the things Father had said about the man. That he seemed a coward for deserting his Army. But the first time Jaran had walked in his dreams, the things she saw there made her question her own fortitude. Made her wonder if she would join her parents or run away like some of her ancestors.

The Soup Soldier's memories and dreams, they weren't like those other soldiers'. The Soup Soldier hated war. Hated killing. Maybe it was her pity for the man that kept her returning to his dreams.

The Soup Soldier had lost his arm someplace far to the South.

Bomb.

That was the word. But she understood the word through feelings rather than language. It came as a terror of bright flashes. As air forced from his lungs. As confusion. As loss.

He had been walking on a trail with other soldiers. That terror had come from the sky and fell down all around and consumed his friends in noise and light.

After losing his arm, the Soup Solider was taken in a big truck to a small Army camp far to the north to heal. There he made more friends. In his dreams Jaran had seen smiling faces over steaming bowls of meaty soup he had prepared for them.

But his Army didn't need cooks. They needed soldiers and workers.

When his superiors felt he was well enough, and because he could no longer fight without an arm, they ordered the Soup Soldier to return south to work as a repair man on that same trail. Repairing damage from other bombs.

The fear he had felt upon hearing that haunted Jaran's own dreams. He was afraid to go back to that place where he had seen so many people die. So many friends.

He just wanted to live.

The night before he was supposed to be taken south, he had fled into the jungle.

After many days of walking and getting turned around in the jungle, he had come to a giant crescent-shaped wall of stone. It rose high and spread wide. As if the earth itself were reaching out to him with a warm and welcoming embrace. In his memories of the wall, Jaran felt a peace so absolute it blocked out any notions of pain or fear or suffering.

Water spilled down from the rock face into a fresh pool beneath. The Soup Soldier had drunk until he could continue on. A few days later, he had found Jaran's village.

Since the Vietnamese soldiers had left, Jaran's mind had been a chaos of horror and hate and other feelings she didn't have words for. Feelings that made her chest tight and her eyes sting.

After meditation, when lying down to sleep at night, she thought of that crescent wall and its pool. Longed to feel more than the secondhand experience from the Soup Soldier's memory and dream. She wanted to immerse herself in that wall's quiet solitude.

She had spoken once to the Soup Soldier about the place. Disguising her questions as small talk so as to not give out that she had intruded into his sleeping mind.

Lying to the Soup Soldier, she had said that a wanderer passing through the village had mentioned a big wall in the jungle. Said it was one of the most peaceful places he ever saw.

A soft smile had appeared in the Soup Soldier's eyes. He told her that he had seen such a place. That it was as peaceful as the other traveler had claimed.

"I'd like to go there someday," Jaran had said to him.

"Walk about three days that way and you'll find it." The Soup Soldier had pointed across the river. "It's hard to miss."

Of all travelers and wanderers to pass through Jaran's village, she was glad the Soup Soldier had wanted to stay.

Jaran often wondered if he would eventually sense the evil hanging over their village. Most outsiders did. They usually departed of their own will soon after arriving.

But the Soup Soldier stayed. And the months had gone on. He became another friendly face in the village. Making people happy with his soup.

Making Jaran happy.

"Let's get you dressed," Grandmother said, pulling Jaran from her thoughts.

It felt as though only two heartbeats had passed since Grandmother had reminded her to breathe. Yes. Pain did funny things to time. Grandmother tugged Jaran's robes up, flaring out the back to avoid the gashes.

But the fabric dragged across a yawning wound. Jaran hissed and slapped Grandmother's hand away. She regretted it instantly, worrying Grandmother might mistake her reaction as more insolence. Meekly Jaran said, "Forgive me, Grandmother. It hurts more this time."

Whatever fury Jaran was expecting did not come. There was only a kind understanding on Grandmother's face. She let go of the robes and they fell back down around Jaran's waist. She cupped Jaran's face. Thumbs caressing Jaran's cheeks. "We'll stay a while longer, then."

Grandmother sat in the grass beside her and looked down into the valley. Down toward the village. She nodded to herself for a while. "I was harsh on you," she said after a while. "I must ask your forgiveness."

Grandmother had never apologized for whipping her before. Or burning her. Or any other of the little tortures she inflicted. Pain, Grandmother had told her a long time ago, was her family's ultimate teacher. Only through pain could they shed their mortal skin. Taken aback, Jaran said, "I will heal."

"You mistake me, Granddaughter. You deserved every lick of the whip. I meant my words were harsh." Gazing out across the river, Grandmother's eyes scaled the mountain. Climbed to the spire jutting black into the sun. "What I said was said out of anger. And fear. I want to believe that what you said was also said out of anger."

Jaran said nothing.

"My time with you is nearing its end, Granddaughter. You were right. I have hidden things about the world from you. These new beliefs you have. This anger you carry. I am partly to blame. If not for this war I would take you to other places to see. Give you a chance to help others. Show you how good people really can be. I don't believe I can help you rediscover the goodness of the world with the time I have left. But perhaps I can correct your path in my dream life."

Jaran felt the weight of what Grandmother was suggesting and already a guilty feeling descended on her. "Mother already missed the opportunity to take Grandfather's spirt. I can't deny her yours, too."

"Your mother is already a powerful shaman. You still need my guidance. If she believes my spirit will make you stronger, I'm sure she would make that sacrifice. I will ask your mother to let my spirit pass into your dreams. If you'll allow me."

Jaran was honored. Still, Mother had been deeply saddened when she learned she could not carry Grandfather on in her dreams. He had been on a walk when his heart had given out. There had been no time for him to sing the song. His daughter, his only living blood, had not been prepared. Her only solace was in knowing she could still take Grandmother's spirit into her dreams when it was Grandmother's time.

"Your mother and I will be reunited when she passes her spirit into your dreams." Grandmother smiled sadly.

"Besides, your mother has your father to keep her company. I'm sure she won't mind."

They sat in the rising sun's warmth and smiled.

After a time, Jaran asked, "Will the boy recover?"

Grandmother pulled the little glass vial from the neck of her robes. Held it swinging on its leather cord. The black liquid sloshed inside.

"As you bathe I will see to the boy. It will take some nights of soothing to undo.... Well. I believe I can help him." Grandmother dropped the vial back into her robes. A breeze came. "Do you smell something cooking?"

Now that Grandmother mentioned it, she did.

Grandmother stood. "After your bath we should call on the Soup Soldier and see what he has for us. Are you ready?"

Jaran nodded. Grandmother helped her dress and together they made their way slowly down the hill to the dirt path beside the river. Jaran walked beside Grandmother. Her robe sticking in the gashes and to the drying blood on her back. Despite her efforts not to move her upper body too much, here and there the fabric tugged free and stung. The morning sun sat atop the jungle-covered mountains. Far away, beyond the tall and wild grass, soft hazy sunlight set the thatched roofs of her village aglow. Home.

The breeze was stronger by the river. It bent the tall grass and reeds in the water. The black boulders in the river peeked out from their hiding places amidst the browns and greens.

The rich aroma came again. Breathing it in, Jaran's mouth watered and her empty stomach rumbled. She picked out the different scents. Fresh noodles. Meat and tendon. A thick brown broth of hours-boiled oxtail.

The Soup Soldier truly was a divine gift. What a waste for his army to use him for war. He could have brought so much happiness to people with his cooking.

Jaran was glad he could do that here.

When those other soldiers had come he was frightened they might shoot him for deserting. Father had prepared a lie to tell the commander, but none of the soldiers even acknowledged the Soup Soldier's existence.

After a time, the Soup Soldier fell into the village's rhythm. Rising in the mornings, he had taken to watching as Mother and Father took their small boat across the river to the far shore. Stood by the docks and watched as they returned in the evenings. He must have noticed that *only* Mother and Father ever traveled to the far shore. But he never asked where they went after they left the boat. Or why.

But on an evening some months later, curiosity finally overcame him. Jaran had gone to stand beside him as he looked across the river to the dock hidden in the overgrowth.

"Will you join them one day?" the Soup Soldier had asked her.

"One day."

He nodded as if he understood everything. He stared across the river. "When I came here, I told your parents I could protect the village. Somehow, I feel I can't protect anyone from what's over there. Not even myself."

He was right. But the First Oath forbade her to speak on it.

She had tried to sound brave when she said, "That is very humble of you to say." But she had failed to hide the fear in her voice

When she thought about the far side of the river there was always fear in her. Suppressed only by the complete faith she had in her parents to protect her. To protect the village. The faith that Grandmother would teach Jaran to one day join her parents. One day take their place. To make Jaran as strong as Mother and Father.

She had stood with the Soup Soldier in the fading evening light and they watched Mother and Father emerge from the jungle and motor across the wide river to the village.

"It's not human," the Soup Soldier had said. "Is it?"

Jaran had said nothing for a time. Besides the First Oath keeping them silent, Mother and Father believed the villagers were not prepared to carry the burden of knowledge. Jaran agreed. She knew what was hidden over there. Most times she wished she didn't. The Soup Soldier had seen enough horror in his life to be burdened with that knowledge. Even some of Jaran's ancestors—powerful shamans all—Grandmother had told her stories of how after they had gained that knowledge, they simply walked off into the jungle and never returned. Some lost their minds. Some even took their own lives, ashamed they did not have the courage to keep the Three Oaths.

When Jaran was old enough to begin her training as a shaman, Grandmother talked with her about her family's purpose in this world. Running away or the taking of one's own life might seem cowardly to some. But for years, Jaran's purpose was the focus of her daily meditations. For the horror they might have to face, she discovered she could hold no grudge against any of her ancestors.

"It is no man," Jaran had said to the Soup Soldier. "But I would say to you that if there was ever a time when men came to our village to do us harm, I would be honored to have you protecting us."

"Well..." The Soup Soldier had rubbed absently at the stump of his lost arm. The day's last light welling in his eyes. "Then until the day you need me, shaman girl, I will keep your belly full with soup."

On the trail beside Grandmother, Jaran looked across the river. It had been nine years since Jaran set foot on that far shore. Grandfather had been alive then and he had summoned her to the mountaintop on the day she began her lessons with Grandmother.

Motoring Jaran across the river in a boat, Grandmother had said, "You must take your lessons seriously, child. Your first lesson is to see what you may face at the end of your training."

I'll get her, Shaman....

Nine years. But Jaran still remembered the fear that seeped from that jungle shadow and wormed into her mind. It followed her as Grandmother led her up the foot-worn paths and rocky switchbacks. Followed her to the mountaintop. Into the cave. Down into darkness.

I'll get her....

"Grab hold, child," Grandfather had said. "Hold tight to me."

Mother and Father had looked on as Grandfather took her down. In Mother's wide eyes there was a look Jaran had never seen, but one that Jaran would come to know well.

Father lowered them down hand-over-hand on the old rope. Grandfather's glass vial hung around his neck. The same kind Jaran received that day. The dark, thick liquid inside shining in his lantern's flame.

At the bottom, Jaran had clung to Grandfather's robes as he lifted the lantern to the dark. And how that dark had hated the light. Pressed back against it. The light halted at the shackled man's feet, as if the flame feared to illuminate what lay chained in the darkness.

Two white eyes, dull and glowing, had lifted in the dark with the sound of chains pulling tight. Then the voice had come. Terrifyingly sweet. The outline of a shackled hand lifted, beckoned her closer.

"A new child, shaman?" The chained man had said. "Oh! Another sweet *girl*." His voice warm sugar melting on Jaran's tongue. Oh, how stupid she was to feel safe. "Come to me, child."

What a stupid, stupid girl she had been.

The *urge* to go to him. *Stupid*.

Grandfather's strong hand snatched her shoulder before she could take her first step toward the sweet man.

"No?" The chained man cooed. "You're not *afraid* are you? Don't be. I knew your mother and father when they were young. And your grandfather and grandmother, too."

Vaguely Jaran remembered being confused. The chained man must have been very old to have known her grandparents as children.

She would learn.

"I have sweet children of my own," the chained man said. "Nine daughters and nine sons." In his voice she could hear his pout. "Oh, but I haven't seen them in so long. Maybe you can meet them. Would you like to meet my children, little one?"

Jaran flushed. Hating her younger self for nodding. For wanting anything from him.

"Wonderful." Those two white eyes narrowed, betraying something sinister beneath his happy voice. "You'll meet them. Soon. I promise…"

Jaran arched her back, letting the pain of torn flesh dull the memory. Even now, after all that time he still made her feel so small. And he would never go away. He was still up there. Chained in that pit. Never eating. Never drinking. Never dying.

Just waiting. Waiting for a shaman to make a mistake.

The chained man had spoken to Grandfather then, but he had kept his eyes locked on Jaran's. So sweetly he had said, "I think I'll get this one, shaman. Yes. I'll get her."

"I doubt it, Khan." But even Grandfather's voice, the voice that was always so strong, it had cracked in the chained man's presence.

"Doubt?"

The chained man's next words came from nowhere. Sweet whispers from the dark. *Would you like to see what's waiting for you?*

Before Jaran had even known what she was doing, she had answered in her mind.

Yes.

Her first mistake.

The chained man took her. With those eyes he took her.

Later, Grandmother told her she had never left Grandfather's side. That she really didn't go to the place the chained man took her. That it was all in her head. Told her that what she had seen wasn't real. What she had felt. Her family circled around her, they made her say it wasn't real.

Her tiny face in Grandmother's rough hands. "Look at me, girl!" Patting her face, Grandmother told her, "Say it, Jaran!" Pleading, "You must say it's not real!"

Maybe they thought if Jaran said it enough times she would believe it. Believe she had just imagined it. Believe it was just a dream that someone else had put in her head.

"It's not real!" Jaran had cried out. That was the first time she had said it. She had said it a million times quietly to herself over the years. It didn't matter how many times she said it. It was always real for her.

Always.

There by the river, tears behind Jaran's eyes pounded to be let out. She would not let them fall.

Always so real.

Those white eyes had grown and swallowed her. And she had fallen. White turned deep black. Black flame burning beneath a cauldron as big as the world. A cauldron so big it hurt her mind to remember. Things couldn't be that big.

She fell into screams. Black and sucking. Boiling.

From boiling tar came nine pairs of hands. They grabbed her. Nine long, unloving things inside her. Tearing. Ripping. On and on.

Somehow she was on her back at the top of the pit in the cave. Vomiting everywhere. Clutching her little belly. Screaming for Mother to make the hurt stop.

The grating, howling laughter from the darkness. "All nine of my boys!" He cackled. "That's what she got!" The chained man screamed to her, "Come back, girl! Come be my whore in Hell!"

By the river Jaran's eyes stung and her throat burned

and in a heaving sigh she dropped her head and let the tears come.

Grandmother said nothing. She knew.

That devil up there, he showed each of Jaran's family members something before their lessons began. They all had their secret torments. They each carried their own little piece of Hell with them. To remind them. Remind them that they must never let him escape those chains. That dark pit. So long as he inhabited human flesh, her family would guard Erlik Khan.

As they've done for seven-hundred years.

To protect the good.

The glass vial hung on its cord against Jaran's chest. She touched it through her robes.

She drew a shuddering breath and blew it out. The anguish pouring from her slowed to a trickle and Jaran wiped away her tears and wiped her hand on her robes. She put up her hood.

A faint drone came from the river. She hadn't heard it over her weeping. In the water, almost to the village docks, a boat was returning from the far side. Mother and Father? But they never came back before evening.

Jaran's confusion gave way to a happy relief. She'd be glad for the rare chance to sit and speak with them before they fell asleep from exhaustion. They tried to offer her comfort when she needed it, but with what they went through each day it was difficult.

From far away it looked like just one person in the boat. The sun still hovered above the mountain and Jaran squinted at the boat in the yellow glare. She pulled the binoculars from her satchel and put them to her eyes and focused on the boat.

Her heart froze.

"Grandmother," Jaran said. "That's not Mother and Father."

Grandmother squinted as she looked out. "What do you see?"

Jaran described the man in the boat. A tall, dark-skinned man with short black hair. He wore a strange type of blue and gray striped clothing. He had something long and black in one hand. A rifle maybe. Like the long wooden rifle the Soup Soldier had given to Father.

Jaran had never seen anyone like this man. Maybe he was from the country the Soup Soldier's Army was fighting.

He was nearly to the village docks, but he wasn't slowing the boat.

Jaran swung the binoculars toward where the man aimed his boat. And gasped. Three little naked children up to their knees in the river smiled and splashed. Their mothers washed clothes in the water nearby.

The man in the boat, he steered toward them.

"No," Jaran said, scanning between the boat and the children. Jaran screamed to them, "Move! Look out!"

But they were so far away. They couldn't hear her over the splashing and laughing.

"Grandmother, what—"

A little boy bent and grabbed handfuls of water and jumped and threw up his hands. Sparkles rained down around his smiling face. The boat plowed him, hands slapping forward on the wood, little body breaking backward.

Jaran went rigid and screamed. Screamed until only wisps of air squeezed from her throat.

Grandmother grabbed her and shoved her down in the reeds.

Grandmother! Jaran tried to say. But her throat wrenched closed in terror.

Grandmother grabbed the binoculars and shoved them into Jaran's hands. "I need you to watch, child. Tell me where he goes."

Jaran lay in the grass and shook her head. Finding her voice, she said, "Please, Grandmother, please. I don't want to look. The little *boy!* I don't want to look!" Jaran pushed the binoculars toward Grandmother, wishing she would take them.

Grandmother slapped Jaran hard. "We need to see where he goes. We'll get the Soup Soldier. He'll know what to do. But we need to see where he *goes*. Now watch him!"

Jaran blinked away terrified tears and breathed out hard and rolled to her knees. Brought the binoculars up. The man stood knee deep in the water. One knee raised as if standing on a submerged rock. A mother came running, splashing toward him in the water, insane anguish twisting her face. She held out her arms to the little body floating crooked in the water. The man pulled something small and silver from his hip and pointed it at the woman's screaming-open mouth.

Run away! Jaran pleaded silently. *Run!*

A line of red blasted out the back of the mother's head and she jerked and fell, splashing into the water.

Another woman snatched up her little naked girl and held her tight against her chest. Tiny arms wrapped around her neck, the mother held out a defensive hand. Silent from distance, through the binoculars the word on her lips was *PLEASE!* Over and over again, *PLEASE!*

Her fingers snapped back as the man shot. The girl and woman twitched as bullets tore through them.

The third mother ran away toward the village, hands waving. Where was her baby? The man shot her in the back and she dropped hard, face-down in the mud. She clawed at the muddy beach and dragged herself away, her legs were crooked and crossed and not moving, dragging muddy grooves behind her as she crawled.

The man fired once more and the hair on the back of her head twitched. She thumped in the mud and was still.

"He killed them all!" Jaran cried. "Grandmother, he killed them *all!*"

"Be strong, girl. We can't help them. The Soup Soldier must have heard that noise. He'll help. Watch where the man goes."

She needed Mother and Father. She wanted to run to them. She needed their strength. But they wouldn't be able to get back to the village. That man had taken their boat.

A sickening realization crept up her throat like vomit. If he had their boat then—

No!

She pushed the thought away. Maybe the man didn't go up the path. Up the mountain. Maybe Mother and Father were still alive.

No, not maybe. They are *alive.*

She forced herself to believe. They had to be alive. Had to be.

Jaran watched. The circles of the binoculars shaking. The man looked down at the water. Raised his foot. As he did, a tiny naked body bobbed up from the brown water and it spun dead in the current and floated out into the river.

Monster!

The man's chest inflated and he stretched his arms like he had just woken from a long sleep.

Then he opened his eyes and looked downriver. Toward Jaran. His eyes—

Jaran's heart fell out of her chest. "No…"

Terror, like thousands of creeping, unnatural hands reached from the grass and clutched her.

I'll get her…

Jaran fell in the grass and put her hands to her ears. Sucking in panicked breaths. Trembling.

"It's not real," she gasped. "It's not real."

Grandmother's face appeared. "I told you to watch!"

I'll get her.

"It's not real."

Over and over she said it, but still the gunshots rang out. Father said she would never have to worry. Said he would protect her. Always protect her. Father said he would never escape.

"Jaran!" Grandmother shouted. "Where did he go?

What did you see?"

Jaran sucked in air. Through tears and rapid breaths she said it. Said the thing she thought she would never have to say.

"Erlik Kha-Khan," Jaran said.

Grandmother's eyes shot wide open.

"Erlik Khan is free…."

CHAPTER TWO

John lay in the humid night with the detonator in his hand.

In the deep and thick Laotian jungle, far from the nearest U.S. forces, a long line of soft glowing lanterns bobbed like fireflies in the woods back home. The lights, dimmed so low, illuminated tired faces sheened with sweat. NVA soldiers. Behind them in the dark, the growl of a diesel-engine. A truck. Maybe two. Hard to tell. Vehicles kept their headlights off in the night so patrolling U.S. aircraft couldn't see them moving along the Ho Chi Minh Trail.

John watched. Counted lanterns and the men between them. One lantern for every ten or so men. A hundred men so far, give or take.

At least a hundred NVA infantry against John and his eight men lying in the shadows. But only if it came down to a fight: something John was doing everything in his power to avoid. If everything went smooth it would be just another recon. Watch. Count. Mark the grid coordinates.

Observe and report.

The soldiers walked slowly. Each carried an AK-47, some in better condition than others. They carried a few extra mags in cloth bandoleers. Some men, if they were lucky enough to have slings, slung their rifles over their backs. Some men held onto the muzzle and good-ole-boy carried it over a shoulder.

John was so close he could smell their heavy sweat. So close that clouds of bulbous cigarette smoke rolled over him.

He held his breath while the gray smoke wrapped around his face. A cough was a death sentence. His thumb twitched on the *clacker*—the claymore mine detonator.

Chris—three men down the line—took his job as a Special Forces engineer beyond love. The Army had taught him how to do two things really well. One: build things. Two: blow things up. There were enough explosives planted along that curve in the Trail that if John couldn't fight his body's reaction, if he had to cough, most of those soldiers wouldn't even have time to turn around and look to see what had made the noise. There would be a flash and the NVA leadership would have to count boots to figure out how many men had disappeared in that twenty-meter span.

The smoke passed. John breathed. Shifted his eyes. Only his eyes, to Brandon, John's new commander. Sweating face outlined in a dull luster of lantern-light. It was the kid's first mission with the team, so John had kept him close. Guys new to the recon teams, you could never tell how they were going to react the first time they got within grabbing distance of a very large, very *hostile* element.

Brandon was looking at John, wide-eyed. Pupils two little flecks of light. A bead of amber sweat trickled from the kid's hair and down his cheek. His face twitched. John gently, *gently,* held out his hand, spread his fingers and motioned downward.

Do not scratch that.

Brandon nodded. It could have been the swinging, bouncing lights, but Brandon's face seemed to tremble.

Not a good sign. Not then. Not there. John emphasized the downward motion. *Steady...*

More troops marched out of the dark and Brandon's mouth hung open.

The diesel-engine rumble grew louder and a single truck appeared, hood and headlights illuminated by lanterns. It inched forward, slower than the men marching. The truck's bed was uncovered and, as it passed he could see that inside the bed were long, rounded shapes wrapped in cloth. Wrapped in shrouds.

Bodies. Lots of them. Pyramid-packed like logs. There must have been a big fight somewhere.

It was hard to get a good estimate. Maybe a hundred corpses? The NVA and Viet Cong dedicated a lot of effort into concealing their dead from the Americans. You could kill these guys all night, but by the following morning you would have only guesstimates of the dead based on blood trails. Maybe some pieces of dropped equipment.

The NVA marched on. The truck crawled behind them, wheels dropping in ruts. In a few minutes the truck rounded the curve and disappeared into the dark. The lanterns faded. The diesel-rumble was slow in dying, but eventually the cloak of absolute jungle dark and silence draped back over the American recon team.

Brandon let out a long, slow breath.

John held out a fist. "Shh…"

John waited. Gave it time. Some NVA commanders split their marching element into smaller groups in case of U.S. bombing runs. John gave it five minutes.

Nothing came.

Nothing moved.

John gave it five more minutes.

Nothing.

That was probably a wrap.

John propped himself up on his elbows and looked toward Brandon. Whispered, "Good job."

"That's all?" Brandon asked.

"That's all."

"We didn't gather any intelligence."

"We got a body count. That helps Big Army."

"*Actionable* intelligence."

"Well that's our mission," John said. "Recon. I don't know what else I can do to help you understand that."

A few heartbeats passed. Brandon said, "What exactly are you trying to tell me, Sergeant?"

"Take it easy."

"Sir."

"Say again?"

"You're in the Army, I'm your commander. You'll address me as 'sir.'"

John's head drooped. This kid wasn't going to fit in. Not here.

For whatever reason, each of the six recon teams in SOG had been assigned a non-Special Forces qualified captain. The colonel called them *Team Commanders*. John trusted the colonel. He was a good commander. Stuck up for his men. But…

But Brandon had been a nightmare from day-one, about two weeks ago. A really good way to shatter the morale of a well-functioning team of senior NCOs is to throw in an uptight junior officer.

The kid might have excelled at leading regular Joes in the infantry. Maybe. There had to be some reason Brandon was selected for SOG, right? But this kid, he was not adjusting well to the recon team's approach to operations.

"Listen," John said. "I told you we're professionals here. Every man is equal. Every man has a voice. It's why we're so effective. That's why we're on a first-name basis instead of regular Army—"

"That changes now," Brandon said, pushing himself up to his knees. "And a lot more things are going to change when I finally take over. First, we're not going to waste our time out here. We're going to get some results. We're going to get some actionable intelligence for the colonel."

Brandon clicked on his red flashlight. In the spreading light, Chris's and Phil's crimson faces floated over Brandon's shoulder. They hadn't made a sound.

Chris lifted his chin and slid a finger across his throat.

John shook his head.

Face turning down in an exaggerated frown, Chris pulled his finger down from his eye, miming a tear—saddened he would not get to watch John murder their new commanding officer.

Brandon opened the flap on his rucksack and shined the light on the radio face and reached for the handset.

Heart hammering, John slapped his hand over the handset. "What the fuck do you think you're doing?"

Brandon's head jerked up. Face angry. "We're going to follow that NVA column. I'm telling our extraction to wait."

"Like Hell you are. We're heading for exfil. On schedule."

"You're out of your fucking mind talking to me like that."

"You're not touching that radio until you're calling for an extraction. We're over the border, understand? Laos. The NVA knows our teams are out here mapping the Trail. They triangulate our radio transmissions. If you touch that radio for any other reason than calling in an immediate extraction, you're going to get us all killed."

Brandon growled. "Then we'll just keep *moving* after we call out."

Chris chuckled.

Brandon started and spun around.

Chris, his face glowing in red light said, "Johnny. You didn't tell the poor kid about Counter Recon?"

Brandon said nothing.

"There's a bounty on us recon teams," Chris said. "Pays more if they take us alive. You know, so they can torture us. The NVA disbanded an entire unit of Sappers and turned them into hunter-killer teams."

"The NVA knows we're out here," John said. "That's no bullshit. But they're not happy about it."

"These Counter Recon guys," Chris exaggerated a cold shiver. "These are the kind of guys that the Boogey Man is afraid of. Skinny guys. Tiny. Just AKs, satchel charges, and RPGs."

Phil nodded. "Knives."

"Mmm. Yeah," Chris said. "Real *sharp*, too."

Brandon's head went back and forth between Phil and Chris.

John said, "That's enough, guys."

Brandon turned to him. "This some hazing thing? You trying to scare me—"

"Oh, we are," John said. "You should be scared of them."

"Why?"

"Because *we're* scared of them," Chris said.

"Ohio," Phil said.

"Tell him about Ohio," Chris said.

Brandon looked at John.

"Later," John said. Suppressing a very real shiver. He had known every man on that team—

"No," Brandon said defiantly. "Tell me about Ohio."

John looked at Chris and Phil. Cleared his throat. "Ohio got delayed on a mission one night. Couldn't make it to their extraction. They called HQ when they dug-in for the night. Said they were going to move to the extraction site at first light. They called in SIT-REPs every hour. Then an hour went by with no call. Then two hours. When Ohio's comms went dark, when the extraction birds reported negative contact the next morning, HQ sent us in to go look for them. We found their grid. Found where they had dug in. But we never found the bodies. Just five big pools of blood."

"Like they were too big to come from men," Chris said flatly. The mocking fear from a few moments ago was gone, replaced, perhaps, with genuine fear.

"There was nothing else," John said. "No expended brass. Nothing. Just blood. Each man bled to death in his fighting position without firing a single round."

Brandon looked at each man. Watched them. Maybe looking for some sign of a joke he wasn't in on. When none of them so much as blinked, he closed the flap on his pack.

"Alright," John said. "Let's get—"

Someone yelled. The voice angry-loud. A lantern jerked out of the darkness.

John froze. Phil and Chris whipped their rifles toward the light and the voice.

The lantern jerked this way and that. John sank to the ground.

Another column?

But it was just a single lantern. It drifted closer. The voice grew louder. Grumbling. Something wet. Slurping. A single man came into view. He carried no rifle, but there was a pistol holstered on his hip. In one hand he carried the lantern, in the other, a bottle. When he was directly in front of them, John could just make out the stripes on his uniform that identified him as—

"An officer," Brandon whispered. "Sounds drunk."

Then Brandon was up and running towards the lantern light.

John reached out to grab the kid but he wasn't fast enough.

"*Stop!*" John hissed. He sprang up and ran after, slinging his CAR-15 and drawing the suppressed 1911 from his hip. That marching element was still close. Ten minutes of tired walking didn't take you far. If they made any noise….

The NVA officer mumbled something and turned toward the thrashing, toward Brandon bulling through foliage. The officer raised the oil lantern just as Brandon baseball-bat swung the butt of his rifle at his jaw.

The rifle smashed the glass lantern. Shards flew. Liquid flame spewed out on both men's chest and legs and they went up. Brandon dropped his rifle. Both men screamed and flailed and patted at themselves. John leveled his pistol at the NVA officer, but Brandon danced into his sights.

John sidestepped in time to see the officer yanking his sidearm.

"Get down, Brandon!" John shouted, and Brandon dropped screaming just as a hail of wild, swinging shots barked from the officer's pistol.

The flames screwed with John's sight-picture. He blew out a breath. Saw the man's head. Aimed a little lower.

John fired once, his suppressed pistol coughing and the mechanical action ringing out in a *ca-chink*. The officer's head jerked.

Face slack in odd confusion, the officer clapped his hand to his neck. Suddenly not at all concerned about the flames climbing his torso. His jaw worked like he was chewing something tough and sticky. Looked directly into John's eyes. A black bulge pushed out from beneath his hand. Chest still aflame, black-orange jets of flame-illuminated blood spurted between his fingers.

The officer dropped his pistol. He sat down, thudding hard. He held his neck. Clothing burned, turned black and fizzled away. The fire gnawed the man's skin. He might have been trying to scream. His mouth opened, but let out only wet, gurgling coughs. The blood spurting from beneath his jaw splattered in the fire raging in his lap and it hissed and spit and steam rose into the darkness above like his soul was rising into that giant dark.

Out of pity, John put a second round of .45 ACP between the man's eyes. It knocked the officer's head back and his flaming torso followed, toppling over in a wet *thwack*. His hand fell lifelessly away from his neck. The blood slowed to a dribble and he lay still beneath dancing and dying flames.

Brandon rolled on the ground. When he extinguished

the flames he sat up, looked from John to the officer and back again. Then clambered to his feet and rushed over and dropped down next to the still-burning dead officer. He rummaged through his pockets.

The dying flames were the only light source and the jungle pushed back hard against it. New York would need the dark for their escape. Ten minutes was a shitty lead time. A sprint would bring that column back quick. God forbid the NVA had stopped for a rest just beyond that curve.

John ran up, holstering his pistol. "Gotta go, kid."

"Wait, we need to check—" John grabbed Brandon's LCE and jerked him to his feet.

Brandon shoved John off and dropped and searched the corpse, shouting, "We need intel!" The excitement of the last moments had obviously killed Brandon's noise discipline.

John yanked him up and grabbed him by the front of his shirt. "Open your fucking eyes! He's some drunk fuck! He doesn't have anything." John was inches from Brandon's face, furious.

Over Brandon's shoulder, fireflies. Lots of them. John's guts went cold. He shoved Brandon towards the team and stood on the Trail. Brought up his rifle. Aimed. Front sight leading a lantern light. "Get ready, Chris."

"You got it, boss."

Inhale. Patience. John estimated the distance to the lanterns, eyed the Trail's curve. *Just a little closer...*

A lantern illuminated a crisp silhouette. Another. Another.

John fired, transitioned, fired, transitioned, fired.

Silhouettes fell and screamed.

Lanterns went down and one broke open on the packed clay and the NVA who had been following the dead men halted in their tracks. The men rushing behind them plowed into their halted comrades and they stumbled right into a place they really didn't want to be.

John yelled, "Claymore! Claymore! Clay—"

It was like calling down lightning. The entire jungle flashed brilliant white for the briefest of moments. When the light winked out, the frightened eyes of the NVA soldiers burned in an afterimage. This close to the claymores Chris had planted, the detonation was just a loud *pop* in John's ears. But when John opened his eyes he was on the ground, ears ringing. Splinters and dirt clods rained down in the musty air.

Small lights twinkled in the dark. John couldn't hear it, but he knew his team had kicked off the *Mad Minute*. Recon team New York threw everything they had at the NVA element. Full auto. Going cyclic. John felt the *pig* in his belly—the M60's thrumming, oinking grunt.

"Chris!" John yelled over the ringing and thumping. He pushed himself to his feet and stumbled toward the line. "Chris!"

Someone grabbed him. Red flashlight illuminated a face. Chris. His mouth moved.

John pointed to his ears. "I can't fucking hear!"

Chris stopped. Grinned. He threw up a series of hand signals. Pinky and thumb to his ear, then two fingers and mouthing the word *Bravo*. He whirled his finger and showed a thumbs-up.

John nodded. Grabbed Brandon and shoved him into the jungle, toward the direction of the Bravo extraction site. John told Chris to take the lead and New York retreated through the jungle. Phil, Boing, Mike, and Howard provided covering fire as Dan, Chris, Brandon, Terry, and John fell back about twenty meters.

John's group turned and fired, covering the others as they bounded back.

This they repeated. And repeated.

"More claymores!" John yelled over the gunfire.

Chris and Dan ripped the claymores out of their packs and duct-taped the mines in the trees about chest-high and staked tripwire in the ground.

Then they leapfrogged, red lenses bouncing in the dark.

After six or seven bounds and putting a significant distance between themselves and their attackers, John pulled his map from his cargo pocket—checked it, checked his compass. They had been retreating south and east, but they needed to cut over south and west to reach their extraction. John relayed this to Chris.

Chris nodded and with a chopping-hand he signaled the direction for the others to run. They turned out their lights. Leapfrogging ceased and New York ran. Hard. With luck, the NVA would pursue southeast.

And as New York ran, a pocket of light blossomed in the dark behind them. Bright lines shot through the trees.

About two seconds later came the *boom*.

Brandon tripped, sprawling out. Chris was on him, heaving Brandon's LCE, yanking the kid to his feet. They ran.

The second claymore went off a few minutes later. It was an even longer time before the third went off, the sound muffled by the jungle. The NVA were taking it slow now.

It doesn't matter what country a soldier comes from. When they realize they're in a minefield, the approach is universal. When the first mine goes off and the victim is flailing on the ground with big chunks of himself missing, everyone left standing gets real cautious. That would give New York some extra time.

And they used that time to run. In a while, the muffled ring in John's ears subsided. His head filled instead with the sound of his sprinting breath. A little later and he could hear the slapping and stomps of men running for their lives through elephant grass.

Chris called a halt and knelt next to John, breathing heavily. His big shoulders heaving. "I think," Chris said, "they broke contact." Chris panted. "I haven't heard anything. For a while."

John looked back the way they had come. "Maybe the

Mad Minute worked. NVA commander probably broke contact instead of getting more men killed. I don't think they knew how small we were."

But something didn't sit well with John. New York's reaction to contact had been extremely effective, but it was a textbook SOG reaction. If you have to fight, make it seem like you have the whole Army with you. If the NVA commander was smart…

Chris said, "What do you want to do?"

John shook his head and re-checked his map and compass. "File formation. Take it slow and quiet. We'll listen and see if anyone followed us. I want you on the rear-security. Listen real good."

"You got it."

They stood and John called for a file. As the men spread out, John clicked on the radio in Brandon's pack and handed him the handset.

John said, "Call HQ and tell them we're thirty mikes out from EP Bravo. You can keep the radio on, but *only* to listen. Don't transmit. You remember what we told you?"

Brandon nodded.

"New York," John said. "On me."

John moved up the line. Phil took point. John fell-in about five meters behind him.

It was still dark when they reached the extraction point, some unremarkable clearing. John checked his watch. A little after 0400. He signaled for a loose three-sixty and New York lay prone in a defensive ring.

Brandon came over to John and said, "HQ says to dig-in and wait for the choppers. They'll fly at first light."

"That gives us about two hours. Okay. Guys, find what cover you can. How many more claymores we got?"

"Six," Chris said.

John nodded. "Put 'em all out. Wide trip wires."

They waited. Darkness turned to dull, misty gray. Then a chill blue.

Big dew droplets gathered on the tall grass and

gathered on the men hiding there. Black rifles shined with wet. There wasn't much for cover, so digging-in amounted to hiding in the foliage just outside the clearing.

Brandon lay facing out behind a mound of earth and John knelt down next to him.

"Let's get this outta the way," John said. "What you did back there was pretty fucking stupid."

Brandon didn't look at him. His jaw muscles worked, contempt showing clear on his face in the gray morning light. Like a sulking teenager. But that probably wasn't too far from accurate.

"It was a target of opportunity," Brandon grumbled. "An officer. We could have—"

"You need to learn to *see*. It was a *drunk* officer at the extreme ass-end of a column carrying nothing but dead bodies. Holy God, Brandon, the fucker was probably just relieved of command. Maybe heading north for some punishment. You expect him to be carrying anything important? Do they even teach you to ask your NCOs for advice anymore?"

Brandon said nothing. John looked out at the circle of men. No one looked at him, but at this distance there was no doubt that they were hearing everything. John had never liked getting his ass chewed in front of people, much less his subordinates. Brandon probably didn't like it any more than John did.

John leaned forward and lowered his voice. "Listen, if you're going to command New York, you need to understand that you can't just waltz in here and expect these guys to assume you know what you're doing. A lot of men have died to learn the best ways to survive out here. We're not a bunch of teenage infantrymen. To lead, on these teams, is a *privilege*. And it's earned by pulling your weight and listening to the guys who know what's going on."

"You should go check on the men," Brandon said. "Some of them might need your advice."

"They get it when they need it. And *I* get it when *I* need it. New York *lets* me lead. If there was ever a second when they started doubting me, I'd get voted out and someone else would take over. That little saying you officers have about not being able to lead when you're aiming down the sights, we have one, too. 'Ain't nothing gonna change but your mind.'"

Brandon grunted.

John watched him. It was hard to have your shortcomings thrown in your face. But it was necessary if you wanted to stay alive. If you wanted to keep your men alive.

John sighed. He'd figure out how to handle this kid over a beer. Or twelve. The most important thing was that the men were alive. This was just a hiccup. This whole change in leadership might work out. Somehow. John just needed to work with Brandon and find out what made him so resistant. John would mentor him like John had been mentored. Whether Brandon liked it or not. It might work.

The gray light warmed to orange and the sun brought the slapping sounds of the Hueys. Chris popped a smoke grenade and tossed it into the clearing. Violet smoke billowed into the air. Two helicopters circled in a wide arc around the landing zone. One descended while the other, the gunship, hovered over the landing zone.

John offered his hand to Brandon. "It's a new day. The men are alive, and we have some intel. Some *results*. We don't have to report the hiccup with the officer. We'll just say someone spotted us. We'll figure something out."

Brandon looked at John's hand, ignored it and stood. The hardness had returned to his eyes. Brandon shouted over the rotor wash, "I have the *responsibility* to lead you men. It's given to me by the Army. It's not a privilege given by the grace of a noncommissioned officer. If the Army says I lead, *I* lead. *Your* job is to follow *my* orders." Brandon pushed by. Over his shoulder, he said, "We'll report everything as it happened, including your insubordination." Leaning low against the wind, Brandon stalked off toward the Huey.

"Hey!" Chris called to Brandon.

Brandon turned.

"John goes out first."

"Is that so, Sergeant?" Brandon cocked his head. "Is that another privilege I get to earn from you?"

"Not a privilege," Chris laughed. "The guy who goes out first is usually the guy who gets shot."

Brandon stared hard at Chris. Then turned and ran to the Huey and climbed aboard.

That NVA officer had fired about six shots. Close range. If John had not warned Brandon to drop to the ground, what would have been the outcome?

John scolded himself for even thinking it. It wasn't his place to decide who had the right to live. Regardless of how big an asshole they were.

John approached the aircraft and stood alongside the skids. The din of engines and blowing rotors drowning out every other sound. Brandon slumped into the webbing seat on the far side of the Huey. Arms folded on his chest, he stared out the open door into the jungle.

John counted each man as they boarded the aircraft. Phil came last. He clapped John on the shoulder, nodded. They'd communicated without words for so long, John knew exactly what that nod meant. He smiled and took Phil by the shoulder and guided his friend into the Huey.

Over the sound of the engine there was a quiet popping. In the air, the hovering gunship's door gunner was going full auto.

The door gunner next to John tensed in his chair, his black and bug-like tinted face-shield swiveled, looking out over John and Phil. He swung his M60 machine gun and waved John out of the way.

John went cold. He knew. He knew exactly what was behind him. His hand on Phil's shoulder tightened, grabbing shirt, grabbing flesh, tensing to shove Phil aboard.

The M60 barked loud, belching flame.

John shoved. Phil jerked. Wet sprayed on John's face and suddenly he held all of Phil's weight in his hand. He was falling.

John wrapped both arms around Phil's belly, like a wrestler he shoved with his legs and heaved and threw them both onto the Huey. Above him, a fan of rifle muzzles unfurled as New York aimed and fired. Brass casings clinked on the floor, dropping hot on his head. John lay on Phil, shielding him. Wrapped his hands around Phil's head, fingers sliding across something coarse and jagged. Pressing against something soft and spongy.

All around was noise and John's gut dropped as the Huey shot hard and fast into the sky. The Huey banked. John grabbed a crossbar under a seat and spared a glance down, the grass and jungle falling away beneath his feet. And he saw them.

"No."

Five or six shirtless men emerged from the jungle, one carried the instantly recognizable tube of an RPG. The others raised AK-47s to the climbing Huey and yellow sparked from their muzzles. At their feet were other shirtless men sprawled on the ground. Green straps slung across their bloody and ripped-open chests. Satchel charges.

The door gunner's M60 roared full-auto. Chris leaned back, kicking his foot against the seat across from him, bracing himself. He fired controlled pairs out the door. The enemy soldier with the RPG aimed up, even at this distance John could see he was leading the Huey.

John screamed, "RPG! Chris! RPG! Shoot him! Shoot—"

Chris went full-auto. The door gunner churned the earth, walking rounds toward the man.

A flash on the ground. Smoke. The pilot jerked the Huey and the RPG's smoke trail arced wide. On the ground, the man who fired the rocket convulsed from the M60's punching impact.

There were dead men on all sides of the landing zone. New York had been surrounded and not even known it. Those men... They'd made it through the claymores. Snuck right into New York's perimeter. Shirtless men. AKs. RPGs. Satchel charges. *Christ,* John thought. *Oh, Christ.*

It was Counter Recon.

How?

Adrenaline and confusion coursed through him. John's heart pounded so hard he thought it might beat itself to pieces against his ribs. John put his hand to his face, pressed his wet and sticky fingers against his eyelids, eyes throbbing against his fingertips.

How?

He breathed deep. Exhaled hard.

The Huey screamed over the jungle. The guns went silent. The door-gunner swiveled his silent and smoking M60, scanning.

They gained altitude. John rolled over. Got to his knees. Phil—

Oh, God.

Blood.

Blood covered John from chest to knees. His fingers black with it. John tried to pull a bandage from the pouch at his shoulder, but his slick and frantic fingers kept slipping on the brass button. Phil's eyes were rolled up into his head and white. His face sunken and pale. The side of his head blown out, a soft pile of twisted yellow and gray flopped on the floor.

"Medic!" John screamed. Searched the cabin for Mike. But Mike had been on the floor with him all along, now wrapping a gigantic white bandage around Phil's head.

"Plug him up, goddamnit!" John shouted. His words lost amidst the chirp-chirping rotors. Even as the words left his lips he knew it was useless, but.

You never fucking give up on your men.

Mike worked. Deft hands cocooning Phil's head in padding and cloth. Phil's mouth hung open beneath the giant bandage. The aircraft's rotors rattled the fuselage. The blood pooling beneath Phil's pale face rippled in shivering waves.

John slumped against the seat. Energy poured from him like he had been cut open. He looked around the cabin at the other team members. No one looked at him. At one time or another, everyone on the team just needed a minute to themselves. They all understood that this was John's minute.

And John locked eyes with Brandon.

Brandon.

Brandon looked away. Looked out the door. Into the sky.

That kid. That fucking idiot kid brought Counter Recon down on John's men. A cold rage came. And John let it come.

Brandon, sitting right next to the door.

Right next to the door.

John stood, stepped over the men and their gear. He reached out.

The slap hit John hard on the face and he stumbled. Chris was on him, grabbing John's shirt, shoving his face into his.

"Look at me!" Chris shouted over the roar.

But John turned to Brandon.

Chris shook him. "*Me!* You son of a bitch, look! Look at me!"

John looked at him.

Chris held on. His face hard.

They stayed like that for a long time. When the strength went out of John, Chris relaxed his grip and let go. John slumped on the floor.

They drifted over jungle-covered mountains. Orange morning sun shooting in through the open door, over

Brandon's shoulder, consuming him. Blinding John. Even in that murderous rage, John couldn't muster the strength to put a hand to his eyes. He let his head drop.

Hanging by its chain on John's chest, stuck in the blood on his ripped-open shirt, was his gold cross. Light glinted off the gold. John heaved a trembling sigh.

"Not very Christian of me," John said. Words lost in the wind.

John leaned his head back on the seat and closed his eyes. Let the sun warm his face. He asked God for restraint. Restraint so he didn't shove Brandon out into the sky.

CHAPTER THREE

Brandon sat alone at the command bunker's U-shaped collection of folding tables waiting for the debriefing to begin. Dim lights hung above gridded maps tacked to the plywood walls. Overhead views of various sections of Vietnam and Laos. Red string strung between pushpins marked confirmed sections of the Ho Chi Minh Trail. Yellow string marked suspected arteries. Brandon's eyes searched absently for the place he and New York had been extracted from that morning.

The colonel's enlisted aide, some staff sergeant, had driven Brandon over from the helipad.

"You still got about twenty minutes before anyone shows up, sir," the staff sergeant had said. "Have a seat. Make yourself comfortable."

Brandon had sat. But there was no way in hell he could make himself comfortable. Not after what had happened that morning.

He put his elbows on the table and rubbed his eyes. In twenty minutes he'd have a lot of explaining to do. Left alone with his thoughts, it was going to be a long twenty minutes.

He thought about how he would explain the death of

one of his men. How he could spin it so his actions with the NVA officer wouldn't seem rash. Wouldn't seem *fucking stupid…*

He thought about how resistant New York was to accept him as their commander. He thought about requesting a transfer. The SOG Recon Teams, he had discovered, were a voluntary force. A rare thing in the military. If Brandon wanted to quit he just had to say so. He thought about where they might send him. Probably back to the Infantry.

It should've been you.

God, he couldn't go back to the Infantry.

By some miracle Brandon's reputation had not followed him here to SOG. That would not be the case if he was sent back to the Infantry.

He thought about how he ended up here in the first place. In SOG. Why Brandon? Why any of the six new captains? Special Forces had loads of qualified captains. What made Brandon and the five others so special?

That was hard. To admit to himself that maybe he wasn't fit to lead New York. John and his men presented a leadership challenge beyond anything he'd ever come up against. Brandon had tried to do what was asked of him during their recon in Laos. Had he misunderstood his instructions?

Keep them in line. The voice had said. *We're not getting the results we want.* Brandon thought about his plane ride from Okinawa and that mysterious crackling voice on the C-130. He thought about how he could have possibly misunderstood such simple instructions.

When Brandon had received his orders and read them, he had a feeling this tour in Vietnam would be different. The orders were strange. Different than those he received for his first tour with the Infantry. These new orders assigned him to the *Studies and Observations Group*. A unit he'd never heard of. None of his friends had heard of it, either.

In California, Brandon had boarded the civilian charter plane loaded with fresh troops of all ranks. Their faces young. Their uniforms clean and dark green. Half a day later he'd landed in Okinawa.

When he had handed his orders to the enlisted clerk at the processing station, the Sergeant had told him, "We're still waiting for the rest of your group to show up before we load the plane."

So Brandon had milled about all morning. All afternoon. Most of the evening. All day watching hundreds of soldiers pack ninety-men tight into Air Force C-130s and fly off to wherever they were going.

Late that night, a different enlisted clerk woke him. The sergeant said, "Captain Doran? Your flight is ready."

With sleep still in his eyes, Brandon had grabbed his duffel bag and went out to the flight-line, expecting to be packed in with ninety other troops.

Instead, he found five other captains as sleepy and confused as he was. The clerk led them to the far end of the airfield to a C-130 painted flat gray. That was the first thing the struck Brandon as being slightly off. The color. But then he noticed the aircraft had no military markings. The only marking he saw on the plane was a tail number.

Aside from the crew, Brandon and the five other captains were the only people aboard. They found headsets in the webbing seats and put them on. The headsets allowed for intra-aircraft communication and the captains introduced themselves and made small pleasantries as the plane hurtled down the runway.

Captain Conway, one of the few African American officers Brandon had ever met, was the first to ask, "Anyone know what the hell this Studies and Observations Group is?"

That was when a different voice came over the headset. A man's voice with a hard Boston accent. It said, "Let me answer a few of the questions you might have." The man might have been on the plane with them. Might not have been.

The captains had looked at each other. They listened.

The voice said, "We call it *SOG* for short. We have a few different arms, all focused on unconventional warfare. You six men will be assigned to the recon teams. I'm afraid you won't learn anything further until you've all signed your non-disclosure agreements.

"What I *can* tell you is that there are currently no officers below the staff level assigned to the teams. The operational teams are made entirely of enlisted Special Forces soldiers. That's where you gentlemen will fit in.

"You will each be assigned to a team as the *Team Commander*. We haven't been seeing the results we've predicted, so we need men within the teams that will, shall we say, keep the teams honest. Make sure they're focused on accomplishing their assigned tasks. Our hope is that with an additional layer of oversight we'll increase our effectiveness on the whole."

Seemed easy enough.

"But," the voice said. "These teams are already well-established. These men are highly skilled and highly efficient. They might not appreciate the sudden change in structure. If you run into any resistance, you are to remind them they are still in the Army and must still respect the chain of command."

That hadn't proved to be so easy.

"You will all learn more when you arrive," the voice said. "You gentlemen pull this off and there'll be recommendations for each of you for assignments at the Pentagon. Best of luck in your endeavors."

And that was the last they heard from him. Whoever he was.

Captain Conway had attempted to ask a follow-up question, but the voice never came back on.

That was two weeks ago. Since then Brandon had been in-processed, given his gear, and assigned a bunk. Then he was assigned to Recon Team New York. And that's when he met his NCOIC, John.

And that insufferable bastard, Chris.

"What's your blood type?" Chris had asked around a mouthful of chewing tobacco."

"O negative," Brandon had said. Thinking there must have been some important reason Chris was asking.

Spitting a shiny brown stream, Chris shrugged and clapped John on the shoulder and said, "At least he ain't completely useless."

These men had been a nightmare from day-one.

The door opened in the command bunker and white daylight sliced across the tables. Men filed in, stretching their eyes open wide in the gloom. Brandon stood and said hello to the officers coming in. The fat, rusty spring thrummed and yanked the door, slapping it shut.

The two majors, the J-2 and J-3 nodded to him and took their seats at the head of the table. A large, abused but comfortable-looking leather chair took up the space between them.

Captain Jones peered at Brandon, his eyes probably not yet adjusted to the dark. After a moment of awkward staring, Jones said, "Brandon, God, we heard you guys got into some serious shit."

Brandon nodded. "We hit a few snags."

"Fuck, man. I'm glad you had Saint Nick watching over you. My guys won't shut up about him. My senior NCO idolizes that guy."

"Who?"

"Saint Nick. Sergeant Nicholas. John. Your NCOIC."

"Oh." *Saint Nick?* "Yeah. He's something."

"I think the word you're searching for is 'legend'. The guys on Illinois said he gets New York out of the craziest shit. Said he never lost a man."

Brandon's hand tightened on his rifle. "I hadn't heard."

The door-spring groaned. Brandon turned. An unbelievably large silhouette of a man stood in the doorframe.

"On your feet!" someone called out. Metal folding chairs squeaked as the officers stood at the position of attention. Their commander strode towards the head of the table. Boots thumped loud on the plywood floor.

Brandon had never really spoken to Colonel Murphy, aside from a quasi-welcome-brief which amounted to each new captain merely stating his name. But he had seemed approachable enough. The recon teams were just a small part of what the colonel managed. He had a demeanor of a father with too many children.

But how would Colonel Murphy react to hearing Brandon was thinking about quitting New York? Would he even *let* Brandon quit?

Brandon stifled a nervous chuckle. *Just wait until you brief your mission. You won't have to quit. They'll fire you. Relieve your ass for cause.*

"Take your seats, gentlemen," Colonel Murphy said. He sat in the leather chair between his two staff officers. Squinted as he surveyed those in attendance. A yellow blotch of light from the dim bulb above his chair reflected on the top of his freshly shaved head.

Major Black, the J-2, placed a few sheets of paper in front of the colonel and he shuffled through them.

The colonel asked, "Everyone here?"

Major Riley, the J-3, said, "Florida is still out."

It was barely noticeable, but Brandon caught the slightest interruption in the colonel's shuffling before he nodded in acknowledgement.

With the rotating mission schedule and high op-tempo, the captains didn't get a lot of time to sit and talk with each other, so Brandon still didn't know to which team each of the captains had been assigned.

But looking around the tables, Captain Conway was the only one absent. He must have been assigned to Florida.

"Alright," the colonel said, tapping the papers on the table. "Let's get started. I trust you've each had enough time to get acquainted with your teams and learn how we do things around here. Don't be afraid to ask any of your non-coms for help if you need it. Pride should be the one thing you *don't* pack in your ruck when you head out. With odds already stacked against you, you don't need hurt feelings getting in the way of the mission."

That was one hell of a contradiction to what was said on the plane. All that talk about bringing these NCOs to heel. But the colonel's statement prompted a lot of head nodding and murmurs of "Yes, sir".

The colonel said, "I'll hold one, maybe two more of these group sessions, but then I want you reporting directly to the Two and Three individually for debrief when you come off-mission. Flying back and forth between here and Saigon takes up too much of my time already."

In the mess tent one evening, Major Black had told Brandon that Big Army was worried about the interception of classified radio traffic. The standing policy was that any classified information had to be discussed in-person. With regard to SOG, that meant everything. From large operations to minor pay and personnel issues.

"Our friends at the Department of State," Colonel Murphy continued, "are still restricting bombing missions on the Ho Chi Minh Trail outside of Vietnam. Anything you find in Laos is off-limits to Arc Light runs. But we still need to get out there and map the trail in case the bureaucrats change their minds. I've briefed the Marine Corps and Army area commanders on Trail sections located in their AORs. They'll monitor those so we can focus on Laos." The colonel sat back in his chair and looked at the captains. "Okay, let's hear what you've been up to. Brandon, go ahead and start us off."

Brandon stiffened. He'd spent all that time thinking about quitting and none of it thinking about what he was going to say.

The four captains turned and looked at him. The J-2 and J-3 clicked their ballpoint pens.

Brandon cleared his throat. Stalling for time he pulled his map from his cargo pocket. It was damp with sweat and humidity.

John had given him the map before New York inserted into Laos. On it, John had traced every confirmed artery of the Ho Chi Minh Trail.

"Good morning, sir." Brandon said. He nodded to the other officers. "Gentlemen. Recon Team New York…"

Just tell them what happened.

Brandon said, "Recon Team New York conducted a reconnaissance of the area located at the following coordinates." Major Black wrote them down. "Recon confirmed a section of the Ho Chi Minh Trial that parallels a stretch of the Xe Xou River. This section remains hidden from aerial reconnaissance by," *what was it John had said?* "a crude method of interweaving palm fronds. During our night reconnaissance, we witnessed a troop movement of approximately one-hundred enemy soldiers followed by an M35 deuce-and-a-half carrying at least another one hundred corpses." Although Brandon did not actually *see* the dead, he thought John's estimate would sound better in the report.

Major Black interrupted. "Were the dead enemy or civilians?"

"Unknown, sir. I was only able to see the bodies in dim lantern light."

"NVA or VC troops?" asked Major Riley.

"NVA, sir," Brandon said. "I spotted an officer at the rear of the column. His uniform was clearly visible."

"Clearly visible?" Colonel Murphy leaned forward in his chair, thumped his big elbows on the table. The lightbulb above his bald head cast deep, skull-like shadows and his eyes disappeared in the dark. "Tell me how you could see him so clearly. In the *dark*. How close were you?"

Brandon's face burned. He looked down at his place at the table as if a sensible answer might be waiting there like a meal. "I was," Brandon cleared his throat, "within arm's reach, sir."

Captain Jones leaned forward. Down the line, the other officers were leaning in as well.

That stunt you pulled was pretty fucking stupid.

There had to be a way Brandon could describe his actions as calculated, not stupid. Charging that officer was the impetus that led to Phil's death. These moments would be what those men at the head of the table would scrutinize when they talked about firing him.

Brandon took a breath and said, "I spotted a drunken NVA officer straggling a significant distance behind the main marching element. He did not appear to be armed and I attempted to take him prisoner for interrogation. I intended to overpower him, but by the time I saw his pistol, he had already drawn it and fired wildly. Ultimately, the decision was made to neutralize the officer," *although not by me,* "as he had succeeded in alerting the larger element. It was at this point New York and I began our evasion and radioed for extraction. Before retreating, I searched the officer's corpse for intelligence, but discovered nothing of value."

Brandon swallowed, sliding his arm down into his lap to hide his singed sleeve. Hopefully no one would ask him to elaborate.

Colonel Murphy interlaced his fingers and rested his chin upon his hands. The dark holes of his eyes focused on Brandon. The look of a man going over the details. Looking for holes in a story. Brandon's hands trembled and he clasped them beneath the table. At last, the colonel said, "Friendly casualties?"

Brandon winced at the flood of heat inside him. Of course the colonel knew what had happened. The pilot would have radioed ahead. Why did the whole room need to know how badly Brandon had fucked up?

A chance for a shining career squandered. This was the end of it. He should just tell it like it happened. That might grant him some sympathy. Get him transferred to some office job in Saigon.

Brandon sighed and said, "One friendly KIA, sir. My point man. We were ambushed at the extraction point." Brandon hung his head.

And started when a hand clapped him on the shoulder. He looked up. Jones had leaned over to console Brandon. Staring at him with big, sorrowful eyes.

"The NVA commander didn't break contact?" Colonel Murphy asked. "Seems strange they would pursue you so far." The two majors, still writing on their pads, nodded in agreement.

What the hell was happening? These men were supposed to accuse Brandon of dereliction of duty, not feel sorry for him!

Brandon squirmed in his chair. "It was, ah, not the same element from the previous engagement, sir." Some heads perked up around the table. Brandon dropped his eyes to his map. He wondered if maybe he should have worded that differently. "My senior enlisted man identified the secondary attackers as a unit with which I was previously unfamiliar. Something called *Counter Recon* if I'm not mistaken."

The scratching pens stopped. All heads turned.

"Holy *shit*," Jones whispered. Hands going to his head and leaning far back in his chair, like Brandon was carrying some plague.

"Describe them," Colonel Murphy said. Voice a mixture of urgency and restrained excitement.

Brandon described what he had seen. Shirtless men in shorts, carrying rifles, RPGs, and satchel charges. Of the tactic in which they encircled the landing zone at the extraction point and waited for the aircraft to land before attacking.

The colonel and his staff officers exchanged glances. The three at the head of the table nodded and spoke quietly amongst themselves.

The leather of Colonel Murphy's chair rubbed and groaned as the mammoth man leaned back. The shadows vanished from his eyes and he looked at Brandon. "You're lucky to have made it out with just the one casualty, son. Those sons-of-bitches are no joke. They took an entire team from me. You kill any of them?"

Brandon nodded. "We did, sir. Although we weren't on the ground long enough to confirm a count."

With a dismissive wave, the colonel said, "Doesn't matter. As long as you taught 'em they aren't invincible. Colonel Murphy ran his finger along his lip, eyes going far away as if remembering something. As if savoring something. Then he grunted and said, "It was some damn fine leadership that got you all out of that mess. Good job."

Brandon stared. Meekly, he said, "Yes, sir." It probably wasn't appropriate to say *thank you*; it wasn't Brandon's leadership that got New York out. Brandon bit down to stop his teeth grinding.

Colonel Murphy watched Brandon a moment. Then said, "I want to talk with you more after this." Then he called on Jones.

No longer the room's focus, Brandon relaxed. Slouched in his chair. He listened to the other officers and was surprised to learn that Jones and the other captains had absolutely nothing to report.

Brandon sat there dumbfounded and listened to Captain Alexander explain that the MEDEVAC he called for was for him. He had tripped and broken his ankle and had to be carried out of the jungle by his team. Brandon stole a glance under the table at the comically large cast around Alexander's foot. By the time each of the captains had finished, Brandon felt like he had just won some contest. As far as results were concerned, without a doubt Brandon had outshined his peers.

Losing a man, to Brandon's morbid surprise, seemed to be a non-issue. Just a fact. He didn't sense that the leadership was callous. Colonel Murphy and the majors seemed to care about the teams. Were friendly casualties that common around here?

Later, when the briefings concluded, Colonel Murphy whispered to Major Black, who nodded and said to the captains, "Alright gentlemen, good work. We'll have more missions coming your way soon. Refit and get some rest. For now, I need you to clear out. The commander needs the room." Major Black stood and snapped to attention. "On your feet!"

Brandon and the other captains stood and saluted, ceremoniously concluding the end of the meeting. Colonel Murphy stood and saluted, then turned away from the table to rummage in a cupboard.

Wasn't so bad.

Brandon slung his rifle over his shoulder. Still, he wasn't sure he belonged here. He'd give it some time. Get a meal in his belly and get some sleep. Then he'd ask to speak privately with the commander about a transfer.

He turned to follow the other captains out.

"Not you, Brandon." Colonel Murphy said, almost grumbling. "You sit."

Shit.

Captain Jones's eyebrows went up in sympathy and he patted Brandon on the shoulder on his way out.

The door's spring thrummed as the men departed and banged shut when the last man exited. Brandon sat back down at the table. Alone with his commander.

It should've been you.

Brandon winced at the voice in his head and gripped the fabric of his trousers.

He watched the colonel, unsure of what he was doing. Cupboards opened. Closed. Glass clinked.

Brandon went over New York's recon in his mind. If the colonel had kept him behind to chew his ass, he'd have to keep his story straight. And if the colonel was of the opinion that Brandon wasn't fit for duty here, he could ask for a reassign—

The colonel placed three short, thick glasses on the table in front of Brandon. He twisted the cap off a bottle of whiskey and poured each glass half-full.

Colonel Murphy sat in one of the steel chairs next to Brandon and crossed his legs and rested his glass on his knee. He nodded to Brandon's glass. "Go ahead, son."

What?

Brandon picked up the glass and took a small swallow. The burn filled his throat. His eyes drifted to the third glass, wondering who it was for.

But Colonel Murphy said nothing about it. In one long pull, he downed his whiskey. He winced then smacked his lips and refilled his glass.

Brandon was about to ask the colonel if he was expecting someone else when the door opened. A man dressed in civilian clothes carrying a black leather briefcase came in and placed it on the table.

Colonel Murphy remained seated. Brandon, unsure of the etiquette, remained seated as well.

"Good morning, colonel," The man said. Brandon's ears perked up instantly at the Boston accent.

Colonel Murphy nodded and gestured to the third glass with his own. "This is Captain Doran." He drank. And with a hard exhale, like blowing out fire, he said, "He's your man."

"I see," that new man said, picking up the glass. He took a swallow and held the glass up and nodded approvingly to the colonel.

The man pulled out a topographic map from the briefcase and laid it on the table. He then pulled out a clear plastic sheet, similar to those used with overhead projectors, but this particular sheet was marked with various symbols, circles, and numbers arranged in grid coordinates. The man placed his glass of whiskey on the corner of the map to hold the sheet in place.

"My men aren't expendable," Colonel Murphy said. "I

want Florida back." He knocked back his whiskey and thumped the empty glass on the table. "Regardless of the condition in which you find them."

The man looked up. "Of course, Colonel. I have hopes of recovering my own man as well."

Brandon sipped at his whiskey, trying to hide his confusion. What did Brandon have to do with a conversation about Florida?

The man looked at Brandon. "We should begin planning immediately." He held his hand out to Brandon. Brandon took it and they shook hands. The man had a strong grip. In fact, now that Brandon looked closer, beneath his loose cotton shirt and khaki pants the man bristled with dense muscle. "My name is Smith. I'll be your handler."

"Pleasure."

Handler?

The CIA? Brandon had heard that the SOG program was started by the agency, but the unit had been handed over to the Army Special Forces. He didn't think he'd ever actually meet an operative.

The colonel seemed more interested in his whiskey than whatever Brandon and Smith had to talk about. He refilled yet another glass for himself. Brandon, sensing some tension between his commander and the operative, was unsure if he should make himself seem eager to assist with the mission. But Colonel Murphy had clearly offered Brandon to help with whatever it was.

For want of something to say, Brandon asked, "Where are we going?"

Smith pointed to the map, and Brandon followed his finger. "Just south of the northern border. Specifically to Florida's last reported location. They went missing along with one of my men. You and I are going to find them."

"They went missing near the DMZ?" Brandon asked. The border between North and South Vietnam was a pretty hot location. It seemed dangerous to take such a small team there.

Colonel Murphy grunted. "Not *that* northern border."

Brandon set his near-empty glass on the table and leaned over to see where Smith pointed. With the waving contour lines on the map and the plastic overlay, it was difficult to discern immediately where in Vietnam Smith was pointing. Then Brandon saw the thick black borderline that ran roughly west to east, all the way to the South China Sea.

There was a clink of glass on glass and a soft gurgling as Colonel Murphy poured Brandon another drink.

A heavy feeling settled in Brandon's guts. He looked up at Smith. "We're going to *China?*"

CHAPTER FOUR

John felt the rain coming as he stepped out of the quartermaster's hut into a wash of red pastels. Bulging gray clouds screened the setting sun. Diffused sunlight painted the corrugated steel Quonset huts autumnal reds and bronzes. Oaks and Hickories.

In one hand he carried a flattened cardboard box. In the other, a green duffel bag stuffed with fresh uniforms for New York. Any clothing with Phil's blood on it John had told the men to incinerate.

Thunder blasted overhead. Pelting rain pinged on the metal huts and churned the brown clay walkways. He ran, hefting the canvass duffel over his shoulder and holding the box close. His O.D. green uniform turned a wet black.

The recon barracks were separated from those of the regular Joes by a single roll of concertina wire. A simple wooden sign stood at the walkway through the wire: *Authorized Personnel Only*.

And it was effective.

The support soldiers on the compound knew there were a bunch of Green Berets running around. They didn't know why. They didn't ask. Non-SF troops considered this quiet duty station a privilege and, without complaint, they pulled guard-duty on the perimeter, operated the mess hall, and ran the various S-shops. They learned fast that life on a secret, well-funded Special Operations outpost in the middle of nowhere was nice and relaxing compared to the alternative. Nobody wanted to risk getting sent back to the bush for poking their noses where they shouldn't.

John slipped through the gap in the C-wire and ran to New York's hut. Their Q-hut was just like every other team's, the only difference being that New York's had a plywood porch and awning just outside the front door, under which Chris presently stood in a cloud of blue cigarette smoke.

Chris was New York's only tobacco-user, but he used enough for the whole team. The guy smoked cigarettes, chewed tobacco, and would occasionally pull out a pipe. The team was never happy when they returned to the hut and all of their stuff reeked of ash and smoke.

When Phil had complained about the smell, Chris had said, "What the hell do you expect me to do? Go *outside*? In the *rain*?"

"Sorry, man," John had told him. "Outside with it."

And John had flown down to Saigon with the colonel for a briefing the next day. When he returned, the Q-hut had a brand-new porch with an awning and, in the pouring rain, Chris sat beneath it in a cloud of pipe smoke.

John had stood beneath the awning, admiring Chris's work, and asked, "Should I even ask where you got the wood?"

With his pipe in his teeth, Chris said, "Probably better if you didn't."

"Anyone going to be upset?"

Chris pulled out the pipe and held it while he gazed thoughtfully at the sky. "I'd imagine so."

But now, stepping beneath the awning to join Chris with the duffel bag and the box, it was a more somber experience.

Twin streams of bull-smoke blew out from Chris's

nose as he nodded to the box. "That for his stuff?"

"Yeah."

Chris looked out at the mud.

"Take the guys over to the Lizard," John said. "Get an early start."

Chris took a drag. Blew out smoke. "Captain Ahab take care of the debriefing?"

"Yeah."

"I guess he's good for something, then." Chris shrugged. "Well if you don't need me thinkin', I might as well be drinkin'." Chris poked his head in the door. "Hey! Drinks are on Saint Nick!"

Above the rain on the steel and wood there came muffled hoots and cries of "Amen!" and "Hallelujah!" The men came through the door and slapped John on the shoulder as they ran off through the rain toward recon's personal bar.

"I'll get the first round." John said. He held up his finger to Chris. "The *first* round. I've got a wife at home. I'd like to keep it that way."

Chris shook his head. "You're not paying for a thing. Not today. I just didn't want them boys holdin' back."

John watched him. Chris's easy grin was missing, but John caught that glimmer. That glimmer that appeared right before Chris made things go boom. Horror settled in John's gut.

"Jesus, Chris, you're not putting it on Phil's tab, are you?"

Chris's mouth hung open. The mocking look of shock did absolutely nothing to ease John's mind. "It hurts me deeply that you think I could stoop *so* low."

"I. *Know. You*. Who's paying?"

Chris held up his hands. The smile came. Stretched his face wide. "Now, listen. Don't worry. I know that an officer of Brandon's caliber would want to spoil his team on a day like today."

"No!"

But Chris sprang off the porch. Hooting and cackling as he ran. Running so fast the rain didn't touch him.

John squeezed his eyes shut, already imagining the conversation. The explanation to Brandon about how an officer's name somehow appeared on a bar-tab at a club reserved for NCOs.

But another round of thunder came like an artillery salvo and it punched John from his thoughts. He watched Chris catch up to the group. Just coming off-mission, New York had a whole forty-eight hours to drink themselves senseless. It'd probably be good for them. He watched them go. When they turned on the main roadway and disappeared into the rain, John went inside.

He stood there dripping in the quiet and listened to the rain. The team's rucksacks sat at the foot of their bunks. Phil's missing pack was instantly conspicuous.

That absence would be conspicuous for the rest of the tour. Phil's normal seat on the helicopter. His permanent position as point man. The position that was typically rotated between men due to its inherent danger. It was always Phil's.

None of you fuckers ever see shit until it starts shooting at us. That had been Phil's reasoning.

John chuckled softly. Sadly. There would be a million small, but constant, reminders that Phil was gone.

John placed the cardboard box on Phil's bunk and went to his room at the back of the hut. New York had surprised him by building a simple plywood partition to give John some privacy. Stenciled on that partition in simple black spray paint was *SFC Nicholas*. He winced at the word *Saint* scrawled in black marker above the *SFC*.

"I guess I don't deserve it anymore."

New York had christened him *Saint Nick* because, despite their wild, sometimes desperate encounters, somehow or another, New York always came back together. Sometimes wounded. Always alive.

The way John saw it, the team got *themselves* back safe.

They were every bit as brave and as committed to each other as he was to them. Maybe more. John was just the guy lucky enough to be in charge of a good team.

But all that was about to change. One small change in the team's dynamic by adding Brandon, suddenly everything went to hell. It was John's job to have a serious talk with Brandon about his role. It was Brandon's job to approach this assignment as something personal. You didn't lead a team like New York by pointing at a hill and telling the men to charge it. *You* charged the hill and knew, you *knew* the team would be right behind you.

Saint Nick.

The writing taunted him.

New York heavily embellished most of John's actions that earned him the nickname when they swapped stories with the other teams at the Lizard. It always devolved into a sort of *my-dad-can-beat-up-your-dad* contest. With the added alcohol, the ribbing turned into brawls. John once had to pull Phil off a guy from the Illinois team who refused to believe one of Phil's stories about John.

John smiled, remembering when he and Phil had to report to Colonel Murphy's bunker for disciplinary action.

"Explain to me why you assaulted Sergeant First Class Burke." The colonel had asked Phil.

Phil had cleared his throat and said meekly, "Sir, Sergeant Burke did not believe me when I told him that Sergeant Nicholas saved Christmas."

Colonel Murphy had leaned back in his chair then. His mouth hanging open. He looked at John and said, "I thought everyone knew that was true."

John had never really taken the nickname seriously. But thinking back, it seemed like the team did. They believed in him.

So what changes now?

Now that the reality of war had finally set its sights on New York? Now that the team knew deep down that John couldn't guarantee their survival?

John opened his footlocker and took out a set of keys. Spares for each man's footlocker. Each key had a white paper tag. Each tag had a name. He slid them one-by-one until he found Phil's. He took Phil's key off the ring and held it up. Hoped it would be the last key he would ever take off that ring. He put the others gently back in his footlocker and walked back into the common area and down the line of bunks.

What changes?

Nothing, he decided, kneeling down beside Phil's footlocker. The leadership might have changed, but that didn't change how John would approach the missions. He'd be there to guide Brandon whether the kid wanted it or not. John couldn't mitigate the risk of the missions completely, they were always dangerous. But he could make sure Brandon wasn't unnecessarily putting New York in harm's way.

If John had to lose more sleep planning and going over maps and rehearsing everything in his mind, so be it. That was his job: to worry. He'd think of everything. He'd think of everything that could go right and everything that could go wrong. Plan for every possible contingency. If he could plan for war, he could plan for Brandon.

There was surprisingly little inside Phil's footlocker. Some photos of his wife and two boys. His mom and dad. Not much else. An unsent letter. John held this up. Stamped and sealed. Addressed to Phil's wife.

"Shit."

He thought of burning it.

In a few days, a black car with government plates would pull up to Phil's house. Two men in uniform would get out. They'd knock. Phil's wife would be there on the floor holding her boys. The two men would leave.

A few days later, maybe a week, this letter from Phil would come. She'd have that brief moment of hope that the two men had made a mistake. That it was some other woman's husband being shipped home in a box. Then she'd see the postage date marked on the envelope and relive Phil's death all over again.

John really wanted to burn it.

But he had to send it. Phil's wife and kids would appreciate it. Someday.

"I hope."

He set the letter aside on Phil's bunk to mail out later and he took out Phil's socks and razors and soap and packed them in the box. He took out Phil's Bible. Turned it over in his hands. A few months ago, John had given it to him brand-new from the chaplain's office. Now the cover was folded back and the binding was worn and creased white.

Phil hadn't been religious when he had showed up to Vietnam. But religion during wartime was an odd thing. Sometimes you'd get a guy who, back in the world, couldn't give a damn about God. But something would happen. Everyone had a different *something* that sent them searching for answers amidst the horrors of war.

For Phil, his something was a village. New York had stumbled upon it near the border of Laos and Vietnam. It was still smoking when they found it. Burned to the ground. Families slaughtered.

The whole team was real quiet for some time after that. But the sight seemed to hit Phil the hardest. He had come to John drunk one night and demanded to be transferred out of recon. He wanted to get on one of the direct-action teams. Wanted to pull a trigger. It didn't seem to matter to Phil if the person on the other end had anything to do with the village or not.

As a rule, John didn't discuss religion with anyone. Not anymore. Everyone knew John was religious. He didn't keep it a secret. But after enlisting in the Army, in his teenage-naivety, he found out the hard way that a lot of people were set in their own beliefs. He had unwittingly started a lot of heated arguments, some of which turned into fights. Other soldiers threw his faith back in his face or went out of their way to stomp it into the dirt. After a few years of this he gave up sharing his faith with anyone unless someone approached him.

Some time ago, on a clear night, John had found Phil sitting alone at the base perimeter. When Phil saw him standing there, he quickly wiped the streaks of moonlight from his face and asked, "What kind of God lets this shit happen, John?"

John had stood there for a while but said nothing. He went to the chaplain's office, picked up a field-Bible from the stack and walked back out to the perimeter.

"You might find some answers in here," John had said. He left it on the ground next to Phil and walked away. That was all that was said.

After a while, after a few more missions, Phil's attitude changed. He wasn't the same as before, but he wasn't as angry as he had been.

Sitting on Phil's cot, John flipped through the pages of that same Bible, hoping Phil had found what he was looking for.

For every non-religious guy who found God during war, there was a religious guy out there whose faith was starting to crumble. And though he didn't want to admit it, John was that guy. He was raised Christian and had always felt his faith was solid. But the strain of war was punching a lot of holes in it.

He flipped in Phil's Bible to a dog-eared page. There was a pencil mark next to one of the passages. John rested his elbows on his legs and read.

Luke 6:37 Judge not, and ye shall not be judged: condemn not, and ye shall not be condemned: forgive, and ye shall be forgiven:

Phil was kind of a reserved guy, so it was difficult to really know what about that passage stood out to him. But it made John think about Brandon. What the passage said to John was that blaming Brandon for Phil's death wasn't going to solve anything.

What kind of God lets this shit happen?

"I wish I knew, brother," John said to the pages. Exhaling, John's shoulders slumped and his hands dropped between his knees. His thumbs wedged between the pages. It was so easy to blame Brandon. If he would have just *listened*.

How could John forgive a man he was beginning to hate? A man who took someone he loved?

John didn't have an answer for that. He placed the Bible in the box and finished packing. He set the box beneath Phil's bunk and walked toward the front door, picking up Phil's letter as he passed and went out onto the porch. Rain drummed the metal trashcan lid. Thick tendrils of rain fell on the far-away hilltops and wind gusts fanned and dropped them like fingers dancing some unseen marionette in the valley below. John stood beneath the awning watching. Stood there for a long time as the puddles rippled. He wanted to wait until the rain stopped before dropping off Phil's things. He didn't want the box getting shipped home a soggy mess.

Closing his eyes, John leaned back against the wall, thumbing through the pages of his own Bible. He stopped randomly and looked at the pages.

"Of all the possible...."

Psalm 13:1 How long wilt thou forget me, O LORD? for ever? how long wilt thou hide thy face from me?

John searched for more uplifting passages. But even when he went back to the ones that helped him in his adolescence, he failed to find any solace in their words. The thunder came again, farther off, but the rain showed no signs of letting up.

John's watch showed 1630. The supply guys would be closing up soon to grab their evening meal. New York was scheduled down for forty-eight. He could send Phil's stuff out tomorrow. And he could get blackout drunk tonight. He tapped his breast pocket. Phil's dog tags jingled inside.

John was about to go inside and lock up, but stopped when a lone figure, carrying a rifle by the fore-grips, came running toward him through the rain.

Brandon. His black hair wet and slicked down his forehead. John's hand tightened on his Bible.

"Sergeant Nicholas!" Brandon shouted over the rain. He slipped in under the awning and stopped. Breathless, he said, "Gather up the team. I've just received a WARNO."

"A warning order?" John reminded himself to keep it cordial. He held up his hand. "Hang on, sir. New York just came off-mission. We're down for forty-eight. That's the colonel's policy."

"Then his policy just changed. I received this mission personally from him. It's a CIA operation. The colonel specifically said he wanted New York."

If John told Brandon to pound sand it would probably cause more harm than good.

"Sir," John said. "The guys are exhausted. We just lost a man. They're off at the Lizard right now. They won't be able to see straight by the time I stop them."

Brandon's head cocked to the side, like a dog trying to comprehend human speech. "Then go stop them *now*, sergeant. We're leaving well before first light."

It might have been John's exhaustion. Maybe his grief. Something was eating him. The pressure in John's head dizzied him. Blurred his vision. He rubbed his eyes.

Brandon said, "Did you hear me, Serg—"

"*You* go fucking stop them!" John roared. "They're off getting shitfaced because *you* got Phil killed!"

The release of anger and despair felt so good he couldn't stop himself. John said, "You're alive today because New York got you out of that jungle. The price was a fucking life. Phil is dead because you refused to listen. Because of your fucking *stupidity!* And you want to put us right back out on some bullshit mission?" John pointed off toward the Lizard. "If you walk into that bar and try and stop *my men* because you're so goddamned eager to please the colonel—"

"At ease, sergeant!" Brandon screamed. So loud it reverberated in the hut's metal. Brandon stepped up to John, snarling, "As a matter of fact, I *am* eager to please the colonel. You should be eager, too, *Saint* Nick. You're the one who does miracles, right? Do you take requests? Because I've got one for you. Bring Florida back alive."

John stared at him. "Florida?" It was all John could make his mouth say.

"Florida," Brandon said. "This *bullshit mission*, it's a search-and-rescue."

That hit John like a mortar round. He would never refuse a search-and-rescue. No one in SOG would ever say no to that. They knew how easy it was to become the team that needed to be rescued.

"Nothing to say?" Brandon said. "Let me fill you in. The longer we stand here," Brandon raised his hand toward the jungle. "The longer Florida is out there waiting to be rescued. Now get your ass over to that bar and round up *my* team."

They stared at each other. John's anger and pride swirled and swelled inside him. He shook. Thought he might be sick. He grabbed the railing and bent over. Exhaled. The fight that was in him deflated with his breath. John bowed his head and looked at Brandon over his arms. "Where do you want us?"

Brandon lifted his chin, looked down his nose at John. John's elbow tingled at the opportunity to crush that fucker's trachea. "Command bunker in thirty minutes. Colonel Murphy cleared it out for our mission planning."

That was an odd place to do the planning, but if Brandon wanted New York stumbling and puking all over the colonel's toys, well, that wasn't John's problem anymore.

"We'll be there."

Brandon's eyes lingered on him. Then he turned and jogged off through the rain toward the officers' huts. John, still shaking, watched him disappear into the gloom.

"Goddamnit!" John roared, and drove his boot into the trashcan. The side imploded with a hollow bang, and the can lifted and tumbled, cardboard C-ration cartons and empty packs of cigarettes blew out into the mud.

Stooping to right the trashcan, John's Bible slipped from his hand and splashed in a mud puddle. He snatched it up quick. Thick muddy rivulets ran down the paper cover. The pages swelled with red water.

How long wilt thou forget me?
How long wilt thou hide thy face from me?

John looked up into the clouds. The rain pelted and stung his face. And though he stared at the sky for a long time, no answers came. No epiphanies. No comfort.

He held the Bible up in his trembling hand. "Keep hiding," he said to the sky. "I'm done looking." He slammed the book in the trashcan. The empty metal tolled like a bell and the sound followed him through the beating rain as he set off to collect his men.

CHAPTER FIVE

The C-130 shuddered. Slammed hard in the sky. Brandon sat in the dark cargo hold and gripped the baggy fabric of his trouser leg. Crushed and balled it in his shaking, sweating hands.

Just turbulence. We're fine. Just turbulence.

In a few moments the shaking stopped. The aircraft settled. Vibrated with its low, four-engined hum.

They were running dark. No unnecessary light. The soft illumination of tiny control panel lights throughout the cargo hold outlined bulky black shapes. Parachutes. Rucksacks. Men seated in a row.

Keep them in line, Smith had said. *Keep them following orders.*

Easier said than done.

Before New York had even boarded the aircraft, John had bombarded Brandon with questions. When Brandon answered, John criticized his every decision.

Standing outside the C-130's lowered ramp as the rest of New York shuffled aboard, heavy with their parachutes and rucksacks, John had said, "I'm better suited to be jumpmaster. I have the experience."

Brandon, exhausted from lack of sleep and John's countless questions said, "I've got my jumpmaster wings same as you. *I'm* supervising the jump. That's what Smith wants."

"I'm telling you the jump order needs to change. This is Boing's first jump. I want him close to me."

"It's not changing," Brandon said. "Smith jumps first, followed by the most experienced gunfighters. That's you and Chris. That's what Smith wants—"

"I don't give a shit what Smith wants."

"*I* do!" Brandon pointed to the ramp. "Get on that fucking aircraft! Now!"

That was about four hours ago.

In that time the cargo hold grew hot and muggy. Brandon pulled a spare bandana from his cargo pocket. Wiped his hands and sweating neck.

Boing sat at the end of the jump order, toward the cockpit—doubled over in his seat, head in his hands. Maybe it *was* a good idea to move the interpreter up in the order instead of having him jump last. If Boing got squirrely at the door, Brandon would be the only one left to deal with the problem.

Boing's knees bounced.

And that didn't sit well with Brandon. He'd seen the same behavior in lots of trainees at the Airborne Department. Some of the trainees, they got up to the door, took one look out into open sky and their hands shot out and death-gripped anything they could get their hands on.

Who could really blame them? A lot of things could go wrong as soon as you stepped out that door. Even if you knew what you were doing, most of those things were still deadly.

Well. One way or another, Boing was going to earn his jump-pay. If Brandon had to kick him out, so be it.

Keep them in line, Smith had said. *Recommendations for each of you for assignments at the Pentagon.*

Brandon shook his head. Jesus, these guys were making things difficult. If it wasn't John's arguing or Boing's fear, it was Chris's mouth. Chris seemed to go out of his way to irritate Brandon. To embarrass him in front of Smith. Make him seem an incompetent commander.

In the command bunker during New York's briefing, Smith had dropped two duffle bags on the floor by Brandon's feet. Stenciled on one was the word *TOPS*. On the other, *BOTTOMS*.

"Grab some new uniforms, gentlemen," Smith had said. "You won't be Americans on this operation."

Chris, stinking drunk, asked, "Who we gonna be?"

Smith, eyes dark with annoyance, said, "Anyone but American."

Chris came over and stooped by the bags. Pulled out a blue and black tiger-striped jacket. His words came out in a haze of alcohol. "I *love* playing pretend!" He scrunched the fabric and nuzzled it. "Mmm. I want to be Russian. Can I be Russian?" He stuck his nose in Smith's face. "Comrade?"

Face burning, Brandon growled, "That's enough."

Chris pouted. Whispered loudly to Smith, "I think I know who *he* wants to pretend as." And he clacked his heels together and Nazi saluted Brandon.

"Goddamnit, I said *enough*!"

Chris waved the jacket around. "A bunch of white boys hangin' out in the jungle with a black guy, a Mexican, and a Vietnamese interpreter. No! No one will know we're American Special Forces *at all*—"

John had grabbed Chris by the collar and dragged him stumbling and giggling to the wall of maps on the far side of the bunker. Quiet words were exchanged. Chris had shut his mouth after that. Brandon seriously doubted it would stay shut.

Even hours later, Brandon's anger still simmered. Chris had refused to shut up when his commander warned him. *Twice*. But one fucking word from John....

Down the line, Chris leaned back against the cargo webbing. Mouth hanging open. Passed out.

Keep them in line.

And just how the hell was Brandon going to do that? Any of Brandon's perceived control over New York was obliterated by John's constant arguing and Chris's...

Chris's...

Incessant fuckery!

These men laughed at the UCMJ. As long as they didn't assault Brandon, or kill him, there was virtually nothing Brandon could do to them. He had shared his concerns with Captain Jones at dinner just a few hours prior.

"You know how long it takes the Army to grow a Green Beret?" Jones had said. "Then they have to *volunteer* for recon. Then there's a selection process." He shook his head. "No way. Word gets out that guys are being punished for shooting their mouths off, that volunteer pool is gonna dry up. For these guys there's no way the colonel would recommend punishment for anything less than murder."

Brandon's grinding teeth drowned out the four propellers droning outside the plane.

Keep them in line, Smith had said. *Out where we're going, one man can make or break the mission.*

Smith stood up from his seat across from Brandon. His metallic voice came over the headset. "Alright, gentlemen. I've just been notified that we will *not* be aborting the mission. Let me fill you in on some further details."

Shadowy heads turned toward Smith. Someone nudged Chris and his head shot up.

"First," Smith said. "Welcome to Northern Vietnam." Smith handed Brandon a bulging manila envelope.

Brandon clicked on the red light at his shoulder. Scrawled in pen across the envelope was the word *Mercury*.

Smith handed John a similar package.

"What's Mercury?" Brandon asked.

"Just an in-house designation for our operations," Smith said. "Nothing to concern yourself with."

Brandon nodded and clicked off his light.

"Inside those envelopes you'll find your maps of the

mission area. And there's larger maps of every square kilometer from our insertion all the way back to Da Nang."

"We're walking home?" John asked.

"I don't plan on it," Smith said. "But I planned *for* it."

John nodded in the dark.

"We'll be over the drop zone in about ten minutes. It's a small rice paddy on the outskirts of a small remote village. We won't have a lot of time over it. As for our objective—"

"Objective?" John asked. "I was told this was a rescue."

"That's *partly* accurate. Three days ago, Recon Team Florida, along with my colleague as their handler, inserted into the jungle near the same village we're heading to now. Their mission was to locate and secure a High Value Target. A man. My agency wants this man. Our mission is to pick up where Florida left off. If we find survivors, we'll help them as best we can. For the others, we'll mark the grid coordinates and your Mortuary Affairs will handle recovering their remains."

There was a log silence before a deep baritone voice cut in on the headset. Mike, New York's medic. "You suspect your HVT is in the village?"

"Unknown. I was hoping Florida would have been able to confirm that. That didn't happen."

"What do we know about your target?" John asked.

"Not much. Reclusive. Hasn't been seen for a long time. But intelligence and recent developments suggest he's at least *near* the village."

Chris said, "What's Florida's status?"

"Dire. With the site being so far north, we needed to use a re-trans aircraft to forward their radio traffic. We only had a two-hour window in the mornings and evenings to speak with them. We'll have the same problem on the ground, I'm afraid. I monitored every radio call Florida made. I won't sugarcoat it, gentlemen. Things went south really fast for Florida."

"Could they have been captured?" Brandon asked.

"I highly doubt it. But keep your capsule readily available in case that happens. There's no shame in it."

Brandon's heart iced up at the mention of the cyanide. The death sentence nestled in his shirt pocket. Smith had stood on the lowered C-130 ramp and handed a tiny orange pill bottle to each man as they boarded the aircraft.

"The first call to come in," Smith said, "was from my colleague. He reported Florida had reached the village and had established an extended recon site from which to observe the village and its people. During the evening commo-window, Florida's senior NCO reported in and said my colleague was investigating a lead on the HVT. The senior NCO and another Florida man stayed behind at the recon site. The rest of the team followed my colleague. That was the last contact we had with them."

"Any idea what happened to the guys who stayed at the recon site?" John asked.

"No. Each subsequent retrans aircraft reported negative contact with Florida."

Brandon stared at Smith in disbelief. A whole team wiped out? One or two men surviving on their own in hostile territory for the past forty-eight hours? *Maybe* surviving? What the hell was Brandon getting into? Why hadn't Smith requested a bigger unit for this? Requested a fucking Infantry company for Christ's sake?

"What type of opposition was Florida up against?" John asked.

"I wish I knew."

Chris said, "Sounds a lot like Counter Recon."

Smith shook his head. "Doubtful. NVA stay away from the village from what we can tell. But that has recently changed as well. We picked up some NVA chatter. A company-sized element is heading toward the village."

"Why?" John asked. "They pick up Florida's radio traffic?"

"Enemy RADAR picked up one of our aircraft circling. The NVA area commanders want to know who is snooping around and why they're so interested in the place."

"How long do we have before the NVA arrive?"

"Unknown."

John sighed and looked around at the team. "Are the villagers hostile? You think they had anything to do with Florida's disappearance?"

"Our first assessment was that they were just fishermen. There's some farmland nearby that the women tend. But..." Smith blew out a long breath. "Everything we thought we knew changed in the last forty-eight hours. Given the fluid situation, we've been authorized..." Smith held up his palms, maybe weighing his next words. "*Relaxed* rules of engagement."

"Well?" John said. "What are they?"

"They don't exist," Smith said. "There are no rules of engagement. Your actions will not be questioned by your government. If you come across a toddler and you don't like the way he's looking at you, well, like I said, you're not Americans on this mission."

What the fuck did Brandon just walk into? He rubbed his eyes. A few hours ago, Smith was promising Brandon a job at the Pentagon, but Jesus, he didn't think he'd have to consider slaughtering women and children to get it.

Maybe it wouldn't have to come to that.

Maybe?

No. No, it *would not* come to that. Nobody needed to die unless they were a threat. These guys were recon. The best, right? Ghosts. Invisible. If nobody saw them, there was no reason for a gunfight. Brandon's knees were bouncing so hard the manila envelope slid off his lap and slapped on the floor.

He picked it up and clicked on his red light. He pulled the documents from the envelope. Flipped through them. Just maps and aerial photographs. He looked at them carefully and tried to get his mind back on track. On an objective overview of the mission. He flipped through all the documents and looked up at Smith. "I don't see anything in here about your HVT. Who is he? What's he look like?"

Smith rubbed his red-lit chin. "Who he is doesn't concern you. And we couldn't find any photos of him, so even *I* don't know what he looks like. As I understand it, we'll know him when we see him."

"How?" Brandon asked.

"His eyes."

The aircraft's warning light clicked on, bathing the cargo area in dim red light.

A crew-member's voice crackled over the headset. "Two minutes, guys."

"Gentlemen," Smith raised his hands and the men stood. "Our jump window is small. Maybe fifteen seconds. You miss it and you're going in the trees, or worse, landing in the middle of the village. When the light turns green, get your ass out the door."

Brandon stuffed the envelope in his rucksack and hung his headset on a hook. He stood and went to the aft door. Pulled the handle and yanked the door inward. Wind and engine roar blew into the cargo hold.

Brandon swept the door seams and stomped the platform. He finished his checks just as the green light flashed. *Fifteen seconds.* He turned and waved Smith forward. Smith passed him his static line.

Brandon shot out his arm. "Go!"

Smith was gone.

John came, passed his line over. Before Brandon could say anything, John was out the door.

Prick.

Two-one-thousand. Chris, Terry, Mike, their faces illuminated in green light. Gone. The next alien face. *Three-one-thousand.* Gone.

Howard, Dan, and George went out the door, faces

calm like they were on their commute to work. Brandon checked outside, *four-one-thousand,* and parachute canopies billowed out like tiny clouds and drifted away behind the aircraft. *Plenty of time.*

"Let's go, Boing…"

But Boing wasn't there.

Shielding his eyes against the harsh green light, Brandon peered into the darkness at the front of the aircraft. And into this darkness he lunged, lumbering with the cumbersome rucksack between his legs. Rushed toward the front of the C-130. And there he was. Doubled over and shaking. Chunks of neon green-lighted vomit plastered to his rucksack.

Seven-one-thousand.

Panic buzzed electric in Brandon's chest.

"Get the fuck up!" Brandon screamed. "We'll miss the jump!"

Boing wouldn't look at him. Just kept shaking his head.

Eight-one-thousand.

Brandon grabbed the parachute straps over Boing's shoulders and heaved. Boing dropped his weight so hard Brandon nearly toppled over. If that fucker wasn't New York's only interpreter, Brandon would have just left him.

Nine. Ten-one-thousand.

Brandon hauled again, screamed in Boing's ear. "Get up, you sonofabitch! Get! Up!" Brandon heaved.

A flash. Pain. Blurry vision. Brandon's jaw throbbed.

He fucking hit me.

The green light clicked off and the red light switched on.

He missed it. His belly went numb. Holy shit. He missed the jump.

Don't fuck up. Keep them in line.

He snatched Boing's sweaty wet hair and pulled his head back. And punched Boing in the jaw. Dull pain in Brandon's knuckles. Boing's face dropped onto his puke-covered rucksack.

Chest heaving with panicked breaths, Brandon rolled Boing onto his back. Grabbed the shoulder straps and hauled Boing's unconscious bulk toward the door.

A crew-chief or co-pilot or someone appeared. Probably to close the door after the team had jumped. The man waved his hands, mouthing something. Brandon dropped Boing's dead weight and slipped his 1911 from the holster and leveled it at the man. His hands stopped waving and he reached for the sky. Stumbled backward away from that howling door.

Holstering his pistol, Brandon grabbed Boing and hauled him to the door.

Boing stirred. Brandon pulled him to his feet. Turned him with his back toward the door. Brandon grabbed Boing's static line and hooked it to the steel cable overhead.

Boing shook his dazed head. Confusion in his red-lit eyes. The roaring wind must have drawn his attention. He looked behind him into that hurricane dark. And terror stretched across his face. Groggy arms shot out to grab helplessly at the door frame.

"Sorry about this." Brandon put his boot into Boing's chest and shoved. Boing's shaking, vomit-soaked fingertips slipped from the doorframe and he went sailing out into the night and the wind.

Brandon tugged at his own static line and found it secure. There was moonlight above and darkness below.

Trees or the village.

Brandon hoped for the trees.

And he leapt.

CHAPTER SIX

John lay prone. Piss-warm water soaked his uniform, spilled into his boots. Chin-deep in the rice paddy muck he aimed his rifle into that giant dark. That rolling, black, moonlight-lined jungle mass.

Smith lay five meters away.

Tethered rucksacks splashed down from the sky. Moments later their owners hit the muck and grunted and rolled in the wet. Metal scrapes and clinks. Unbuckling. They shed their parachutes and sank low on their bellies in the rice paddy. Aimed their rifles into the dark.

There was no need to watch the men descend. John counted the splashes. There should have been two more. But they didn't come. And still didn't come.

"John!" Chris hissed. "Oh shit, John!"

The fear in Chris's voice already kicked John's heart up in gear. But it bang-shifted when he saw beyond Chris's arm stabbing at the sky. Stabbing at the twirling, flapping streamer silhouetted against the moon and rocketing to Earth.

John sprang out of the muck. "On me!" He plowed through the shin-deep water. Abandoning noise-discipline. Abandoning caution. "New York, on me!"

He ran, high-stepping. Like jumping over hurdles. Pumping and pulling his legs from the sucking muck. Leg muscles burning.

No way that was Brandon up there. Brandon was Jump Master qualified. He would've pulled his reserve chute by now. That had to be Boing.

"Fuck!" John cried. Running. Panting. "Jesus, Boing! Pull your reserve!"

Closer now. In the moonlight, the spinning figure's arms stretched overhead. Hands death-gripped on the thick rigging.

Too slow. The mire New York ran through grabbed their feet, tripped them up. They'd never make it to Boing before he hit. But what could they do even if they did?

Gasping for air, John stopped dead in the slush, cupped his hands to his mouth and screamed to Boing. "Pull the reserve!" He sucked in air and nearly puked, screaming, "Pull the reserve!"

Heavy wet sounds all around him. Other voices joined. "Reserve!"

"Pull the reserve!"

"Reserve!"

All the voices together devolved into a screaming, cult-like chant. Like calling forth some ancient God. "Reserve! Reserve! Reserve!"

In that thumb's distance between moon and jungle canopy, a black tentacle spit out from Boing like ink in water. The reserve chute.

The men fell silent.

Water ran off them and trickled in the rice paddy.

They watched the chute streaming and flapping and finally catching air and billow and…

Reality slipped its cruel hands around the throat of John's hope. And squeezed.

Boing had been nearly to the ground and still rocketing when the reserve chute finally deployed. John slapped his hands over his eyes.

Two heartbeats later, the sound came. The sound of impact.

John fought to crack his eyes open. He didn't want to see.

He knew what he'd see. He shifted his eyes skyward. And he saw a black dome silhouetted against the moon. A fully deployed chute drifting down and down. Out in the distance there was a tiny splash.

Brandon...

John was running. Running toward the end of the rice paddy. Running toward the flaring parachute. Running toward the figure yanking it down.

John hit Brandon at a dead run. Grabbing shirt. Grabbing flesh beneath it in his fists. Brandon and John toppled in the water. John, retching from the sprint, grabbed Brandon up by the shirt and snarled. "What the fuck happened?"

Brandon's mouth worked like something short-circuited in his mind. Every time he opened his mouth, he didn't speak.

And every time Brandon didn't speak, John shook him and said, "What happened?"

Finally something shook loose.

Brandon stammered, "I don't know."

"You don't *know*? You're the Jump Master! What the fuck do you mean you don't know?"

"I—"

Someone splashed behind John. Called to him.

Not taking his eyes off Brandon's, so furious he didn't even know who had called to him. "I'm busy!"

"No, man," the voice said. "Boing's alive! The fall knocked him out. Mike needs you." Wet footsteps receded into the night. "Come on!"

John looked at Brandon. Hard. Moonlight in his wet hair. Shadows in his eyes. He let go of Brandon's shirt and the kid sank in the water. "Grab your shit." Then John turned and trudged toward the group.

And as he went, a sound came out of the night. A sound that reached inside John's chest and clawed his heart.

Screaming.

He came upon Chris sitting in the muck. Boing hauled up into his lap. "I gottcha, Boing," Chris said. "I'm here. We're here."

Silence as Boing inhaled long. His arms flapped, hands splashing in the rice paddy, fists beating against Chris's thighs.

Then Boing screamed.

Chris slipped a hand over Boing's mouth. "I know, man. Let it out. Scream all you want. I just need to keep it quiet." Chris slipped his other arm around Boing's chest and cradled him. He looked up at John. Mouth hanging open. Shaking his head.

Mike thrust his big aid bag into John's hands and pulled him down to crouch in the water beside Boing. "Keep the bag out of the water."

"His legs?" John asked.

"I'll know in a minute."

John unzipped the aid bag and clicked on his red flashlight and shined the light into the kit and held it out for Mike.

Mike's hands disappeared beneath the water and he felt around Boing's legs. Boing jerked. His wails muffled beneath Chris's hand.

When Mike lifted his hands dripping from the water, the look on his face conjured images John did not want to see. Images of despair. Images of hopelessness.

Glass vials clinked as Mike dug around in his aid bag. Yanked open snapped pouches. "Sit tight, Boing. Got something real nice for you."

Moonlight spilled from Boing's eyes and he sobbed through Chris's fingers.

Mike punched Boing's thigh. Held his fist there. Boing cried out and pulled away. When Mike withdrew his fist there was a pinprick of reflected light. He capped the sharp thing and threw it away into the water.

Morphine.

"Litter!" Mike called.

Dan and Terry already had it assembled. They pushed through and set it down, submerging it in the water beside Boing.

Chris rocked Boing in his lap. "We're gonna get you outta here, Boing. See that? We got the king's chair for you. You ready to go?"

Groans, drunken and muffled was all Boing could manage.

In the soft blue moonlight John could see the shaking in Boing's torso slowing. His flapping, beating hands went lethargic. Then they collapsed, splashing in the rice paddy.

"He's out," Mike said. "Load him up. Careful with his legs."

"Head for the treeline," John said. "We need to get out of the open."

The team loaded Boing onto the litter, strapping him down about the chest and waist. John rallied the men and led them from the rice paddy's wide openness into the black jungle's concealment. He assigned men to bury the parachutes and they disappeared with their e-tools.

He stood over Boing. Chris and Mike joined him.

Brandon stood beside Smith.

"We need a MEDEVAC," John said.

"I can't help you," Smith said. "Not until the retrans aircraft arrives in the morning."

"Call the bird that dropped us. They can retransmit."

"It's out of range."

"It *just* dropped us," John said. "It's worth a shot."

"Counter Recon. Too much of a risk."

"I'll risk it."

Smith's blacked-out head turned to Brandon. "Captain?"

Blood pounded in John's neck. Throbbing with each

moment that Brandon did not speak.

"Counter Recon," Brandon mumbled. "It's too much of a risk."

John lunged. "You mother—"

Smith stepped between them. "You don't even know what's wrong with that man."

"I know exactly what's wrong with him," Mike said. "His legs are shattered to the knee."

"Life-threatening?"

Mike scoffed. "You're damn right it's life-threatening."

"Gentlemen." Smith held up his palms. "It's unfortunate. I'm sorry. But the damage is done. That man is going to lose his legs if we get him help now or eight hours from now." Smith brushed by John to stand over Boing. He looked at him. He looked at Mike. "I know you're more than capable of keeping him comfortable until morning. Are you so quick to abandon your missing team?"

"Florida is *dead*," John said. "You said it yourself. I don't want Boing ending up the same way."

Smith turned to John. "I said their situation was dire. They could still be very much alive."

John looked at Boing. He didn't want to admit it, but Smith had a point. There could be survivors out there.

"Can you keep him comfortable, Mike?" Feeling very tired, John rubbed his eyes. "Will he keep until morning?"

Mike said nothing.

John nodded. Understanding completely. "I'm not leaving Mike here alone."

"Of course not." Smith placed a hand on John's shoulder. "Simple fix. We'll split our group. A small security team will stay here. I'll give them the grid coordinates for our objective and they can meet us once your medic determines your interpreter can safely be moved."

John considered that. Splitting the team was never a good idea. God, why did this have to happen? Why now?

What had John done to deserve such a—

"Sergeant?" Smith said. "We have a lot of searching to do before sunrise."

John sighed. "Right." He walked over to Brandon. Whispered, "Mike needs to work on Boing. You're going to stay with him while I go with Smith."

Brandon looked at Boing. Looked at John. "I want to stay with Smith."

Shivers rippled through John's shoulders. "I don't care what you want. I don't care what Smith wants." Pointing at Boing, he whispered, "I *do* care what happens to Boing. You were the Jump Master. What happened to Boing, that was *your* fault. You don't get to brush that off. Not this time. Whatever Mike needs, you're going to give him. You're going to remember what you did so you don't do it again."

Brandon opened his mouth to speak, but shut it when John grabbed a fistful of his shirt.

"The next words out of your mouth better be 'I'll stay with Boing'."

Through his knuckles John felt Brandon's torso trembling.

"I'll stay with Boing," Brandon said.

John let out a long breath. He let go of Brandon's shirt. "I'll leave Chris with you. When Mike feels ready, you come to us."

Brandon said nothing.

John didn't expect him to. He left the young captain standing there and found Chris. Told him what he wanted to happen.

Chris shrugged. "I might lose the captain somewhere between here and the objective."

"I believe it." John lightly punched Chris in the chest. "At least make an effort not to overtly kill him. It'll look good on your NCOER."

How the hell was John going to fix this mess? Could he even fix it?

Smith scribbled some coordinates on a piece of torn-out notepad paper and handed it to Chris.

John threw his rucksack onto his shoulders. "One more thing." He motioned Chris close. Whispered in his ear. "Let Brandon lead a bit, huh? I gave him a hard enough time about all this. He doesn't need it from everyone else. It might make our lives easier in the long run if he feels like a commander."

Chris recoiled. "Are you out of your fucking mind?"

"Just..." John held up his hand. "Just do this one thing for me."

Chris looked at Brandon. Back to John. "No promises."

"Howard and Dan," John said. "You're with me and Smith. The rest of you stay here." He turned to Smith. "We're ready. Give Howard the coordinates. He'll take point."

Smith clicked on his red flashlight. Howard leaned over Smith's proffered map and Smith pointed at a spot and said, "Maintain this azimuth for about a kilometer."

"Anything else?" Howard asked.

"Just keep an accurate pace-count and let me know when you've gone a klik."

Howard shrugged. "Okey-dokey. On me."

John looked back as they moved out. Chris's red light shined down on Boing and Mike. Brandon knelt, obscured by shadow. Soon, the jungle swallowed up the men he had left behind.

Whatever happened in the plane, it must have been something with Boing. It was the kid's first jump. He had *told* Brandon that. John should've done something. Something *more* to make sure Boing went out the door first.

They moved on, following Howard deeper into the jungle.

Thoughts weighed him down on the walk. Phil. Boing. Eventually the ground leveled out. Still damp and soft.

Each sucking step pulled from the muck coughed up puffs of stinking rot.

They walked for some time. Slipped deeper and deeper into that dark. John was still brooding over his regrets when something—some odd feeling—reached out of the black. John paused. Listened.

Unable to grasp what had bothered him, he continued on, trying to puzzle out what he felt. The jungle seemed old. Untouched by humans. That wasn't what bothered him. There was something else. John had crept through lots of similar places. But he couldn't quite place what was off. All he knew was that he didn't like it. He kept these feelings to himself. His fingers slipped up to the cross beneath his shirt and he rubbed it.

Just nerves. A lot on my mind.

John checked his watch frequently. The green luminescent hands brilliant in the near-total darkness. They had been marching for nearly an hour when Smith signaled Howard.

Moments later, Howard materialized from the gloom. A shadow against shadows. "What's up?"

"What's your pace count?" Smith asked.

"Nearly there. About another fifty meters."

"That's my estimate, too." Smith turned to John. "What about you?"

"About that, yeah," John said. "Fifty or sixty meters."

Smith said, "Take it a little slower from here. I don't know what to expect. Florida—or whoever came for them—could have left surprises."

Howard grunted. "Step where I step." He turned and eased through the foliage.

John swallowed hard. He wouldn't be happy if he lost Howard to a friendly claymore.

They moved on. Slow and deliberate movements. Silence descended heavy on them.

John's thoughts drifted. To Boing. To Brandon. To how the hell could you screw up jumping out of an airplane—

John squeezed his hands into fists and breathed out slow.

Focus.

There would be plenty of time to be pissed off at Brandon. He had to keep his thoughts on the mission. On the here and now. Think about what kind of enemy he might be up against.

What did he know?

He knew it was a considerable feat to take out an entire recon team. That's why the Counter Recon teams were born. Because the NVA regulars couldn't manage it. Whoever was lurking out here, they were dangerous. Or maybe they just had the bigger numbers. For all John knew, they could be walking into an NVA headquarters. Or a Counter Recon training ground. Whatever was out there, he hoped—

John bumped into Smith. The operative was kneeling on the ground, fist raised. John crept forward to Howard. "What's up?"

"You smell it?" Howard whispered.

John took in a few short sniffs. "I don't…"

But he did.

When he opened his mouth to speak, the lightest tinge of something acrid brushed his tongue. The taste moved into his throat. He inhaled deeply. "Yes."

"Gunpowder?" Smith asked.

Howard clicked his tongue. "Not unless someone fired off about a thousand rounds just a few minutes ago. My guess is that something went boom."

"Smells like Laos," John said.

Howard grunted. "Uh huh."

"What happened in Laos?" Smith asked.

"Detonated a lot of claymores," John said.

"Yeah." Howard sniffed long and low. "Florida was here."

John nodded. They waited there in the dark. Listened.

He rubbed his palm up and down a tree until tiny jagged splinters poked his skin. He thumbed the splinters. Found a hole about the size of his fingertip. Found another. And another.

One claymore would blow seven-hundred tiny metal balls at anyone unlucky enough to be in front of it. By the smell of that little patch of jungle, a lot more than one had been detonated.

Florida *had* been there. It didn't worry John that there was no sign of the missing team. It was a standard tactic to deploy claymores against pursuers while evading. What worried him was that there were no pieces of whoever had attacked them.

John asked, "Was this Florida's recon site?"

"Yeah," Smith said. "My man said they were dug in pretty well."

New guys. Cherries. Out in the bush a cherry might jump at shadows. Might blow claymores if something spooked them. But not a recon team. If Florida blew a bunch of claymores, they had a reason.

What was out there in the dark that had spooked them?

Adrenaline came. John breathed in deep against it.

Smith said, "We should start searching here."

"What are you hoping to find?" Howard asked.

"I'd be happy if you could find me anything that doesn't grow out of the ground. Radios. Maybe a body."

Dan suggested using paracord strung between trees to mark off grids to make their search more methodical.

Smith and John agreed.

They set their packs on the ground and went to work stringing individual lengths of cord. The method gave them designated places to start and end. Prevented them from going over the same ground. Extremely helpful in the dark.

They advanced on-line, sliding their feet along the ground, clicking on a red-lensed flashlight when something they kicked didn't make the typical swish of grass.

Anything that went thud warranted inspection. But when they clicked on their lights all they found were clods of dirt knotted with weed roots.

They finished their first pass, untied their cords and shifted. Tied off new grids. After the second pass John untied his cord and wrapped it around his elbow and palm. He stopped, cord mid-wrap.

There was something again. A feeling. Something out in the dark. He stood dead still. Listened. He heard…

Nothing.

But the longer he listened in that absolute absence of sound, the more his guts fluttered. Anywhere in the jungle— Vietnam, Laos, wherever—there was always *something* moving. Something making a sound. But not here. He parted his lips. Tasted the air. This place, this air. It all seemed…*dead*.

He listened for a long time. He recognized the swishing and sweeping of Smith and Howard and Dan searching their grids. He listened for anything else.

John's gut feelings had saved his ass more times than he could count. But was this just his nerves? Counter Recon had been on his mind a lot. And Florida going missing. Now Boing. There were a lot of similarities between Ohio's and Florida's disappearances. Was John just paranoid? Losing his nerve?

He listened.

Silence.

There weren't many soldiers in *any* country's military, capable of moving in absolute silence through this type of foliage. He knew some snipers who had incredible stealth skills, but that type of movement required a lot of practice. Required self-discipline forged of iron. He listened hard. Tasted C-4 on his tongue. Maybe the blasts had scared off all the life. Maybe whatever creeped or crawled or flew around there didn't like the taste of explosives any more than John did.

He relaxed at the thought. No. If there was someone

there, someone creeping toward them, John would have heard them.

John found Smith's line and kept a hand on it and followed it to find a tree to mark his own grid. God, if the whole team were there they would have finished this fucking search by now. John felt at his elbow for the end of the cord wrapped around it and—

Something thudded hollow against his boot.

He froze. Flexed his foot inside his boot. A shape. Round. He could feel it through his boot leather. He clicked on his flashlight with his free hand and shined it at his feet. In the red light, motor-oil black liquid streaked down his pant leg to the dark oval shape resting against his boot. Whatever the liquid was, he hadn't kicked the thing hard enough for it to splatter his leg like that. Unless it had fallen. Maybe a coconut. He squinted at the thing on the ground, covered in a black and sticky wet mass of something like a cat's hacked-up hairball.

Jesus, that *was* hair.

John's senses exploded. Pores yawned and spewed sweat. He dropped to his knee, reached around and grasped at his rifle slung over his back. The paracord yanked tight around his elbow and palm. He pulled his arm tight to unwrap it.

"Fuck."

A shriveled eye peered up at him from beneath tangled, matted hair. A girl's face. Her mouth hung open in a voiceless groan. The skin at her neck mangled and chopped apart.

Wheezing came from somewhere out in the darkness. Like a dying thing taking a last deep breath. Then the dark vibrated with a grating laughter. John swung the light toward the noise. Muscles electric. Buzzing.

A man. Asian. Shirtless. Paces away. One arm ended short at a scarred and smooth stump below the elbow. His face. His eyes.

Oh Jesus, his eyes—

The man lunged, cackling, hand contorted in a grotesque claw. John fell on his back. Tried to bring up his rifle.

"Shit!" John yelled. The paracord wrapped around his elbow had trapped his arm. He couldn't aim.

The man fell on him. Plowed his knee into John's groin. Squishing balls against bone. Tight pressure ballooned in John's gut and he howled in pain. In fear. The red flashlight reflected in the man's eyes. All white. All red in the light. The cripple batted the flashlight and it went flying. Total darkness. Filthy fingers slithered in John's mouth. Fingernails clawed at his gums and tongue and cheek and the roof of his mouth. John pushed with his free hand. Tried to grab. But only found sweat-slick skin and tight muscle.

Fingernails in his mouth tore open soft flesh. Blood leaked in John's mouth. John gnashed his teeth. Bit hard on fingers. Rancid filth and skin stuck in his teeth.

John thrashed and bucked his hips. His trapped hand brushed something hard at his hip.

His 1911.

John let his rifle fall and he yanked the pistol from the holster and thumbed off the safety. The paracord trapped his arm, but he could work it just enough.

He rammed the pistol beneath the man's ribcage and pulled the trigger once. Twice. The pop deafening. Bells rang over gunfire.

The man rocked back. His weight lifted from John's chest. In the dark, John threw his free hand up and swatted around until he found the man's slippery neck. Cupped the back of the man's head. John pulled the man down to his chest in a murderous embrace. Screaming, John rammed the 1911's muzzle into the man's ear. Metal clunked on skull under skin.

John pulled the trigger.

Warm slop sprayed John's face. The cripple jerked and went limp. Dead weight collapsed on John's belly and drove out the air from his burning lungs. John bucked his hips. Heaved the lifeless body off. It rolled limp to the side. The torso's weight pulling the dead arms across John's face and flopped to the ground.

John's head went heavy and he let it thump in the grass. Red lights swirled above him. Red dots leaving long, fading-red trails. Shouting voices from somewhere far off beyond the lights. He could focus on none of it. He didn't *want* to focus.

The red lights blurred and shifted into other colors he had never seen before. The shouting voices faded. But the empty silence they left was filled with…

Something crawled inside him. Something filthy. He couldn't stop it. He strained. Tried to push it out, but it poured into him.

Oh, God…

Miles away, John's heart thundered. His arm, it fought against him. He reached. Pulled. Reached. Reached for the only thing he could think to reach for.

His cross.

His skin laughed at him.

He clutched the cross in a fist through his shirt.

God!

Invisible hands grabbed John's fist. His fingers. Pulled. Pried. John clutched the cross.

From the dark. From inside. From inside John's mind, a voice. A terrifyingly sweet voice. It cooed at him. It said, *Yes! Resist!* It howled and thrust itself into John's soul. It screamed, *I fucking love it when you fight!*

CHAPTER SEVEN

Brandon ran in the dark. Tried to keep up with the men running ahead of him. Their red lights flicked on and off. On long enough to make sure they didn't smash into a tree at a dead run. Off again. On.

Chris had been on point, moving them toward Smith and the others. George and Terry on rear-security. Mike and Brandon had been carrying Boing on the litter. Few words had been exchanged when the gunshots had cracked in the night. They set Boing down. They all dropped their packs. They ran.

Anxiety spread through Brandon's chest as they slapped through foliage. But he didn't know what he was running toward. Only that there was gunfire.

Or, there *had been* gunfire.

Now, running through the dark, there was the sound of his breath. Sucking and blowing.

But the gunfire; it had ceased.

Chris called a halt by flashing a cone of red light at his feet. Mike and George knelt around him. Gasping, Brandon caught up and joined them.

"We're here," Chris whispered. "I haven't heard anything else? Any of you?"

No one spoke.

Chris rotated around, checking his compass. He jabbed his hand out. "That way. Get on-line. Five-meter spread."

Chris clicked off his light and that was all that was said. No other planning. Brandon had so many questions. But the men disappeared before he could ask any of them.

A hand came out of the dark and patted Brandon's shoulder. Every muscle in Brandon tensed.

"You remember the challenge and password?" Chris asked.

"Jesus," Brandon gasped.

"No, that's not it."

Brandon wiped the sweat from his face. Breathed deep. Exhaled. "Tiny and bubbles."

"Good." Chris knuckled Brandon's chest. "This'll be easy. Just shoot anyone who doesn't know the password."

In the dark, Chris's hands patted around on Brandon's gear. They stopped on the 1911 holstered at his hip. "Mmm. Sling your rifle. Keep your compass in one hand and the pistol in the other. That way you won't walk in front of us. Holler if you need something." And then he was gone.

Brandon stood in the dark and the silence. Alone.

Not alone. No. Five meters. There were only five meters between him and the next man.

He licked away sweat from his sandpapered lip. Swiveled his head. Neck-skin rubbing against his shirt collar loud in the silence. He slung his rifle. Taking a breath he brought his pistol up to his waist. Exhaling slow he pushed pistol-first into the foliage.

He held his compass by his hip and it kept him moving straight. His boot kicked something soft. He knelt. Touched it. Bulging pockets. Canvass straps.

A rucksack.

The word *tiny* formed on his lips. But the breath caught in his throat before he could call out in the night. He still didn't know if any of the men who had gone ahead were still alive. A tremble started in his biceps and went up his shoulders and arced down to his belly. Something told him not to call out. Not yet.

He went on. Torso trembling. Trembling so much that he didn't feel the thin tightness stretching across his thighs until he had taken all the slack out of the trip wire.

"Oh." Brandon whimpered. "Shit."

He froze. Squeezed his eyes shut. Prickling cold crawled up his back. The bead of sweat shaking on the tip of his nose fell and splatted on his thumb.

And nothing happened. No flash. No boom. Pistol in hand, he hooked his thumb around the wire. Ran it side to side. A slight elasticity. Fabric…

Paracord.

Not a trip wire.

The tension poured from his chest. Down his legs and into the grass. He nearly collapsed with relief. He stepped back from the cord. "Holy fucking *shit*." He waited for his heart to crawl out of his ass before moving on.

He reminded himself that Smith and the others had gone ahead to start their search. They must have been doing it by grid.

Dipping beneath the cord, Brandon continued on.

He pushed through the foliage into a small pocket in the jungle illuminated by three dim crimson stars. The red flashlights aimed up at him like some three-eyed demon looking up from a meal.

"Tiny!" one of the stars hissed.

1911 shaking in Brandon's hand, he said, "Buh-bubbles."

The lights hesitated. Then dipped back down. Their light spreading across a man—

"Jesus," Brandon said.

It was John. Bathed in the red light, he lay sprawled on his back. His fist clutched tight on his chest. His face and lips covered in blood. In gore. Slimy white chunks. Brandon fought the urge to puke.

"What…" Brandon gagged. "What happened?"

The three men said nothing. They did not move. Their lights held steady. Illuminating the red and black wetness. As if holding silent vigil over a thing stillborn from Hell.

Leaves rattled. A figure emerged from the jungle and shoved past Brandon. Chris. He stood there, looking. His hands shook. Curled into fists. And when Chris fell to his knees the air came out of him in a squeaking groan. The air Chris managed to take in, he used it to say, "Who…?" Used it to say, "Where are they?" He gasped and his hands fell upon John's chest. He said, "I'll kill 'em." Exhaling hard, he said, "I'll fucking kill them *all*. Where *are* they?"

Chris's despair must have broken some spell over Howard. His light shifted to Chris. "Chill out, man. John's fine. He's just unconscious. We already checked him for holes."

Chris looked up at him. Quietly, he said, "What?"

"It was just this one guy, man," Howard said. He shined his light on the wrecked visage of a man crumpled in the underbrush. "He tussled with John. John zapped him."

Chris stood and looked at the dead man. He looked at John. He looked at the group of men watching him. "Well why the fuck is he just *lying* there?" He kicked John's boot, it wavered and lay still.

Mike appeared. He knelt beside John and ran his hands over him. Put his ear to John's nose. Wiped away something black and greasy from John's neck and pushed his fingers into John's carotid artery.

Brandon stepped forward. "Someone tell me what happened."

"Ain't much to tell, man," Howard said. "This guy attacked John. John blasted the fucker to bits. That was that. And John just…" Howard held out his palms, "Just passed out."

"No one else came?"

Howard shook his head. "We hunkered down and

waited. You were the first ones to show up."

Brandon holstered his pistol and went to the dead man and shined his light down. A large trickle of blood from his ear. On the other side, his temple was blown open from where the .45 ACP exited. Eyeball bulging from his eyelid. Shirtless and shoeless. Counter Recon?

Maybe. But he didn't appear to have any weapons. And Counter Recon attacked in groups, but there hadn't been any follow-up attack.

It was difficult to look at the man for long. Covered in filth. Black grime squished into the lines and wrinkles of his destroyed face. He was missing an arm, but the scar tissue on the stump looked as though it had healed a long time ago.

Brandon looked to New York. "How did he sneak up on you?"

"Beats me," Howard said. "We were searching the area and John went to start a new grid. Next thing you know, he's screaming and shooting."

Chris shoved some snuff in his lip and wiped his hand on his pants. "I ain't never heard John scream before. If it wasn't you telling it, I'd never believe it."

"Having trouble believing it myself," Howard said. "Scared the shit outta me."

What nobody mentioned was that half the team had to stay behind because of Brandon. That they were somewhere else with their commander when they could have been watching John's back. Whatever was wrong with John, if he was hurt, these men would blame Brandon. Just as they blamed him for Phil. Just as John blamed him for Boing. Sweat beaded and rolled down Brandon's face. He rubbed at it with his sleeve, smearing the salt-sting into his eye. He should have just left Boing on the aircraft.

"Why is he unconscious?" Brandon asked. "Head injury?"

Mike's fingers worked around John's scalp. "Hard to

say. Mental trauma, maybe."

"Bullshit," Chris said. Half-heartedly kicking John again. "Wake up, Johnny. This ain't your first time killing someone."

"Do something useful," Mike said to Chris. "Help me clean this shit off him."

They poured canteen water on clean kerchiefs and wiped the gore from John's face, flinging the filthy rags into the underbrush when they had finished. Mike took a pen light from his shirt pocket, pulled John's eyelids open with his thumb and shined intense white light in John's eyes. Dipped it away. Shined it in his eyes again. John's pupils remained dilated, but there was some sort of cloudy haze coating them.

Mike asked, "He say anything before he lost consciousness?"

"Yeah," Howard said. And Howard rubbed his arm. Like rubbing away a chill.

"Well?"

"God," Howard said. "He was, I don't know. Calling out to God, I guess?"

"That's John for you." Chris bent down and wiped a chunk of congealing blood from John's shirt and lifted it to his nose. Sniffed. He held it out to Howard. "Cherry or strawberry?"

Howard swatted Chris's hand away. "Fuck off, man."

Brandon's stomach turned. "You're not helping, Sergeant."

Chris flicked the blood off his finger. Wiped his finger on his trousers. In the halo of Mike's pen light Chris's eyes lingered on Brandon. "I might have been here to help if the jump had gone right."

There it was. It had come sooner rather than later. Brandon looked at Smith, but he seemed more interested in John.

Keep them in line...

Brandon stood up straight and looked at Chris. Cleared

his throat so his voice wouldn't crack. "Stand down, Sergeant."

Mike clicked off his penlight. The jungle returned to that infernal red glow.

No one spoke. No one breathed. Brandon's neck tensed, the hair on it stood. Eyes adjusting in the dark, eyes flitting to the red-black shadows surrounding him. He suddenly felt terribly alone.

There were stories. Rumors. Of cherry officers. Inept lieutenants. They would lead their men out on a combat patrol. A firefight would break out. The only casualty would be the young officer. Killed by enemy forces.

Allegedly.

They called it *fragging*.

Prominent in Brandon's mind just then was the fact that Chris had nearly turned into a killing machine until he found out John was merely unconscious. What would he do when he found out what happened with Boing aboard the aircraft? When he found out the accident might not have been an accident?

Brandon held his breath. Sweat trickled down behind his ear.

Smith cleared his throat. "I suggest we finish our search, gentlemen. We've got two casualties and we haven't even started the mission." He shined his light up in the trees. "And in case you haven't noticed, daylight is coming."

Chris snorted and he stooped and patted John's face. "Come on, John. Time to move."

John groaned and Brandon let out his breath. Cleared his throat. "Right. Let's finish up here. This is where Florida sent their last call?"

"It is," Smith said.

"Alright," Brandon said. "I need some men to go back for Boing and the gear we left behind. Mike, you tend the wounded. Everyone else continue the search. Smith and I will figure out what to do next."

Chris looked down at John. "MEDEVAC is where I would start."

"I told you," Smith said, absently looking around the jungle. "We're not putting blips on enemy radar until we're ready to leave."

Chris turned on Smith. "That a fact, spook?"

Not paying attention, Smith said, "That's a fact."

Chris went after Smith. "I'll fucking remember that when you're the one lying there."

But Terry and George took Chris's arms and pulled him away. One of them saying, "Florida is out here, too. Let's find 'em." Howard followed them into the jungle.

What an absolute mess. Everything from insertion up to now had gone wrong. Everything. Brandon would be the laughing stock of the unit. Nothing new. Right then, Brandon just wanted to go home and bury his head in the sand.

Smith had offered him a chance to start over. An assignment at the Pentagon. He wondered, with everything that had gone wrong, if that offer would still stand.

Gray light filtered through the jungle canopy. So much time wasted. But maybe a daytime search might yield something of value. If they could recover just a scrap of clothing, Brandon would deem it sufficient and they could move on. Poke around a bit looking for Smith's HVT. Find the village and send a few men to recon it. If they reported nothing of significance, he could scrub the entire mission.

Smith shined his light on the wasted cripple's face.

Brandon looked at that bulging eye for as long as he could. But soon warm torrents of saliva spilled into his mouth and his belly rumbled and he looked away.

Chewing back chunks, Brandon walked over to Smith. "What's our extraction plan when we're ready to leave?"

The operative stood motionless, rifle hanging across his chest. His red light slid over the dead cripple. He shined it on John. "We have a remote airbase about two-hundred kilometers from here. Air America aircraft use it. We'll call for a Huey extraction when we're done here."

"Hueys can't make that roundtrip."

"These can," Smith said. "Experimental aircraft. Outfitted with oversized fuel tanks for long range operations."

"Didn't know we had those."

"Officially, we don't."

It was still dark on the jungle floor. Brandon doubted Smith saw him roll his eyes. "When can we contact them?"

"The C-130 will arrive in orbit at zero seven-hundred and depart at zero nine-hundred. They'll retransmit our radio traffic."

"Why so little coverage?"

"To keep our footprint small. We're not equipped to handle much if the NVA or VC get curious and come looking."

"What about the NVA on their way here?"

"I intend to be gone by the time they get here."

Brandon checked his watch. "Did you find anything during the search? I mean, before all this happened?"

Smith shook his head. "Nothing but this fellow here. And the girl's head."

Brandon had deliberately avoided looking at the thing. What little he had seen of it was enough. The neck skin hanging at sharp angles. Like it wasn't cut off but *torn* off.

Smith knelt down and went through the cripple's pockets and pulled something out. He opened his hand and shined the light on the thing in his palm. Brandon leaned in. A metal fishhook.

"Do you think him and the girl are from the village?" Brandon asked.

Smith turned the hook over in his hand. Examined it. As if the fishhook were an answer to some ancient question. "I believe they are. Our intelligence suggests it's a fishing village."

Brandon locked his eyes on the fishhook in Smith's

palm. Tried not to look at the girl's head. But his eyes were oddly drawn.

"God," Brandon said. "What makes someone do that? You ever seen shit like this before?"

Smith stood and dropped the fishhook on the dead man's chest. "Decapitations have been used to frighten one's enemies for as long as there have been blades to cut with. This is nothing new."

That didn't make any sense at all.

"Seems like he cut off the wrong head," Brandon said.

"What?"

"If he was trying to frighten us, why didn't he bring an American's head? Why kill a girl from his own village?"

They talked about different theories for a time, but were interrupted when Mike came out of the dark. A nervousness in his voice when he said, "Hey, sir. We have to get Boing outta here. His legs feel like bags of gravel and he's already getting a fever." Mike leaned in close. "He won't last long if I don't get him into surgery. Soon."

"How soon is soon?"

"Immediately is the more precise word."

That was all Brandon needed to hear. He'd use any reasonable excuse to un-ass this shithole. Sure, there were enough able-bodied men to continue Smith's mission. But with the senior NCO out of the fight and the interpreter about to die, well, those were good enough reasons to abort. He just needed to do his due diligence with the search here. Then a quick recon of the village. Should be a wrap after that. Maybe he could convince Smith to call for the extraction and search the village while it was still inbound.

"Smith," Brandon said. "I think it'd be a good idea to call for extraction when the re-trans aircraft arrives in orbit."

"I hardly think that will be enough time to complete our work here. We haven't even started looking for the HVT."

"I know. I'm sorry. But we've had too many failures. We need to cut it short." Brandon looked at his watch. "If you call when the window opens, we'd have about four hours to look around. If we use that time wisely, I think—"

"Would you join me for a moment, please?" Smith looked down at the cripple. And he turned and walked into the jungle.

Brandon sighed and looked at Mike. "Give me a minute."

Mike stopped him with a gentle hand on the shoulder. "If you hang out with us long enough, you'll learn why we don't trust these guys. Don't let that civilian push you around."

What was that supposed to mean? In the dark he couldn't read the expression on Mike's face. "I won't," he said. And he trailed after Smith.

He caught up to Smith and they walked for a while. Abruptly Smith stopped and rounded on Brandon.

"Listen carefully, Captain." Words wet like he was foaming at the mouth.

Brandon backed off a step, but Smith closed the space between them. "Do not presume you have the authority to give *me* orders. I'll call for an extraction when *I* deem it appropriate. Not any sooner. This is *my* operation. You and your men are *my* security element. You are OPCON to *me*."

Brandon stammered the first thing that came to mind. "I have injured men—"

"And they are *your* concern. Not mine. You have a Special Forces qualified medic assigned to you, yes? Michael is his name?"

"Yes, but—"

"And I assume he has brought with him his medical supplies?"

"Of course—"

"Then it seems you have everything you need for

tending to your injured personnel."

"Mike doesn't think so."

"Then *you* have improperly prepared for the mission," Smith snarled. "I have a fucking job to do. It requires my full attention. I refuse to deviate from *my* mission to teach *you* how to command your men. Your colonel praised this team's skill. I'm honestly quite skeptical of his assessment."

Brandon bit down hard, face flushing hot. They stood there in silence.

Smith sighed and pinched the bridge of his nose. "Forgive me. That was harsh. Blame it on stress, huh? It's easy to forget you're the fish-out-of-water on this team." He wagged a finger at Brandon. "But I told you. I told you it would be a challenge commanding these teams. I warned you not to let these men walk all over you. And that's what they're doing. Every time they question you. *Disagree* with you." Smith put a hand on Brandon's shoulder. "It's a challenge. I know it is. If you don't think you can handle the responsibility—"

"I can handle it," Brandon said.

Was that the truth?

Smith nodded. "I'm not heartless. I don't want any of your men to die. I can tell Mike feels the same way. But don't you think he's being overly cautious in asking you to abort the mission? I need more time. This is our last chance at finding this HVT. I need to at least confirm that he's not in the village.

"You'll benefit from my success, too." Smith looked up through the canopy to the coming dawn. "Success in a unit like this guarantees you a prestigious position when you DEROS. But success is only part of it. You need a recommendation from your handler. That's me. Pull this off and you're on your way to the Pentagon." Smith leaned in to whisper, "Of course, I'm sure the Infantry would always welcome you back."

Brandon stared at Smith. The voice in his mind

mocking him.

It should've been you...

No. The Infantry would certainly *not* welcome Brandon back.

Brandon exhaled. He needed that Pentagon assignment more than Smith could possibly know.

"What do you say?" Smith asked.

"It'll be hard for me to get those men to do anything if I don't at least get a MEDEVAC for Boing."

Smith crossed his arms. He rubbed his chin. The jungle brightened with the coming morning light.

"I'll get you your MEDEVAC. But from now on you're in my corner. You're the green-suiter. It's easier for those men to take orders from you. I'll get your MEDEVAC, and you get those men to do what I need them do. Deal?"

Seemed like a fair trade. And it would add time before anyone on the team found out what happened to Boing. What *really* happened.

"Deal," Brandon said.

Boing was laid next to John when Smith and Brandon returned to the search site. Chris and Terry waited with Mike.

"Found something," Chris said.

"What is it?"

"Come with me."

Brandon followed them through the jungle. The vegetation thinned and the gray morning light soaked the team's grim faces.

After a while Chris stopped and pointed.

Brandon recoiled. Hand going to his mouth. "Oh my God."

"Yeah," Chris said.

Bodies.

Here a woman lay sprawled on her back. Half-dollar sized pools of blood filled her eye sockets. And there, a child, knees to chest. Chubby hands curled over his face as if rubbing away sleep. And there, a woman, her face and neck lodged against a tree. Arm extended as if she had been trying to claw her way up to escape. And there. And there and there and there and there—

Warmth shot up Brandon's throat and he bent over and puked in the grass.

Retching, stomach spasms forcing his words out in a roar, Brandon said, "Jesus!" Clutching his stomach he said, "When the hell did this happen?"

"Wasn't anytime recently," Terry said. "Looks like there's twenty in all. Yonder we found the rest of that little girl."

"What—" Brandon retched. "What happened?"

"They were running from something," Chris said. "I'm thinking it was the cripple."

"He couldn't have," Brandon said. "He was unarm—"

But in one hand Terry held up an AK-47. Bolt locked open. In the other hand he held up an empty thirty-round banana mag. "Looks like he ran outta ammo. Lucky for John."

Wiping his shirt cuff across his mouth, Brandon stood and said, "Where'd they all come from?"

Chris gestured out through the thinned trees. Out into the soft gray. "Where do you think?"

Brandon came forward and looked. Looked down a gentle slope of waist-high grass into a deep, sprawling valley. Within a swirling, glacial mist, boxy shapes materialized and disappeared and materialized again. This was it. They had found it. He thumbed absently at his rifle's safety switch as he stood there and beheld the dark and silent village.

CHAPTER EIGHT

Get out of my fucking head! Please!
Only laughter answered.

CHAPTER NINE

Brandon lay prone in the grass with the binoculars to his eyes. He watched the village. Dim in the gray light. Dead. The sun was coming behind him but had yet to penetrate that thick mist creeping through the valley.

From the photos he had studied on the aircraft, he knew that beneath the mist there was a wide river. But those aerial photographs, taken on some cloudless afternoon, they did not evoke the feeling of dread Brandon felt now. The feeling that no single man could have caused so much death. The feeling that somewhere down in those huts something sinister waited.

Far away, beyond the unseen river, the other side of the valley rose up sharply in all manner of jagged, jungle covered hills and peaks. One single black escarpment shot out high above the jungle like a tower.

The bamboo huts, maggot-pink, were raised upon thin, stilted legs. The river probably swelled when the heavy rains came. That veiling mist crept through the village, reaching up to caress outer walls as if it, too, searched for something lost there. The huts pulsed and squirmed like insects feeding upon whatever might lay obscured beneath the gray. In places, the mist peeled back like skin and revealed the dark shapes of doors and windows. Like eyes with no life in them.

All was still down in the village. Where light ought to be, there was darkness. Where sound ought to be, silence. From Brandon's elevated position, atop the slope leading down, only the thatched roofs completely broke free of the fog. At the village's south end, a cluster of four tall and thin shed-looking huts stood apart like silent onlookers of whatever events had transpired there.

Chris, lying next to Brandon, held his own binoculars steady. "Doesn't look good for the villagers." He spit tobacco juice. "In every village I've ever seen that's been attacked, the survivors didn't just abandon the place. They'd be burying their dead. Mourning them." Flicking his chin toward the village, he said, "Ain't a thing moving down there."

"Probably ain't nobody left to do the burying," Terry said.

"Hard to believe one guy killed all those people," George said.

"We don't know it was just one guy," Chris said.

Great. Just great.

Brandon shook his head as he listened to the men. First the mission was a search and rescue, then a snatch-and-grab, now there was the potential of fighting an unknown-sized enemy element that had no problem slaughtering women and children. And New York was already down two guns.

The men were probably right. No survivors. Brandon had been watching the village for a long time and he hadn't seen anything moving either. He couldn't even guess at what happened down there. At what happened to those people. But if the village was populated by farmers and fishermen, if anyone was left alive, they would be up and about. The rice farmers he had seen during his patrols with the Infantry were usually heading to the paddies well before the sun came up. *But,* he thought. *If there were no survivors, there might not be an HVT.*

"We need to get down there and have a look," Chris said.

"No," Brandon said. "We wait until the fog lifts. Until then, nobody goes near that place. Not until we confirm there are no hostiles." Florida got wrapped up in something bad. Until Brandon figured out what that *something* was, nobody was stepping foot in that village.

Chris spat. "How else are we gonna confirm there's no hostiles unless we search it?"

Brandon sighed and turned to Smith. "Do you have any more intel on this place?"

Smith watched through his binoculars. Jaw muscles twitching.

"Smith?"

"There was a lot of activity a few days ago," Smith said quietly. Eyes locked in his binoculars. "I ordered a Blackbird recon. Those photos I gave you are from just twenty-four hours before Florida came. Photos showed people working in the rice paddy we jumped into. People in boats. People working in that field."

Brandon thought about that. Looked back at the village. "There's no other villages out here? NVA or VC bases? No—"

"Nothing," Smith said. "There's nothing out here. Just this place."

"Then who killed all these people? Why?"

"Maybe," Chris said, "Charlie picked up Florida's radio traffic and came looking. Maybe they thought the villagers were helping Florida."

"Or Florida wiped out the villagers," Brandon said absently.

"Most of those people we found were women and children," Chris said. "They were unarmed. How about you save that baby-killer bullshit for those liberal-arts motherfuckers back in the world."

Brandon let his binoculars slip and he glared at Chris.

"Are you still drunk? What I meant was that if those people were fleeing the same force that attacked Florida, they might have been caught in the crossfire."

Chris spat and shook his head and put his eyes back to his binoculars. Apparently, apologies were beyond him.

Brandon needed to talk to Smith. Alone. Make him see his HVT was wasted. Convince him the team was only equipped to recon the village. They couldn't extend their stay just to go looking for something they would never find. Especially not with carrying wounded men. God, but there was no way Smith would call for extraction until they searched the village.

Against his better judgement, Brandon said, "Chris."

"Yeah?"

"We need to search the village."

"No shit."

"I want you in charge of the fire team that goes down there. Make it happen."

Chris eyed him sidelong from behind the binoculars. "Not feeling up to coming along?"

Brandon's face flushed. "Smith and I will guard the wounded and coordinate Boing's MEDEVAC."

Chris pushed himself up. "Of course you will." He called the other men to him and they receded into the jungle.

Brandon checked his watch. *0655*. The retrans aircraft would be circling soon.

He looked at Smith and was about to speak, but the sight of the man made him shut his mouth. Smith held his binoculars to his eyes, but his eyes were wide and focused on something far away. Or maybe focused on nothing at all. Sweat beaded in the brown hair of his eyebrow. Trembling with the beating of his heart. When it slid down and fell upon his eyelash, he did not blink.

"Smith," Brandon said.

Smith's head jerked at the sound.

"Listen," Brandon said. "I'm in your corner, but this is

fucked. We don't even know what we're going up against. I'll send my guys down to take a look and see if they can find your HVT, but I think we need to consider that he's either dead or gone. We seriously need to think about getting out of here."

Smith stared at him. His eyes drifted slowly away until he once again gazed out at the village. Stayed there for so long Brandon started to think Smith hadn't understood what he said.

But then Smith rubbed his chin, "I was just thinking the same thing." Smith pulled himself up to a crouch and opened the flap of his pack.

Smith *agreed*? Brandon felt his jaw hanging open and he shut it. He wanted to ask Smith what had changed his mind but thought better of it, lest Smith change his mind again and decide to stay.

After pulling the whip antennae out of the pack, Smith switched his radio on. In the pack there was the face of a radio Brandon had never seen before. Switches and dials and buttons.

"Interesting radio," Brandon said.

"Latest and greatest," Smith said. "Doesn't matter if the NVA gets ahold of it. These have an external encryption device and we change the fills every week. No need to change frequencies if the radio falls into the wrong hands. In a week it'll just be a paperweight."

"Did you bring an encryption device?"

"Of course not."

Brandon held up his hands. "Didn't know if you were planning on being out here more than a week."

"No," Smith said, thumbing rubberized buttons. "I wasn't."

Neither was Florida.

Despite his joy over finally getting out of there, Brandon couldn't fight off the stirring disillusionment he felt toward Smith. The chat in the jungle left a bad taste in his mouth. He didn't like being someone's *yes-man*. He'd be glad to get back to base and forget Smith even existed. Pentagon or no Pentagon.

Smith hailed the retrans aircraft and provided a SITREP. Looking to the sky, Brandon neither saw nor heard the C-130.

"Affirmative," Smith said. "Alert Echo element. Mercury team will secure Lima Zulu."

Smith listened. He looked up to the sky and said, "Roger. Mercury-actual out." He clicked the handset onto the radio's face and collapsed the whip antennae.

"Why Mercury?" Chris asked from behind. He was flanked by Terry, Dan, George, and Howard.

Smith shot him a look. "I don't pick the call-signs." He closed his pack and tugged the straps.

"Me and John worked with a Mercury team. Eldest-Son operation. I figured you college boys would be smart enough to come up with more than one callsign."

Smith hefted his pack onto his shoulders. "We aren't assigned permanent callsigns. The callsigns are operational."

"Meaning?" asked George.

Smith sighed and put the binoculars back to his eyes to look out across the village. "We order them based on the position from the sun. The handler's callsign assigned to Florida was Venus."

"Is there a Sun team on standby to come get us if we don't make it back?" Chris asked.

"No." Smith looked at the men gathered around. "Mercury designations mean the mission is abandoned if it should fail. Most missions of this particular nature get a Venus and Mercury, but I've seen some Earth and Mars designations. Since we've started the naming conventions, there has only been one Icarus team deployed. But that takes approval from the Director."

"The fuck is an *Icarus*?" Terry asked.

"I don't have time to educate you on mythology."

Ice crept up Brandon's shoulders. He understood.

Icarus. If an Icarus team was ordered to fly too close to the sun, it meant the Mercury team was already standing in it. Brandon looked down at the village. "Mercury," he muttered.

Brandon stood and looked at Chris. "What's your plan?"

"Break things and hurt people is what I was thinking."

"Let's hear your plan, Sergeant," Smith said. "The captain and I are going with you."

"What?" Chris and Brandon said.

"I don't want your men killing my HVT," Smith said to Brandon. "You will ensure that doesn't happen."

Chris scratched the back of his head and looked around at the men. "This kinda changes things a bit." He pointed a finger at each man and softly counted. He shrugged and said, "Alright Cap." Voice glum. Like a teenage boy forced to bring his little sister along with his friends. "I guess Mike and George are gonna stay with Boing and John."

Brandon took up his rifle and reached for his rucksack.

"Leave the pack," Chris said. "You won't need it."

Chris took Brandon and Smith to the treeline and explained how they would advance on the village. He pointed out three egress routes that would lead everyone back to this spot in case they were separated or had to retreat. Listening to the man, it was like Chris flipped a switch and turned off his arrogance and clicked over to a detached tactician.

"Sound good?" Chris asked.

Brandon thought about the plan. "No. We'll be too slow. We can't sneak in like it's a recon. The EVAC is on its way. There's only about four hours to search before they get here."

"Creeping?" Chris sounded confused.

"He thinks we're doing it like Laos," Terry said.

Chris's eyes opened wide and he laughed. "Yeah, we're not reconning the village." Chris stepped out from the trees onto the hill and held out his hand to his side. The other men formed in a loose wedge-formation behind him. "We're assaulting it."

The four enlisted men clicked their rifles to semi.

"New York," Chris said. "On me."

And the men flew down the hill into the mist.

CHAPTER TEN

New York ran through the field. Brandon's boots sunk ankle-deep in tilled soil. Trampling lush, leafy greens that crunched and snapped underfoot. It called to mind the Army's poor-quality training films. Projected on the canvass wall of some tent.

Booby-traps, the static-muffled narrator's voice said, *may be present near villages sympathetic to enemy forces. The observant soldier notes and records the movements exhibited by local nationals. If locals are aware of hidden dangers, they will avoid them.*

Parting shot of an American NCO walking down a dusty road. Fading music. Iris-out. Camera holds on Sergeant Smiley's shit-eating grin. Happy that he still has his legs. *Remember,* the narrator says. *Step where they step.* Fade to black.

A USARV production.

But where were the training films explaining what to do if enemy forces were trying to kill villagers?

Brandon kept his eyes on the men in front of him. They ran fast and they out-distanced him. Beneath the lactic-acid burn, his legs buzzed with anticipation that the next time he put his foot down it might be blown off in a white flash. Even if Brandon had the breath to call a halt, New York was out in the open. Exposed. They would have to move anyway.

New York had their rifles trained on the huts. That was good. Brandon could focus on the ground. He shifted so he ran directly behind Terry. Put his boots precisely in Terry's bootprints.

He had heard all of the men click their safeties off. Brandon kept his rifle switched to safe. Regardless of how good the enlisted men might be, sprinting with the safety off seemed an egregious safety hazard. Brandon had been trained to switch it off only after identifying a target and that's what he was going to continue doing. He didn't even carry his 1911 with a round chambered. A round in the chamber with the hammer cocked was just inviting an accidental discharge. He'd seen it before. Some colonel walking up to a clearing barrel and blasting a hole in it. If Brandon ever *needed* his pistol, how hard would it be to rack the slide?

They came out of the field onto hard-packed dirt. A path running between the two rows of huts. Chris threw up a flurry of hand signals. The wedge formation broke. Like birds breaking from a *V*. Terry, Howard, and Dan curved left, stopping at the corner of the first hut. Chris broke right of the path, coming to a stop at the corner of the first hut in the row closest to the river. Chris waved to Brandon and Smith to fall-in behind him.

Brandon hit the hut's wall and leaned his back up against it. Panting. Breath loud in his head. He tried to keep it quiet, breathing deep through his nose and exhaling slowly through his mouth. He felt like he was about to die and everyone else looked like they had just taken a leisurely stroll.

Well inside the fog now, he saw things that were previously invisible from top of the hill. The river, not far from where he stood against the hut. But the mist still obscured the far bank. Three wooden docks were spaced out in the water. Their planks grey and cracked from sun. Tied-up on either side of each dock were small boats with outboard motors. Only one boat was moored at the most southern dock and it rocked lonesome in the current.

"Smith," Chris whispered. "You pull security out here. Waste anything that isn't us." Chris waved a hand along the dirt path between the huts. "This is a good kill zone. Nowhere to run." Chris signaled Terry on the opposite side. "Stay with Smith."

Terry nodded.

Chris looked at Brandon. A grin tugged at the corner of his mouth. Falling in behind Brandon, Chris nudged him to the corner of the hut.

Brandon looked back at him. "What are you doing?"

Chris cinched up on his rifle and sank into a slight crouch. "John wants to make sure you learn the ropes." He nodded at the hut. "Just kick in the door."

Brandon looked at the door. Looked at Chris. "What if someone's *in* there?"

Chris's eyebrows went up. "If they have a weapon you should probably shoot 'em."

"Oh shit."

Chris shoved him. "Go!"

The adrenaline. The pressure in his head. Like being too deep underwater. Thoughts. Plans. Worries. Everything was purged from his mind and there was only the bright and crisp here and now.

Brandon was up the steps of the first hut and putting his boot into the door. It groaned, bent, nearly cracked from the force and slammed open. Brandon was inside the single room and jerking his rifle right to left. Nothing. Empty. In his periphery Chris's rifle muzzle hovered over his shoulder.

Chris spun, checked behind the door. The hut was clear. They looked at the room; big enough for maybe ten or twelve people. Probably one extended family to a hut. The only things there were the typical items you'd find in any of the huts in rural Vietnam. Cooking pots. Bedrolls. A few chests for what little clothing these people had. There was a mat laid out in the middle of the room with some wooden chopsticks and deep spoons set for a meal that was never finished. Half-eaten bowls of rice and greasy brown soup. Gray congealed bubbles of fat floating on top. The rich smell of broth.

Chris nodded to Brandon and whispered, "Clear." He reached his hand out through the kicked-in door and waved to indicate they were coming out.

"Next one," Chris whispered. "Go!"

They were down the steps and up the next set in mere seconds. Dan and Howard emerged at the same time and kicked in the next door in their line.

Chris and Brandon cleared the next hut. And the next. And the next. Watching New York work like this was eye-opening. Smith had left out a word when he had described New York as instruments. They were *precision* instruments. The one recon mission Brandon had gone on with New York was not the proper arena for these men to showcase their abilities. The way they moved, operated. These men were deadly.

Brandon went through another door and scanned the room and there was a shape, some movement out of the corner of his eye and he jerked his rifle back and thumbed off the safety and slipped his finger on the trigger and Chris's head was in his sights but Chris nudged Brandon with his shoulder to keep him moving and Chris's non-firing hand waved out and guided Brandon's rifle to the center of the room.

Brandon's heart pounded hard. His hands went cold and numb. He had nearly blown Chris's brains out. But Chris kept moving, spun and scanned the place where Brandon saw movement. But Chris fired no shot and when Brandon looked back to the shape, to the movement he thought he had seen, it was merely a dark robe hanging in the corner.

"Clear," Chris grumbled. Eyes narrowing as he looked down at Brandon's rifle.

Brandon clicked on his safety switch. "Sorry."

This was the last hut in the row. Chris clicked on his safety and stood a little more relaxed. He waved out the door and went out. Howard and Dan came out and joined him on the path. Brandon looked around the empty hut. Confused by the lack of...

Anything.

But as he looked around the hut, not really seeing it, confusion gave way to a growing sense of frustration. Brandon's adrenaline tweak dissipated. Now that all was silent, now that he had a few moments to just think, he found himself dwelling on a nagging sense of inadequacy. That he was somehow beneath these men. Their warfighting skill. Their tactics. The things that win battles. These men were superior to him in all of it. During the entire sweep of these huts, Brandon had not issued one single command. Hadn't *needed* to.

These men know what to do, he heard John saying.

The longer he thought about it, the surer he became. Brandon didn't belong on this team.

Yet there he was.

Did the other captains feel this way?

The team gathered on the path. Brandon stepped out into the fog and stood on the top step.

Chris waved Smith and Terry up.

Smith strolled up casually. Inspecting huts as if they were works of art hung in a museum. When he reached the group on the path, Smith stopped. Turned. Looked. He looked across the river. Looked back at the tilled field. "This doesn't make any sense," he said to no one in particular.

There was no sign of anyone aside from the twenty or so people they had found on the hill. But this village could house a lot more than that. Smith was right. It didn't make sense.

Smith continued looking around. Maybe searching for some anchor for an argument against abandoning the mission.

A breeze drifted through the river valley and came down along the path. Brandon turned to it and lifted his head. Let the cool of it roll over his sweating skin. The breeze pushed the fog tumbling down the dirt path and it opened up like stage curtains at the start of a show.

"You smell that?" Chris asked. Prompting deep sniffs and questioning looks from the team.

"Yeah," Dan said. "Smells like cooked meat."

Brandon sniffed. He smelled it too.

Through the gap in the fog he saw it. He hadn't seen it through his binoculars. The fog must have obscured it. A large, darkened mound.

Brandon stared. It wasn't a pile of dirt. It wasn't a pile of hay. The hellish details crawled out amidst the wisps of smoke and reached out to him. Everything black, slashes of red. Reaching arms. Contorted torsos. Black, hollow eyes.

"Jesus Marry and Joseph..." Brandon said.

Smith came and stood beside him. "I think we've found the other villagers."

"Holy shit, man," Howard said. "You think Florida is in there?"

Chris spat. Brown tobacco juice smacking in the dirt. He said nothing.

A tiny skull with no teeth yawned at him. Brandon retched and turned away.

Pull yourself together.

Brandon spat sour chunks in the dirt.

"We have to search it," Chris said. "Volunteers?"

Dan darted out through the doorway of the last hut Brandon and Chris had cleared. "Hey," he hissed. "We got company!"

All heads turned toward him and his thumb pointing over his shoulder. They all ran inside the hut and went to the small window overlooking the river. All straining to see.

Brandon pushed himself forward, but Chris pulled him back from the window. Finger over his mouth, he said, "Don't make yourself a target."

Brandon nodded and stepped back. He and the men crouched and watched from low in the shadows.

Through the mist floating over the river, a small boat plodded toward them. The outboard motor sputtered and whined. From the distance, it was hard to be sure, but it looked like two occupants were aboard.

"Anyone have binos?" Brandon asked.

None of them did.

"Alright," Chris said. "We sit tight until they come ashore. Everyone take a hut. When they walk through on the path, we take them on my signal. If they're armed, waste 'em."

"No!" Smith blurted. "The HVT."

"Okay…" Chris rolled his eyes. "If they're armed, ask them to pretty-please drop their weapons. Try to take one alive. Go."

Brandon stayed put. Smith and New York vanished into the other huts. Whoever these two men were, they were about to get a big surprise.

There had been no sign of Florida, but this was a start. At least Brandon would have something to show for this scrubbed mission. It wouldn't be a total waste of time. Smith could take these two guys back, interrogate them, then use whatever intelligence he gathered to launch another attempt for his HVT. Whatever Smith did with these people, Brandon didn't care. They could disappear for a while. Or forever. Brandon just wanted this to be over.

One of the cloaked figures hopped from the boat to the dock. He had the springing, lively steps of youth. The other man sitting in the boat was short and his hooded robe flowed over a fat body. The young one pulled the boat close to the dock with a line of rope and moored it.

Brandon went to the wall adjacent the door. If they came into this hut, how would he take them? He fidgeted with his rifle. Long and bulky. He might have to use his hands to grab one of them. He slung his rifle and drew his pistol. God, he didn't want to kill anyone. Adrenaline came. Icy. Head pounding. But he might have to kill the teenager. He peeked out the window. He saw no weapons—

The teenager hopped back into the boat and his robes billowed and a leather-wrapped handle extended from a long leather sheath belted at his hip.

A fucking sword?

"Shit."

Chris will take care of it. Or one of the others would. Brandon wouldn't have to do anything. He was sure of it. He looked around the hut. Looked at the hooded robe hanging in the corner. The exact same kind those two men wore.

"Oh *shit!*" He pushed himself against the wall.

Maybe all the villagers wore those robes. He thought back. Thought of the people in the jungle. Linen pants and shirts. No robes. The folds of dark fabric draped there on the wall sneered at him.

"Oh fucking *shit...*"

The youth killed the boat's motor and helped the older man climb on wary legs from the boat to the dock. The young one picked up a bulging burlap sack from the boat and slung it over his shoulder.

The pair approached the huts on the path. The older one, stooped and wobbling on bowed legs, held the youth's elbow. They neared the huts and they spoke low in some other language. It didn't have the same tones as Vietnamese. Maybe it was a Northern dialect. Their voices higher pitched, like women's voices.

Keep walking. Please!

Through gaps in the bamboo door Brandon saw them

walking along the central dirt path. Then they stopped right in front of Brandon's hut.

"No," Brandon breathed. "Keep walking…"

His heart pounded. It beat through his back and thumped against the wall. He took a step toward the door. Blood pounded in his palms gripped tight around the pistol.

Why couldn't they just keep walking? Let someone else do this. *Just keep walking.* But they didn't. They turned and climbed the steps toward Brandon.

Brandon raised his pistol to the door.

Shadows crept up through the slits in the door. The thumping shuffle of slow, unsteady footsteps approached.

Oh Jesus. Oh Christ.

The kid had a sword. Chris said to kill them if they had a weapon. Did the old one have one, too? Jesus, he'd have to shoot them if they reached for their weapons. The young one would be fast. He might open Brandon's throat if he hesitated. Brandon had to. He put his finger on the trigger.

The door creaked open. Brandon shook with nervous energy. Gold morning light lay upon the two cloaked figures.

The old one stood in front of the teenager. Brandon aimed.

What the fuck do I do?

Brandon slammed his boot in the old man's chest. A mass of flesh. Somewhere deep inside the man Brandon felt a *crack* through his boot. Despite the man's stocky frame there was barely any weight to him and he launched into the air. But he still clung to the teenager and the kid went somersaulting backward down the steps.

But the youth was up again just as fast and he rounded on Brandon, stared up at him from the dirt path. The kid's hand went to the handle at his belt. Brandon brought the pistol up, aiming somewhere between the boy's shocked-open eyes.

And Brandon pulled the trigger.

There was no click. There was no bang. The trigger barely moved. His eyes flicked to the pistol in his hands and to the trigger that was resisting his finger. To the hammer that was not cocked back. He looked back to the teenager's wide eyes. Brandon's armpits went numb.

He hadn't put a round in the chamber.

The teenager's dirty face contorted in rage and a high-pitched scream erupted. The sword was out. The kid crouched, ready to lunge.

Chris was out the opposite door and down the steps before the old man could even attempt to sit up.

Brandon grabbed the pistol's slide with a sweaty palm and racked it back and the pistol let out a muffled click as round fed into the chamber.

"Wait!" Chris yelled. And Brandon lowered his pistol, heart hammering so hard he almost jerked the trigger.

The teenager spun toward Chris. And as he spun Brandon saw soft features beneath the hood. They seemed—

"It's a girl," Brandon mumbled.

"Flag on the play!" Chris bellowed as he ran. "Unnecessary roughness!" and Chris swung the butt of his rifle.

It blasted her in the jaw and with a wet smack her head jerked to the side and her knees buckled and she collapsed in the dirt.

Chris shouldered his rifle like an axe. Hooking a thumb in his belt and looking down at the girl, he triumphantly proclaimed, "Personally, I'd call it *necessary* roughness."

Brandon holstered his pistol and hurried down the steps. Hands held out between Chris and the girl, he said, "Stop!"

Chris looked up at him. "Why?"

"Because it's a fucking girl."

"Impossible." Chris looked down. "I would never hit a girl." But he cocked his head at her as if he couldn't trust his own statement.

"Well you just did." Brandon tugged her hood back, revealing long dark hair and soft features. Her dark, tanned skin around her chin cut and bleeding and swelling purple.

"Ouch." Chris stooped and looked at the girl's chin and sucked his teeth. "Sorry, princess."

Brandon waved his arms in frustration. Scratched his fingers through his hair. "Check the other one."

Chris knelt down and pulled the old man's hood back. He stared for a moment. When he stood he was laughing. "What's worse? Butt-stroking a girl or drop-kicking her grandmother?"

With the hood lowered, with the gray hair and wrinkled features displayed, the old *man* was obviously an old *woman*.

"*Goddamnit.*" Squeezing his eyes with his fingers, Brandon said, "Check that sack. Find out what are they're carrying."

Another mess.

He hadn't wanted anyone to get hurt, yet here they were beating the shit out of two women.

The girl's eyes fluttered and searched around. Focused on Brandon. He held out his hand to help her up. He smiled, trying to soften his face, trying to apologize without words for the misunderstanding. Maybe she might trust him. Might come along with New York willingly and offer some insight as to what happened here. The girl looked at his hand warily and then to her grandmother. If it *was* her grandmother. The old woman pushed herself up on her elbows and nodded to the girl. These were some tough ladies to shrug off hits like that.

The girl took Brandon's hand and he pulled her up.

She was about a head shorter than him. Shoulders back, she stared at him with defiant, deep brown eyes.

"Guys!"

Brandon turned.

Howard held the opened sack and stared inside. Jaw hanging open.

"What is it?" Brandon asked.

Howard upended the bag. Dirty clothing and muddy boots spilled out into a pile on the dusty path. The clothing looked exactly like—

"What the hell?" Brandon looked back in time to see the flash of a knife coming for his gut.

He tensed. Shot his arms across his belly in a protective X. Already knowing the knife would simply fillet his forearms before plunging into his belly.

But Chris drove his boot into the back of the girl's knee. Her leg went disgustingly sideways and her knee plowed into the dirt. She wavered, face screwed up in pain. Her wild eyes locked with Brandon's. Her bleeding lips pulled apart in a wet snarl. She twitched and the knife swung out wide and she lunged from her knees. Chris held his rifle aloft in both hands, as if offering it to God. The rifle's buttstock came down on the back of her neck and the *crunch* sounded wet beneath her skin.

She went limp and the knife fell from her hands and she collapsed once again, head slamming the packed dirt. But despite Chris's brutality, the girl's fingers still searched the dirt like legs of a dying spider. They curled around the knife's handle. Chris came alongside her. Laid his boot upon the back of her hand. Slowly put his weight down until her fingers shot out straight and trembling. Chris kicked the knife away in a dusty *puff*.

"Have you ever considered using a punch?" Dan asked. "You could've fucking paralyzed her."

Chris held up his index and middle fingers like a gun. He said, "You ever try to finger-blast a hooker with broken fingers?"

Dan shook his head in disgust.

Howard lifted up one of the shirts that had spilled from the bag. Chris's wry smile faded when he looked at it. The morning sun shone through four holes in the back. Around the holes were thick mounds of maroon congealed blood.

The shirt was the same odd camouflage pattern Brandon and New York wore.

Chris nodded his head as he inspected the uniform. He sighed and his face remained eerily calm as his eyes fell upon the girl trembling in the dirt. "You think Mike can see us from here?"

"Doubt it," Terry said.

"Good."

Whatever that meant.

Chris slung his rifle and drew his 1911. Put the toe of his boot into the girl's ribcage and rolled her onto her back. She grunted and her eyes rolled and eventually focused on Chris. Then on his pistol.

Stepping on the girl's chest, Chris's boot covered her from navel to collarbone. She cried out and grabbed the black leather. Wheezed as Chris leaned on her and forced the air from her. Chris raised the pistol. The hollow grinding of metal on metal as he unscrewed the suppressor.

Brandon stepped forward. "Stop." But Terry grabbed a handful of Brandon's shirt and pushed him back against the hut. Shaking his head, Terry put a finger to his lips.

Real quiet, voice like a bass line, Terry said, "That bitch just tried to kill you." He glanced over his shoulder and then turned back to Brandon. "This is one of those things you don't see. Got it? Don't say anything. Don't interrupt. Don't give orders. Don't even look if you don't have the stomach for it."

"How…" But the notion of reprimanding Terry for such blatant insolence evaporated when he looked, when Brandon really *looked* into the man's eyes. The razor-sharp edge in his voice and the steel coldness in his eyes told Brandon that if he didn't keep his mouth shut, Terry would shut it for him. Maybe permanently. Brandon put up his hands. Terry nodded and let him go.

Chris slipped the suppressor into his cargo pocket and bent over the girl. He aimed the 1911 between her eyes.

Unlike Brandon, these men carried their pistols with a round in the chamber. Brandon would bet everything he owned that the girl was moments away from getting her brains blown into the dirt. The old woman, firmly held in Smith's big hands, gasped.

Fishing a lighter and cigarette out of his shirt pocket, Chris stuck it in his mouth and lit it. "You speak English?" Chris asked through the exhaled smoke.

The girl looked up at him with the same defiant look she had given Brandon.

Chris clicked the pistol's safety down and slid his finger onto the trigger.

The fog encased them. Like this was the only thing happening on the planet. Like Chris was the master of this little piece of earth. Like there were no people left in the world and Chris was the absolute authority in deciding who lived and who died.

Dan took a step closer to Chris. "Come on, man."

The slight waiver in Dan's voice, the ever-so-slight fear in his voice screamed out loud that even Chris's teammates didn't know what he was about to do.

The river bubbled and hissed. Bugs buzzed.

The pistol barked. Everyone jumped. The ejected casing flashed gold and pinged off a bamboo wall. The old woman screamed, shook wildly in Smith's grasp. Brandon spun away, eyes going anywhere but the mess of brain and skull Chris had just made.

He fucking murdered her! Oh Jesus oh holy fucking Christ I can't hide this! Everyone saw! I can't hide this!

The gunshot's echo died slow and the old woman's wailing sobs filled the space between huts. Over her cries, Brandon heard the sound of the old woman slumping in the dirt.

He's crazy. Chris is fucking crazy. He's—

Chris cleared his throat. "I said. Do. You. Speak. English?"

Brandon spun.

The girl stared up at Chris. She was alive? She was alive. A tiny dust cloud hung over her face, kicked up by the bullet. A tiny pock-mark was etched in the ground inches from the girl's head. The dust swirled about her face and she merely coughed when she breathed it in. Had she even flinched when the gun went off?

"Ee-"she said, straining beneath Chris's weight. "Ee…"

"English," Chris said.

"Ee-ngrish."

"Yeah." He gestured to his mouth. "English."

She shook her head.

Chris took his foot off the girl and retrieved the suppressor from his pocket and screwed it onto his 1911. "We'll take them back to Boing. Have a little chat. They'll tell us what happened to Florida."

"Wh-wh-what makes you so sure?" Brandon asked.

Chris shrugged. "I just needed to show her what might happen if she doesn't talk."

Brandon had no desire to find out what he meant by that. This had gotten way too far out of hand. He had to find a way to reestablish his authority over these men. Especially Chris. Had he even had any to begin with?

Was this what won their respect? Violence?

You won't be Americans on this operation.

Chris holstered the pistol and picked up the girl's knife and sword. Tossed the sword to Terry as he walked over to the old woman. She sat up timidly and looked up at him. With the knife's point, Chris dug some grit from beneath his thumbnail. "That girl is pretty tough. Seems like the type that won't talk no matter how much you hurt her." He flicked his eyes toward the girl as he got closer to the old woman. He squatted on his haunches. Sucked the cigarette down to the filter and flicked the butt away. Blowing out smoke he put the knife-point gently against the woman's forehead. Chris turned and watched the girl as he let the knife thump down the woman's wrinkled brow. Thud down on the folding loose skin of her dark and sunken eye socket. Now he watched the woman. He slid the knife closer. Paused. Let it hover a microscopic distance from her twitching eye. Her slapping eyelashes brushed the dust from the blade.

The girl tensed, but she looked on. She watched for a long time. Everyone did. When the old woman closed her eyes, Chris snatched the woman's head and pulled it against his leg. Held it there as she squirmed. He pried open her eyelid with his thumb and she rolled her eye up until only the yellowish white showed. The knife point was on her eyelid now and Brandon swore he saw a tear running down the blade. The girl started shaking. Brandon started shaking. The girl put up a protesting hand and called something out.

And when she did, Chris released the woman. He stood and slid the knife in his thick green LCE belt. Nodding to himself, he looked at the girl. "I think they'll have lots to say."

CHAPTER ELEVEN

With the women in tow, New York climbed the incline toward Mike and George and the wounded men. Brandon's legs burned. The hill seemed so much steeper than it had on their descent. He stopped midway up and looked back and wiped the sweat from his face. The fog that had obscured the village during their assault had evaporated and he saw the village clearly, dwarfed by the hills surrounding the valley. Like toys. The bamboo huts glowed with a peaceful gold in the morning light. He turned away and followed his men.

Mike stood, emerging from early shadows, rifle hanging in his hands. He signaled all was clear and waved the team in. When he saw the two women he smiled and said, "I would've set more places at the table if I'd known guests were coming to breakfast."

But Mike's smile faded when the team responded with nothing but grim and dour faces. "You found Florida," he said flatly.

"We'll talk about that in a minute," Chris said.

Chris held the girl's arm in a chicken wing, holding her wrist tight in the small of her back. She walked stooped over. When she looked up at Mike she gasped and tensed and dug her heels in the ground.

"None of that." Chris yanked her wrist like a dog's choke-chain and she cried out. He nudged her with his hip and they went on.

Terry had the old woman. When they came up the hill she squinted at Mike a moment. But when she saw Brandon looking, she dropped her eyes and kept walking. Maybe these people spent their lives secluded here in the village. Maybe they didn't get much of a chance to interact with other races.

But Captain Conway was black, too. He was the only black man on Florida's team. And he was missing. The women had been carrying some of Florida's clothing.

"Don't let them see the wounded men," Brandon called out. "In case they get the chance to talk to someone." Brandon turned to Mike. "Everything good here?"

"John is still out," Mike said. "I gave Boing another morphine syrette. He's flying high."

Brandon glanced at his watch. "When will he be able to talk?"

Mike shook his head. "It'll be a while before he even knows what planet he's on."

"Where is he?"

He followed Mike back a ways into the jungle. Boing lay next to John. Mike knelt and poured a bit of water from a canteen on a rag and wiped away the beads of sweat trembling on Boing's forehead.

New York's only interpreter. Incapacitated. Brandon sighed with irritation. "Why would you dope him up?"

Mike screwed the cap onto the canteen and he let it thud on the ground as he stood. "Because he's in excruciating pain from shattering his legs. Because I didn't anticipate prisoners from a village that you said was deserted."

Smith emerged from the trees. "Figure out who to blame later. Figure out another way to talk to these women now."

Brandon turned to Smith. "Did you receive any language training?"

"No."

"I know some rudimentary Vietnamese," Mike said. "I can try."

"Come on, then," Brandon said. And they went through the bushes.

The girl sat opposite the woman. Chris stood between them. Mike knelt in front of the girl. He spoke slow in what Brandon assumed was Vietnamese.

The girl looked up at him. Then to the woman. The woman nodded.

Looking back to Mike, the girl said, "Jaran."

Mike's face warmed into a smile. That smile doctors put on when they talk to children. "I'm Mike." He placed his palm on his chest. "Mike."

"Mike," Jaran said.

Mike talked to the women for a while. Laughed occasionally. Maybe just building rapport with them. Neither of the women so much as grinned. Brandon glanced around the circle of men as they listened.

None of them had stepped in when Chris put that gun to Jaran's head. Brandon should have never allowed things to get that far out of hand. If there was ever an opportunity for Brandon to claim his position over these men, telling Chris to put the gun down was probably it…

Don't say anything. Don't give orders. Don't even look if you don't have the stomach for it.

But he had blown it.

He probably shouldn't have even let Chris lead the assault on the village. It had seemed like a good idea at the time. Seemed safe. Let an experienced man lead the team. But Brandon was the commander. He should have taken charge.

These men know what to do.

Then they should know that if they're going to pull

some crazy shit like fire a weapon inches from a prisoner's face, they should ask their commander's approval.

You won't be Americans on this operation.
Keep them in line.

So much contradictory bullshit from Smith. From everyone. What else could be expected from these men? How was Brandon supposed to expect a bunch of attack dogs to obey? How? When Smith had already let them off their leashes before they learned who their new master was?

All eyes were on Mike as he talked. Nobody paid any attention to Brandon. He needed to establish his authority. Now. But he couldn't just demand it. Couldn't just *command* them to obey him.

Nobody had stopped Chris. Was that it? Did they respect violence.

Mike looked up at Chris and said, "I'll try and ask if they've seen any more soldiers like us."

Christ, it was like Brandon wasn't even there.

Mike asked his question. Jaran looked to the old woman. But this time the woman said nothing. The girl looked back to Mike and shook her head.

Brandon squinted at Jaran. Finally aware of what was happening. She wouldn't answer without getting the old woman's approval. Anger rising, the answer to cementing his place as New York's leader became clear.

"Ask her again," Brandon said.

Mike looked at him, eyebrows going up.

"Ask her again."

But when Mike turned back and spoke to Jaran, still she shook her head.

Brandon pushed between Mike and Jaran and yanked the girl's knife from Chris's belt. Turned and stomped toward the old woman. Grabbed her by her filthy, stringy hair and wrenched her head back. Shoving the knife against her carotid artery, Brandon shouted, "Ask her again!"

Mike held up his hands. "Woah! Take it easy! Flies with honey, man!"

"The only flies here are from all the bullshit she's feeding you!" Brandon's voice cracked. "Ask her *again*!"

Mike kept his eyes on Brandon as he spoke to Jaran.

Chris lit a cigarette and took a drag. He watched Brandon through exhaled smoke.

Jaran's eyes flitted from Mike to Brandon to the woman to Mike. Jaran nodded.

"Where?" Brandon said, tugging the woman's hair.

Mike spoke.

Jaran pointed down to the village.

"Where are they now?" Brandon growled.

Mike spoke.

The woman called out, her throat pulsing on the blade as she spoke.

"What did she say?" Brandon demanded.

"I think she told the girl not to say anything else," Mike said.

Brandon looked down at the old woman. She stared right back at him, jaw muscles clenching. Brandon raised the knife high. Everything in him screamed for him not to do it. But he had to. *Had to*. But he had to work himself up to it. His chest rose and fell. Short, quick breaths. Waiting. The adrenaline came, pumping fury through his skull.

"Wrong answer," Brandon whispered. And he slammed the knife's thick metal handle into the woman's face. The skin between handle and cheekbone *popped* and split open.

The old woman groaned. Her trembling hand came up to block any further blows. Hoarse squeals filled the jungle. The sound of her pain. When she spoke again she repeated over and over the last thing she had said. Not to tell them anything. Brandon hit her again. She screamed. But still, with the blood pouring watery purple down her face, still she repeated it.

Brandon looked at Mike. "*Ask her again!*"

But Mike looked at the ground and rubbed his temples. The woman's cries quieted to a rumbling sob. Mike said nothing.

"Fine," Brandon said. He shoved the woman down on her stomach. "Hold this." He tossed the knife at Chris's feet. Chris didn't move.

Brandon snatched the woman's hair and yanked her head up. Drawing his 1911, he put barrel to the back of her skull. He looked into Jaran's eyes and growled, "What happened to our soldiers?"

Jaran shook, exhaling and inhaling hard through her nose. Snot blew out and oozed over her lips. But there was no fear in her eyes. It was a blazing hatred. She turned her chin up. She watched him. Eyes going wet and blurry, she spoke.

"What did she say?"

"I'll tell you." Mike cleared his throat. "Put the gun down and I'll tell you."

Brandon raised the pistol as if to strike the woman. "Tell me!"

Mike looked at the girl. Then slowly back to Brandon. "She said she's not afraid."

Spit and blood bubbled from the old woman's trembling mouth. She was whispering. Quietly repeating the phrase over and over. *I'm not afraid.* Like a prayer. Like an insult. Jaran, her face clinched and shaking, inclined her head, refusing to let fall the tears welling in her eyes.

Brandon snarled. "Ask her again."

There was a brief silence. Then Mike, softly, spoke.

Jaran's trembling lips pulled back in a grimace. She whispered something. Then shut her eyes. And when she shut them, the tears fell.

A frustrated sigh blew out from Mike as he dropped his head.

"What did she say?"

"Goodbye." Mike looked up at Brandon. Disgust plain on his face. "She said fucking goodbye to her grandmother. Put that goddamn gun away. She called your bluff."

The men stared at him.

Brandon's guts blazed. What the hell had Brandon done that was so wrong? Terry was about to punch Brandon in the face for trying to stop Chris, and now no one would support Brandon? For using the same methods?

Frustration burst from him in a roar and he released his grip on the woman's hair. What the hell did he have to do to get this team's respect? What did he have to do for them to accept him as their commander? He hadn't done anything to this woman that Chris hadn't done to the girl, and now Mike looked at Brandon as if he were subhuman. "What do you suggest we do, Sergeant?" he yelled at Mike. "Sit here? Laugh with them until they confess to Florida's murder? Huh? What do we do?"

"Something *else!*" Mike yelled back.

In the quiet, beneath the eyes of the team, he shook his head and holstered the pistol. The two women had the look of people who knew their lives were over. He'd seen it on the faces of captured NVA Prisoners of War. The NVA and Viet Cong didn't know they would be treated relatively well if they were captured by U.S. forces. Enemy commanders lied to their men. Told their troops Americans would torture them. Cut them open and leave them alive while the birds ate their guts. The lies made the little bastards fight to their last breath. So he had heard…

These women. They had the look. In their hearts they knew they would not leave this place alive. Which wasn't true at all. That is, at least New York wasn't going to kill them. Brandon stepped away and looked down through the trees at the village. He looked back at the men. At the women.

Jaran crawled forward and grabbed the old woman. Held her in a hard embrace. Spoke to her softly. With the sleeve of her threadbare robe she wiped away blood from the woman's face.

Brandon wouldn't kill these women. And he wouldn't allow New York to harm them anymore than they already had. Than *he* already had.

"They aren't going to talk," Brandon said, turning back toward the village. "Not yet."

"What makes you so sure?" Smith asked. The tone in his voice had an eerie calm. An indifference. Like the operative didn't care at all that Brandon had just brutalized the old woman.

If Smith knew anything about Brandon's background, he was probably wondering how Brandon could possibly know what these women would or would not do. He wasn't going to open himself up to ridicule over his inexperience.

"Gut feeling," Brandon said.

"She said she wasn't afraid," Chris said to Mike. "She happen to mention what she *was* scared of?"

Mike shook his head.

"In case you didn't notice," Brandon grumbled. "I was *trying* to scare her."

"Oh, I noticed," Chris said. Voice cool as the smoke he breathed out. "But maybe we ain't the big dogs in the fight."

Smith stepped between the circle of men and women and went to his pack. Pulled out his binoculars and went to the treeline and looked down at the village. The last whisper of mist had burned off and the river's far bank was now visible. Dappled in shadow. The river was wide, and from the smooth surface, Brandon guessed it was deep.

Smith said, "Ask them if they're of Mongolian descent, please."

Mike looked over his shoulder at the operative. Clearly frustrated with the way things were going. "Why?"

"Indulge me, please, sergeant."

"I don't know the Vietnamese word for Mongolian."

Smith held the binoculars a bit high, as if examining something on the far side of the river. "Mon Co." He said it as if the answer to the question was of little consequence.

"I thought you didn't speak Vietnamese," Mike said.

Smith said nothing.

Mike shook his head and asked the women.

Jaran held her cheek against the old woman's head. When she looked up at Mike there was hair stuck to her sweating, tear-soaked face. After a moment, the girl nodded.

"They are," Mike said.

"Interesting," Smith said. "Now if you would please ask them where the path on the far side of the river leads."

Smith held out the binos to Brandon. He took them and looked to where Smith gestured. And there it was. On the far river bank, a tiny dock. Barely visible in the high grass. Beyond the grass and vegetation, there was a thin, brown trail disappearing into the jungle.

Brandon handed back the binoculars.

Mike had a difficult time, but through the use of hand signals and broken Vietnamese, he seemed to get the point across. Smith turned to watch the exchange.

Jaran looked at the ground and shook her head.

"*Very* interesting," Smith said. Taking Brandon's shoulder and leading him away from the group, Smith whispered, "We need to get up that path and have a look."

Brandon glanced at his watch and said, "We only have about two hours before the extraction."

"Then we go as a small team. Say, you and me. The girl will lead us. We'll move faster that way. Your men will stay with the wounded and if we don't make it back in time, they can exfil without us. The agency will send another extraction for you and me."

WHAT?

Brandon tried to keep his face tight. Tried to keep his jaw from dropping onto the jungle floor. An entire village had been slaughtered. A whole SOG team vanished and these women most certainly had *something* to do with that. And Smith wanted to take a two-man team into the jungle?

Why couldn't Smith see he wasn't going to get what he came for? There was no sign of his HVT. Florida was dead. Florida's handler was dead. The only thing missing were the bodies. And they were probably stacked and burned in that pile down by the river. There were enough uniforms in that bag the women carried to account for almost every man on Florida's team. There wasn't going to be some naked survivor out there in the jungle. The mission was over.

As calm as he could manage, hoping to change Smith's mind, Brandon said, "Going up there doesn't sit well with me." Brandon's mind raced, trying to come up with some excuse to leave. "I'm nervous about the NVA getting here before we exfil."

Smith squinted at him. Then he nodded. "I hadn't thought of that, Captain. You're probably right. We should call off the extraction. We'll keep the SOG team here in case enemy troops come poking around. We'll need the extra guns. Good thinking."

Not Brandon's day for bluffs.

"On the other hand," Brandon said. "We should probably get these women somewhere safe for a proper interrogation. If they're the only ones who know what happened here, I don't want that information getting away from us. But…" Brandon leaned in whisper-close. "You're willing to stay out here with only one other guy to watch your back? Why take such a big risk?"

Smith's eyes went rigid, obviously seeing exactly how Brandon was trying to manipulate him. "My agency wants this HVT. They're going to get him. Or they're going to get the confirmation that he is dead or has fled the area. And there's the matter of my missing man. These women had Florida's clothing. They were clearly returning from the far side of the river. I would say there is compelling evidence that someone, either my HVT or our men are up that path."

Brandon looked over Smith's shoulder at New York. From a tactical standpoint, they weren't in too bad a shape. So long as they didn't have to do much fighting or evasion. He looked at the river and the far shore. The dock. The path now invisible without the binoculars. "We should bring some more guns with us."

"I disagree. Securing the landing zone is what's most important. The helicopters will need security on the ground in case whoever slaughtered these people comes back. Or if the NVA show up."

Brandon threw his arm out toward the river. "And what if you and me run into them up *there*? If the girl leads us into a trap?"

Smith shrugged. "Then we break contact. If we're killed your men will exfil with the old woman."

If we're killed! Brandon's jaw did drop open at that. God, he just wanted to get the fuck out of there.

Brandon had to walk away. He turned and pushed through the reaching leaves to where John and Boing lay unconscious. Squatting on his haunches, Brandon ran his hand through his hair.

"What would you do?" he asked John.

John's half-open eyes stared at the sky.

Sunlight glinted on something metal on John's chest. A gold chain. Brandon reached down and pried open John's rubber-like fingers clutched around the end of the chain. There was a gold cross on the end of the chain, smudged with fingerprints.

Brandon thought hard as he looked at the shining metal. Thought about everything that had happened since New York arrived. But as he thought, he realized how little had actually happened. Aside from the cripple, that hamburger-faced anomaly, the operation up until this point seemed, relatively, *safe*.

He imagined missing the extraction. If things stayed

this quiet while he and Smith waited for another helicopter there was the chance for him to gain some respect from the team. Sending his men back to safety while he and Smith stayed out in the bush to accomplish the mission sounded like something John would do. He and Smith might have to hide from the NVA, but how hard would that be? Brandon had laid right at their feat in Laos and had not been seen. He rubbed his chin.

Fear.

It was fear. Fear was telling Brandon to run. But at that moment what was there truly to fear out there? He sighed. In the long run, going with Smith across the river might make commanding this team easier. He didn't like the idea of staying out here alone. Didn't like the idea of going across the river as a two-man team. But despite the plan not sounding good, the rewards might be worth the risk.

Brandon looked at his watch. The second-hand *tick-ticked*. "Fuck," he whispered. Then he looked down at the cross on John's chest. He nearly laughed. He could barely remember the last time he prayed. "Mind if I borrow this?"

John said nothing.

Brandon dropped the cross and chain in his shirt pocket and buttoned it. He pushed through the trees and said, "Chris. Smith and I are leaving. You're in charge while I'm gone. Clear an LZ in the field and use Smith's radio to relay the coordinates to the retrans aircraft. Keep that woman safe while we're gone. If the helicopters get here before Smith and I return, tell them we're following up on the HVT's possible location. If we don't return, you are to extract the team, the woman, and the wounded and instruct the pilots to return to this location as soon as they hear from us."

"That's a great plan," Chris said. "I like everything about it except all the parts that are completely fucked. You're not going anywhere without us."

"I gave you an order, goddamnit." Walking toward the

men, he said, "Give me enough paracord to bind the girl's hands. Set out as many claymores as you can. Clackers. Not tripwires. If we're not back by the time you leave, just leave them for us."

Brandon hoped to God he wouldn't need to use them.

CHAPTER TWELVE

The current was strong and the river wide. Brandon sat in the little wooden boat's stern and revved the motor and the boat lurched forward. Smith sat at the bow, rifle resting on the gunwale. Jaran sat between them with her legs crossed and her wrists bound behind her back. To the north the river disappeared into the mountains from where it flowed. To the south it stretched long into the distance, gradually curving and disappearing beneath a blotch of shadow cast by mountain and jungle.

Brandon pushed the little boat hard. It took them a long time to cross the four-hundred-some meters to the far shore.

Closing in on the overgrown dock, Brandon let off the motor and guided the boat along the up-current side. Smith threw a loop of hempen rope around a post and pulled them in. Brandon and Smith disembarked and stood on the dock. In the current, the boat rocked and thumped against the thick wooden pilings. Jaran stared up at them.

Beckoning her with a waving hand, Brandon said, "Let's go."

She sat there. Eyes hard.

Brandon hopped down into the rocking boat and grabbed her up. "I'm not going to hurt you. Now come *on!*" And he shoved her up on the dock and Smith took her shoulders and steadied her.

The rising sun lit the far side of the river and the jungle beyond the tiny village. A pleasant breeze tousled Brandon's hair and the jungle foliage swished around him. Birds called. Insects skittered in the grass. Jaran turned her head this way and that, squinting hard as if she had never heard the sounds of life before.

Strange. Standing there on the dock with the river bubbling and the breeze sighing, it seemed so peaceful.

But Jaran interrupted it. Saying something. Nodding forcefully to the village.

Across the river, Brandon could just barely make out Chris on the opposite dock. Binoculars up to his eyes. Watching them.

"Your grandmother will be fine," Brandon said. "Let's go." And he took her by the arm and pulled her up the hill.

Was Chris actually concerned for them? It was encouraging to think he was. He had an unorthodox way of doing things that Brandon didn't care for.

And a mouth that won't quit.

But keeping the team safe seemed important to him. Brandon still didn't know the men all that well. If he was honest, he didn't *like* Chris. But the man was competent. Cared about the team. Pushing into the jungle, Brandon found himself feeling glad that Chris had slipped into the role of the team's NCOIC in John's absence.

Even though Brandon didn't look back once they started up through the overgrown trail, he had a feeling that Chris would be watching.

Brandon nudged Jaran along in front of him while Smith took up the rear. It wasn't long before the sound of the river was lost behind the wall of jungle. It was still early and here and there they walked through refreshing pockets of cool night air not yet baked by the sun.

They leaned into the inclining trail and kept a quick pace. Brandon grunted at the burning in his legs.

"Lock out your knees," Smith said.

"What?"

"It'll give your legs a moment of rest between each step."

Brandon tried it, being careful not to hyperextend his knees. But while his legs still burned, it actually seemed to alleviate some of the ache.

After a time of walking in silence, Brandon said over his shoulder, "How did you know they were Mongol?"

"Do they look Vietnamese to you?"

"I don't know."

"Well," Smith said. "I do."

"But I don't understand why you brought it up. We were trying to find out what happened to Florida. Something prompted you to interject. What does their race have to do with the operation?"

Smith said nothing for a time. When he finally spoke, it was as if he was carefully choosing each word. "The HVT. I've been led to believe he is Mongol. I'm not at liberty to discuss the specifics with you, Captain."

Brandon rolled his eyes. If Smith wanted to keep secrets, fine. Mongol. Vietnamese. Their race didn't matter. Brandon just wanted to finish this search and get back before the helicopters came.

Jaran led them, but after a time it seemed that Smith and Brandon could have left the girl behind. The trail didn't fork off or disappear at all. Beyond the overgrowth near the river, the trail was worn and well-traveled. Here and there, off-colored soil was packed down, probably a repair for a rut or some other defect. Water damage maybe, from heavy rainfall and washout. Odd that the trail would be so well maintained but the dock and the trailhead were practically hidden.

Maybe whoever maintained the trail went out of their way to keep it hidden.

The thought sent a suspicious tightness through Brandon's chest and he slid his eyes back and forth. Looked carefully at the ground before him. Listened.

With nervous awareness Brandon followed Jaran. She neither stopped nor protested. Probably thinking about what would happen to the old woman should she return without the two Americans. That was good. Hopefully neither of the women would cause trouble simply to ensure the other's safety. As long as they believed that illusion of potential danger, this mess would be easier for everyone.

They went on.

It was easy to fall into the trap of drifting thought. The memory, the *feel* of the knife handle bashing the old woman's face pounced on Brandon. He winced. The image wouldn't leave him and he dwelled on his behavior during that long, monotonous climb. His barbarism when trying to extract information from the two women. That wasn't like him. Not at all. He had barely gotten anything from them by shoving a gun in their faces. Yet the women seemed to open up to Mike when he simply asked them nicely. Was it better to be loved or feared?

Flies with honey.

The path curved sharp and abrupt, contorting into a series of steep inclining switchbacks. Long, smooth grooves gouged in the ground exposed softball-sized boulders that helped a bit as stepping stones.

Jaran plodded on. Working her way from rock to rock, her soft leather boots padding on the rough stone.

She jumped suddenly upon a boulder and turned to look at Brandon and Smith. They stopped and watched. She stepped down from the stone and continued up.

Brandon looked over his shoulder. Smith shrugged.

"Hey," Brandon said, turning back. "Jaran."

She stopped, eyes invisible in the shadow of her matted hair.

"Slow down." He didn't expect her to understand, but

she stood there and waited for him to catch up. When he reached her, he nodded forward and gave her shoulder a gentle nudge. She moved on.

Smith and Brandon only carried their rifles, pistols, and ammunition. But even without the added weight of their rucksacks they both breathed heavy against the path's perpetual incline. Jaran, however, showed no signs of fatigue.

Higher up, the path narrowed to a span of about three men abreast. The jungle thinned and the sun bathed the path in hard light. A steep cliff dropped away to the side, but still the path continued upward. They walked on and eventually the trees stopped growing along the path. Instead of dirt on the ground it was hard, smooth stone. The only green left was that of the jungle canopy reaching up, but not overtaking the cliff's edge. A hard wind blew, growling in Brandon's ears. Without the blanket of jungle blocking the view, he saw that they walked beside a mammoth black escarpment that stabbed into the steel-blue sky.

Brandon knew this place. He had seen it from across the river. Far below on the far bank, through a thin haze, tiny rooftops and the dark rectangle of the tilled field. Somewhere in those far away trees New York waited.

Jaran slowed and looked again over her shoulder, glancing sidelong at Brandon.

The look chilled him and he was overcome by a hyperawareness of how close he stood to that high, high edge. He watched her hard and he sidestepped as far from the cliff edge as he could. He raised his rifle slow, muzzle pointed at her back. Raised it so he was sure she could see it. "Don't get any fucking ideas."

Even with her hands tied behind her back she was potentially lethal. All it would take was one good kick to send him over the edge. He might end up in the trees, but doubted they would do much to slow his fall. No, sir. If she managed to shove him, he was dead.

Jaran might not have understood English, but she seemed to understand rifle just fine. She moved on.

The trio walked in silence until the path ended abruptly at another cliff. Brandon groaned and his leg muscles turned to jelly when he saw the way ahead. A frayed rope bridge anchored with clusters of bamboo poles.

"Fuck that," Brandon said.

He had crossed a lot of rope bridges before. Army obstacle courses always had them. But those bridges stood about chest-high off the ground and, if you fell, you only fell onto soft gravel or into a pool of muddy water. He closed his eyes. Tried to dam the flow of images of his crushed, ripped-open, impact-mangled body.

Smith shouldered by. "What do you think your obstacle courses were preparing you for?"

"You don't have to cross them with someone who wants to murder you."

Smith looked at Jaran. "Captain," Smith sighed. "If you want to be on the first bird out of here you need to get this over with."

"You first."

Smith slung his CAR-15 across his back. "Fine." And he grabbed the two handholds. "Oh," he said over his shoulder. "Cut the girl loose. I'm sure you can appreciate the need for one's hands. Given the circumstances."

Smith started across the bridge, placing one foot in front of the other along two thick wooden planks. The bridge swayed back and forth, but seemed steady.

When Smith was safely across, Brandon undid the knots binding Jaran's hands and stuffed the paracord in a cargo pocket. He pointed across the bridge and nodded to the girl and she darted across. A squirrel couldn't have negotiated that bridge any faster.

Showoff.

When she was across, Smith pointed to the ground and she sat. He motioned for her to lie down on her stomach, facing away from the bridge. Brandon appreciated that.

Jaran had tried to shank Brandon before. She might not hesitate to try and shove them both off the cliff when he reached the far side.

Brandon's hands were slick with nervous sweat. He grabbed ahold of the coarse, dry ropes. He held tight. Sliding a foot forward, and then bringing his toe to his heel. He shimmied across, reminding himself not to look down, not to look down, not to look down…

He was fine with helicopters. He was fine with planes. Even parachuting didn't bother him. But something about heights where there was nothing to slow your descent except the skull-exploding earth unnerved him.

He shut his eyes and felt his way across.

When he reached the far side, Smith held out a hand and they clasped wrists. Smith pulled him to solid ground, but even the ground felt unstable beneath his trembling legs. Brandon bent over. Hands on his knees he stared at the ground, tried to calm his spinning head. Panting like he had just sprinted a mile.

"Looks like we've arrived," Smith said.

"Where?" Brandon had no idea where they were supposed to be going. Smith stepped aside. Brandon looked up and sucked in a deep, trembling breath. A flow of thick vines spilled down over blackness. Streaks of rust-red clay stained the rocky edges and pooled in the pits of dull grey stone. As if human sacrifices had once been performed there.

Legs weary from the climb, from the bridge crossing, from adrenaline, from fear, Brandon sank to one knee and slipped his rifle from his back and raised it, aiming into a thick blackness contrasted against the bright morning sky. He aimed into the dark, yawning mouth of a cave.

The front sight-post blurred and focused and blurred against the cave's gloom. Brandon breathed out slow behind his rifle.

He should have listened to Chris. He should have brought the whole team.

Smith would never agree to turn back. Not now. No way. Going home meant going forward. Going in. This thing needed to be done.

There had been no resistance on the trail. Did that mean there was no one inside? No one waiting? Brandon blew out hard.

Fine.

If Smith wanted to look in the cave, Brandon would look in the cave. There was probably nothing in there but spiders and rats.

Fine.

Placate Smith. Have a look. When they didn't find anything they could get their asses back to the boat and go home and forget about this shithole.

Brandon searched between the vines. Waited. "Get up," he whispered to Jaran. But Jaran didn't move.

Duck-walking to where she lay pronated, Brandon patted her on the back. She turned her head to him, chin dragging in the dirt and gray pebbles.

"Up," Brandon said. Punctuating the word with a flick of his rifle.

Jaran got to her hands and knees. Eyes on his rifle's muzzle. She stood warily and faced Brandon.

Swiping his rifle, Brandon said, "Turn around." She turned and faced the cave. Brandon slung his rifle and slid in behind her. Pulled the cord from his pocket and tied her wrists behind her back. He grabbed one of her wrists and held it tight. Tight enough to stop her from pulling any stunts. From running. Tight enough to let her know he was there.

Slipping his 1911 from his holster he rested the suppressor on Jaran's shoulder.

He was spitting in the face of the Geneva Conventions. Using a non-combatant as a human shield. He was glad Mike wasn't here to see this. Smith, however, didn't seem to give a shit. Why would he? They weren't Americans on this operation.

"Ready?" Brandon said over his shoulder.

Smith pulled his flashlight from his LCE. "Yeah."

Brandon prodded Jaran forward.

Smith kept a few paces behind and off to the side and he clicked on his flashlight, shining the beam over Brandon's head and into the cave. But in the brilliant morning light, the red lens illuminated nothing.

"Switch to white," Brandon said. "If anyone's in there I want to see them coming."

Smith clicked off the light. Plastic scraped as Smith unscrewed the flashlight's head and put the little red plastic disc into the storage compartment. Smith clicked on the light and white light ate away the dark inside.

Nothing.

No one.

Dangling vines cast harsh black shadows against gray stone and he pushed Jaran through. Leafy fingers caressed Brandon's pistol and wrist. They went in. Their gravel-scraping steps echoed off the damp stone walls. The temperature plummeted as they passed beyond the opening, but despite the growing heat outside, the chill brought no comfort.

The cave was wide, about four men could stand side by side. But in Smith's light, further on, the passage narrowed to single-file width.

Large shadows leapt from the walls as Smith swept the light left and right. Brandon had to take a minute and steady himself. Steady his heart. He was literally jumping at shadows. If he couldn't get his mind under control, he would be worthless if something real jumped out.

A glance at his watch was enough to sober him. There wasn't much time left before the extraction.

Brandon prodded the girl on. "Come on." But he said it more to himself than to the girl. He had to move. The sooner he confirmed nothing was here, the sooner they could get back to New York. But something in his gut tugged at him. He prayed hard for this cave to be empty.

But the path. The bridge. The cave itself. These things, by virtue of their existence, Brandon had the feeling that his prayer would go unanswered. Everything in him told him to run. Told him that somewhere in that dark, there was something waiting. It was against this fear that Brandon fought as he pushed Jaran faster, sacrificing caution for speed.

Smith's light swept across the passage and froze upon a three-legged stool. A rugged thing made of bamboo. Behind the stool, along the wall, stood another bamboo structure. Tall and rectangular. Lashed at the corners with rope. Brandon tightened his grip on Jaran's wrist.

"What do you think that is?" Smith asked.

"Weapons rack."

"But it's—"

"Yeah," Brandon said. "Empty."

The rack looked almost medieval in its construction. Not made for rifles. The high grooves suggested it was made to hold long and slim weapons. Bows, maybe. Spears.

The lower notches, very slim and cut about thigh-high. Those were for swords.

Pushing into the narrowing passageway, Smith fell in behind Brandon and held the light high over his shoulder. The air was still humid, and the deeper they went, the cooler it became. Brandon told himself lies. That it was the chill that set his teeth to chattering. That it wasn't his fear.

In the light, deep, irregular gouges ran black upon the walls like claw-marks of some beast. Grooved and smooth, but here and there a sharp chunk missing. These marks ran straight ahead in the walls and ceiling, disappearing into the darkness, marking the way forward in that ever-narrowing passage. But they weren't just on the walls and ceiling, Brandon felt them in the floor through his unsure footing.

Tool marks. Someone dug this. By hand.

Excavated. That was the *how*. But that wasn't what

worried Brandon. What worried him was the *why?*

There must have been a reason to crudely excavate this much rock. Back in the world a bunch of guys would work for days dynamiting a project like this. Brandon flexed his muscles, attempting in vain to mask the trembling in his hands. The NVA and VC had extensive tunnel networks that simultaneously awed American commanders and terrified the men ordered to crawl through them.

Had Jaran led them into the entrance of a tunnel network? Or the exit? Was this a base? Some hidden fortress? Why would the NVA put so much effort into a hidden structure so far from any fighting? Maybe it was old. Maybe it was made during a different war. Or in anticipation for some future war. Brandon's palm sweated against Jaran's wrist. Maybe it was a place where a defending force could stockpile artillery rounds and hide troops.

But if this was an active base, where were the sentries and signs of soldiers? Where were the latrines and trash points? Where were the firepits for cooking. There was none of it.

Why hadn't he listened to Chris?

He tried to remember as he pushed Jaran deeper. Tried to remember every briefing on hidden NVA structures. No matter how much thought he gave it, he could find no logical explanation for a project such as this. This was different.

It was like the deep insides of Egyptian pyramids he had seen in *National Geographic*. The foreboding entrances. The long, narrow hallways. But pyramids were—

His breath caught. That was it: This place was like the entrance of a tomb.

Jaran breathed heavy. Pressed up against her, Brandon felt the slightest ripple in her muscles. The smallest resistance in her steps. Was she afraid, too?

In Smith's light the tunnel seemed to dead-end at a rock wall in front of them. Brandon squinted, trying to see if there was a curve or a corner in the passageway. In front of him, the tool marks changed direction. No longer horizontal. They ran vertical—

The twitch in Jaran's muscles telegraphed her attack and Brandon was ready when she planted her feet and squatted low. Just before she threw herself back at him he wrenched her wrist straight up to the back of her skull. Her shoulder popped staccato like a deep, tough root ripped from the earth. Brandon felt the reverberations all the way down in her wrist. The fight poured from her and she screamed like a thing dying. Banshee screams echoed from all around the cave.

Grabbing Jaran's bulging dislocated shoulder, Brandon spun her around to face him. In Smith's light her brown eyes were wide and bright and frantic and her jaw hung slack. Spit hung on her quivering lips.

"Stupid girl!" Brandon growled. He slammed the pistol grip square into her face. The *crunch* of splitting cartilage vibrated through the grip. Blood flowed bright red from her nose onto her robes.

The sound spilling from her face as she tried to breathe was like boots pulling from wet and sucking mud. She wavered a moment. Then sat down hard.

"Stupid girl," Brandon said. "Fucking stupid, stupid girl!" He grabbed a handful of her hair and yanked her to her feet. She howled and he snatched her other wrist and held it tight behind her back. She hunched over, her dislocated arm hung awkward, flopped over her side like nothing kept it attached but the cord binding her wrists. She trembled and let out lip-biting grunts as her arm swayed in its bag of skin.

"You behave yourself," Brandon panted. "And I might pop that back in for you."

He was just about to nudge her forward when Smith's ambient light illuminated a black, gaping hole in the floor next to Brandon's feet.

"Holy shit," Brandon whispered.

"What?"

"I think she just tried to throw me down there."

"Down where?" Smith looked over Brandon's shoulder. "Holy shit."

"Yeah. Get the light up here and take a look."

Brandon pressed Jaran against the wall, kept his knee between her legs to keep her off balance. Smith slid past them.

Smith got down on his belly and pulled himself to the edge and shined his flashlight into the pit and looked around. The flashlight revealed a coil of thick braded rope tied off to two fat metal spikes driven into the rock. After a few moments of searching, Smith gasped.

"What is it?" Brandon asked.

"Hello!" Smith yelled, and Brandon jumped at the sudden noise. "Oh my God. Hello!"

Brandon's heart raced. "What is it?"

"Are you alive?" Smith called down into the echoing dark.

"Smith!" Brandon yelled. "What the fuck do you see?"

Smith looked up at him, his flashlight illuminating the confusion and surprise on his face. "I think it's one of our men."

CHAPTER THIRTEEN

Brandon knelt at the pit's edge, running his hand over the two rusted iron spikes driven in the rock. Peering down into darkness. Into nothing. His eyes had not yet adjusted to the gloom. Were human eyes even capable of adjusting to such absolute dark? The rope looped around the spikes had a familiar roughness. The same thick and fraying braid used for the rope bridge outside. Strong. Still, he tugged on it. Grabbed tight with both hands and threw his weight against it. To check. To double-check. To triple-check the anchor points. The rope had a slight give, an elasticity that he didn't like. But the rope held.

Knowing his recent luck, the rope probably led down to a viper's nest. Brandon turned away from the pit to tell Smith to give him some extra light—

Jaran stared at him. The look in her eyes shoved the words back down his throat.

Face still wet with blood, she lay on her side near the wall and stared up at him. Chest rising and falling with the uneven breaths of a wounded animal. The look on her face...

He would have been comfortable seeing anger in her eyes. Rage. He deserved rage. He would not have given a moment's pause for a look of anger. But the look in her wide-open eyes, it was terror.

"What's wrong?" Smith said.

"What?"

"Why do always say 'what' after I ask you a question?"

It was hard to take his eyes off the girl. He watched her a few moments more. Then turned to Smith and said, "Give me some extra light."

Smith lay alongside the rim and shined his light down.

Brandon knelt beside him and added his own light. The pit was deep. Brandon had to lie down on his belly and reach his arm down into the pit. Reach out with the flashlight. Had to will the light to illuminate something.

"I don't see anything," Brandon said.

"He's down there," Smith said. "Keep looking."

Smith had said he saw someone, but Brandon saw no one. Nothing.

He held the light steady, as if sustained light would somehow melt away the dark like sunlight on ice. He looked. He watched. Shifted his gaze. A shape appeared so subtly that Brandon thought it was a trick of the light. He squeezed his eyes shut. Opened them. Still there.

"I see him," Brandon whispered. Far down, naked flesh materialized from the dark. Arms. Legs. Torso. Like the darkness was giving birth to a man. The longer he looked the more of the man seeped from the dark. When the face materialized, a slow cold climbed up Brandon's neck. The man down there, Brandon had spent nearly two weeks with him. Sitting with him and waiting while they in-processed with the other captains. Brandon had talked with him on the plane from Okinawa. The man's deep baritone thrumming in his mind.

Anyone know what the hell this Studies and Observations Group is?

"I know him," Brandon said.

"Who is it?"

"Florida's commander."

Captain Conway. He lay down there in the dark. Spread-eagle and naked. It had to be him. Captain Conway was the only other black man assigned to the recon teams besides Mike. It had to be him.

"Think he fell?" Smith asked.

"Fell?" Brandon would have considered it if Jaran had not just tried to shove him in. The image of Jaran carrying a sack of bloody uniforms crept into his mind. The light trembled in his hand. "No. I don't think he fell." He brought the light up and shined it at the girl. "I think she *pushed* him."

Jaran's wide, unblinking eyes shined in the white light. Her lips moved but only silence spilled out.

"Regardless," Smith said. "We need to get down there and investigate. How he got down there is irrelevant."

Brandon grinded his teeth and looked back down into the pit. Throwing his friends away like garbage didn't fit Brandon's definition of 'irrelevant'.

"How do you want to get him out?" Brandon asked. "I think the best way is to tie—"

"Mortuary Affairs will handle all recoveries," Smith said. "We have the grid coordinates."

That didn't feel right. Leaving Conway down there. That didn't feel right at all. If the whole team were here they could haul him up and carry him down the mountain no problem. Or if Smith and Brandon had thought to bring a litter. Leaving Conway behind would be another addition to the growing list of things Brandon would mull over on the helicopter ride home.

"How big is this thing?" Smith asked.

Brandon shined the light around the pit's circumference. "Big."

"See anything else?"

Completing a cursory inspection around the perimeter, only tiny dust motes swirled in the light. At the bottom there were still dark places that the light would not go.

"No," Brandon said. "I don't see anything else."

"Okay. I'll keep an eye on our friend up here. Make sure you look around the entire bottom. See if you can find any arteries."

Brandon's heart quickened. He hadn't considered other tunnels. Of who or what could be waiting for him. The adrenaline drip. The peripheral panic. It must be how the tunnel rats feel…

"Let's get down there," Smith said.

"Yeah," Brandon said under his breath. "*Let's.*" As if Smith had even thought about going down there. One of them had to stay with Jaran, that was true. Lest she somehow cut the rope and leave them both down there to rot.

What a way to go. Starving to death and listening to Smith tell him how it was all Brandon's fault.

Brandon was just as capable of babysitting. What Brandon *wanted* to say was: *It's your mission, you fucking climb down there.* He wanted to order one of the recon men down there.

But would any one of New York's men protest if he ordered them to go down there? The answer came instantly.

No.

Those men would fight amongst themselves to be the one who went down.

Brandon grunted as he stood. Slung his rifle across his back. He clipped the flashlight to his LCE. There was a pecking order. Smith was at the top of it. Despite being in charge. In *command*. Brandon only commanded the enlisted soldiers. As far as the government saw it, Smith outranked Brandon.

Smith pushed himself up to one knee and laid his rifle over his raised thigh. Leveled it at Jaran. "Yell if you get in trouble. I'll pull you out."

"Thanks," Brandon grumbled, and he snaked his arm around the rope and gripped it tight. Stirred his leg and wrapped the rope around his thigh and calf and pinched the rope between his feet. With his weight on his legs, Brandon inched backward and descended hand-over-hand into the dark.

Down.

Down.

The flashlight at his shoulder blasted a brilliant white spot against gray rock in front of him and he had to look away over his shoulder.

Down.

The cold air grew thick. Breathing in a smell—

Brandon's stomach revolted and he gripped the rope hard. Pulled his face into his arms. Buried his nose and mouth in his elbow. He sucked in air through his uniform's fabric. Not good enough. The smell got through. Mouth slimy, Brandon retched, dry heaving into his arm.

The stench of shit and rot assaulted him. Poked at any cracked openings in his mouth and nose and eyes. The palpable odor clinging to him like a layer of filth on his skin.

He couldn't stay paused on the rope. If he started puking he didn't know how long he could hang on. The fall would be long.

Brandon spit out a thick wet string that clung yellow on the wall. Waited for any surprise vomit. When it didn't come, Brandon eased off his grip and continued down. Sucking in rancid breaths and sliding, holding his breath as long as he could. Shoving his face in his arm and sucking in a breath.

Down.

The odor hung in the cool, still air. There was no getting accustomed to it. There was a dampness to the stench like the inside of a mouth, and it grew with each inch that Brandon dropped.

When Brandon's feet touched firm ground, he held the rope tight and tapped around with his foot to make sure he was at the bottom. There was no sense in winding up like Boing.

Brandon winced at the image of Boing flying out into the night. The sound when he hit… If that kid would have just jumped out of the goddamn plane like he was supposed to.

What was Brandon supposed to have done? Let the team jump without their interpreter? Ask the pilot to risk his life—his *crews'* lives—to swing back around for another pass to drop Brandon and Boing? Risk getting picked up on enemy radar?

The pilot would've denied another pass, anyway. He wasn't even an Army aviator, he was a spook contractor. Brandon would have had no control over what the pilot did or didn't do. Wouldn't be able to change the pilot's mind unless he held a gun to his head. And when the pilot called Brandon's bluff…

Brandon laughed sardonically into his elbow. If the pilot had denied another pass, Brandon would be, at this moment, back at base having coffee.

Having coffee and getting ready for a mammoth ass-chewing.

Was that so bad? Compared to this?

If things didn't improve on this mission, if they didn't find anything earth-shattering out here Brandon was going to get that ass-chewing anyway. Boing was crippled and John was…

John was whatever he was.

He's your man, the colonel had said.

"Hey!" Smith's voice echoed from above. "Still alive?"

Feeling nothing but firm ground, Brandon let go of the rope and took the flashlight from his shoulder. Face still buried in his elbow, he swept the light around the pit and surveyed the bottom.

"Yeah," Brandon called absently. Flashlight washing over Conway's body. "I'm still alive."

Conway's corpse laid in the approximate center of the floor. Whether it was an artifact of dust or the humid air, Conway's skin glowed bronze in the harsh white light, as if covered in a sheen of feverish sweat. A few days' worth of facial hair had grown on Conway's face. Gnarled. Caked with blood.

"What the hell?" In the light were four dull metal spikes like the ones anchoring the rope at the top. He hadn't seen them from above. A spike for each hand. A spike for each foot. Heavy rusted chains ran from the spikes to shackles clasping Conway's hands and ankles.

Brandon shined the light around the pit. Nearly a perfect circle. No additional arteries. No holes for people to hide. Scrapes and gouges like the horizontal ones in the passage ran vertical here. All the way down to the bottom. Brandon marveled at the walls, held by a mesmerizing disbelief that somebody dug this by hand. Confounded by the questions of *why* someone would and what purpose it served?

A glance at his watch pulled him back to the now. Whatever the answers were, they were things for other minds to ponder.

He stepped toward the center, but there the heavy and wet tastes of shit and blood and piss were far worse. Like a physical barrier he had to claw through. He clenched his jaw. Tried to shut out the taste and the smell. He shut his eyes against it. Beneath the smell of filth, there was another, familiar odor. It had hung in the air on his first recon with New York in Laos. It had mingled with the cloud of diesel exhaust coming from the truck.

Decaying flesh. Faint, but it was there. That struck him as odd. Despite the obvious, Conway's corpse looked okay. He could have only been dead two days at most. Bodies didn't decompose that fast, did they?

The smell was awful, and he didn't want to get any closer to Conway than he had to. But he should at least try to figure out how he died. Mike might be able determine what killed him if Brandon could locate his wounds. That might give Smith and the team, or whoever analyzed this mess afterward, some clue to go on. And it would at least show that Brandon had done his due diligence. He'd be able to provide an answer. An answer that would undoubtedly raise more questions, but answers to questions seemed to placate Smith. All Brandon had to do to get home was have a quick look at Conway.

Simple.

Stepping forward, opening his eyes, he peeked out over his elbow and scanned the floor. Kept the white circle of light out in front of him as he inched closer to Conway through the filthy cloud. The ambient light rolled over a bulging shape off to the side. Brandon swung the light at it and reached for his pistol.

"Jesus!" he gasped. And instead of grabbing his pistol, he grabbed his heart. Pressed his chest like he could force it to slow.

In a small, shadowy alcove, maybe just tall enough for a man to sit, two more naked bodies lay. One man atop the other. Stacked.

These men weren't wearing dog tags, and he didn't expect them to be. Recon missions were hardly ever officially sanctioned by the government. Before the recon teams went out they were stripped of anything that could identify them as Americans. ID cards. Dog tags. Name tags on uniforms. All of it. Brandon barely knew his own team, he would have no way of knowing who these two men were by sight alone. But every recon man was photographed when they arrived in SOG. In case they went missing. He could identify them that way. He'd just have to get a good look at their faces.

If Smith would have agreed to let one of New York's enlisted men come along, identities could have been confirmed immediately.

Brandon kept to the wall and went to the men. After each step the stench thickened and Brandon's mouth ran wet and sour. He stood over them and shined his light down. A young blond man gazed up with waxy, dead eyes. He lay on top of the shorter man beneath. Only legs and an arm stuck out. Maybe it was Florida's interpreter.

He looked at the blond man. As expected, Brandon didn't recognize him. The fringes of his wavy yellow hair were dark with dirt and blood. In his forehead was a black spot. Brandon knelt and brushed aside the hair plastered to the wound.

Bullet wound. Small. Right above his dim, half-open blue eye. And, to Brandon's horror, about the size of a 5.56. A quick sweep of his light revealed several other tiny holes in the man's chest and abdomen.

One of our rifles did this?

How? Brandon shined the light around the pit. No rifles. No weapons of any kind. So who shot him? He looked up. Thought of Jaran and the old woman. Not them, either. New York had searched all of the huts and hadn't seen any of Florida's weapons. The cripple? No. He had carried an AK-47. A 7.62's holes would be a hell of a lot bigger.

Brandon sighed with frustration. There was a lot to figure out down there, but he didn't have time for puzzling out any mysteries.

He looked at the blond. Stared hard, committing the man's face to memory. He'd have to do the same for the other.

Brandon reached out his hand to the blond man's chin. Fingers hovered over it. "Sorry about this." He grabbed the cold skin and pushed his head aside and leaned forward and shined the light on—

"Fuck!" Brandon yelped and fell back on his ass. Kicking on the floor. Squirming away from the dead men. Images of empty eye sockets. Of desiccated bone-gray skin. Stretched tight. A gaping mouth.

A big black hole in the center of his skull.

"You okay?" Smith called down. "What happened?"

Brandon lay panting on the floor, inhaling filth and gagging. Flashlight aimed at the dead men. Hand gripping his still-holstered pistol.

"Captain?" Smith called.

Brandon slowly got to his feet. "I'm fine!"

He was *not* fine.

"Good. Hurry up. Burning daylight."

"Fuck you," Brandon mumbled. Straightened his uniform and mumbled, "Asshole." Patted off the dust and mumbled, "Motherfucker."

He went and knelt again next to the gray man. He shook his head in revulsion. This…

This was *not* a recon man. Whoever he was, he looked like he was hundreds of years dead. But just like the blond man, he had a hole in his head. Much bigger than a 5.56. Maybe a .45. "Hmmm…"

Brandon turned and flicked his flashlight around the floor. Put his ear to the ground, scanning. Looking for a—

There. The gold sparkle of an ejected casing. Far away in the center of the room, it lay near Conway. Brandon went to it. Stood over Conway and looked at his head.

No hole.

Conway's bicep was torn open and chunky yellow meat hung from the wound and spilled on the floor. But nothing particularly fatal presented itself. Maybe he *was* pushed.

Brandon picked up the casing. Sniffed it. The sharp smell of gunpowder stung his nostrils. Fired fairly recently. He went back to the gray man. With thumb and forefinger he held the casing next to the hole in his head.

"Yeah." Brandon dropped the casing which reverberated on the stone floor. He wiped his fingers on his trousers. "That's probably what did it. But…"

He stood and drew his pistol. Pointed it at the gray man. He looked at the pistol's slide. Looked at the ejection port. Looked at the wall and tried to figure how the hell an ejected casing would have had enough energy to come to rest all the way over in the center of the pit.

Re-holstering his pistol, he looked at Conway. It was just too far. And it was in the opposite direction. If the gray man was shot where he lay, then the casing *should* have landed near the rope that Brandon came down.

"Which means…"

Brandon stooped and put the flashlight low to the floor again. And in the oblique light, there they were. Drag marks in the dust.

Brandon took the gray man's hand, skin papery and pliable like a hornet's nest. Turned the hand over and looked at it in the light. Discolored. Red like rust. A faint impression encircled the man's wrist. Same on his ankles.

He shined his light around the walls. The floor. No extra shackles or spikes. He looked back to Conway. And he came up with no explanation.

Frustrated, he shook his head. There was no time for this. Brandon was no detective. He'd tell Smith what he found. If Smith or the Army wanted to solve the mystery of who shot the dried-up mummy, they could send fucking CID out here.

He'd done all he could. He had come looking for answers and found only more questions. He took one last look around the bottom, making sure he found everything there was to find.

Yeah. He was done here.

Crossing the floor toward the rope, he thought about what had brought these dead men down here. Tried to imagine Florida standing at the top of the pit and why they would send a man down to investigate. Imagined a man coming down and finding…

What? A hundred-year-old corpse staked to the rock? But why shoot him….

Brandon's toe caught something hard and he tripped and crashed down onto a soft mass. Conway's belly. Hands slapping the rock, Brandon's flashlight went spinning and scraping across the rough stone floor and it smacked the wall and shined bright in his face, blinding him with white. He turned away from it. He saw the thing he'd tripped over. One of the spikes that kept Conway shackled to the floor.

Something squirmed beneath him. Writhed. Sucking gasps echoed in the pit. Brandon froze, eyes locked on the thing making the sound. Conway's face.

He couldn't move. The gasping din like a boot on Brandon's neck. Shoving him into the ground. Pressing him into Conway's flesh. The dead man's belly jerked and spasmed.

In the light, against the wall, a shadow. Long and black. A hand creeping on the wall. Conway's hand. It raised until the chains snapped taut. The fingers hooked into trembling claws. Then struck out like a viper. Fingers wrapped around Brandon's paralyzed calf.

And Conway's head rose. A ghoulish face in the hard light. Pale-gray and waxy skin caked with dried black blood. Conway's lips cracked apart. Jaw coming open animal-wide.

The ice in Brandon's arms thawed just enough.

The pit exploded with the dead man's screams.

Brandon grabbed his pistol.

CHAPTER FOURTEEN

John could fight no longer.
Something tugged the last strip of his soul into a gaping maw. Teeth bit down. Claws ripped.
You were a tough one.

CHAPTER FIFTEEN

The other hand came up. Torn-out muscle flapped from the open wound in Conway's arm.

Brandon yanked his pistol from its holster.

Aimed.

Conway's dead hand came blindly down. Pinned the pistol to Brandon's leg. Wet fingers slithered over Brandon's trigger finger. Wrapped around the 1911's slide and grabbed tight. The whole time Conway screamed.

Brandon's voice wouldn't work with the panic stuffed down his throat. But his hand. His hand worked. So he did the only thing he could. He pulled the trigger.

Gas spat from the suppressor. A sigh, like screaming ghosts whirled around the pit. Conway jerked. Armpit meat split apart. Conway's lips curled back and he howled.

Brandon pulled the trigger again. Nothing.

Conway's grip on the slide was so tight that the pistol didn't cycle. Conway's other hand clawed. Reached. Pulled at Brandon's pants, trying to draw him closer to his screaming mouth. When Brandon finally found his voice, he added his own screams to the echoes.

The screaming shattered the ice in him. Brandon twisted hard and flopped onto his belly and kicked at the dead man's screaming face. Tore at naked legs. Scrambled away. When he was clear of the dead man, he got to his feet and sprinted for the wall, flattening his back against the cold rock. The metal of his rifle slung on his back dug into his flesh and he yelped. His *rifle*. He slipped it from his back.

In the white cone of flashlight the dead man flailed. Metal chains grinded and clinked. Hands and feet punched and kicked against the bindings, trying to tear the spikes from the stone floor. Blood flew from the torn-open bullet wound and spattered in black spots on the floor. Conway held Brandon's pistol by the slide and he beat the grip against the stone as he thrashed.

Brandon brought up his rifle and aimed at Conway's head.

"Hey!" Someone shouted.

Brandon jerked his rifle up toward the noise.

"What the fuck is happening down there?" Smith shouted down.

Gasping, Brandon shouted, "He's dead!" Aiming back to Conway, Brandon screamed, "Conway's dead and he's moving!"

Conway slammed his hands against the chains. Punching until the chains snapped taut. Punching again. With each blow a wet grunt spewed from his mouth. In the shadows cast by Brandon's flashlight it looked like one of the spikes might give.

Brandon clicked off the safety.

"You fucking moron!" Smith shouted at him.

"They're all dead down here!" Brandon screamed.

The other two. Unchained...

He jerked the rifle toward the other dead men. He couldn't see them in the dark. Jesus, he couldn't see them. He jerked the rifle left. Swung it back right. Nothing but dark.

"If he's moving," Smith yelled. "It means he's still alive!"

How could a dead man still be alive?

"Help him, Brandon!"

Help him?

Help him…

Brandon gripped his rifle. He watched Conway. The calmness, almost incredulousness in Smith's voice blew away the fog of terror clouding Brandon's mind. He still trembled with some residual nervous fear, but his mind was working. He could think.

He stood there and inhaled. Long and slow. Exhaled. Let his mind reset. As long as his mind was calm, his nerves would follow. Brandon breathed deep. In and out. His nerves would follow.

The two other men, the blond and the old corpse, they both had bullet holes in their heads. But Conway…

Conway had no such wounds.

You idiot.

The pit seemed to widen. The snarling screams of some undead movie monster faded away to the choking sobs of a frightened and seriously injured friend.

He's still alive. You fucking idiot.

Help him.

Conway quieted. Convulsing, he let out thick, wet coughs. The chains rattled around him.

"He's still alive," Brandon whispered. "Help him." Brandon clicked on his rifle's safety and slung it. Picked up the flashlight.

He went to his friend.

Standing over Conway, he shined his light on him. Shined it on his abdomen so he didn't blind the man. Let the ambient light illuminate his face. There was no telling how long Conway had been down in the dark. Even that little light could be blinding to him.

Had Conway been asleep while Brandon was poking around down there? Kicking the spike and falling on him probably scared him half to death. Probably thought some animal had found its way down here.

Brandon looked at him.

His wounds looked bad. God, his armpit.

Brandon cupped his hands and shouted up. "Smith! Conway's hurt! We have to get him out of here!"

"Bandage his wounds and find out what happened!"

"He's going to die!"

"And everything he knows will die with him!"

Brandon looked at him.

The space between Conway's legs was damp. A small mound of filth piled about his crotch. Brandon shook his head in disgust. Who could do this to a man?

And why?

Brandon knelt beside Conway. Tilted the light up so he could see his face.

"Hey, Conway," Brandon said.

Conway's eyes shot wide open. Locked on Brandon's.

Brandon nearly recoiled, but fought the urge. "It's Captain Doran. It's Brandon. Remember me? Colonel Murphy sent my team to rescue you." Hopefully Conway would recognize the names. Maybe they would help keep him calm.

Conway parted his lips. A raspy whisper escaped.

Brandon leaned in closer. "What's that?"

"Water," Conway said.

"Yeah," Brandon said as soothingly as he could manage. "Yeah, sure. Got some right here." Brandon put the flashlight between his knees to keep the light on himself. He reached around behind him and pulled a canteen from its pouch. He unscrewed the cap and lifted Conway's head. Skin burning with fever. Brandon was no medic, but bad things happened to people with fevers this high. He tilted the canteen at Conway's lips. Small rivulets ran down the sides of his chin, leaving clean streaks in the grime.

Brandon asked, "Do you know your name?"

Sucking down the water, through heavy breaths, he said, "Conway."

"That's good, man. Do you know what team you were on?"

"F…f…f…" His lips trembled. "Florida."

Brandon laid Conway's head back on the ground. "It's okay, man. I'll get you outta here. Who did this to you?"

Brandon thought he saw a dim flash wipe across Conway's eyes. "I killed him." Conway said. "He got me. But I got away." Conway nodded. "I got away…"

"That's good. I'm glad you got away." Feverish. Delirious. Poor guy didn't even know he was trapped in a hole. How long had it been since he had any food? Water? Brandon hadn't even thought to bring any rations. He wasn't expecting to find a survivor. That was careless of him. Add it to the list of things he shouldn't do again. Brandon lifted Conway's head and gave him another sip.

"Must've been one of my guys who killed me," Conway said. "Don't know who. Girl brought me back. Got me out." Conway clenched his eyes shut and shook his head. "I got out. She rescued me. I'm safe here. I'm safe. Don't let me go back. I don't want to go back there."

Brandon let him talk. Conway was delirious. Even men that had been seriously injured, lost enormous amounts of blood, Brandon had never heard someone talk about being dead and coming back to life. The fever must—

"Wait," Brandon said. "The girl? What girl?"

"The *girl!*" Conway rasped. Words punctuated by heaving sobs. "I heard her voice. She brought me back. I got out. It was black there. Burning. I drowned. Someone drowned me. That's how I died. I came back through the water."

"Came back from where?"

Conway's shackled hand grabbed Brandon's. Gripped it tight. Conway stared hard at Brandon. His eyes clear and bright. When Conway said where he had been, it was with absolute conviction. He said, "*Hell.*"

Brandon leaned back.

Conway's hand slipped out of Brandon's and fell on

the floor.

Hell.

"Okay," Brandon said. "I need to get you out of—"

"When he gets inside he makes you do things. You feel what he feels. I was happy. I—" Conway's eyes lost focus and drifted around the pit. "I...*enjoyed* it. I saw the things he made me do. But I couldn't stop it. I couldn't stop *him*."

"Who makes you do things? What things?"

Conway's lip trembled. "I killed them. I remember. My hand. My rifle." His voice turning to airy sobs. "My men are down there! Florida! They're waiting for me. Screaming!"

Just tell me what fucking happened for Christ's sake!

Tears poured from Conway's eyes. "The children! I killed them! I didn't want to!"

"The villagers? *You* killed them?"

Conway's head dropped on the floor and he shook as he wept.

Brandon sat back on his heels. Confused. Why would Conway say he killed the children? It had been the cripple, hadn't it?

He's delirious, Brandon reminded himself. The fever. It was the only explanation. He'd have to talk to Mike about this.

"Are your men still here? Did anyone survive?"

"Dead. All dead. Sergeant Sutton, he was the first. He killed the shamans. Then he killed my men. I should've listened. I should've cut the rope. Should've cut the rope…"

Brandon looked over his shoulder. The rope hung there in the shadows against the wall.

Brandon put his hand on Conway's shoulder. Skin hot. "It's okay. We'll get them home. We'll get them all home." Aside from the blond man in the pit with them, Brandon had no idea where to start looking for Conway's team. "Where are they?"

Just tell me they're piled with the burned villagers and we can all go home.

Conway tensed. Arms and legs straining against the chains. Pulling them tight. His sorrowful scream filled the chamber. "He made me *kill* them!"

Brandon pressed his hands against Conway's chest. Tried to hold him down. Conway bucked. Knocked over the pile of shit. Brandon breathed in the foul odor. Gagging, Brandon shouted, "*Who* made you kill them?"

"I can *feel* him! He's close! Don't let me go back! Don't let me go back! He's coming! He's—"

Conway gagged and white frothy vomit erupted from his mouth. All the water Brandon had given him spewed out and splashed stomach-warm and slick on Brandon's face. Brandon squeezed shut his mouth and eyes and turned away as it slimed down his neck into his shirt.

"Goddamnit!" Brandon yelled. "Who's coming?"

Conway strained against the chains. Brandon squinted open an eye. The metal chain links grinded and rust flakes fluttered down onto Conway's shaking skin. In the light, beneath Conway's armpit, a giant pool of blood spread across the stone.

"*Shit!*" Brandon smacked his hands over the bullet wound. Pressed hard.

But Brandon felt the life going out of him. Tense muscles relaxing. Conway's body slapped down on the rock. All of his energy drained onto the hard stone floor. His head rolled back and forth, lips moving. And soon, even that movement ceased. Conway lay still. His eyes went far away and waxy. A word came out long and airy on Conway's throaty exhale. The word sounded like: *Lick*.

Brandon knelt there in shit and blood and vomit with his hands pressed on Conway's skin. He stared. Waiting for his friend to speak again. But when the hissing echoes of Conway's last word had bled into the stone, Conway still had not drawn another breath.

He was gone.

Brandon looked at his hands. Covered in blood. They

started to shake. Not from fear. Not from sadness. From shame. If Brandon hadn't been so fucking stupid. Hadn't been such a fucking coward, Conway would still be alive.

Brandon did this.

I killed him.

It should've been you.

"Fuck you," he whispered to the past.

The silence and dark pressed in on Brandon's little light.

He had to move. Had to get back to New York. Get back to base. He had to get back so he could quit this God forsaken unit. He had to get out of the Army. He wasn't made for this.

He shined the light in Conway's eyes and the pupils, large and black, did not contract in the light. Conway's last fevered words lingered in his mind.

I killed them. He made me kill them. Hell.

Fever dreams. They must have been. What else could they be?

The girl rescued me.

The girl.

A forge sparked in his belly. And as he slid the light from Conway's face, it illuminated the chains. The shackles. When Brandon looked, took the next few moments to really look, to *see,* what had been done to his friend, the bellows blew. And all that shame welling up in him, it burned.

But it was no cleansing fire. It left something in the ashes. Something sinister. It wasn't anger. It wasn't rage.

It was hate.

That girl didn't *rescue* Conway. He looked up to the top of the pit. To where Jaran waited.

And the longer he looked, the hotter his hate for her burned.

He took his pistol. Racked the slide. The spent casing ejected and a fresh round locked in the chamber. He holstered the pistol and stood. He went to the rope.

Climbed.

At the top, Smith grabbed his wrist and hauled him up out of the dark. Beyond Smith's shoulder Jaran—

"What did he tell you?" Smith asked, shifting in front of Brandon. "Florida's commander. What did he say?"

"Move."

"Stop." Smith put a hand on Brandon's chest. "We're not going anywhere until you tell me what that man told you."

"Conway," Brandon said. "*That man's* name is Conway."

Smith looked at him. His hand still pressed hard against Brandon's chest. Fingers stiff. His face unreadable. "Tell me what Conway said."

"Ramblings," Brandon said. "He had a fever so bad I'm surprised he could even talk. He told me he escaped." Brandon gestured down. "Does it look like he escaped?"

Smith's fingers relaxed and his hand slid off Brandon's chest.

Brandon tried to step around him but Smith blocked his path. "When I ask you a question I want it answered," Smith said. He looked at Brandon. Eyes hard. "I told you, it's not your job to *think*. It's to follow orders. *My* orders."

All the hate burning in Brandon needed to be vented before he exploded. And if Smith didn't get out of his fucking way the wrong person was going to die.

"He said he killed some kids," Brandon said. "Said someone made him do it. Then one of his own men killed his team. Whoever it was, Conway said he was close. The last thing he said sounded like 'Lick'. Now move—"

"Erlik?" Smith's eyes went wide. "You're sure? Did he say where he went? Quickly now!"

"No!" Brandon snapped, frustrated. "I don't even know who—"

"We're leaving," Smith said. "Get the girl."

"I'm getting those men out of that pit."

Smith grabbed him by his LCE, "Get that fucking girl

and get *moving!*" And he shoved him toward Jaran.

Brandon shined his light on the girl. She squinted. Wet streaks glistened on her cheeks.

A haze closed in on Brandon's vision. Like he watched her through falling snow. Or ash. Conway. The torture he endured. His dead eyes. Brandon's hands shook with violence.

The pit. The dark. Every detail was seared into his mind. He'd carry that forever.

Smith was talking. Droning somewhere beyond the snow. Brandon heard none of what the man said.

The girl. The *murderer*. Her dislocated shoulder bulged beneath her filthy robes. Hung rotated and askew. Beneath distant eyes, squinting in the light, her mouth moved. Whispering. Praying, maybe. Praying would be a good idea.

Praying because you think you know what I'll do to you.

The macabre scene down in the hole pounded Brandon's mind. Jaran's mouth kept moving.

You have no fucking idea.

Brandon's hatred for her radiated outward to his limbs and his guts. Blood pounded in his ears. He drew his 1911.

"Let's go," Brandon snarled. He snatched Jaran's dislocated arm and pulled her to her feet. The arm heavy and wet-towel limp. Jaran wailed like a beaten dog and kicked her feet, trying to get up as fast as she could. Screaming, she twisted and contorted her body, trying to follow wherever Brandon took her arm. Through her clothing, her arm swiveled and stuck fast, like the ball of her shoulder snagged in the skin. She screamed. Drew breath. And screamed again.

Screamed so much her voice cracked and went gravely. Tears and spit flew from her lips. She screamed until nothing came out. She chewed the air. Her cries and her resistance to move sent a numbing rage through Brandon's hands. He dropped her arm and grabbed a fistful of her hair at the back of her head, his fingernails scraping skin from her scalp. He yanked her head back.

Her face squeezed with pain.

Every sound the bitch made stoked his fury. Every time she made a sound, he yanked. Jerked back. Wanting her to shut up. Forward. Wanting her scream more. Side to side. With each movement she cried out. And each time she cried out he pulled harder. Her knees buckled. She dragged her feet. She wouldn't move.

He wrapped his other arm around her waist. She was so thin he carried her on his forearm. He dragged her out through the cave opening into the muggy, piss-colored morning and he squinted his dark-adjusted eyes against the intense sunlight. Brandon dropped her, shoved her toward the cliff. When her toes hit the edge he jerked her hair and she stopped.

She teetered there. With Brandon's fingers tangled tight in her hair she gasped at the jungle below. Her fear trembled through her scalp. Brandon pushed a little harder. Forced her head out over the edge. Her legs tensed. She jammed herself at the edge, pushing back against him. She let out a long, cracking breath. Must have finally used up all her screams.

Pity.

Brandon leaned his head in close to her ear. Rested his chin on his wrist. Smelled the dirt and smoke in her hair. He whispered in her ear, "You enjoy torturing people?" Whispered through clenched teeth. "You enjoy making people shit all over themselves before they die? You enjoy *humiliating* people?"

Brandon put the 1911's suppressor into the nape of her neck. "I'm going to blow your throat out. Then I'm going to let you fall." He caressed the trigger.

"Easy," Smith said from somewhere beyond the hate. His voice soothing. Motherly. "Easy, Brandon. We need her."

"You have the grandmother," Brandon said. "I'd say one is enough to get the information you need."

Jaran whispered something. Brandon reached up his

thumb and clicked off the pistol's safety.

You won't be Americans on this operation…

Smith said, "I'm willing to bet that this girl didn't kill your friend."

Brandon's eyes shifted to Smith. "No bet." And he looked at the girl's head.

Smith held up his hands. "Even if she *did* have something to do with it, what if she was protecting herself?" Protecting her friends and family?"

"Protecting herself from what? Our soldiers don't fucking murder civilians. Conway would have let these people be. Even if Conway did kill some of those dink kids," Brandon shoved the suppressor under Jaran's ear. "This *bitch* probably had something to do with it." His fingers shook in her hair. "These sadistic fucks murdered a whole team and threw their commander in a hole like fucking garbage. To rot. To—"

"Your friend. Conway. He told you *exactly* who was responsible. Conway gave you his killer's name. Erlik. Erlik Khan to be exact."

Jaran's trembling ceased. She didn't move. Seemed like she didn't even breathe. Conway hadn't mentioned the name *Khan*. What the hell did Smith know about all this?

"How do you know his name?" Brandon asked.

"He's the man Florida was looking for. He's the man *we* are looking for. And we need this girl's help to find him."

"Erlik Khan," Brandon said.

Jaran flinched.

Brandon relaxed his finger off the trigger. How odd. How odd that with a gun to her head, with the only thing preventing her from plummeting to her death being the failing strength of Brandon's fingers, she seemed to fear a name even more.

"That's it," Smith said. "I'm glad you're listening to reason. Khan is who we're looking for. He's responsible. I'm almost certain. If those women did anything to

Florida, Khan probably had something to do with it. If you kill that girl the old woman won't talk. We need them if we're going to find Khan. That's the mission. If you help me find him, I'll let you sit in on the interrogations. They'll be long and slow and they won't be pretty. I promise."

"Who…" Brandon's vision went blurry and he squeezed his eyes shut against the sudden dizziness. "Who is he?" Brandon asked.

"I don't know."

Brandon looked at him.

Smith raised his hands. "I'm being honest. I don't know a lot. He's just an HVT we're after. I'll tell you everything I know. I'll tell you. But you *must* let her help us. If you kill her, you'll never get your shot at the man responsible for your friend's death."

Brandon looked at the back of Jaran's head. Looked at the pistol.

Smith's boots scraped across the bare stone. A gentle hand came down on Brandon's wrist.

The touch wiped away the fog. Doused the raging forge. And with no fire burning, exhaustion overtook him. His legs went weak. His hand, once holding Jaran from falling, was now the only thing keeping him upright. A clear bead of sweat glided down from Jaran's hair, down behind her ear. It arced down around the fat black suppressor. Brandon eased Jaran back from the cliff's edge. He thumbed on the 1911's safety. Then he holstered it.

"Good," Smith said. "That's good. You'll be glad you didn't go through with that."

Brandon looked away from the girl still hunched there at the edge. He looked out over the cliff. The dense, dark-green jungle rolled like waves over the surrounding hills. He shook his head. Tried to shake off the daze. He had never been so vicious in his life. To anyone. What the hell was happening to him? Where had that rage come from? What the fuck was happening to him? One minute he was helping a hurt friend drink, the next he became a monster. Tortured this girl.

Sighing, Brandon put a weak hand on Jaran's uninjured shoulder and backed her away from the edge. Turned her around. She kept her head down, eyes on the ground. For that Brandon was grateful. He doubted he could have looked her in the eye. An apology seemed somehow insignificant.

Brandon helped her sit. He untied her hands and helped her lie down. She winced as she pulled her elbow across her belly and held her dislocated arm.

Brandon pressed and felt around her injured shoulder. Rotated her arm just slightly. She jerked away from him and he held up his hands, trying to show he meant no harm. She undoubtedly did not believe him. He tried to put on one of Mike's reassuring smiles. To her he probably looked like some sadistic devil smiling at the pain he was causing her. But she finally let him touch her.

For once he was thankful for having stupid friends in his neighborhood growing up. Thankful that their idea of fun was jumping off rooftops. He had set dislocated shoulders enough times…

Jaran winced when he put his hands on the bulge where her shoulder had come out of the socket. He laid perpendicular to her, sliding a foot under her neck and the other under her rib cage. Her arm, he gently pulled up between his legs and held it by the wrist with both hands.

"This'll hurt," Brandon said, soft. Not like she would understand.

Rotating her wrist and gently pulling her arm toward him, Brandon pushed out with his legs. Jaran gasped and screwed up her face in breathless agony. The scraping *pop* vibrated in Brandon's legs when the shoulder slid home. Jaran's mouth opened wide and she breathed in deep. Deep.

Her scream rattled Brandon's eyeballs in his skull. He sat holding Jaran's arm until the valley swallowed up the lingering echoes of her agony.

"Yeah," Brandon said. "Told you."

Jaran watched the sky. Her opposite hand rested on her set shoulder. After some long inhales and exhales, she nodded and whispered something.

Brandon stood and helped her to her feet. She rotated her shoulder in delicate circles, wincing when she raised it too high. But it seemed she had regained most of her mobility. She stood with her head down. She didn't look at Brandon.

Brandon shook his head, but no amount of shaking was going to clear his mind of the shame he felt. An overwhelming tiredness filled his body. How long had it been since he slept? He turned to Smith.

Smith nodded at him. "Let's go."

CHAPTER SIXTEEN

They moved as fast as they could down into the dense jungle. Down into the humid air. On the mountaintop, in the open sky, it had been easy for Brandon to forget about the humidity. Going down, there were still pockets of mild coolness in the places where the sun had yet to penetrate and bake the air. But before long, Brandon's skin shined with sweat. He kept his hand loose on Jaran's arm. The rough fabric of her robe going dark from his sweating palm. His own uniform hung damp and heavy and he undid the buttons and flapped a nearly imperceptible breeze with his hanging-open shirt. Hoping a slight flow of air might help wick the moisture.

It didn't.

"How are we on time?" Brandon asked. He just wanted to hear something positive. The extraction was the most positive thing he could think of.

Smith, taking point in their formation, said, "Doesn't matter." He swatted aside some encroaching leaves with a loud *slap*. "I'm calling off the extraction."

"What?" Brandon nearly tripped on his own feet. "Why?"

"Your friend said Khan was close. We need to follow

up on that."

"Conway was crazy with fever! He didn't know what he was saying."

Smith smacked a mosquito on his neck. "I think he knew exactly what he was saying." His calloused palm came away with a spot of blood. Tiny black flecks. Smith looked at it and wiped his hand on his pants.

You spook fuck.

Brandon winced. New York's attitude was rubbing off on him. He'd have to watch that. But he couldn't help the frustration and fear sizzling in his chest. How else was he supposed to feel? When he had been so close to going home. When he had tasted *hope*. Brandon fixed his eyes on Smith's back. Watched the man damn-near sprint down the path in the places that he could. With just a few words Smith had slapped that sweet taste of hope right out of Brandon's mouth.

The NVA were coming and Smith wanted to stay out there and go looking around because of a dying man's ramblings?

Brandon had no intention of ending up like Conway.

"Are you going to tell me about Erlik Khan?" Brandon asked.

"I told you. I don't know anything."

Such bullshit.

"Hey," Brandon said. "My friend died trying to accomplish your mission. His whole team died. I want to know what they died for. What my men *might* die for."

What I might die for.

Smith walked on, his voice bored and uninterested when he said, "Everything I know is in that file I gave you."

That file had nothing but aerial photographs and maps and Smith knew it.

"Stop," Brandon said. More forcefully than he expected.

Smith skidded to a halt. Turned around. His mouth

hung open and he was panting quietly.

"Tell me what you know," Brandon said.

A look of genuine puzzlement wiped across Smith's face. Then his lips pulled back in a snarl. "I'll tell you what you *need* to know. Right now, all you need to know is that you'll regret it for the rest of your fucking career if you don't move your ass."

Jaran tried to pull to the side of the path. Probably didn't want to be standing between two men growling at each other. Brandon let her go and she stepped aside and squatted down.

"Well?" Smith asked. "Move it, *Captain.*" He spat that last word out like it was phlegm.

Smith's radio was a heavy thing and he hadn't brought it with him. If he wanted to abort the extraction, Smith would have to make it down the mountain and across the river before the helicopters came. Brandon wasn't going to make that any easier for him. When Smith saw that Brandon wasn't going to move, he stomped up the path. Got right in Brandon's face. Squinting, Smith looked Brandon up and down like he was examining a pile of dog shit on his living room floor.

Where Brandon stood on the path, on the steep incline, he stood head and shoulders taller than Smith, but it was still easy to feel small under a glare like that.

Even so, Brandon refused to move.

"Worthless," Smith whispered. "Stay here then. If this is how you're going to act, I'll be glad to be rid of you." Smith turned and started down.

"You said you'd tell me what you know," Brandon said to Smith's back.

Smith kept walking.

"I won't let New York go blindly to their deaths like Florida did."

Smith kept walking, turned on a switchback and went down into the foliage.

Grabbing Jaran's arm, Brandon hopped and skidded

down the path after his handler. Boots churning up gray dirt clouds. When they caught Smith, Brandon called, "One word from me and those men will disobey every order you give."

Smith spun around, eyes dark with fury. Brandon tried to stop, but he slipped and his sweating hand jerked free of Jaran's arm. He fell on his ass and slid down the hard path and nearly plowed into Smith's shins, stopping just short. Smith towered over him.

"One word from *you?*" Smith growled. "From *you?* Who the fuck do you think is in charge out here? One word from *me* and you're relieved of command. One word from *me* and *your* men become *my* men." Shoving his finger in Brandon's face, Smith said, "Don't fuck with me you little shit."

Brandon stared up at him. Breathed hard. Breath blowing out onto Smith's pointed finger. Pieces of Brandon, smaller parts of him, begged him to keep his mouth shut. Begged him to do as he was told. Obey his superior. Follow orders.

But instead, voice trembling, Brandon said, "You really think New York will follow *you?*"

What the hell are you thinking? Those smaller pieces screamed.

Smith glared at him.

Screamed, *This man will crush your career!*

But Brandon said, "You think they'll obey your orders after they find out *why* you relieved me?"

"They'll do as they're told because they are professional soldiers. Unlike—"

"They're professional *assholes*," Brandon said. "They just happen to be soldiers. Have you even met Chris?"

Brandon got his feet under him and tried to stand. "Those men—"

Smith shoved him back down.

He hit the ground with an, "Oof." Brandon held up his hands. "Those men are a team. In the truest sense. You and me, we're not part of that team. And they know it."

Smith stared at him. After a while he lowered his finger. Slow. But his face stayed hard.

That's right. Listen to reason.

"*This*," Brandon said, tugging his camouflaged shirt, holding out the fabric for Smith to see. "This is why they'll listen to me. I know they don't like me. But to them I'm a soldier. You..." He flicked his fingers at Smith. "To them you're just some civilian playing dress-up. If I tell them you relieved me because I was looking out for them—" Brandon couldn't help laughing. "Well, good luck getting them to do anything."

Smith's eyes searched Brandon's face. A few moments passed. Then he backed away down the path, watching Brandon. Tapping his finger in the air. The look of a man committing something to memory. "You seditious little prick," Smith said. And he turned away and started down.

A dumfounded laugh hissed from Brandon's throat. He had actually thought for a moment that Smith would start talking. *There goes your career. Dad will be so proud...*

"Hurry your ass up if you want to hear this," Smith shouted from the jungle.

Brandon looked at Jaran. Her eyes went to where Smith had disappeared down the path. Back to Brandon. Confusion plain in her eyes. Shrugging, Brandon said, "I'm as surprised as you are. Come on."

Smith kept a quick pace. Grip loose around Jaran's bicep, Brandon struggled to catch up.

They were on a rutted and steep switchback, leaning back into the uphill and sidestepping down when Smith started talking.

"This information stays between you and me," Smith said. "That's the deal. Don't go talking to your men about this."

"Sure."

Picking his way carefully down, Smith said, "I don't really know too much about Khan," Smith's voice was tight and frustrated. "That much is true." He gestured to the deep green around them. "We were alerted to this location when we intercepted some radio traffic. NVA commanders discussing troop movements. A junior NVA commander suggested using this village to stockpile munitions and rice. It made sense from a strategic standpoint. The villagers produce a lot of rice and could move the NVA's beans and bullets quickly on the river. But for some reason the senior commander forbade anyone from coming near here." Smith shrugged. "Well, *specifically*, the senior commander said, 'Don't go near the *shamans*.'"

"Shamans?"

"That's right. The first of our analysts to review the interception thought the NVA commander's decision was a bit strange. There's still a lot of rural villages in Vietnam that practice some forms of shamanism, but the NVA never had a problem hiding weapons in those villages. At any rate, eventually the analyst's report made its way to my office for action deemed appropriate. And that's where it died. For some time anyway."

"Why did it sit so long?"

Smith grunted. "Because honestly, Captain, nobody gives a shit about tiny villages in the middle of nowhere unless they serve some strategic purpose. Or if the people there are aiding the enemy somehow. The NVA leadership denied permission to use the village, so we didn't care. Why would we? And if they *did* end up using the village, our fast movers would've napalmed it and solved the problem."

Jaran kept her eyes down on the path in front of her. It was probably for the best she didn't understand English. Probably best not to know she and her family could've died screaming because of decisions made by people she would never meet. A move made by some Vietnamese commander. A counter-move made by some American commander.

Brandon's stomach turned a bit with revulsion as he remembered the villagers' bodies sprawled in the jungle. The burned bodies smoldering in that pile.

They had died screaming anyway.

"So why are we here?" Brandon asked. "Why do you care about this place now?"

"My agency employs some interesting people. People who are more fascinated with research than anything else. They love figuring out how bits of information fit together. How one event influences another. An agency librarian came to drop off some files and got to chatting with one of our analysts. The question of what reasons an enemy commander might have for avoiding shamans came up. The two of them looked at the interception's transcript and tried to puzzle it out. That's when they discovered our linguist had inadvertently left a word untranslated."

"Which one?"

"*Mong Co*," Smith said.

Jaran's head perked up.

"The librarian," Smith said. "He did some digging. He found a telegram from 1942. An Austrian archeologist commissioned by the Nazis sent it from Hanoi to Berlin. A progress report of sorts. It described a site secluded in the mountains of northern Vietnam that was guarded by Mongol shamans. The name *Erlik Khan* was mentioned."

"An archeologist? What did he find?"

"We'll never know," Smith said. "The Austrian and his team disappeared."

Brandon's guts tightened. "Like Florida."

Smith nodded. "Just like Florida. My superiors weren't happy about the similarities. The Austrian team disappearing back in the forties, Florida disappearing a few days ago, this whole situation turned a lot of high-ranking heads. Some reputations were...*tarnished*. So, to answer your question, we're here to finish what Florida started. We're here to find Erlik Khan."

Brandon shuffled around a boulder. "I still think it's a

mistake to make a decision based on what Conway said. What if we can't find your HVT? What if he's gone?"

"If we can't find him, we take the next best thing. I'll take the women back with me and obtain an entire oral history of this place. Find out what Khan's role was in whatever happened here. Once I have that documented, the director can figure out what he wants to do."

The way Smith laid it out, his confidence that the women would tell him what he wanted to know, it was a little concerning. Brandon pulled out his canteen and sipped some water. Offered some to Jaran. She refused. Of course she did. She walked on and kept her eyes on the ground. Oblivious of Smith's intentions. Taking her prisoner. Holding her for God knows how long. Interrogating her.

...long and slow...

Brandon stifled a regretful laugh. Not too long ago he was going to shoot the girl. *Wanted* to. He shook his head. Now? Was he actually *worried* about what Smith would do to her?

"What if the women don't know anything?" Brandon asked.

"That'll get sorted out eventually. One way or another."

Jaran hadn't said a word or protested since starting the trek down the mountain. Back at the pit, the look in her eyes, before Brandon had gone down, that fear. Was it fear of what he would find down there? Or fear of something else?

"You asked Mike if the women were Mongol," Brandon said. "Why does that matter to you?"

"It doesn't matter to me. The NVA commander told his men to stay away from the Mongol shamans." Smith waved his hand at Jaran. "The girl said she's Mongol. She's just a sign-post that tells me I'm in the right place." After a moment, he added. "I suppose it is a little curious though."

"Why?"

"We're a few thousand miles from Mongolia."

Brandon shrugged. "Airplanes. Cars. People travel. It's not like they walked here."

"Even so, what reasons would a tribe of Mongols have for setting up a permanent residence in Vietnam? They're a nomadic people, so why have they stayed here? Why did they come at all? There's nothing about that village to identify them as Mongol. No yurts. No herds of animals. Why would they give up everything about their culture unless they were deliberately trying to blend in?"

"Maybe they haven't been here that long. That village looks like it could have been built in a few months."

Smith shot him a look that was thick with condescension. "Do you ever observe the world around you? Did you not see the marks on the cave walls? These people have been here long enough to dig through almost three-hundred feet of solid stone. With *hand-tools* I might add."

"But—" Brandon caught himself. He had let Smith steer the whole conversation away from Khan. And Smith seemed more than happy to let it drift.

"Khan," Brandon said. "Why do you want him?"

Smith nodded to himself. "Between you and me. That stipulation still stands." Smith looked at Brandon over his shoulder.

Brandon thought about that. Even if he was sworn to secrecy, at the very least he could still make decisions based on the information. He nodded.

Smith turned back and continued down. "Florida's Venus operation was launched not only to find Khan, but to ascertain his value. We're not entirely sure he's valuable at all. What interested us is that he *could* be. If NVA commanders are hesitant, or even frightened of something up here, and that 'something' has to do with this Erlik Khan fellow, then we want whatever 'it' is. Maybe it's something we can exploit. Give us an edge in the war. But to determine his value, first we have to find him. After that we can figure out whether he's worth having or not."

A sick feeling bubbled in Brandon's guts. Brandon had stopped walking right around the time Smith said he wasn't sure if Khan was valuable. He had to force his feet to move to keep up with Smith.

Whether he's worth having or not?
He doesn't know?

There had to be more to this. Smith had to be withholding some crucial piece of information that would make this mission seem *worth* the lives it had already cost. If capturing Khan could somehow end the war, then Brandon could understand. It was worth the risk. But the way Smith told it, the way Brandon understood it, Florida was sent out to die for…

What? A guess? An archaeological expedition?

That cave. It had felt like a tomb. The pit. The old, leathery gray corpse—

Brandon's temple throbbed with his heartbeat.

Was that…

He was getting a headache.

"No," Brandon mumbled. "No, it can't be him." He almost didn't ask the question forming in his mind. He wasn't sure he wanted to know the answer. Wasn't sure how he would react if he knew the answer.

Brandon rubbed his eyes. And he asked, "Is Erlik Khan even alive?"

Smith scoffed.

"I found a dead guy in the pit. He looked like he'd been dead for a hundred years. Could that be Khan?"

"You think a dead man in a hole is what's spooking the NVA? That's why you think they avoid this place?"

Brandon rubbed his eyes. Watched the operative over his pressing fingers.

Smith looked at him. "Now you know what I know, Captain. Satisfied?"

Brandon nodded, nervous frustration threatening to tear his lungs apart.

"Did your friend in the pit say anything else that could

be useful in finding Khan?"

"No," Brandon croaked. He suddenly didn't want to talk anymore. Was afraid of having any more knowledge. He had to let his brain rest before it started bleeding.

And so they went on. Tired. Brandon was just tired. Exhausted was more like it. Emotionally drained. To keep his legs moving he fantasized of Smith aborting the mission. Of getting aboard the extraction helicopter. He ached for a nice long nap in the vibrating seats. The helicopters didn't just mean safety and an end to all this, they were the first step in forgetting Smith. Forgetting everything that happened here. But what he'd just been told, the *ridiculousness* of this mission, it turned his daydream to shit. He put one foot in front of the other. Sometime today he'd be able to sleep. But he'd have to wait for it. And he'd have to wait even longer to go home.

CHAPTER SEVENTEEN

They stepped through the foliage onto the grassy riverbank. Into the quiet sounds of water and buzzing life. The boat waited where they'd left it. Moored and rocking at the overgrown dock. A breeze blew down the river valley and Brandon faced it. Lifted his arms and let the air flow through his unbuttoned shirt. Let it cool his sweaty hair and skin.

The dock far across the river, where Chris had stood before, was empty. He scanned up and down the shore, no sign of New York. But they were probably waiting. Hidden somewhere in the treeline. Maybe watching from the huts.

Brandon winced when he looked at the huts. Searching the village with the team was probably the stupidest thing he had done on this mission. It had given New York a chance to see how inexperienced he was. It had only been Chris observing him during the search, but Chris would talk. Tell the other men how poorly Brandon had performed. How it was obvious Brandon didn't know the first thing about small-unit tactics. How he didn't know how to clear a room and had nearly shot Chris in the head. How he had forgotten to even load his fucking pistol.

Brandon let the river carry his eyes south and he

wondered how far south it went. Did it flow near the hill?

The hill where he had been a lieutenant. The hill where, a little over a year ago, he had been a platoon leader in the Infantry. He had commanded thirty men. He could only remember a handful of their names. Of the names he still remembered, he would probably forget them too. Forget them all. Eventually.

All but two.

Cox and Davis. He'd remember their names forever. Their faces.

Cox and Davis. With their too-long hair and their unclean feet and their unshaven faces and their *fuck-you-sirs* and their *I-ain't-gonna-changes*.

You'd threaten to charge them with insubordination and they'd ask when the bird would come to take them back to the rear. You'd threaten to take their pay and they'd say the Army had given them everything they needed to survive. Except pussy.

You'd threaten to take *that* away and they'd spit in their palm and wave it at you.

Brandon's father had commanded an Infantry company in WWII. In his den, darkened with evening shadows, Dad would talk quietly to the turned-off television. Or talk to the corner of the room. Always over a sloshing glass of scotch he would talk about the *good ones*. Talked about how the men he had commanded, they were the bravest goddamned sons-a-bitches you'd ever seen.

He used to tell Brandon about them. The good ones. Fall asleep in church or stay out too late or maybe hide Dad's trusty bottle of scotch and, later, when Brandon's pants were down, Dad would tell him all about the men he had commanded. Every time the belt *whapped* Brandon's bare thighs, Dad told him. Told Brandon that he'd never, *never* be half the man that those men were.

You're too goddamned stupid!

Brandon would never be a *good one*.

I fucking hate stupidity, Dad had said.

Maybe Dad forgot about the *bad ones*. Maybe that's why he never talked about them. Or maybe he just wanted to forget.

How would Dad have handled Cox and Davis? A little over a year ago, it was a question Brandon asked himself nearly every day. Cox and Davis made sure everyone knew they wouldn't fight the war they'd been torn from their lives to go and fight. They weren't going to follow the orders of anyone who claimed to be in charge of anything. So they slacked off. Did things wrong. They were stupid. *Deliberately* stupid. The only things you'd ever see them carry were their rucksacks and their weapons and a dense, heavy resentment for the Army. And for anyone to whom the Army had given even a sliver of authority.

I fucking hate stupidity.

Brandon stared at the huts across the river and spoke quietly to them. He wanted to pop thermite grenades and watch the electric white flash consume every last stick. And when the blaze was steel-melting hot, he'd toss in his memories. Memories of a place far south of here. Of a firebase on a hill.

The way Brandon hated Cox and Davis, was that how New York hated Brandon? Did Colonel Murphy know about Brandon's hill? If he did, then why was Brandon even in this unit? A unit where only the best were allowed to reside?

Why?

Was that the right question to ask? The Army was a system built on systems. You could ask a hundred different men why the Army did a thing and you'd get a hundred different answers. When a system didn't work, it was abandoned for a better system. No. *Why* was not the right question. Was it who?

Smith and Jaran stood on the dock. Smith pointed to the boat and she climbed down into it and sat. From the shore, Brandon said, "Who made the decision to assign the captains to the recon teams?"

Smith started and looked quickly at Brandon. His jaw going round and round for some time behind tight lips. Chewing something. Finally, Smith asked, "Does it matter?"

"I think so."

Smith relaxed. His cat-that-just-saw-movement stare vanished. "What did I tell you about thinking?"

"Does Colonel Murphy know about me?"

The stare returned.

"No."

Embarrassment burned hot in Brandon's neck. "But you do."

Smith stooped slowly and loosened the mooring line and pulled it long and wrapped it and pulled it long and wrapped it like a whip, watching Brandon all the while. He tossed the rope into the boat. "So what if I do? Pull off this mission and it goes away. You'll be assigned—"

"To the Pentagon, yeah. Great assignment. But why me? Why any of the captains?"

"It's not obvious?"

Brandon looked at him.

"The captains keep the teams honest." Smith smiled. "*I* keep the *captains* honest."

"You—" Brandon swallowed. "You're holding my *record* over me?"

"Have I had to use it against you? You've had little hiccups here and there, but you're doing fine." Smith shrugged. "Forget it. All six of you captains stepped on your dicks back in your former units. Nobody knows anything about you guys except me and my superiors. Cheer up. Colonel Murphy said you're my man, right? That man was a Green Beret before there even *were* Green Berets." Smith shrugged. "He's a tough man to impress. But you did."

He's your man.

He's your man. When Colonel Murphy had made the statement Brandon's heart had soared. He couldn't remember the last time a superior officer had complimented him.

For six months Brandon had led that Infantry platoon and at every morning meeting with the company commander, with the other lieutenants watching, it was always Captain Goode saying, "Lieutenant Doran, Fourth Platoon is on sandbag-filling detail."

And if there weren't sandbags to fill there was the perimeter to guard. And when another platoon wanted a break and took the perimeter, then there were shit-pots to burn. And if there wasn't shit to burn, there were latrines to dig. And no matter how much Cox and Davis and the other men like them tried to dodge the work, no matter how much Brandon micromanaged the men until the work was done to standard, it was never enough for Captain Goode.

Fourth Platoon had dug a trench latrine so perfectly rectangular and so perfectly five-feet deep that Robert McNamara himself would have had a hard time finding a better place to cut sling-load.

But then the rains had come. And they had kept coming. And after two days of hard rain, the clay around the outhouse's 4X6 supports had washed out and poured down into that squishy pit. And boy did Big Country pick the wrong time to flop his fat ass down on the throne.

"It's a hole, Doran!" Captain Goode had screamed in the rain. Standing on the edge of that trench latrine and stomping on the outhouse roof. Where the floor *used* to be. Big Country, trapped in a rising pool of rain and piss and communal shit, screaming from inside the box. Pounding his ham-fists against the ceiling. Men all around in the rain, hacking the wood with e-tools to free the big man trapped inside before the soupy every-shade-of-brown rose up around the collapsed outhouse. Neck straining, Captain Goode screamed, "How do you fuck up a *hole?*"

And that was the way of things. First, Second, and Third Platoons fought the war. Fourth Platoon fucked things up.

It could get worse, Brandon remembered thinking.

And it did.

It had gotten worse when, one night, the rains had taken a break. When the night was clear and cool and had not yet thought of turning to morning. It got worse when Cox and Davis fell asleep on the perimeter in their sandbag-covered foxhole.

It got worse when the sound of legs pushing through tall grass or a cough, or *something*, Davis couldn't remember; something out beyond the perimeter spooked Davis awake. And there in the grass, Davis had seen, or at least he said he saw, advancing in the moonlight, a pack of blue, sweat-gleaming faces.

Charlie had finally come knocking at their door.

And when Davis saw the faces, he panicked. The different expressions on his face when he told the story to Captain Goode and Brandon and the two CID men in the lantern-lit command bunker—the expressions were those Brandon was sure Davis had never worn before.

Shame. Guilt. Sorrow.

Davis had grabbed the clacker, pumped it with trembling hands and called down thunder. The claymores daisy-chained beyond his foxhole blasted the faces back into the night.

Brandon had been lying on his cot, reading. When the shockwave had snapped the dust from the pages of Brandon's book, when the *bang* squeezed his heart, Brandon had grabbed his rifle and run out of his tent to see everyone else had come out, too.

Come out to see. To hear. To run toward the sounds. But not toward the sounds of a battle. Not the sounds of an NVA probe or a full-on assault. Not a single shot had been fired after the claymores detonated.

It was screaming. That was the sound they ran to. They ran to so many different screams in the night. Some were screams of pain. Some were wet and terrified. Some were hard and furious.

But they were all in voices Brandon knew. All in a language he understood.

Charlie had not come to Alpha Company's doorstep.

It was First Platoon. Returning from a night reconnaissance.

A pencil. That's what the CID man taking notes had used to scribble Brandon's name down in his little spiral notebook when he had asked Davis who his lieutenant was.

"Second or First Lieutenant?" The CID man had asked.

"First," Brandon and Davis had said.

The same pencil jotted down the last time Davis had slept. And the last logged time First Lieutenant Brandon Doran, Fourth Platoon, Alpha Company, had conducted his perimeter checks and made sure Private Gerald Davis and Private Francis Cox were not sleeping in their foxhole.

Brandon knew the answer before the pencil had stopped writing Davis's previous answer.

Brandon *hadn't* checked on them.

"Why not?" Asked the CID man, pencil held over paper, looking at Brandon.

"I must've overlooked them," Brandon had said. "I checked the rest of the men. I logged it. The other men will tell you." But it wasn't the truth. Not really. It *was* true that Brandon had checked on the other Fourth Platoon men manning the perimeter. But when he had made it around to Cox and Davis, when Brandon had stood there in the night and looked at the little sandbag-covered foxhole, Brandon had simply spat on it and walked away.

Why?

Because fuck them, that's why.

But those words were never spoken. And so the pencil never wrote them down.

A pen. That's what Captain Goode had used to transfer Brandon back to the rear where, as Captain Goode put it,

"All the pieces of shit belong." No screaming. One of the few times the company commander had not yelled at Brandon. Captain Goode had shoved the orders into Brandon's hand and pointed to a stack of letters on his desk. Real quiet, Captain Goode said, "It should be your family I'm writing a letter to."

Brandon had tried to take the crumpled paper from his commander, but Captain Goode held on. When Brandon looked at him, Captain Goode said, "You ever come near any hill I hold, and your family *will* get a letter."

Captain Goode let go of the paper and went back to his desk and his letters and when Brandon turned to leave, Captain Goode said, "You'll never be half the man those men were."

Relieved for cause and a General Officer's Memorandum of Reprimand and a Court Martial for dereliction of duty. At least he had been acquitted at the Court Martial. Fourth Platoon's soldiers hated Cox and Davis as much as Brandon did. All the combined statements painted a picture for the judge and the panel. A picture of two shit-bag soldiers that, even *had* Brandon checked on them, would have deliberately gone back to sleep anyway.

Still, a relief for cause and a GOMOR were career killers by themselves. Together, Christ, Brandon was surprised he was promoted to captain at all. And then to suddenly be handed orders for SOG...

You didn't get hand-selected for elite units when you had a record like Brandon's.

Brandon looked at Smith.

Smith looked back at him and nodded. Nodded as if he was following along with Brandon's thoughts and was surprised it had taken Brandon this long to figure things out.

Brandon shook his head. What was it Mike had said? There's a reason we don't trust these guys?

So long as Smith held this over his head, he was in

Smith's pocket. So long as Brandon was on the team, he was Smith's yes-man. But that was an easy problem to fix, though, wasn't it?

Just quit. That was all Brandon had to do.

Brandon didn't belong on this team anyway. He looked at the sky. Thought about the helicopters that would come. Smith was going to call off the extraction? Fine. Brandon could stick it out for a few more days with New York. But Brandon would make sure Boing got on those helicopters when they came. And John too, if he wasn't awake yet. And then, after a few days, when everyone finally made it back to base, Brandon would quit SOG. Disappear back into the Army. And he would take his secrets with him.

"You hear that?" Smith asked.

Brandon listened. Nothing. But after a moment, quiet echoes, like drumming, drifted across the river.

Smith's mouth hung open, head cocked, he stared at Brandon.

"Helicopters!" Smith said. "Come on!"

CHAPTER EIGHTEEN

Brandon's legs jolted into motion. Like a puppet watching as someone else bent his legs. Made him jump down into the rocking boat and yank the engine's pull-start.

The engine grumbled. Brandon yanked again and again, fist and elbow pistoning. The engine chugged like a reluctant lawnmower.

Brandon yanked. "Come on you fuck!" And he yanked. The engine sputtered to life and belched out blue smoke, whining loud and swallowing the helicopters' distant rumble.

Gunning the throttle, Brandon reversed from the dock and whipped the handle and angled the boat toward the village.

The helicopters weren't yet visible. But if he could hear them, they were close. There might still be time to get across the river and to the landing zone. To stop New York from extracting. But that thought was dashed when thick red smoke billowed from the jungle still so far away and drifted skyward. You didn't give away the landing zone's position too early, so you didn't pop smoke until the bird was ready to land.

And when they *did* land, they were on the ground only long enough for you to get your ass onboard. Brandon had already seen how fast New York could board a Huey. They didn't waste time exposing their ride home. The boat slowly picked up speed and Brandon clung to the shred of hope that they might make it across before the helicopters landed.

But as they inched toward the far river bank and its waiting docks, a Huey screamed in low over the treetops and banked in an arc so tight the aircraft's belly turned perpendicular to the ground. It leveled out. Its nose flared and the helicopter slowed, barely pausing to hover over the smoke before disappearing behind the tall grass growing wild and swaying along the river bank.

The Huey, a tiny thing from so far away, electrocuted Brandon's hope, leaving it black and smoking in the bottom of his soul. There was no way, absolutely no way they were getting to that aircraft before it took off.

"Faster!" Smith shouted. "Faster or we won't make it!"

Throat clenched, Brandon dropped his head in resignation. Fought back the urge to weep.

Somewhere far away, Chris's voice shouted in his mind. Running through the Laotian jungle in the night. Bullets snapping. Hot air exploding. Lungs raw from running and running. Brandon falling face-down. Mouth full of dirt. Chris had been there. Had snatched Brandon's LCE and pulled him to his feet. The whole time shouting, "You can make it!" Shoving him, shouting, "Come on! You can make it!"

The docks were still far. But the boat was moving faster. That shoreline growing bigger every second. Brandon clutched the throttle. Squeezed. Squeezed out every bit of speed the engine could give him. Squeezed harder. Demanded more.

"We'll make it" Brandon whispered. Throat stinging. Teeth clenched, he said, "We can make it."

Still, even in this bright and blazing determination,

thoughts of failure taunted him from peripheral shadows.

If Smith couldn't halt the Huey, if the pilot denied a radio request to turn around, Chris and the others would be back the next day at the latest. Maybe even that very evening. But all the same, Brandon's heart pounded. He couldn't spend a night out here without them.

He needed them.

We can make it.

Faster now. The boat skimmed over tiny waves. Smith and Jaran rocked and thumped. Jaran kept low in the center. Leaned on the gunwale.

"Go!" Smith yelled, voice dampened by wind and splash and engine din. "Faster!"

The docks were diagonally upriver, right outside village. After docking, the three of them would have to sprint another three-hundred-some meters to the landing zone through that tilled and soft soil. They could cut a considerable distance off their run if...

Brandon cranked the stick and veered towards the smoke.

Smith looked back, eyes wide in confusion. He yelled over the engine, "What are you doing?"

Brandon pointed. "Getting us to that bird!"

There was no proper shoreline to beach the boat. Just tall grass and reeds. It was a gamble. And from the slight apprehension pulling at Smith's face, he knew it too.

If only they had brought a radio. Brandon cursed himself for not bringing one. But at the same time he was thankful they *hadn't* brought one. They were heavy things. Even swapping the pack between the two of them would have slowed their descent off the mountain.

A second Huey broke over the trees. Not far now. Close enough to see the long and fat extended fuel tank mounted like a pontoon along the aircraft's side. Close enough to see the flat gray paint job like the C-130 that had brought New York here. No markings. Gray, not OD green. These weren't Army helicopters. It hovered just a moment and descended into the grass and red smoke.

Brandon aimed the boat at the Huey. Keeping his eye on it as it disappeared.

Closer. Blurred rotors just visible over the tall shoreline grass. On the hill above, leading into the jungle, tiny figures emerged. Hope brimmed in him.

"See us! Please!"

But if anyone had seen them, no one made any overt gestures. No one pointed or waved. He could fire his rifle. Get New York's attention that way. No. That wouldn't work. Over the Huey's rotor wash nobody would hear a gunshot from that far away. Somebody *had* to have seen them. The pilots or crew-chiefs from the air. They might wait if the crew had seen them.

Nearly there. But he couldn't see a good place to beach the boat through the veil of grass. But there was no time to change his mind and steer toward the docks. He picked a spot in the grass and committed.

"Hey," Brandon yelled to Smith. He pointed at Jaran. "Cut her loose!"

"Why?"

He nodded to the shore. "I'm sure you can appreciate the need for one's hands."

Smith looked back to the shoreline. Then to Brandon. "Oh, shit!" And with the boat skipping, Smith clumsily crawled along the boat's floor and undid Jaran's wrists and threw the cord overboard.

Smith grabbed his rifle and put a foot on the boat's prow. Crouched. Ready to jump. Brandon rapped Jaran's shoulder. She looked back and Brandon waved his hand up, pointed at Smith. "Get up!"

Warily she obeyed. Crouched with a foot on the gunwale. But she canted her head toward the sky. Her mouth hung open in subdued fear.

Don't run.

There wasn't time to chase her if she bolted.

"Get ready!" Brandon shouted.

Men filtered out from the jungle. But still no sign anyone had seen them. He watched the activity near the hilltop. He *should* have been watching where he was going. At the shoreline, the reeds and tall grass waved and fanned in a breeze. And just for a moment, amidst the browns and greens, a giant gray mass peaked out from the bending grass. A boulder. And all its sharp angles.

They were going too fast.

Body going electric-numb, Brandon cut the boat to the side, Smith and Jaran jerked and bent over and clung to the wood.

Too fast.

Too late.

The only thing louder than the bang was the thunderclap *crack* of splitting wood. Brandon mousetrap-snapped, slammed his chest against his knees, crunched his face and teeth against his shins.

Guts tense in weightlessness. Brandon's head snapped up. Spinning globs of blood lingered in the air in front of his face. Beyond a muffled ringing in his ears, a high-pitched staccato whine, the propeller whizzing, followed him through the air.

The boat rolled right and Smith and Jaran rolled left, floated out into air and away from the boat.

But Brandon remained in his seat. The cause of the whine, Brandon's white death-grip on the throttle, it had kept his ass in his seat.

The boat rolled.

Dazed, head stuffy from headbutting his shins, Brandon looked up at the green grass blackening beneath the revolving boat's shadow.

Incomplete images flashed in his mind. Most of them he missed. Some of them he caught.

Intestines. Torn yellow. Skull. Stringy. Rupture. Pink fluid. Shatter.

Brandon released the throttle. The whine died. He crossed his arms over his belly and tucked his head.

And plowed into the ground flat on his back. Air blasted from his lungs, tore at his throat in a roaring cough. The seat hammered his ass and spine into the ground. From his lower back a sickening crinkle erupted up his spine. Echoed in his ears.

The gunwales slammed the earth. A split-second of complete darkness, then light as the boat bounced and went tumbling into the tall grass. Brandon lay in a dazed silence. Stared at blue sky and sunlight. Then…

Oh, the pain came. Reached inside him and grabbed his bones. Put its thumbs against his spine and tried to snap it like a twig.

Hands shaking, Brandon opened his mouth to scream away his agony. But he had no air for screaming. Or breathing. Something hollow throbbed between his shoulders. He tried to inhale but he made only sucking frog sounds. His screams turned to airy, phantom whispers. His abdomen convulsed. Deep in his belly something spasmed.

Oh, Jesus.

Unable to draw air, he clawed at his chest. Wrenched his LCE aside and tore at his undershirt until he exposed bare skin. Brandon croaked, drew in a whisper's worth of air and held onto it as he felt for blood. Felt for broken ribs. Felt for holes. If his lungs were punctured he was dead. If his diaphragm wouldn't work he was dead. His pressing fingers found only fabric and unbroken skin. Damp from sweat, but not blood.

Just the wind knocked outta me.

He hoped.

Letting his head fall back, he tried to relax. Slowly, in its own time, the air came. He tried to let his body figure itself out. With each stomach spasm a faint stream of air worked its way down his raw throat and into his lungs.

Just the wind knocked outta me.

But now that he had air, his attention went to his spine and that sound, that *crinkle* he had heard. The rubbery discs between his vertebrae compressing. Squeezed thin between bone. Bulbous protrusions popping out from his spinal column. Panic crawled its way up, bulging in his throat.

"Captain!"

Brandon jerked his head toward the voice.

"Captain!" Smith shouted.

Here! Brandon tried to scream.

"Captain!" The voice moved away.

Brandon tried to sit up and jolts of electric pain discharged from his spine, shot into his guts. He flopped on the ground—

"Captain!" Further.

—he sucked air through his teeth.

I'm here! I'm alive!

That crinkle. The violin-string plucking he had heard. His spine—

Oh, God, please don't be broken.

He tried to move his legs.

He felt nothing.

The little air in his lungs, he used it to whisper, "No, no, no, no…"

The sharp grass towered over him. Above the green, the remnants of red smoke drifted into the cloudless blue sky. Without the boat's engine, there was only the chirping whine of distant helicopter engines and rotors.

He couldn't stand. He couldn't scream. Nobody would be able to see him lying in the chest-high grass. If Smith could make it to the helicopter in time—

"Captain!" Smith's shouted. Closer.

Brandon's despair flared. "Go stop them you idiot," Brandon groaned in a raw whisper. "Don't let them leave." The pain pulled his spine. "Fuck, I need a medic."

"Captain!"

God, he was done for. If Smith didn't somehow get the team's attention, the Hueys would extract New York and be gone. If nobody was watching when Brandon hit the ground, it would be almost impossible to find him. Smith had to run. Had to run *now!* Tell them to wait. Even with larger fuel tanks the pilots couldn't spare the time it would take for New York to search for their crippled commander. He couldn't stay out here like this.

Smith needed to get to the helicopters. Or to his radio if they left. Tell them to turn around. Maybe they would refuel and circle back for him before the sun went down.

Mercury.

Flying too close to the sun meant—

"Oh, shit." In a panic he tried to shove himself up. But panic only dulled his pain for so long. His arms wobbled and he collapsed. Fear's cold fingers closed around his heart.

No one comes back for a Mercury team.

"Fuck," Brandon gasped. *My men aren't expendable,* Colonel Murphy had said. The NVA were coming and Brandon would be left there to die. Crippled and alone. A tear welled and slid down his face. He blinked the next one away. His rifle was gone. Lost when the boat tumbled in the air.

If the NVA found him…

They pay more if they take us alive.

Brandon groped his hip. Felt the 1911 secure in its holster and he squeezed his eyes shut. How long could he hide out here? How long before he would have to put his pistol in his—

A silhouette blotted out the sun.

"God *damn*, Cap!" Chris said. Smiling wide. "Where'd you learn to fly a boat?"

"Oh," Brandon groaned. "Thank God." The words blew out with the force of pure relief. Brandon raised his hand and reached out. Chris clasped Brandon's wrist and the touch was like God touching him. He didn't even try to fight the stinging in his eyes.

Chris tried to pull him to his feet and something ground in Brandon's pelvis. Brandon screamed, agony driving him to near unconsciousness.

Chris let him back down. "What the hell happened to you?"

"My back," Brandon gagged, words vomiting out. "I think it's broken. My legs. Fuckin' boat. Landed on me."

Chris's face turned serious. "Oh, shit." He stood tall and cupped his hands to his mouth. "Mike!" He waved his hands. "Mike! Brandon's fucked!" Chris bent down. "Mike's coming. We'll get you outta here. Choppers are waiting for you."

He tried to say *thank you*, but didn't think he could without bursting into tears. He focused on the pain. Focused on anything else to keep from crying in front of Chris. "Smith and Jaran okay?"

"Yeah," Chris said. "Mike kissed their boo-boos. They're fine. They can walk. I mean, a boat didn't land on them."

"How is everyone else?"

"Boing is still in a lot of pain. Mike did all he could to keep him comfortable. John is finally up and walking around. But Mike says we should MEDEVAC him anyway. His eyes are all fucked up. Infection, maybe."

Brandon looked at Chris. The fear of John discovering what happened to Boing, or how Brandon had shot another soldier, those fears were conspicuously absent. Instead, he thought of Captain Conway.

Not dead. Unconscious.

He thought of the terrified look on Jaran's face when Brandon had come out of the pit.

What if she was protecting herself?

Conway chained down. Not dead.

"John is awake?"

"Yep. Been up for maybe half an hour. We told him to sit tight and wait for the helicopters, but he wanted to help out. He's out recovering claymores." Chris scratched his head. "Crazy thing though. That old lady attacked him as soon as she saw him."

That was odd. She seemed to be the peaceful one of the pair. "What did you do with her?"

"Tied her up. Had to gag her too. Kept screaming. We put her on the first Huey as soon as it landed. Howard's riding with her and all the rucksacks. He'll keep an eye on her."

"What was she saying?"

"Dunno. Seemed like the same thing over and over, though."

"Mike couldn't understand her?"

"Nope."

"John say anything?"

"Not really. Still a little groggy. Says he doesn't remember much. I told him where you guys went. He said he'd like to talk to the girl when she came back."

"The girl?" Brandon muttered.

How did John even know about her? Maybe the team told him.

Mike pushed through the grass. Eyes cold. Clinical. He looked at Brandon a few seconds and said, "Can you walk, sir?"

"No," Brandon said. "I don't know if my back is broken or if I'm paralyzed or—"

Mike knelt and pulled a morphine syrette from his aid-bag.

"No!" Brandon said.

Plastic cap in his fingers, silver needle sticking up sharp in the others, Mike paused there looking at him. "You sure?"

Brandon could think of nothing better than slipping into a chemical coma. But something, a lot of things maybe, told him to wait until he was somewhere safe before allowing himself the luxury of narcotics.

"No morphine," Brandon said.

Mike capped the needle. "Suit yourself, hero."

Chris knelt down with Mike. Brandon threw his arms around their shoulders. They interlocked their arms and made a seat beneath him and lifted. Brandon grimaced at the jarring movement. But, rising, his pain went suddenly far away. Head above the grass, there they were. Helicopters. Waiting for him. Door gunners sweeping their big M60s. Keeping watch.

Not being able to walk, that was his ticket home. He didn't have the heart to tell the men that Smith would be keeping them out there.

Navigating through the tall grass, Mike and Chris tried to hold him steady. They failed miserably. His spine stretched and creaked.

Smith and Jaran noticed them struggling through the grass and came back for them. At least Smith had been able to retain his rifle in the chaos.

Chris stepped in a hole and stumbled. Pain blossomed from Brandon's spine and he shot his head back and screamed, "God damn you!"

"Sorry," Mike said. "Sorry. Almost there."

"*No morphine!*" Chris yelled, laughing.

Brandon cursed at them both through clenched teeth and they went quiet.

They went on. Closer to the Hueys. Closer to home.

Howard and the old woman sat in the first helicopter. Its cargo area filled with bulky rucksacks. It throttled up, getting ready to lift off. Some distance ahead of it, a lone figure stepped from the shadows of the jungle.

"That John?" Brandon asked.

"Yeah," Chris said. "There he is."

Brandon couldn't make out his features in that slash of jungle shadow. Only the tiger-stripes on his uniform stood out. John had his hands behind his back in a sloppy parade-rest. As the first Huey rose, John stepped out and the sun lit up his face. And his hideously large smile.

That smile made Brandon's guts drop with some strange fear. Something old. Primal. "Stop," Brandon said. The word a mere whisper. But the men didn't stop. "Stop, goddamnit!"

They stopped.

"What's wrong?" Mike asked.

"Just..." Brandon said.

Why *did* he stop them? He could think of nothing to say.

He searched the men's faces. Even Smith, once so eager to stop the extraction, looked hesitant. Brandon looked over his shoulder at Jaran. When he saw her face, that old fear in him iced over with pure terror.

He made me kill them...

But Conway was delirious when he had said that.

Still, Jaran trembled. Her chest beneath her robes worked in a barely controlled panic. A few hours ago, Brandon would have said she was simply afraid of the strange flying machines. Jaran's eyes fell on Brandon's. She pointed. Pointed at John. And she said, "Erlik Khan." She danced with panic. She screamed, "*Erlik Khan!*"

He's coming...

Brandon turned back to the Hueys. John held his hands aloft, like Christ on the cross. The sunlight caught something long and thin hanging down from his hand. Then it was gone in shadow. Then it was there. A rope?

He's out recovering the claymores...

"Get down," Brandon muttered. Nobody moved.

"What the hell is he doing?" Chris asked.

"Get down," Brandon said. Voice growing. "Get down *now*."

The first Huey lifted off. When its skids were no higher than John's head. The pilot, through his window in the floor, waved to John.

John ignored him. Turning instead to look upon Brandon and the group around him. And in the sunlight, John's eyes were a flat, dead white. John raised a hand, firing wire hanging from the boxy clacker like a marionette's cut string. He waved to Brandon.

"Goddamnit!" Then Brandon screamed the only other word he could think of to make these men move.

"Claymore! Claymore! Claymore!"

Mike and Chris fell to the ground and dropped him. Brandon cupped his hands over his ears. His back spasmed and his shrieks of agony were loud in his head. The other men buried their heads in the dirt.

The green grass and blue sky disappeared in a silent white flash. In the split-second that followed, the staccato blast of five or six claymore mines rocked through his head. Through his hands over his ears came the screech of rending metal and the *slap slap slap* of rotors pounding earth. Two meaty shockwaves punched through Brandon's lungs and drove out the air. Secondary explosions. The giant fuel tanks. Above the elephant grass two oily black mushroom plumes ascended into the sky. Churned into each other. Swirled apart with slashes of orange fire.

Dazed. Ears ringing. But beyond the ringing, some strange sound, like firewood crackling.

Brandon shook his head, shook off the shockwave-daze. As the ringing subsided, as his head cleared, when dirt around him popped from the ground in tiny plumes, and when shredded grass sprinkled down on his face, with growing terror ripping his mind apart, Brandon knew *exactly* what that sound was.

Conway's voice echoed in his mind. *I killed them. He made me kill them. He made me...*

Brandon hadn't believed him. He had thought Conway was just crazy with fever. Bullets tore at the earth around him, and Brandon slipped his 1911 from its holster. Clicked off the safety. Aimed it shaking at the grass. He knew there was a round in the chamber this time. And if John came walking through the grass, Brandon was going to put it, and all of its friends, right into John's chest.

CHAPTER NINETEEN

"Holy shit!" Chris yelled. Voice cotton-muffled in Brandon's ringing ears. "Holy fucking shit!"

Brandon, on his back, searched the grass for movement. Jerked the pistol this way. That way. Nothing but waving green. On either side of him, Mike and Chris lay prone. Their rifles still slung across their backs. Thank God they had them. Brandon's rifle was somewhere lost. It might as well have been across the river for all the good it would do him now.

Chris jumped to his feet. When he raised his head above the grass, orange light squirmed on his face. His mouth went slack with disbelief. Fingers crept up into his hair and grabbed hold. He inhaled long. Then he screamed, "*Howard!*"

Crack.

Mike dove over Brandon, drove his shoulder into Chris's waist and tackled him. Chris fought to get up.

"Hey!" Mike pinned Chris's arms down. "That's John shooting." Chris fought. Mike grabbed his shirt and shook him. "That's *John* shooting. He'll blow your head off from a mile out."

Through slashes of waving grass Chris's face was pulled back tight with anger. "He fucking killed Howard!"

Mike pulled himself to a crouch. Popped his head up. Dropped it just as fast. An echoing snap blasted above them just as he hit the ground. "Jesus," Mike said, confused terror in his eyes. "Jesus…"

On the Laos operation, even when everything had gone to hell, even when one of New York's own was killed, Brandon had not seen fear overtake a single man on the team. Anger? Yes. Fear? Never. But in Laos they'd had a plan. They had killed as many enemy soldiers as they could and then retreated. This was different. Their backs were to the river. This time they were confronted with an enemy they didn't *want* to kill. How Brandon kept his own head about him, he didn't know.

Crack.

Crack.

John's rifle fire zipped through the grass over their heads, dusted Brandon's face with the scent of mowed lawns.

Mike rose and peaked over the grass. He jerked his hand up. "Hey!" Mike shouted. "Over here! Run!" He screamed, "*Run!*"

"Who is it?" Brandon asked.

"A crew chief. Hey! This way! Come on, run!"

Crack-ack-ack-ack.

"No!" Mike's hands came up short. Then he dropped to his knees beneath the fading echoes of the full-auto burst. Eyes shut tight. Hands balling into fists, he yelled, "What the fuck are you doing, John?"

Mike shook the terror off his face and looked to Chris. "What do you wanna do?"

Pop. Crack.

Chris stared into the elephant grass. Didn't flinch as it shredded around him. He got on his knees, unslung his rifle. Held it. Looked at it. Then he clicked off the safety. "I guess we do what we always do when assholes shoot at us." He eased up into a low crouch, brought the rifle butt to the center of his chest, and slowly raised his head, his shoulders above the grass. Scanned for his target. His finger slid onto the trigger.

A shape burst through the grass. Brandon jerked his pistol toward the movement and fired, suppressor hissing gas.

Jaran.

The grass just behind her head twitched from the .45. Brandon's heart sledgehammered against his sternum. "*Jesus.*"

But she didn't seem to notice she had just been shot at. Or if she did notice, she didn't care. She kept running. Charged Chris. Reached out and dove, grabbed the heat shields on Chris's rifle in both hands and drove the rifle down with her diving body. The rifle discharged, blasting a round into the dirt at Chris's feet. On her knees, Jaran clawed at Chris's belly until she had a handful of shirt and tried to pull him down.

"The fuck are you doing?" Chris yelled.

Crack.

Whack.

Chris jerked. Green fabric shredded. Yellow meat splattered. Dark red sprayed hot and wet on Brandon's face. Chris fell. Swallowed in the grass.

"No!" Brandon lurched toward where Chris had fallen. But his back seized and his legs jerked and he fell back groaning and beat his fist on the ground. Flopping in the grass he screamed, "Mike!" Pointed to Chris. "Mike! Medic!"

Mike looked. Rushed to Chris. His hand clutched his shoulder, stringy yellow meat spilled between his fingers. Cords in his neck strained beneath gritted teeth.

Mike rolled back Chris' fingers and looked at the wound. He shoved Chris's fingers back into place and said, "Hold that." Mike popped open the pouch on Chris's LCE and snatched out the field dressing. Tried to tear the plastic but his bloody fingers slipped on the smooth green packaging. He bit into the plastic covered in Chris' blood and tore it open with his teeth.

Unfurling the bandage, Mike's fluid hands wrapped and tied a pressure dressing around Chris' shoulder in barely any time at all.

Mike wiped his bloody hands on his trousers and spun toward the incoming rifle-fire. He slipped his rifle from his back and into his hands in a movement so smooth it was like the rifle obeyed some unspoken command. Rising in the grass, Mike aimed. But as soon as his rifle flicked to his target, Jaran latched onto his collar and yanked him down.

"Get off," Mike grunted, and shoved her with a giant hand. Jaran tripped over Chris's boot and summersaulted backward into the grass.

"Oh," Chris groaned. Through gritted teeth, clutching his shoulder, he shouted, "John, You mother *fucker*!"

Mike peaked above the grass. "We gotta do something, man. We gotta do something fast."

"I *tried* to do something. Look where it got me."

"Good initiative. Bad judgement."

"Yeah, yeah…"

Jaran pushed though the grass and grabbed Mike's rifle in both hands and slammed a front-kick into his balls. His hands slipped from the rifle and he sat down hard.

When he tried to stand up, Jaran yelled something and raised the rifle high, threatening a butt-stroke. Mike's hands shot up protectively in front of his face. Jaran lowered the rifle.

She knelt and examined the CAR-15, turned it this way and that. She pointed it up in the air and pulled the trigger, blasted a round skyward. The three men flinched.

Mike waved a hand in John's direction. "Little girl, if you're gonna shoot the goddamn thing, shoot it at him!" And he shouted something abrupt in Vietnamese. He looked over his shoulder at Brandon. Eyed the pistol in his hand and flicked his head at Jaran. Brandon nodded and

Mike crawled over to Chris and checked him for more wounds.

Brandon rested the butt of his 1911 on the ground, barrel pointed toward Jaran. If she turned the rifle on any of the men…

But she didn't pay attention to any of them. The way she bobbed her head to look for John, the way she had looked at John before all this, what she had said, Brandon got the feeling she wouldn't be a threat at all.

But why wouldn't she let Mike or Chris shoot back?

Why wasn't *she* shooting?

She knelt there with the rifle resting on her knee, muzzle sticking in the dirt. She closed her eyes and reached into the neckline of her robe. Made a fist beneath the fabric. Her mouth worked silently. Incoming rounds zipped above her head, but she was oblivious to them. Or maybe she didn't know what the sound was. Not everyone knows what it sounds like to be shot at.

Her robe's loose collar slipped down and revealed a thin leather thong hanging around her neck. Her mouth kept working like a silent prayer.

A breeze. The sky brightened blue as if a cloud had drifted away to reveal the sun. But there were no clouds. And then…

Silence. The gunfire ceased. Brandon looked around. Listened. Looked back at Jaran. Eyed her hard, trying to make sense of what just happened.

John was just reloading.

That was what the logical part of Brandon's mind insisted.

Or he's moving to cover. Maneuvering to flank.

The silence did not last. First a piercing scream, cracked and high-pitched and charred with anguish, then rifle fire. But the report had come from somewhere else. Either John had flanked them like Brandon suspected or…

Mike and Jaran lifted their heads above the grass. The girl gasped.

Propping himself painfully up on his elbow, Brandon asked, "Who is it?"

"The old woman," Mike said. "She survived. But Christ, she's burned to hell."

More rifle fire. An answering volley, most likely from John. More raw screams. Brandon couldn't understand what she was saying.

"*Erlik Khan!*" the woman screamed between rifle shots.

"She must've inhaled flames," Mike said. "Scorched her lungs." He rubbed his head. "I can't fix that." More rifle fire. Mike ducked, but kept watching. "She's shooting at John. She's got something in her hand. She's waving it at him. I can't see what it is."

Jaran pulled the thong around her neck up and over her head. A small glass vial slipped from her robes, the thong tied about the vial's neck just below a cork stopper. Some kind of runny black liquid, like water and campfire ashes, sloshed inside.

The old woman let out a long, primal scream. But there were tones beneath the hoarseness. Like singing. Chanting. And on that scream was the name *Erlik Khan*. Over and over. *Erlik Khan*. Then rifle fire.

Jaran chewed her lip hard and watched the exchange without blinking. Gripped the glass vial so tightly it was like to shatter in her trembling hand.

"Mike!" Chris grunted. "We need to move—"

A howl shook the air. Shook Brandon's heart. The cloudless sky darkened, as if the sunlight fled from whatever made the sound.

Mike's hand went to his mouth.

Brandon watched the sky. "What the hell was that?"

"She hit him," Mike said.

"Hooray," Chris grunted as he sat up. "The fucker dead yet?"

"She put him down." Mike stood. Called out to the woman in Vietnamese.

"Careful," Brandon said. "She might shoot you, too."

"I told her she's out of ammo." Mike waved to the woman. "Come to us!" He turned to Jaran and pulled her up by the elbow and she stood. "Tell her to come here," he said to the girl. He squeezed his eyes shut and patted his forehead and then blurted something in Vietnamese.

Jaran nodded and raised a hand and called to the woman.

"Mike," Brandon said. The medic turned to him. "Is John dead?"

Chris and Mike looked at each other. Said nothing. As if not saying it would somehow keep their friend alive. Somehow negate the last minutes. Somehow bring the dead back to life. Regardless of what John had just done, Brandon doubted the two men wanted to feel good about John being dead.

Mike turned to watch the old woman come. But then he dropped down quick, grabbed Jaran's arm and pulled her down with him. "John's up, guys. He's alive. She hit him in the gut. There's lots of blood on his shirt," Mike shot to his feet. "He's running!"

Smith pushed through the grass, crouched low, holding his rifle tight in his hands. He looked down at Brandon. "He's heading into the jungle. We need to go after him."

"Where the fuck you been?" Chris yelled.

Smith ignored him. "Let's go."

"Who's left to chase him?" Mike said. "Howard's dead. Commander can't walk. Chris is shot, and we don't know where the others are."

It was a bad idea to let John wonder off just so he could come at them again. But Mike was right. Who was left to chase him?

"Captain!" Smith said. "Get your men moving!"

Brandon looked at Mike. Opened his mouth to speak. But then Mike said, "We got too many casualties here to worry about. We need to regroup and then we'll figure out what to do."

"He's going to escape!" Smith yelled.

Mike looked out over the grass. Then he shook his head. "He's gut-shot. He won't last long."

"Captain," Smith said. "Do *you* have any input?"

But what he really said was: *You know damn well who's in charge here so get these men moving.*

Brandon lay there in the grass. Looked back and forth between Smith and Mike. How could Smith expect these men to move? Brandon thought carefully about what he was going to say. "We'll reassess after Mike patches us up."

Smith stared at him. Chewed his cheek as he nodded.

The woman stumbled through the grass. Mike was right, she was burned to hell. Her once-long hair reduced to little black balls atop her head. Lips blistered and third-degree pink. Her dark robes singed black and dry except for blotches of perspiration. What unnerved Brandon was the woman's eyes. They couldn't focus on anything. Darted about wildly as if she were drugged. Her mouth hung open, lips trying to form words that did not come. Lips that couldn't hold back rivulets of frothy drool.

Jaran ran to her. Caught the woman just as she collapsed and they both thudded on the ground. Jaran took the woman's head in her lap. Brushed soot and remnants of hair from the woman's sweaty face. She screamed to the woman. Screams accented with deep, heaving sobs.

"She hit?" Brandon asked.

"Even if she was," Mike said. "There's nothing I can do for her. The burns…" Mike helplessly held out his hands. "She's dying."

Dropping to his knees beside the women, Mike's hands hovered over the woman's melted face. Then went to his aid-bag, but his hands moved without urgency. He rummaged through the kit and pulled out thick bandages and bottles of dark yellow liquid. "Keep her talking," Mike said to Jaran, a nervous tremble in his voice.

Brandon looked away, gave the women what small privacy he could. He laid his head back on the hard earth, grimacing at the pain in his back. Eyes closed, he laid there and listened to the sounds of tearing tape and the wrapping of cloth and the clink of glass bottles. And the human sounds of crying. Of whispered goodbyes. Of final breaths.

Brandon ran his hand along his thigh. Massaged it. A removed feeling, like his leg was encased in a cast, but he could feel his hand rubbing. He tried to flex his leg. The muscle just above his knee twitched.

Thank God.

The feeling was coming back. He could only hope that there was no serious damage. Hope that in a while his legs would remember how to move. That he would be able to walk. He focused on his toes and they wiggled beneath the hard boot leather.

Thank you.

"Try pulling them up to your chest."

Brandon opened his eyes. Mike stood over him. Beyond Mike's legs Jaran held the woman. They were surrounded by the discarded paper packaging of bandages. The woman's face was wrapped completely in thick white gauze already stained yellow. Just her nose protruded. She lay unmoving in Jaran's lap. Jaran squeezed one of the woman's papery hands and whispered. Shook the woman and whispered. As if begging her to come back.

"Sir," Mike said. "Pull your legs to your chest."

Brandon nodded and pulled his legs. Slowly. Cautiously. He pulled them up. Flexed them. Grunted at his throbbing back. A spasm jerked him and he cried out.

"Looks like a pinched nerve," Mike said. "You're lucky. Is there pain in your legs when you move them?"

"Yeah," Brandon said. "Here." And he patted the outside of his thigh.

Mike nodded. "L3 or L4. Hopefully it's a herniated disc." He interlaced his fingers and held them out to Brandon. "The muscles in your lower back are gonna get real tight to keep you from moving much. It'll be painful, but you should be able to walk soon. I've got some anti-inflammatories in my kit, but no muscle relaxers. Try to keep moving. Motion's lotion." Then he turned his attention to the women.

"You okay?" Brandon asked.

Mike massaged his eyes. "I'll be fine. I just need to forget everything that happened in the last five minutes."

"Good luck," Chris said. He pushed himself to his feet and came to stand beside Mike. He bent forward, holding his elbow across his belly. Behind Chris, thick oily smoke from the helicopters ascended into the sky. Chris watched the smoke for a moment, and then looked down at Brandon. "John asked me once to take over as NCOIC if he ever decided to leave the team. I think he just made his decision."

Mike nodded. "You got my vote."

Brandon stared at Chris. The way this man compartmentalized mental and physical trauma dumfounded him. His first thought was to scream at Chris. Call him a fucking idiot. Ask him if he was aware of everything that had just happened. But then Chris put his good hand on Mike's shoulder and gave it a squeeze. Together they watched the smoke rise. Both of their faces were hard, but their eyes betrayed them. They were filled with sorrow. Chris and Mike cared about the team. *Their* team. Cared for the men that were lost in the helicopters. Brandon felt his face soften, a weight on his brow lifted.

"Congratulations," Brandon said. "I dub thee NCOIC."

Chris nodded to the sky.

And that was that. Chris turned and reached out his hand to Brandon. Brandon took it, and Chris pulled him painfully to his feet.

Brandon stood crooked, bent awkwardly at the waist and unable to straighten. He followed Mike's and Chris' stares and gasped at the scene before him. It was the first glimpse he was able to get of the destruction. The carnage.

After the blast, the first helicopter had banked violently. Rolled on its head. Now it lay burning. Torn and twisted metal rotor blades lay strewn amidst giant gashes in the field's dark soil.

The other helicopter simply sat where it had landed. It, too, burned. The charred-black pilot and co-pilot sat slumped in the inferno, still buckled in their seats behind soot-caked and cracked cockpit windows. One of them moved. Arms and hands came up lazily to the harness buckled at his chest.

"Jesus!" Brandon gasped. "They're still alive!"

He turned to Mike and Chris, but they didn't move. Just stared. Brandon couldn't understand why the men weren't running toward the Huey to rescue the pilots.

But Mike simply shook his head. "They're long gone." He coiled his arms to his chest, mimicking the two pilots. "The muscles shrivel as they burn."

Brandon turned back and stared into the red and orange flames. Black smoke. Watched in horror as the dead pilot's hooked hands curled toward his chest. Neck and head arched back.

This was all wrong. All fucking wrong. Everyone was dead. Florida. The pilots. The helicopters were destroyed. Brandon was stuck out here. He had almost gotten out. But now he was trapped. Lightheadedness took him. Brandon bent over, holding himself up with his hands on his knees. The earth spun. God, he was thirsty. He pulled the canteen from its pouch and tilted it up. His hand trembled. The water sloshed out and he sucked down whatever got into his mouth. He was trapped. He looked to the sky.

Brandon asked, "C-130 still up there?"

Please, oh please let them be up there.

"No," Smith said, flatly. "We're on our own for the next eight hours."

Brandon straightened as best he could and turned to Smith. "*Eight hours?*" He threw the empty canteen at the operative. It thudded hollow against his chest and dropped on the ground. Smith's eyes went hard and he stared at Brandon. Brandon swept his arm to the helicopters. "Look what that son-of-a-bitch did to us in five minutes! We'll all be dead in eight fucking hours!"

Smith didn't hide his anger when he said, "We'll have to deal with the situation."

"Look at my men!" Brandon screamed. "We're fucked out here! Tell me how the fuck we're supposed to *deal* with this!"

"By surviving long enough to call the retrans aircraft when they come back." Smith inhaled deeply and seemed to grow several inches.

Chris walked over and interrupted them. He put a pinch of tobacco in his lip and said, "Them NVA you said were on their way..." He chewed a moment then spat brown juice. "Well, they got one hell of a smoke signal to follow now."

Brandon kept his eyes locked on Smith. He could tell by Smith's eyes that the realization had come to him at the same moment as it had to Brandon: time was absolutely against them. That they were going to have a big fight on their hands if they didn't move out immediately.

"Chris," Brandon said, trying his best to sound calm. "Check for survivors and salvage whatever gear you can."

Chris nodded and whistled to Mike, twirled his fingers in a *rally* signal. Mike brought up his rifle and Chris drew his pistol and they moved off towards the flaming wreckage.

Brandon took a breath. Looked at Smith. "I think there's some truth to what Conway said in the cave."

Smith nodded. "Tell me everything he said."

Brandon told him. Told him everything. Tried to reason why one of Conway's men killed his own team.

Smith looked up at the rising smoke. "If there's any truth to that, then whatever happened to Conway and his man must've happened to John."

"So what happened to them?" Brandon asked. "What made John…" he gestured to the helicopters.

Smith stared over Brandon's shoulder. Brandon turned. Jaran laid the woman down and knelt beside her. "I don't know," Smith said. "But I think the girl does."

CHAPTER TWENTY

In the field, where the tilled soil was soft and loose and easy to dig up, that was where New York dug the shallow graves.

Dan, George, and Terry, separated from the team during John's attack, had come out of concealment when they saw Mike and Chris searching the burning aircraft. And now they each dragged a different man by their boots.

It was in no way a respectful way to move the dead, but they had tried a two-man carry, one man holding feet and the other holding arms. Cooked-black meat had sloughed off dead arms and Terry had dropped a pilot multiple times, making unintentional mockery of a somber process.

The charred corpses lay in the jungle's shadow, side-by-side in the short grass. The men's final agonizing moments of life scorched upon their faces. Bodies and limbs contorted in hideous attitudes of misery. Black and bony hands clawed at skinless faces. Pilots and crew chiefs, Brandon could tell them by the helmets they wore. Beside them lay a man with no helmet. Howard. Mike had checked the wreckage for the rubber body bags, but they had liquified in the fire. The men would have to be buried without them.

In the field, where there was no jungle to shade him from the sun, Brandon sat atop a small bamboo shed used for storing garden tools. It was the closest structure to the helicopter wreckage and offered an elevated vantage to watch over the team as they worked. He sat his perch and sweated in the noon-day sun. Watched New York dig. Watched them bury the dead.

He ran his fingers over Smith's radio. Over its dents and cracks and the smooth holes peppered in it from the claymores. Absently slipped his finger into a grape-sized hole in the metal housing. It slid to the second knuckle and stuck fleshy. He tugged his finger and it came out black with greasy soot. He wiped his finger on his trouser leg.

Chris had recovered the radio from the first Huey. It had been in Smith's rucksack. When Chris had pulled the shredded pack from the helicopter, when he had held up the radio to examine the holes from the claymores, only a sliver of disappointment had broke through Chris's stolid mask before he dropped the useless thing on the ground and moved on to pulling the next item from the wreckage.

Mike had called Brandon over to the shed. Brandon had taken the radio and gone to the far side of the field.

"You'll want to rest that back of yours before we get moving," Mike had said. "Just relax and watch our backs." He pointed to the top of the bamboo shed. "Up there will give you a good vantage."

Mike had boosted Brandon to the roof, and there he sat with his rifle and his canteen and Smith's destroyed radio. He watched. He thought. He worried. He had kept alert for a time, running on adrenaline, but it had long since bled from him.

As it turned out, Chris had seen Brandon's boat returning from across the river and told the pilots to wait. To save time, Chris had loaded their gear onto the first helicopter with Howard and the woman. He had just stowed Smith's rucksack when he saw the boat launch into the air.

Back throbbing, eyes squinted against the sun, watching the team pull salvage from the smoldering helicopters, Brandon muttered, "Should have just gone to the dock."

But if they had gone to the dock, how would the events have played out? Would John have waited for the entire team to board the helicopters before ambushing them? Was that his plan all along?

It had to have been. Despite Brandon's feelings toward the man, John was nothing if not cunning. The main objective in any ambush is to maximize casualties. John got both helicopters, their crews, Howard, the woman, and had wounded, either directly or indirectly, nearly half the team. All in just a few minutes.

How was Brandon supposed to fight against John?

But was he asking the wrong question again? Asking *how* instead of *why*? Why had John turned on them? Brandon looked across the river. Up to that black spire.

It troubled Brandon that John *didn't* wait for everyone to board the aircraft. He could have killed them all if he had only waited a little longer. So why didn't he?

John knew where Smith and Brandon had gone. Chris had told him. He knew they took Jaran with them. Something had forced John to strike early. Was it something about the cave? Brandon thought about Conway and the other dead men. Thought about their wounds.

What had forced John's hand? What had made him decide to take out the Hueys and risk his life mopping up the rest of the team in a firefight?

The first Huey was lifting off before the main party was ready. Maybe John hadn't anticipated that. *Maybe*.

Terry and Dan scooped the last shovels-full of dirt over the Huey pilots. Jaran had insisted on filling in her grandmother's grave. The row of shallow graves looked like long raised scars in the dark earth. Beneath one of those mounds lay Howard. An open hole was left for Boing. New York was still trying to find his body.

Smith had been furious when he had learned Boing was MIA. It was not a vengeful fury. He wasn't angry at John. It was a fury stoked by the notion that he could not exploit Jaran's knowledge of the area. When Dan reported there was no sign of the interpreter, Brandon was ashamed to admit his first feeling was relief. Relief that no one would find out what he had done to Boing on the C-130.

Brandon canted his head and saw daylight through a hole in the side of the radio. He reached his hand around and gently ran his finger along the exit hole's sharp, mangled edges.

"Claymore, claymore, claymore..." Brandon mumbled. Tapped his fingertip on a gnarled metal point. Brandon pushed until the boxy radio toppled and clunked on the bamboo planks.

The sun was high and midday-hot. It baked the back of his uniform. His neck. Sweat spilled from the pores on his neck and evaporated almost instantly. Left only gritty salt behind. The process repeated. And repeated. Leaving his neck dry and chafed and sunburned.

Brandon stretched. Arched his back. Rotated his shoulders. There was no escaping the heat. The jungle foliage afforded the men and Jaran a large swath of shadow in which to comfortably download salvage from the helicopters. But on Brandon's perch, he took the sun's full intensity.

New York and Smith and Jaran moved about the helicopters in a slow back-and-forth rhythm of *take-an-item-drop-an-item*, and the ants-marching pattern lulled him until his shoulders relaxed into jelly and his eyelids fluttered and maybe Cheryl might consider another date with him when he came home—

CRACK-ACK-ACK-ACK.

Brandon jerked. Snatched up his rifle. Spun his head. Searched. Searched as the echoing gunfire of his dream evaporated. In the air there was only the zipping and buzzing of insects.

And New York and Smith and Jaran moved about the helicopters in a slow back-and-forth rhythm. They had not heard the phantom gunfire because there was nothing to hear. No gunfire. Just dreams.

"Fuck," Brandon groaned and rubbed his palms in his eyes. He shook his head. Stretched again. No matter what he did, the warm haze of sleep still beckoned. Even the tiny adrenaline bump of catching himself dozing did little to make his eyelids any less heavy.

He stretched out his legs, wincing at the dull throb in his back. The electric buzz in his thigh. He needed to stay awake. Needed something to *do*. Laying his rifle across his lap, he put his binoculars to his eyes and scanned the tree line for any sign of John. He scanned as far as he could see downriver and swept as far as he could see upriver. Nothing but jungle, hills, and farmland. He looked over his shoulder toward the river, but doubted John would try coming at them from that way.

But as soon as he doubted the option, hot anxiety sizzled in his gut.

"You *might*."

Brandon might not have liked John's leadership style. Might not have liked the way he questioned Brandon's decisions. But he couldn't deny the man's ruthlessness. That NVA officer that nearly zapped Brandon in Laos, that man never stood a chance against John. John had shot the officer in the neck—*the neck*—from more than twenty paces while Brandon was still between John and his target. The insanity of it. But that led to the big question. The five-million-dollar question. Why would John save Brandon's life only to try and take it less than twenty-four hours later?

Did something out here make John sick? Make him go insane? Was that what happened to Conway and his man? Had they lost their minds?

But why just those two?

Why *John*?

The team. The men John loved. The men for whom John had argued so hard to keep from even coming on this mission.

The pieces were there. The answers. Brandon just had to puzzle them out. When did all this madness start? In the cave? Maybe. Before that?

"The cripple," Brandon said.

He wanted to discuss this with Jaran. Talk to her about what happened in her village. What *really* happened. But Mike's Vietnamese only went so far. Talking to Jaran about all this wouldn't happen any time soon. Not without an interpreter.

Brandon's shoulders and neck burned and he pulled up his collar against the sun. His eyelids fluttered. He tensed. Flexed every muscle trying to get some blood flowing. Get his heartrate up. He wouldn't be able to think straight while he was so tired.

The team worked in near silence. Even Smith picked through the wreckage. Chris, George, and Mike, faces buried in their elbows until they needed to use their hands, searched the helicopters. Dragged blackened pieces of gear to a designated spot away from the smoking machines.

Jaran grabbed equipment and toted it to another consolidation area near Brandon's perch. Rucksacks, aid bags, hell, the team apparently trusted her enough to carry weapons and ammunition. Dan stood amidst the pile of stuff that Jaran gathered and separated equipment into various rucksacks. He divvied out machinegun ammo and grenades and C-rations. Assembled as many complete kits as he could.

Mike disconnected an M60 from its door-gunner's position and handed it to Jaran. She hefted it onto her back, bending over with it. She grasped the barrel with both hands above her head and lugged the mammoth machinegun across the field toward Dan. She dropped it and hurried back to fetch the green cans of belt ammunition.

Brandon kept a running count of the dead. But would the numbers even matter for an unsanctioned operation? These numbers would remain classified until someone declassified the mission sometime in the very distant future. Old habits. Headquarters needed numbers.

Numbers were important in this war. It was one of the first lessons Brandon had learned as a lieutenant commanding his Infantry platoon. After an engagement, the company commander wanted to know the number of enemy dead, wounded, and captured against the same numbers for Americans. These numbers were radioed off to the battalion echelon to the brigade echelon to the division echelon. The American public needed reassurance they were winning the war. So the government gave them numbers.

Land didn't matter here the way it mattered in WWII. A physical piece of land only seemed to matter if the NVA held it. Americans would die to deprive the enemy of a hill in the middle of nowhere. And when the fighting was done they'd abandon it and move on to another hill in the middle of another nowhere. The objective, it seemed, was not taking the hill, but recording the numbers. A hill was just a hill. Nobody cared about a hill. But numbers could sway opinions.

Kill more of them than they kill of you, and you win. A simple metric. Brandon's eyes lingered on the rectangular plots of disturbed earth. On the still-open grave waiting for its body.

Two pilots, two co-pilots, four crew-chiefs, one interpreter, one civilian, one recon man. So, eleven casualties. Plus the eight men assigned to Florida. Their handler. Twenty.

Friendly KIA: Twenty.

Enemy KIA: One cripple.

Brandon winced. Captain Goode would have been less than pleased about that ratio. And Colonel Murphy probably wouldn't be too happy to receive this particular report. Special Forces didn't fill their ranks with recruits fresh out of basic training. You had to grow these men. There was a minimum time-in-service requirement. They had to attend a selection program. Airborne training. It took a long time to grow a Green Beret. Losing nine of them on a goose-chase for a man no one had ever seen was going to make a lot of high-ranking someones in the chain of command lose their shit. And oh boy was it going to roll downhill and bury the poor bastards unlucky enough to be anywhere near a command position.

Kiss that Pentagon assignment goodbye.

Brandon looked at the radio and sighed. With no comms he couldn't send his report, which at least would delay the ass chewing.

Ass chewing?

No.

Might as well not sugar-coat it. If Brandon made it out of this assignment alive, his career would be over.

But to get an ass-chewing he would have to survive. To survive he would need to call for help. Brandon clicked the dials on the dead radio.

In the cloudless sky he searched for some hint of the C-130 he knew was gone. Once the Hueys were within range of New York's organic comms, the C-130, no longer necessary for radio retransmission, would have departed its orbit. Not that it would matter much. Even if the C-130 *was* orbiting, New York didn't have a working radio.

Brandon chewed his thumbnail while waves of options crashed in his mind.

The C-130 would return to its orbit in six hours. And New York couldn't stay here. But they would have to sit somewhere close to here until nightfall. Until the C-130 came back. Then they'd have to come up with some alternate signaling method. They had signaling mirrors, but they would need sunlight. They had flares, but the NVA were coming.

The once-black smoke rising from the Hueys trailed

gray and dying into the sky.
What then? Move south? East? West? North?

It was all hostile territory. Walking north into China was probably the worst idea. They'd most likely be captured by the Chinese military. And New York had no way of identifying themselves as Americans. Not that it would do any good. The Russians and the Chinese supplied the NVA with most of their weaponry. New York would probably be turned over to China's NVA friends and executed. Tortured if they were unlucky enough. There was still a bounty on Recon heads. Christ, New York was barely capable of walking, let alone out-running an enemy element if they made contact.

In Laos, when New York broke contact with the NVA, Brandon's legs had cramped and his lungs had burned during that run through the jungle. In his condition now, barely able to walk, with Chris wounded, if New York ran up against even a platoon-sized enemy element they would be in deep shit.

That's assuming they didn't run into John first. And Brandon had that cold feeling that they would absolutely run into John again.

If only there was a place John couldn't get at them. A place he wouldn't go. *Couldn't* go.

Brandon chuckled in despair. If there was any truth to what New York and the other teams said about John, then there was no place safe on the planet. No place John wouldn't go. Was Conway's man the same way when he went after—

Brandon turned and looked across the river. At the hidden dock and the secluded path. He looked up to the dark spire.

Maybe it was the height of the mountain, or even the relative safety of the cave, but somehow, despite what happened to Conway, being imprisoned like that, something about the top of that mountain felt…

Safe.

Metal clunked on the ground below him. Jaran. She had dropped two dark green ammo cans on the ground next to the M60. Her palms covered in black soot. The M60's barrel, flame-licked black, had gray hand prints from where she had handled it.

"Hey," Brandon said. "Jaran."

She looked up at him, squinting in the hard sun.

He pointed to the men at the helicopter. "Get Chris for me, will ya?" She looked at him with her head dog-cocked.

"Chris." He held out thumb and finger like a gun and said, "Bang". Brandon grabbed his shoulder. "Chris."

Her face lit up with recognition. "Kah ris?"

"Yeah, Chris," and he put his hands to his mouth and mock-yelled the name and then pointed down to the ground.

She nodded and trotted off towards the wreckage.

She seemed eager to help the team despite the way Brandon had treated her. If she had put a gun to Brandon's head, threatened to throw him off a cliff, would he be so eager to hang around and help? Or would he look for every opportunity to escape? And now that her grandmother was dead, what was keeping her from vanishing into the jungle?

She had to know this terrain better than any of these men. There was no way she had maps similar to the sophisticated ones New York carried, but it was doubtful she even needed them. If she grew up here, she would know her way around. If he could only communicate with her she might be able to guide them out of here. Help get them somewhere safe.

Jaran walked over with Chris in tow, his wounded arm in a sling, rifle slung across his back. Greasy black chunks covered his hands and ran down the front of his uniform.

She gestured with both hands, presenting the man. "Kah ris," she said.

Chris spat a wad of brown tobacco juice at his feet.

"Thank you," Brandon said to Jaran. He waved her off.

"You can go now."

But she stood there looking up at him.

Brandon shrugged. "Okay. Stick around." He placed a hand on the radio and looked at Chris. "What are the chances you can get this seventy-seven working again?"

Chris squinted in the sun. Eyed the radio from ground. Chewed his tobacco. Spat. "Snowball's chance in Nam."

"Why's that?"

"They're pretty tough. You can drop 'em off a cliff or set 'em under water for an hour or two and they'll work just fine." Chris picked imaginary berries from the air and tossed them. "When you take their insides and put 'em on the outside, like what that claymore did, they don't work too good after that."

"What do you need to reestablish comms with the air support?"

"A new radio."

Brandon's face tightened. "You're not helping."

Chris rubbed at the sling around his neck. "I'll pull the prick twenty-fives out of the Hueys and see if they work. I didn't see any battery packs. 'Course the crew probably didn't see the need to bring any since the radios are vehicle mounted. But the seventy-seven's battery pack is interchangeable with the twenty-five's. If they survived the fire and the explosions, I should be able to get at least one of them running. How's that seventy-seven's antenna look?"

Brandon held up the shredded ten-foot whip antenna.

Chris spat and shook his head. "Looks like a fuckin' lawn mower ran it over. I'll talk to Smith. Maybe he brought the three-footer with him."

"Comms is priority," Brandon said. "The retrans window opens up around sundown. How's the salvage going?"

"Almost done." Chris looked down at his filthy boots and adjusted his arm in the sling. "The dead are buried. Terry is taking it easy. He's burned pretty bad. He doesn't have any extra holes or nothin'. He can walk, but it hurts him some." Chris chuckled then. Shook his head.

"What's funny?" Brandon asked.

"We found Boing. He's alive." He laughed. It was an odd sound after everything that had just happened. "We found him sleeping on the stretcher in the jungle. Slept right through everything."

A quick bump of adrenaline hit Brandon's heart. He willed his face into dead calm. That solved the problem of communication with Jaran. He looked at the helicopters. George and Mike bore a litter between them. And on it, Boing. Brandon would need to talk with Boing when the morphine wore off. Get out in front of anything Boing might say…

"Should probably keep him sedated," Brandon said. "Until we can radio for another extraction."

"Probably a good idea. I'll see what Mike says."

Voice shaky, Brandon said, "I'm still the commander. Mike will do what I say. I…" Brandon cleared his throat. "I refuse to lose another man on this operation. Keep him sedated."

Chris watched him. Brandon breathed heavy, tried to disguise it by wiping sweat from his brow.

"I'll tell Mike you want to keep him under," Chris said. "Adding to our growing list of problems, John's rucksack is missing. He had our radio. We've accounted for all the other rucks. Howard's spare twenty-five is missing."

"Where did it go?"

"I think John took it with him."

"You do?"

"Yeah, I do."

"If you can get the other radios working," Brandon said. "Then what's the problem? Who is John going to talk to?"

"Who he's talking to ain't the problem. It's who's *listening*. Seventy-sevens are encrypted and harder to triangulate. Twenty-fives, well, I'm sure you remember your first date with us in Laos."

Brandon's guts went cold. "What's the range on John's radio?"

"I know he's got a ten-footer, so about twenty miles. Give or take. Depending on how high up he gets. Mountains and hills interfere some." Chris gestured around. "We've got plenty of those."

Brandon glanced across the river. "Would John deliberately try to call Counter Recon?"

Chris sighed and looked back over his shoulder. Toward the smoldering wreckage. He looked at it for a long time. "I don't know what's wrong with John. I don't know any other way of putting it, but he loved this team. Loved the men on it. For him all the sudden to start killing us…" Chris rubbed his eyes with his palm. "I've been having a hard time believing that he wants us dead. But he does. All of us. That old lady slowed him down, but she ain't stopped him. If something's stopping him from hitting us directly, sooner or later he's gonna find a way to hit us indirectly. Take us apart. One by one."

Chris looked off toward the tree line, the way John had retreated. He spat tobacco juice. Wiped brown dribble from his chin. "John's a whole different kind of mean than what you're used to, Cap. You need to stop thinking in terms of 'what if he tries' and start preparing for 'when he tries'. Don't waste time thinking about *if* he'll try something. Because he will. He'll try everything. You should spend your time thinking about how far away the Counter Recon teams are and how we're going to put as much distance between us and them as we can. If I had to bet, I'd say they're already on their way." Chris looked up at him. "And we're burnin' lots of daylight."

Brandon looked south along the river. North. Looked at the jungle beyond the Huey wreckage. Tensed his muscles to fight off the cold jitters. His eyes kept returning to the dock on the far side of the river. To the mountaintop and that jagged escarpment. If New York couldn't run, they could sure as hell hide.

He looked down at Chris. "Help me off of this thing."

Chris grinned. "Figured that'd get you movin'. Where we going?"

CHAPTER TWENTY-ONE

Brandon pointed to the docks. "Round up the men. Tell them to get whatever gear they can carry and get to the boats." He looked up the spire. "There's a cave up there. It's hidden. Easily defendable."

Chris picked up the radio. He and Jaran followed Brandon as he limped toward the village docks.

"Bad idea to put our backs to the wall," Chris said. "Especially against John."

"Where else can we go?" Brandon asked. "Look at me. I can't even stand up straight. We're in no shape to run. If you know somewhere safer that we can get to faster, tell me. Until you come up with a better idea, we go to the cave."

Chris pulled Brandon's shoulder to stop him and his back spasmed. Brandon jerked and clenched his fists.

Chris asked, "Why are you so sure we'll be safe there?"

"I..."

Why *was* he so sure? The things he had seen in that pit, what made him think of safety? It wasn't something he could explain. It was the sounds, maybe. The sounds of life on the far shore. A *feeling*. "Just meet me at the boats."

Brandon left them behind and walked crookedly down to the docks.

Chris ran off and rallied the team and they picked up their packs and weapons. Terry and Dan carried Boing on the litter. A short time later, the team met Brandon at the docks. They loaded the salvaged gear as evenly as they could among the boats. There were six boats, and they took them all. Leaving none for John or anyone else to follow them. Loaded with personnel and gear, the boats sank low in the water, gunwales barely above the waterline. Up and down the river, echoes of the engines pushing their cumbersome loads. Brandon squinted against the noise. The engines' din like pins in his brain after the complete silence of the village.

Their crossing was slow. In each boat the men fanned out their rifles, aimed at distant jungle shadows. Aimed back at the shoreline they left behind. No one saying out loud that they were looking out for John.

Brandon looked back. If John was watching, if he saw where they landed the boats, he would have a pretty easy time finding the path up the mountain. But the bastard would need a boat. The river was wide and the current was strong. John was wounded in the gut. Not even John was strong enough to swim that long and that far.

It was a morbid hope to cling to, but without serious medical attention John would be dying slow. If New York could wait him out, if they could hide long enough, the problem would solve itself. They'd be safe.

But the look in Jaran's eyes burned away his sureness. Seated at the prow in the boat beside Brandon's, she stared back at the village. Never once on that crossing did she turn to look ahead. To where they were going. Brandon wanted to believe she was thinking about her home. Grieving for her lost family and friends. But the expression on her face, the darkness in her eyes, there was no sadness there. No grief. Brandon had seen that look in her eyes before. And he had seen it in John's eyes. In Captain

Goode's eyes.

Hate.

In her young eyes, the need for violence burned. She was planning something. Maybe what she would do to John. Savoring the bloody images of his annihilation. But, and the thought did not sit well with him; if Jaran was planning vengeance, then she also anticipated meeting John again. A tiny spray of river water spritzed Brandon's neck and, despite the heat, he shivered.

No one spoke as they crossed. Even Chris was silent. The oppressive weight of isolation pressed on Brandon. He'd never felt this before: trapped. Everyone's face was grim, but none of them gave voice to what they all felt. No one acknowledged it. In Laos, when everything had gone to hell, at least they had radios. With radios they had an umbilical to the world. Contact with friendly forces helped them *feel* safe. Reassured them. If Chris could get the twenty-fives working—

Brandon shook his head.

Not if. Chris will get the radios working.

He will.

They reached the opposite shore and the team filed out. Dan and Brandon took a knee on the riverbank and pulled security as the rest of the team downloaded gear. It felt odd when Brandon did his mental headcounts. Felt odd to be missing two. It felt odd to hold Howard's rifle. To look at the rear sight. Brandon put his fingers on the knob to adjust the windage. Played his thumbnail along the knurling. He didn't turn it.

Terry suggested they pull the boats out of the water and hide them in the jungle. If anyone came looking, all there would be left to find would be helicopter wreckage and a bunch of missing boats. It might throw off any would-be pursuers. Make them think New York went downriver. Brandon agreed and, one by one, the men hauled the boats out of the water and dragged them into the thick underbrush and covered them with torn-out elephant grass and palm fronds.

Rucksacks and gear were distributed. Mike lifted a rucksack and Jaran slipped her arms through the straps. He showed her how to cinch the straps down and instructed her to lean forward when she walked up the hill. Smith carried his destroyed radio in his pack. On top he secured the M60.

Chris had pulled two PRC-25 radios from the Huey wreckage. He carried one in his pack and strapped the other at the foot of Boing's litter.

Dan and George carried the litter.

"It's a long climb," Brandon said. "Took us about an hour without gear."

"Then we probably shouldn't stand around," Chris said. "I'll take point."

Brandon informed him of the hazards in the path, told him to watch his ankles on the boulders. Chris nodded and set off up the worn dirt path. Brandon fell in beside Dan and George, hoping that if Boing woke, he'd hear anything Boing might say. And interject if need be.

Putting on the ruck was the most difficult part for Brandon. It hurt to swing the pack up onto his shoulders, but once it was on and cinched down, once he bent over at the waist most of the pain abated.

The climb turned out to be hard on everyone. More so for the litter-bearers, carrying packs *and* a wounded man. Chris halted them frequently for breathers. They stretched aching legs. Sipped cautiously at their canteens. A little over three hours later, legs cramped, clothing sweat-drenched, New York reached the rope bridge. In the open air there was a breeze and each of them took a few moments to savor the coolness.

Dan and George took a long rest. Then they lashed Boing to the litter and hefted him. Mike went ahead of them to steady the swaying bridge, pressing the ropes out wide with his cannon-like arms, and they carried Boing across the sun-grayed planks.

When Brandon reached the other side he found Chris observing the cave.

"This the place?" Chris asked.

"Yeah," Brandon said. "Probably best you guys don't go too far back."

"What's in there?"

"Captain Conway and an enlisted man. I think Jaran…"

Jaran knelt over Boing, helped Mike undo the lashings.

"I mean, I think Conway and the other guy made their last stand here. I was going to tell you, but—"

"You mark the grid?" Chris stared into the cave. His face hard.

"I did."

Chris nodded. "Then we'll pick them up when we come back for the others. There a back door to this place?"

"This is the only way in or out."

Chris paced the width of the opening, glanced back to the rope bridge. "We'll put the sixty here. Pile the rucks around it for some cover. I'll rig the bridge's anchor points with some det cord just in case."

"Any claymores left?"

Chris's eyes narrowed. "No."

Brandon never said another word about claymores.

Brandon stooped to pick up the M60. Winced and groaned at a spasm in his back. "I'll get the fighting position ready. You work on the radios. I need working comms when the retrans window opens."

Chris went over to his ruck and took out the radio. "Won't take long to set them up. I won't know if they're working until there's somebody to talk to. There's only one working battery pack."

He'll get it working. He will.

Brandon extended the M60's bipods and placed it where Chris had indicated in the cave opening. Aimed it at the rope bridge. He stacked the belt ammo-cans next to it. He dragged the rucks, one by one, and laid them around the machinegun like sandbags. Digging a foxhole would be ideal, but all around was solid rock with only a dusting of sand and gravel. It'd take a week to dig a suitable fighting position. But with any luck, they would get ahold of the C-130 and New York would only have to stick it out for a few more hours.

Aside from Chris, everyone retreated into the cool shadow of the cave to wait. Brandon found a place amongst them and sat against the rock wall. Let the cool stone draw the heat from his aching back.

Smith sat behind the M60. Away from the group. Knees raised and rifle draped across his lap. Eyes and face hidden in deep shadows contrasted harshly against the bright platinum sky beyond the opening. Maybe he was watching Brandon. Maybe he was sleeping.

Mike dug through the packs and came down the passage with C-rations. He said they all should get something to eat while they had the time to spare. He held one out for Smith, but Smith refused.

"Suit yourself," Mike said.

Mouths chewed slow beneath dark and distant eyes. Savored every bite as if it were their last meal. Maybe it would be. Another morbid thought. No one spoke. No one traded cheese for peanut butter. No one offered fruit cocktail. Maybe they were just too busy thinking. Or too busy remembering. Or too busy trying not to remember. Maybe they just wanted to focus on the food in their mouths. Just let their bodies run through the survival mechanics of chewing and swallowing and inserting another spoonful of something into their mouths while their minds were far away. Anywhere but there. An hour passed as the quiet clink of plastic spoons in tin cans echoed through the cave.

Dan was the first person to get up. He collected his empty tins, put them aside and took up his rifle and walked out into the light. He crossed the rope bridge and disappeared down the path. Brandon watched him go.

"LP-OP," Mike said around his spoon.

"What?" Brandon asked.

"Listening and observation post," Mike said. "Dan will let us know if anyone comes up the path."

Brandon looked at the bridge. Then back to Mike. "The bridge is rigged to blow."

Mike stared down at his food in the small tin can. Picked at it. "He knows."

Brandon stared at the bridge for a long time. "It's rigged to blow."

But no one responded.

The empty bridge swayed. The shadows of the chest-high anchor-points bled across the rock. Two useless sundials. Two gnomons casting shadows in search of hour-lines that would never exist. Brandon might have slept. It was hard to tell. If he did, he did not dream. When those shadows had grown long, Brandon stood. Pounded the numbness from his ass and thighs with his fist. He slung his rifle and stepped out of the cave and found Chris sitting with a PRC-25 between his legs.

"Need help with anything?" Brandon asked.

Chris watched the reddening sky. "No."

Brandon waited for Chris to say more. Frustration buzzed louder in him with each passing moment. "Can you tell me what you've accomplished, then?"

Chris leaned his head against mossy stone. "I took the seventy-seven's battery pack, antenna, and handset and I stuck them on the twenty-five. Told you it wouldn't take long."

"Okay," Brandon said. "Anything else? Have you tested the radio?"

"No."

"Why the hell not?"

"How am I going to test it? I told you I only have one battery. The radio turns on. It has power. But I need to wait for the plane if I want to talk to someone."

Brandon checked his watch.

Smith came out and stood beside him. Looked at the sky. "Should be about time."

"Try to raise them," Brandon said.

Chris switched on the radio and put the handset to his ear. He listened a moment and pressed the handset's transmit button.

"Anything?" Brandon asked.

"Give me a second," Chris said. He switched the radio off, then on again. The radio, typically olive drab in color, was dark with thick black grime. Wherever Chris touched, the grime wiped away to reveal the original color.

"This one's fucked," Chris said, unscrewing the antennae and unclipping the battery pack. "Get me the other one."

Chris shoved the malfunctioning radio aside and Brandon hefted the other and set it down in front of Chris.

"What's wrong with the other one?" Brandon asked.

Attaching the peripherals to the radio, Chris said, "Ain't got time to find out."

Chris twisted the power nob and listened to the handset and keyed the mic. His jaw tightened and he tossed the handset. Its coiled black cord stretched straight and snapped back, and the handset landed in the dust at Chris's feet. "Fuck."

"What's wrong?"

Chris slapped the radio. "Give me a goddamn second to think!"

Chris picked up the handset and looked in the holes for talking and listening, then turned to Smith and held up the handset. "You cover this up when we went across the river?"

"No," Smith said. "Why?"

Chris scrambled over to the peripherals bag on Smith's ruck. "Fucking remfs," he muttered. "Dumb-ass mother fuckin' remfs." He yanked a spare handset from the bag, ripped off the thick clear plastic and screwed the handset onto the radio. Switched the radio on. Keyed the handset.

Chris grinned. "There we go."

Relief flooded Brandon. "What happened?"

"Box is waterproof. Handset ain't. What's the frequency?"

Smith held out a notepad and Chris dialed it in. Above the clicking and turning of dials, a slight drone fell from the sky. Echoed softly against the escarpment. In the sky, a small gray shape appeared beyond wispy clouds. Joy pulled Brandon's lips back until he was smiling big.

Their tether to the world.

Chris keyed the mic and said, "Air America element, this is New York one-one, over."

They waited.

Chris's eyes flicked up to the barely visible aircraft. "You sure the freq is right?"

Smith checked his notepad. Checked the radio. "It's right."

Brandon asked, "You guys use a rotating frequency during your operations?"

"No." Smith held out his notepad to Chris. "Try this alternate."

Chris dialed in the alternate frequency and keyed the handset. "Air America element, this is New York one-one, over." He squinted up, his mouth open like a panting dog's. "Air America element, this is—" Chris's eyes went wide. "Uh oh."

"What?" Brandon's voice an anxious squeak.

Chris waved him off and his hands flew across the peripherals. He unscrewed the antennae and lay it aside. He picked up the handset and cranked the radio's volume knob all the way up. He put the handset to his ear. But only for an instant. Whatever he heard made his head and shoulders slump. Hopelessness shattered his stoic calm.

Brandon's heart thumped nervous. In the silence, a flat static hiss emitted from the handset. "What's wrong?"

Chris shook his head. "John has your frequencies, doesn't he?"

Smith cleared his throat. "They were in the mission packet I provided him."

"Is there a second-alternate frequency?" Chris asked. "A backup? Any frequency that you *didn't* give to John."

"No."

Chris sighed. Looked back and forth between his radios. His head hung. He nodded. He dropped the handset on the rock. "Get comfy, fellas. We're gonna be here a while."

The static hissed from the handset.

Frustration and fear rattled Brandon's chest. "Somebody fucking tell me something!"

Chris flicked a cigarette out of a pack. Lit it and took a long drag and blew out smoke as he stared out over the river valley. After a while he flicked his finger at the handset. "That static you hear, radio operators call it *noise*. The squelch on the radio normally cancels that out." Chris pointed to the antenna on the ground. "If you suspect you're being jammed, say, if you can't talk to the fuckin' thing you're looking at, a way to test for jamming is to take off the antenna and listen." He held up the handset and wiggled it. "If you don't hear anything, there's nothing interfering with the signal. If you hear static…"

"John is," Brandon said, puzzled. "John is *jamming* us? How is that even possible? He didn't bring any jamming equipment."

"Sure he did," Chris said. "He's got both our twenty-fives, remember? All he has to do is dial in our frequencies and keep the mics keyed. My guess is that he's got both radios turned on with one dialed into the primary and one dialed into the alternate." Chris shook his head. "I told you, Cap. A different kind of mean."

Brandon looked to the sky. The orbiting C-130 faded in and out of sight behind clouds.

"Try again!" Brandon demanded. Pointed his finger up. "And keep trying until you reach those motherfuckers in the sky!"

Chris screwed the tiny antenna back into place. "You're sure you didn't bring a spare ten-footer?" Chris asked Smith. "Because that would really help."

"I'm sure."

"Air America element, this is New York one-one, over."

Brandon paced back and forth between the rope bridge and the cave mouth. There had to be some solution. There *had* to be.

"Is there a way to boost the signal?" Brandon asked.

Chris, in the midst of hailing the aircraft, shook his head.

"You're sure?"

Chris jerked his head up, fury in his eyes. He beat the handset against the radio and yelled, "I'm the fucking demolitions guy, John's the fucking commo guy. If you took the time to get to know your goddamn team, you'd know that."

Heat crept up Brandon's neck. Flooded his face. He chewed his cheek, unable to give voice to the thoughts scattered about by the hurricane in his head.

Chris squeezed his eyes shut. Gripped the handset so hard his hand shook. Quietly, he said, "Listen. Everything I know about the radios I learned from John. Every trick I know, John knows the counter."

Mike appeared beside Brandon. He must've heard the shouting. He said, "We're all cross-trained in each other's skillsets, but each of us is only an expert in our own field. I can tell you that Chris is doing all he can. He's doing everything *I'd* be doing. But in the communications area, John's the expert."

"And Howard was the other expert," Chris said quietly to the radio.

Mike leaned in close and put a big hand on Brandon's shoulder. He kept his voice low. "You're doing fine, sir. We're all problem solvers here. They wouldn't assign you to SOG if you couldn't get yourself out of a jam. We all just need to think of another way outta here."

What fucking problems have any of you solved?

Brandon's staring eyes drifted to Smith. Then up to the sky. To the aircraft directly overhead. This high up on the mountain it seemed close enough to scream at and be heard. The C-130 arced in its continuing orbit. A radio operator was up there, probably hailing the SOG element on the ground. Receiving nothing. Waiting for a radio call that would not come. Each negative response influencing the pilot's decision to abort the mission and go home.

The sound of its engines faded amidst the pounding blood in Brandon's ears.

Think of another way out of here? There is no other way.

He stared at the aircraft.

That! That is our way out of here.

In about an hour that plane would disappear. Forever. The pilots would report that they couldn't raise the New York element and that would be it.

No one comes for a Mercury team.

Brandon shut his eyes against the dizziness attacking him. Swallowed against the stinging throb in his throat.

They think we're dead. Nobody will come back for us.

Brandon looked down at his chest. At the sterile uniform. Nobody would even come back for the bodies. There'd be no need. The government would simply disavow knowledge of New York and they'd be listed as Missing in Action. Forgotten.

Colonel Murphy said his men were not expendable.

Brandon's mind trembled. He fought to keep it from tearing itself apart. Colonel Murphy's voice kept replaying. *My men aren't expendable, my men aren't expendable, mymenarentexpendablemymenarentexpendable.* Brandon jammed his palms in his eyes.

What the fuck do you call this, you son of a bitch? You sent us here to fucking die.

"It's alright," Mike said. "We'll find a way out."

Brandon reached into his cargo pocket on his leg and

yanked out the map John had given him. Flapped it until it unfolded. Shoved the map in Mike's face. "What don't you fucking understand? The only way in or out of this shithole is by aircraft." The map showed pencil markings that snaked along broken paths. "Or do you expect us to just stroll down the Ho Chi Minh Trail to get home?"

Mike's eyes focused on the map.

Chris looked up from the radio. "Say again?"

Brandon turned to look at him, and when he did, Mike snatched the map out of his hands.

Mike turned the map over. "Is this one of John's maps?"

"Who cares whose map it is?" Brandon shouted.

"Holy shit," Mike said. He ignored Brandon and hurried over to Chris and knelt down and held out the map. "It *is* one of John's maps."

Chris leaned over the radio and traced a finger down the map. "Oh, Cap." Chris looked up at Brandon. "I think you just saved our asses."

Brandon stared at the two men, body shaking. "Are you out of your minds? We go anywhere near there and we're dead."

"No shit," Mike said. "But now we know the areas to avoid. Don't get me wrong, it's fucking crazy, but we might be able to skirt the known parts of the trail until we get near a friendly AOR."

Chris clicked off the radio's power knob. "And when we're in range, we radio for extraction."

"Exactly," Mike said. "How many days march you think we'll need to get within radio range?"

"Mmmm," Chris said, traced a finger. "It's a long way cross-country. I'd say, eight? Maybe ten carrying wounded."

"I'm thinking about the same." Mike looked up at Brandon, eyes bright and eager. "This is our way home."

Brandon couldn't shut out the sounds of hundreds of NVA boots marching through dark. Vietnamese voices shouting. His heart blasting in his chest. Claymores. Gunfire.

No.

Not again.

"We have boats," Brandon said. "We'll take them down-river. We can get home that way just as easy."

"Smith," Chris said. "Let me see your map."

Smith pulled it out and handed it down.

Chris and Mike looked down at it. Traced their fingers on it. They looked at each other and back to Brandon. Chris said, "This river runs through Hanoi. You might have heard about that place in a briefing or two."

Brandon said, "Then we go as far south as we can before we reach the city—"

"No good," Smith said. "If we start walking anywhere near that city, we're going to run into enemy elements so big you'd need a battalion of men to even stand a chance. Not to mention the civilians sympathetic to the North. Your men have the right idea. We skirt the trail."

Brandon looked at them. Dumfounded that any one of them would suggest something so utterly insane. "You're all fucking crazy."

Chris shrugged. "Yeah, but when they write the book about us, they'll call us something like 'unconventional'."

I'm going to die here.

I'm going to die for absolutely no reason in some piece of jungle that nobody in the world gives a shit about.

I'm—

All the tension suddenly flushed from Brandon's body. Did his mind just break? Was that what that feeling was? His body weak and liquid. Was this hopelessness? Did it feel like this? Despair? It was all too much, that was it. His mind had simply been exposed to too much stress and it had broken into pieces. He didn't have enough emotion left to be scared.

"I'm—" Brandon stuttered. "I'm—" And he stumbled toward Chris and Mike and lowered himself painfully to the ground. "I need a minute." He leaned back against the escarpment. "Please," he said to the men. Lungs barely able to drive air across his vocal cords. "Just give me a minute."

The men watched him a moment. Then, without a word, they left him to sit.

Brandon looked out over the cliff. Into the descending twilight. Beyond the river, past the barely identifiable shapes of the huts, the mass of dense green jungle rose and fell and rolled on hidden saddles and draws. As he stared, in that moment, it revealed itself to him. He saw it. The absolute immensity of the land. The impossibility of walking through it. Over it. Through that unforgiving and unrelenting mass. Escaping the things that lurked within. Just the thought of taking the first step into that big dark amplified the ache in his legs and the throb in his back.

He sat there. The brush-stroked clouds went by. Brandon just wanted to go to sleep. To slip into a warm dream and never wake. He fingered the 1911 on his hip.

Eight days, maybe ten.

Brandon's belly ached with hopelessness.

"Fucking impossible," he muttered.

The sun slipped behind bulging gray clouds. Their black shadows moved across the valley. The quiet sky flared in blurry reds and oranges. Tiny drops spattered the rock between Brandon's legs. The radio hissed with static. Beneath the hiss of it, some deep thumping. Caused by he didn't know what. Almost sounded like a heart.

They couldn't make it. He wiped his eyes with his wrist. They couldn't make it. He inhaled deep. His breath shuddered. Brandon could die today. His own way. He had the perfect tool for it holstered on his hip. He was in the perfect situation for it. Just open his mouth and with a quick jerk of his finger this nightmare would be over. The river far below was smooth like red glass. Like the blood pouring from his nose and ears. Like the spatter of his brains on the escarpment. A quick jerk and he could sleep.

Jaran stepped out of the cave with only the sound of soft boots on stone. She looked around at the men standing there. Her eyes squinted with queer suspicion. A cool breeze blew at her hair and she hugged herself against the chill. Her eyes settled on Brandon.

Brandon watched her.

And she watched him for a long time. Her eyes slowly widened as if she realized something and she turned away to gaze out over the valley. She bowed her head. Her lips moved silently.

Just a quick jerk of his finger and—

Something brightened inside him. Some little light chased away the darkness. It...*tickled*. He nearly chuckled.

He commanded a team of Green Berets. Trained killers. Experts in survival. He was surrounded by these men and he was giving up hope? No. He had not given up hope. Hope had abandoned *him*. So what was left for him to cling to?

He watched Jaran.

When they crossed the river, she had stared back at her home. How odd. She had seemed so scared before. And there she stood. What could she possibly be hoping for? With everything taken from her? Her family. Her home. What was left for her to hope for?

But that look in her eyes as they had crossed the river. As she watched her village recede, Brandon didn't get the feeling that she was hoping for anything. It seemed that she had accepted what happened to her. It seemed that all she wanted was revenge. Seemed almost eager to chase it. Seemed like she would go after John alone if she had to. Maybe, like Brandon, she had used up all her fear. Maybe the only thing keeping her standing was hate.

Maybe hope wasn't the only thing that could keep you going.

Whoever attacked Jaran's village, whoever slaughtered those people, Jaran had defied them. She had survived. She had spited them.

Brandon could choose to die today. Or he could spite the people who sent him here the only way he could. He could survive.

But he would survive *his* way. He wasn't going to throw his life away. If Chris and Mike thought they'd be using the NVA's superhighway to walk out of this, they were mistaken.

Brandon was the commander. They'd do things his way. They'd use the boats and that was that. They would cut days off their journey and Brandon, *Brandon* would be the savior of this operation. They could take their Saint Nicholas bullshit and shove it. If Chris wanted unconventional, Brandon would give him unconventional.

He imagined drifting down the river, a patrol of American gun boats stopping them. Questioning them. Imagined the look on the crew's faces when they realized they had just rescued a secret commando team. Brandon smiled at that.

It would work. Brandon would make it work. He looked at the men gathered by the mouth of the cave. Those men. Those men who would be left for dead, Brandon would drag them out of this Hell kicking and screaming.

He searched the sky for the aircraft. It was gone. It had abandoned them. Fine. He was getting used to the feeling. Picking up the radio handset, Brandon keyed the mic.

"Air America," Brandon said. "This is New York one-zero. Sorry to see you go. We'll be fine on our own. See you soon. Out."

He let the handset dangle from his hand. Then a click. Then a hiss of static came from the handset. And then Brandon heard it.

A voice! His heart slammed with fierce joy. Someone was there!

Brandon put the handset to his ear and keyed the mic. "This is New York one-zero, say again, over!"

The other men, their heads jerked up. They rushed

over. Gathered around. Eyes bright with surprise.

The voice in the handset, it said, like from somewhere far away, it said… it said something like, "This is… da… one-zero… at… tain…"

So much static. What was he saying?

Brandon said into the mic. "Say again, over!"

And something came through. A clicking sound. A click-click-click like Morse code. But…

No. Not Morse code.

Some primal, some terrible fear screamed from somewhere deep inside Brandon. It wasn't Morse code.

It was laughter.

And then, crystal clear, a deep baritone voice from the handset said, "This is Florida one-zero. I say again. You're going to die on that mountain."

Florida one-zero.

Brandon's eyes darted to the cave.

Conway.

Impossible.

Brandon stared at the handset. The speaker holes staring back at him like tiny eyes.

"Put the gun in your mouth, Brandon," Conway said from the speaker holes. "Before he comes. It's hot here. So hot. The girl can't protect you forever."

Brandon shot his eyes to Jaran. Her eyes clenched shut. Head shaking. Mouth drooling. Forming words impossibly fast.

"He's coming, Brandon," Conway's little voice said. "He'll get you—"

Brandon threw the handset. It clattered on the stone and whipped back at him like a striking viper. He scrambled to his feet, pushed himself up against the rock. Tried to get as far away from the voice as he could.

The others stood around the radio. Stared at it. The sun retreated below the hills. Abandoned them. In the growing dark there was only the sound from the radio. The sound of a dead man's laughter.

Eric Leland

CHAPTER TWENTY-TWO

Brandon watched the handset there on the ground. Silent.

Jaran grunted and staggered to the escarpment and leaned against the rock. Wiping sweat from her face as she slid to the ground.

The girl can't protect you forever.

What did that mean? What had she done?

The men watching Brandon, they whispered questions to him.

"It's…" Brandon said. But he couldn't say the word. The name. Couldn't say it because he didn't believe it. He couldn't make himself say there was a dead man talking to him.

"Was it John?" Smith asked. "What did he say?"

No, not John. Conway.

Wait. John. Yes, of course. Some trick. John was fucking with him. Of course he was.

Brandon tore his eyes from the handset. "It must've been John. He told me…"

Put the gun in your mouth.

"He didn't…" Brandon stammered. "He's laughing at us. That's all."

Chris knelt down next to the radio. His hand went to a switch. He looked up at Brandon, confused. "Radio's off. It's *been* off. You couldn't have been talking to anyone."

"What?" Brandon said. "No, I heard him."

Chris squinted at him.

Frustrated, Brandon said, "Then I must've turned it off. Just now."

"No," Chris said. "*I* turned it off. It was off when—"

"Who cares who turned it off?" Smith said. "Try and get John to talk."

Brandon stared at the radio. "What?"

"Talk to him. Try and raise him. You might be able to get him to let something slip. We can figure out where he is or determine if he knows where we are."

"No," Chris said, and laid a protective hand over the radio dials. "Keep it off. The longer we talk, the easier it is for us to get pinpointed. Trying to hail the plane, that was worth the risk. But this…" Chris gestured at the radio. "Trying to get John to talk, that's just stupid. He's too smart to give you anything. He'll keep giving you misinformation and keep you asking questions until Counter Recon shows up at the bridge."

Dark clouds reached up over the mountains and strangled out the fading sunlight. Washed the escarpment in pink and rose shadows. Brandon picked up the handset, thumb hovering over the black rubber transmit button. He thought about what he had heard. What he thought he had heard.

The radio's off…

Impossible. Brandon *had* seen Chris click the radio off. He remembered seeing that. Brandon couldn't have been talking to anyone. And Conway… Brandon ran his hand through his hair. Christ, Conway was dead. Brandon had killed him.

Trauma. Mental and physical trauma. Stress. That had to be the answer. Infantry guys told stories all the time about being on patrol and halting for the night. Then on guard shift, standing in the dark, so tired, they'd talk to their friend, hold entire conversations. Then someone would grab their shoulder. And they'd realize they were talking to a tree. Realize the friend they were talking to had been dead for a week. Body already sent back to the world in a flag-covered box.

Trauma. That's all it was. Brandon's wires were crossed for a moment. That was all…

But he had heard Conway. Heard him so clear.

So had those Infantry guys…

The radio was still turned off. Brandon held the handset to his ear. Pressed the transmit button. "What do you want, John?"

He waited.

The men watched him.

Nothing.

Brandon breathed out. Just like he thought. Impossible. "Turn it on, Chris."

Chris didn't move.

"Turn it on."

Chris shook his head. "You'll kill us."

Brandon stared at him.

Chris sighed. He clicked on the radio and stood and crossed his arm over his chest. "There. It's your fucking funeral." Then he slapped his forehead. "No, wait," and his eyes popped open in mock epiphany. "It's *my* funeral!"

Brandon pressed the button. Into the mic he said, "What do you want, John?"

There was no answer. The men looked on. Eyes, dark and serious, they stared from beneath concerned brows. All of them knowing each time Brandon pressed that button a little blip was lighting up on NVA commo equipment. Whatever Brandon was going to say, he had to say it fast. Then New York would have to move.

They waited in the silence.

A long time passed.

"See?" Chris said. "He's baiting you. He wants you to

keep talking. I told you—"

Brandon keyed the mic. "You killed a lot of people, John. You killed Howard. He was your friend." Brandon released the button and listened. He didn't know what else to say. What did you say to the man trying to kill you?

Silence lingered. Heavy and dead. Maybe Chris was right. Maybe this was too dangerous. John wasn't going to talk. Brandon reached out to turn the radio off but a crackle came from the handset.

"Friend?" The voice was distinctly John's. But it was distorted with static and a growling contempt. *"Friend? Howard let that fucking cripple sneak up on me. Howard was supposed to have my back. Look what he did to me. Look what his stupidity caused. Howard was worthless. He deserved to die."*

Mike's jaw dropped open.

Chris squeezed his eyes shut.

"But you know all about being stupid, Brandon," John said. "Who got Phil killed? Don't waste any more time thinking about sucking off that pistol. Get on with it. You're just as worthless as Howard. You deserve to die. *It should've been you...*"

Brandon recoiled from the handset. Cold sweat oozed from his palm around the black plastic. That last bit, it wasn't John's voice. It was Captain Goode's.

No.

Brandon shook his head.

Get your shit together.

Clearly, as if John stood right behind Brandon and whispered into his ear, John said, "Let's get on with this. I need to move on. Kill the others up there with you. Kill them all. Start with the faggot. Chris. He disgusts me."

Brandon looked up at Chris. Face calm, he made no indication that he had heard anything. He must have had a strong resolve to not even flinch when a friend—*former friend*—said something like that.

John's voice came again. "If you won't do it, then bring

them down off the mountain. I'll do it for you. I'm waiting down here for you."

"Bullshit," Brandon said into the mic. "You couldn't have swam that river."

"Shut up," Chris said.

"Fuck him," Brandon said. "He's bluffing. He doesn't know—"

Chris grabbed Brandon's shirt. "Shut *up*!" Yanked him close. Even with one arm he tossed Brandon around like he weighed nothing. "Shut your fuckin' mouth! You're giving him information! You just confirmed where we went!"

The realization of what Brandon had just done chilled him.

Chris shook his head and weakly pushed Brandon away. "God damnit, Brandon." He rubbed his temples with thumb and middle finger. "I told you John knows what he's doing."

Brandon dropped the handset clattering to the ground. This was bad. Chris had warned him and he'd walked right into John's trap. Talking to John was useless. Worse than useless. John wasn't going to give up any information.

All that time planning how to hide from John and Brandon had just thrown it all away. Brandon swallowed against the dry fear in his throat. John knew where they went. Brandon had to fix this. The men, elite or not, weren't ready for another fight. Not yet.

Bring them down off the mountain...

Bradon looked out at the countryside. Across the valley. It was *all* mountains here. New York just happened to be standing on the biggest one. John could have been guessing. Bracketing. Guessing wide and narrowing New York's location down with the information Brandon had so carelessly provided. Brandon nodded. John was guessing. He didn't know where they went. Not exactly.

The handset hissed with static. Brandon picked it up and keyed it. "We already came down, John. We loaded up in the boats and we're heading downriver. We'll be out of radio range soon. We'll leave you to deal with Counter Recon. Good luck."

Chris dropped his face in his hand. "If he doesn't buy that, try telling him we fixed the Hueys and flew away."

Thunder growled in the sky and in a few moments a light rain pattered the smooth rock. It didn't take long before the rock became slick underfoot.

John was silent a long time and Brandon wondered if he had believed Brandon's lie. Wondered what trick John would try next.

A sound came. A big insect buzz. Something smacked the bare escarpment above their heads and they all looked up at the rock.

Something tiny, a pebble maybe, tumbled down and fell at Chris's feet. He picked it up and held it out. It had a dull shine to it, and as Chris turned it in his fingers a faint sound whispered to them from somewhere far away.

Chris's eyes went wide and he dropped to his belly. "Get down!"

Brandon dropped. Heart lurching with an adrenaline kick.

Smith sprawled on the rock. Mike grabbed Jaran's robes and yanked her down and he covered her with his bulk. She shoved at him. Clawed. Mike took everything she threw at him, his face passive. But when Jaran looked around, frantic, when she saw all the men pronated and covering their heads, the fight in her ceased and she watched them intently.

"How the *fuck* did he get across the river?" Terry growled.

No one answered.

Panicked thoughts blurred in Brandon's mind as the rifle report faded on the wind. He looked out over the cliff at the smaller hilltops but could see nothing to suggest where John was hiding.

The handset crackled. "Are you sure you're on the

river?" John's voice had the calm, almost bored tone of a forward observer bracketing an artillery target. Matter-of-factly walking one-oh-fives up a hill. Obliterating every living thing with a few words. John said, "Are you sure you're not the ones cowering in fear up there?" John laughed. "Terror suits you, Brandon. You've worn that same terrified expression since Laos."

Boots marched in Brandon's head and he covered his ears against the sound. But the boots just stomped louder. He shut his eyes. The images came. The stench—

"Mmmm," John cooed. "I remember it. The stench of death. But your fear is stronger. I can smell it from here. It's how I found you. It's been pouring off you since the Colonel thrust you upon me. Those men up there with you, they smell it, too. They know you're weak. They know you'll fail them. Just end this, Brandon. You know you can't command those men. When they discover just how weak you really are, they'll leave you behind. They'll leave you behind for me. And I will find you."

Brandon kept his eyes shut. Shot out his hand and clicked off the radio. The static hiss died. But John's voice still came. Clearer than before.

"You're not cut out to lead them," John said. "You're a coward. Cowards can't lead. Put that pistol in your mouth and end it."

A cool relief settled between Brandon's shoulder blades. A feeling like when a long, long drive is nearly over. When he opened his eyes, the faintest sliver of red evening light, like an opened vein, reflected off silver gunmetal. Reflected off the 1911 in his hand. Funny, he didn't remember drawing the pistol.

"*Yes!*" John whispered. "You won't make it out of here alive. I won't let you. I'll be behind you wherever you go. Even if you outrun me, Counter Recon is coming. I called them."

"Oh, Christ," Brandon whimpered. There might have been a chance against John. But not Counter Recon.

"You have no chance, Brandon. None at all. Why continue to suffer?"

Yes. Why suffer?

Brandon laid there on his belly. Took in a long breath. Breathed in the cool air. Smelled the wet rock. He put the 1911's muzzle into the fleshy pad under his chin.

Why suffer?

He thumbed off the safety.

Pain erupted in the back of Brandon's hand and his eyes shot open. Mike's giant black boot swung wide like he had kicked a field goal. The pistol flew from Brandon's hand and smacked against the escarpment and fell on the rock.

Brandon's hand throbbed. His fingers curled into a grotesque, trembling claw. The pain of Mike's kick pulled him, dragged him back from some dream. Some drunken stupor.

"What happened?" Brandon asked.

"You fucking tell me, asshole." Mike screamed at him.

"I don't know," Brandon looked at the radio. "John was talking and—"

"Nobody was talking!" Mike held up the handset. "You turned the radio off and you just laid there. You wouldn't—"

"*GET ON WITH IT!*" John howled from the handset.

Mike's mouth moved but Brandon couldn't hear him over John's screaming.

Brandon slapped his hands over his ears. "There!" Brandon screamed. "There, can't you hear him?"

"Sir!" Mike yelled. "Stop it! Stop!"

"*WORHTLESS, BRANDON! YOU'RE STUPID AND WORTHLESS!*" Conway's voice spewed from the handset.

"Conway's with him!" Brandon wailed. "He's talking, goddamnit! I hear him!"

Mike pulled Brandon to his feet. Tried to pull Brandon's hands away from his ears but Brandon fought him off. The voices were so loud.

"IT SHOULD'VE BEEN YOU!" Captain Goode screamed.

Brandon screamed and elbowed passed Mike. Kicked the radio box and it thumped over on the rock. Still the voices assaulted him.

"END IT!"

Brandon grabbed the handset and beat it against the radio's metal housing. Pounded sharp gouges into the handset's black plastic. Still John's voice came.

"Blow your—"*BANG BANG BANG* "—ucking brai—" *BANG BANG BANG* "—out!"

Brandon threw down the handset and furiously spun the knurled metal connector ring and yanked the handset's cord off the radio and threw the handset toward the bridge where it skidded to a stop on the rock.

But there was no silence. The voices, they didn't stop. They came. They came like F-4 Phantoms screaming in low, wings level, the spaces between words filled with the whirring whine of napalm canisters spinning. Thumping the ground. The *whoosh* of liquid flame. The screams....

And someone's hands were on Brandon's wrists. Pulling. But Brandon clenched every muscle and fought against the pulling. Too much sound. His ears couldn't take any more. Someone's hot breath on his face. Someone's lips moving. Their voice lost amidst the sounds of Hell.

Brandon slumped on the ground and curled up as the sound beat him into the rock. In his throat he felt air being forced out. Felt his vocal cords straining. Shaking. It was the only way he knew he was screaming.

Something small and cool combed through his hair.

Silence came like a car wreck. The complete absence of sound. Brandon jerked and rolled onto his back. Looked up. At Jaran kneeling there.

Deep laughter vomited from the handset. Spurted and coughed. And then it was lost under the soft sound of rain on skin and stone.

And with the sound came the pain. Brandon groaned and lay on the ground with a hangover weakness. The silence was almost as painful as the noise had been. No radio static. No voice. Nothing.

Brandon looked around. The men. They had retreated into the cover of the cave mouth and they watched him in the quiet. Mike leaned up against the cave, he didn't try to hide the annoyance on his face. Smith looked down his nose with doubt.

"Feeling better?" Mike asked. Words singed with sarcasm. "Do you believe me now? That nobody could have been talking to you?"

Brandon pushed himself up and leaned forward. Put his fingers in his eyes and rubbed at the forming headache. He would have admitted that nobody had been talking to him, but his ears were ringing as if he'd gone to the rifle range without hearing protection.

"What did John say to you?" Chris asked.

Mike looked at him. "Don't encourage this shit, Chris."

Chris held up his hand. "What did John say?"

"You really couldn't hear him?" Brandon asked.

Chris said softly. "I want to know what you heard."

"I heard..." Brandon stammered. "I..."

"Let me guess. It's uncomfortable to talk about?"

Brandon watched Chris. Watched his eyes. Searched for any indication that Chris might be fucking with him. There was an eager look in Chris's eyes that Brandon could only identify as belief. Or at least a willingness to believe. Had he heard something different? Something secret only to Chris?

Chris said, "You don't want to talk about it, do you?"

"No." Brandon shook his head. "I don't."

Chris nodded. He stepped out of the cave and gazed across the valley. Then he gestured to the handset. "Keep him talking."

"What?" Brandon and Mike both said.

"Keep him talking. But don't turn the radio on."

"Keep him talking?" Mike said. "Chris, nobody has been talking to begin with."

"Just do as I say."

Mike took a step back from his friend. "You wanna tell me what's going on here?"

Chris kept his eyes on the valley. Tilted his head away from the group. Away from Mike. He sighed. "When I figure out how to say it, you'll be the first to hear. For now, I'm just asking you to trust me. Just for now."

Mike watched Chris back. Then he nodded. "Fair enough."

Chris went to the ruck sacks and rummaged through one. Brandon looked on quietly. Chris looked the way Brandon felt. Beaten. Drained. Had Chris experienced something similar? Chris pulled a pair of binoculars from the rucksack. Craned his neck to look up at the spot where John's bullet had impacted the escarpment and traced a line with his eyes out over the cliff. Going prone at the edge, Chris put the binoculars to his eyes.

"Careful," Mike said.

"Uh-huh."

Keep him talking? What was Brandon supposed to say? Agree with John? Tell him that he was right? That Brandon *was* a coward? List everything he was afraid of? That was a long fucking list. He just wanted to—

"Brandon," Chris said weakly. "Please."

Brandon shoved himself to his feet and picked up the handset. The twisted rubberized cord dangled between his feet. The metal connector ring scraped the rock as it bounced. Brandon held out the handset, hesitant to bring it close to his face. The dark speaker holes like the tiny, anticipant mouths of leeches.

The radio, still turned off, sat heavy and dark and silent. In that lingering, eerie calm, Brandon could clearly see why Mike and the others had looked at him like he was crazy. There should be no way he could have talked to anyone.

Heard anyone. He saw the absurdity of it now, but he had been blinded to it before.

With everyone watching him, the thought of talking into a disconnected mic, into a turned-off radio, it made the words difficult to say. Like performing a play he hadn't rehearsed. Or some kind of confession. But instead of sitting in a dark box with only the priest to hear, he was confessing to the whole congregation. Standing front and center.

Bless me, everyone, for I have sinned.

And, standing there, just when Brandon thought he had rejoined the others in reality, in a place where dead men didn't communicate with the living via radio, just when he was on the verge of accepting the impossibility of the last hour, the sound of labored breathing bubbled from the handset.

Brandon keyed the mic. "You're right, John. I'm terrified. I'm so fucking scared that I won't take one step off this mountain. We're all tired. We're all wounded. Christ, I can barely walk. Come on up if you think you can finish us off. We only have the ammo we brought with us. We won't last long."

Brandon wasn't lying. It was an honest assessment. And with each true word a heavy sorrow pushed down a little bit harder.

The group was kind enough to look elsewhere as Brandon poured his fear into the handset. All except Jaran. She squinted at him, her hard eyes intrigued, like a kid watching a magician perform a trick a second time. Determined to watch every movement to figure it out. She stared so hard she seemed to be looking through him.

John's static-muffled voice startled Brandon. It came weak through the handset, like something interfered with the radio signal. Like it was coming from some other world. The radio was still turned off. The mic was still unplugged. So maybe it was…

"You are a coward." John said. He laughed. "Listening

to cowards beg is my greatest joy. Their wailing as they beg for their lives. The sound of their hope spilling from them. Here's what I'll do for you, Brandon. I'm going to slice you open. But don't worry, I'll sit with you. I'll keep you company while you try to shovel your guts back into your belly. Have a pair of gloves ready. The small intestine is very smooth. Blood just makes it slick. It'll slip and spill through your fingers without gloves. After a few days you'll beg for death…"

John went on. Brandon pulled the handset away from his head, but distance did nothing to keep John's voice from reaching his ears. The horror in John's whispers conjured vibrant, surreal pictures and Brandon's vision blurred and blackened at the edges. There were sounds out there, in the black. Burning sounds. The sounds of Brandon's memories, the few happy ones he possessed, distorting in flame. Perverting. Friends who had encouraged him now taunted him. Cheryl, the woman who promised to wait for him, he saw her. Heard her giggling. The sound muffled and wet with her mouth shoved down on another man's cock. Then his mother, Brandon's head on her lap after falling from his bike, her soft fingers combing through his hair. One moment telling him how much she loved him, the next, how much she resented him being born. Wondering why God had punished her with such a weak crybaby faggot for a son.

The memory of his mother curled and turned to ash and another flashed. He spoke to an Army chaplain.

"I doubt myself so much," Brandon was saying to the chaplain. "I don't think I can lead anymore. I worry I might get more men hurt."

"Worrying that you might make mistakes shows that you care, son," the battalion chaplain had said. "Men need leaders who care. Your doubt should encourage you."

And then the chaplain's face contorted in disgust. "That's what I'm *supposed* to say to you. To keep you from killing yourself. But," and the chaplain leaned in close, breath hot and rank with rotten eggs. "In your case, frankly it makes me sick to my stomach to say anything that might lift you up. *You* got those men killed. A man like you has no place among brave men. You're right to doubt yourself. Everyone else does…"

Chunks of ash flaked from the memory of the chaplain's face. The wind that carried the pieces away hissed, *it should've been you…*

Aside from the chaplain, Brandon had never spoken to anyone about his apprehension to take on another leadership position. Never said anything to Colonel Murphy or anyone else in SOG about how he felt leading New York. But John, somehow he knew. And he knew this was the place to attack. The heart of Brandon's fears. Brandon's weakness as a leader. John's whispers, like water in winter, seeped into the cracks in Brandon's heart. Seeped in and froze. Expanded. Pushed softly. Pushed until Brandon's heart splintered and chipped.

Pushed until Brandon could not lift his eyes to the team gathered on that rocky outcrop. He averted his eyes from the men. The unafraid. The confident. He stared at the cave instead.

Any possible retort that formed in Brandon's mind, any response to what John said to him was glazed with doubt. It dripped with embarrassment. Shame. These feelings churned in his belly like bait worms in a can of dirt. He wanted to shrink into the cave's darkness and curl up in the pit. In the dark. Hide there with the dead men. With Conway.

Conway…

Beneath mounds of ash a cold and forgotten rage flickered to life.

Brandon lifted the handset to his mouth. Dropped it. Emotion ballooned in his throat and choked out the words forming on his lips. Hot tears pushed behind his eyes. He squeezed them shut to hold the tears back, but stinging wetness leaked out and slid down his nose. These men couldn't see him cry.

They'll leave you behind…

Fingers, light and cool pressed the back of his hand. He looked. Through the stinging blur he saw Jaran. She knelt there in front of him. Pointed at the handset. "Erlik Khan," she said. And she put her wrists together. Yanked them apart. Then pointed at the cave. "Erlik Khan." And she put her wrists together. Yanked them apart. Again and again. She repeated it until the force of what she was telling him nearly knocked Brandon back on his heels.

The things Brandon had seen in the pit: the shackles staking Conway to the ground, the ones Jaran now mimed breaking before him…Brandon nodded slowly beneath the dawning realization. The old, desiccated corpse in the pit. The impossibly old one. It had a bullet hole through its head. The blond recon man, he had one, too.

And, like watching it on a drive-in screen, like a black-and-white monster-movie double-feature, Brandon saw the blond man sliding down the rope into the pit. Finding the gray and bone-thin corpse chained down. The fear building in the blond man the way it had built in Brandon. Reaching for his pistol the way Brandon had reached for his. If the corpse had moved the way Conway had moved…

I killed him…

I shot him…

"Erlik Khan…" Brandon croaked. The events unfolded before him.

He made me kill them…

The corpse. The blond man. Conway. The cripple.

"John," Brandon said. And he looked out over the valley.

It all made sense in the way Santa Claus made sense to a child. He goes down chimneys to deliver presents because of course he does. He lives in the North Pole because where else would he live?

Erlik Khan is hiding amongst a group of shamans, Smith had said.

No. Oh, no. Smith had it wrong. Had it all wrong.

Brandon stared through Jaran and into the cave. *Someone dug this.* In his mind he was back in the cave, slowly pushing deeper, going down into the pit. Reexamining every detail under the light of new knowledge. His mind completely focused on arranging the puzzle pieces into place as they fell from oblivion. Erlik Khan wasn't *hiding* amongst the shaman. The shaman were hiding *him*. Erlik Khan was their prisoner.

It wasn't John whispering from the other end of that radio. The rational part of Brandon's mind laughed at the absurdity of it. Pushed back hard against the fairy tale unfolding in this reality. But that same rational part had been conspicuously absent when Brandon was having a conversation with a dead man on a turned-off radio with an unplugged mic. A conversation that apparently only Brandon could hear.

Brandon leaned forward and pushed himself up onto unsteady feet. Jaran stood with him. Stood beside him. Was she a shaman then?

He put the handset to his mouth. His fear. His anxiety. Even the tears that had been dammed behind his eyes, it all evaporated in the heat of the rage flaring from the ashes of his soul.

"You are *not* John," Brandon said. "You might have his body, but you are not him." Brandon barely recognized his own voice. Neither the tone, nor the content of the words. Uttering such insanity, with such anger, he knew he sounded like a raving madman. The men must have thought the same, for in his periphery Brandon saw them turn their heads to each other. Brandon ignored them.

John ignored him as well. The disconnected handset was as dead and quiet as it should be.

But Chris wanted him to keep John talking. Fine.

"Tell me," Brandon said into the handset. "Was it the girl? Was it *this* girl who staked you down in that pit?"

No answer came. Like Brandon's rational mind, John's voice was conspicuously absent.

"Strike a nerve there?" Brandon cast his gaze over Chris and across the valley. To where John must have been watching. He said into the mic, "I'd like to hear that story. Tell me how a little shaman girl captured Erlik Khan."

Blue flashed behind the fat black clouds hovering above the valley. The sky growled.

"I see him," Chris said. "About half a klick out, right at the top of that draw. In the clearing."

The heat in Brandon's belly threatened to engulf him. The only place to vent it was into handset. He broadcasted his fury across the valley. Mouth moving too fast for his mind to adequately supply words, he caught bits here and there of recalled playground insults spewing from his mouth. He hurled them for want of something, anything to say. He kept it up, voice rising to a scream until his voice scratched and his throat dried.

Chris handed the binoculars to Mike. "Spot me." Chris brought up his CAR-15.

Mike laid down and put the binos to his eyes. "Gimmie a second. Mmm…Okay. I see him."

Smith took Jaran by the arm and guided her toward the cave, probably to keep his little asset safe. She resisted at first, stepping back toward Brandon. But Smith held up his hands and motioned gently to the cave, made finger-guns and shooting noises. Eventually Jaran went with him. As he and Jaran neared the cave mouth, Smith called to Chris, "Take him out, Sergeant. First chance you get."

"Pretty much the reason I'm pointing a gun at him." Chris slipped his wounded arm from its sling and curled his elbow around the rifle's magazine. Rolled his shoulders and hunched down behind the rifle. Put his eye to the rear sight.

"Can you hit him from here?" Mike asked.

"I'm gonna find out."

The CAR-15 had a shorter barrel than the standard M-

16 that most soldiers carried. Brandon had a hard time hitting the 300 meter targets with it during rifle qual. At this distance, the CAR-15's front sight-post would obscure John completely. A tough shot.

"Okay," Mike said. "He's in the middle of the clearing. About five-hundred meters."

The rifle's muzzle traversed beyond Chris's elbow. "Contact," Chris said.

A tough shot. But maybe Brandon could talk John into getting a bit closer…

"I've been down in that pit," Brandon said into the mic. "So I refuse to listen to any bullshit about weakness from you. You, who let a girl drag you into a hole and stake you down. Did she laugh when you pissed and shit all over yourself. Fuck, man, I would have."

BANG!

Brandon jerked. Smoke rolled out of Chris's rifle muzzle. Spinning gold brass bounced and dinged off the rock and went careening over the cliff edge. Chris lay completely still.

Lowering the handset, Brandon squinted across the valley. Hopeful he might see the target fall. But with the distance and rain and encroaching dark, John was too difficult to see with the naked eye.

A high scream erupted from the cave. Jaran, held tight in Smith's bear-hug, shoved and shook to get free. He lifted her and her feet kicked against the air.

"Miss," Mike said. "He's not moving. Come to the right about ten meters. Same distance. Reengage." Mike called over his shoulder, "Keep it up, sir. See if you can make him stand still a little longer."

Brandon stepped closer to the cliff and brought the handset to his mouth. Into it he poured every emotion he had tried to hide. Sorrow and shame and worry. With every word his chest went lighter. After a while, a wide smile tugged his face. If what he had felt only moments ago was hopelessness, then this was the feeling of hope flooding back into the vacuum.

"Here's what my report will say at the debriefing," Brandon said. "A little girl subjugated Erlik Khan. We found him covered in his own shit. Sound about right?" Brandon scoffed. "And you have the audacity to call *me* weak?"

Behind the binos, Mike said. "I have no idea what the hell you're talking about, but John looks really pissed off."

In the silence, Chris took a deep breath. His finger squeezed out the trigger's slack.

BANG!

And they all jerked. Chris had not fired a shot. The sound was a burst of thunder directly overhead. It tore open the sky and heavy rain poured and pelted the soldiers on the cliff. The fat drops stinging Brandon's skin and face.

"Reengage!" Mike yelled over the rain. "Still five-hundred meters! Bottom of the clearing!"

Chris hunched behind the rifle, muzzle going side to side, down, up, searching for his target. Searching for John. "Contact!" Chris yelled.

BANG.

The rain smacked Brandon's eyes and lips. He screamed into the handset, "You know what? You sit tight!" He pointed at the clearing across the valley. Somehow *knowing* John could see him. "FRAGO, motherfucker! We're coming off the mountain! We're coming right to you! This team up here. *My* team! They're gonna grab you up and we're going to watch this girl shove your head all the way up your—"

Lightning cracked open the sky and blasted the escarpment above. Thunder exploded. Knocked Brandon back from the cliff edge. In the flash of light, movement.

In Brandon's periphery, there was a form. A man's. But it was out beyond the cliff, in the open air. Then gone. In the next flash of light Brandon jerked upright. Looked to where he had seen the movement.

Now it was directly in front of him at the edge of the cliff. Brandon backed away from the...from the *thing*. Some *thing* in the rain. The pouring raindrops ran together. Streaked down. Curved out. And in. Dripped off sharp things where hands should be. Rivulets ran together and in the next lightning strike he saw a grimacing face. Snarling silently. Brandon went slack in numb disbelief.

It came toward him. Claws out wide.

"Get down!" Someone yelled.

A massive weight plowed Brandon and he went sprawling. Slammed down and slid on the wet rock.

George stood where Brandon had stood. In the path of that... of that *thing*.

"Fire!" George screamed. "Kill it!" And his face lit up, flickered with orange and shadow as he went full-auto.

But the thing kept coming. It turned its attention to George.

More rifle fire. The slick rock lit up white as every rifle New York had shot the thing.

In the lightning and gunfire-flashes, sharp things coalesced from the rain.

George dropped the empty mag from his rifle and it clattered on the ground. He shoved in a fresh mag and slapped the bolt catch.

"Look out!" Brandon screamed.

George aimed his rifle, but the thing was too fast. Lighting lit up sharp edges as the claws shot out and snapped closed around George's waist in a slurping *crunch*.

Lighting. And George's face strained with agony. His rifle fell and smacked the ground.

The thing's mouth opened and a thunderclap roar pounded Brandon's ears. It wrenched its hands, flung them out wide.

George's legs went tumbling over the cliff edge, his top half smacked the rock wall and fell and landed amidst New York. Lighting. Shiny wet ropes stretched out from George's torso and wiggled on the ground. He reached out to the men around him.

"Get the sixty!" someone screamed.

"Kill that fucking thing!" someone else screamed.

"Get over here, Brandon!"

"Run!"

"Medic!"

"Get the fucking sixty!"

"Covering fire!"

"*MEDIC!*"

The thing was between Brandon and the team. Thick blood and rainwater poured from its claws. New York fired. The air above Brandon cracked and ripped apart as hundreds of rounds blasted through the thing and over Brandon's head. He had to get to the team. He had to move.

The thing turned to Brandon. Mouth open. Claws out wide. Something was thumping in Brandon's mind. Maybe his heart. He couldn't tell.

The thing came. Backlit orange from muzzle flash.

A warm wetness spread in Brandon's pants. His legs cold. Unresponsive. He wanted to move. He couldn't. The dripping claws came at him.

The claws stopped short. The thing went dark. The rifle fire ceased.

But it was not silent there on the cliff. A throaty, singing chant reverberated off the rock. Beat in Brandon's mind. Thumped in his chest. Seemed to shake the entire world.

Lighting.

And he saw Jaran though the rain-made body of the thing. She stood there before the men. Fists clenched. Eyes straining hard. Hair soaked with rain. Screaming some deep mantra.

The thing's mouth opened and thunder blasted from its jaws. Its claws went to its head as if to block out the noise. Jaran didn't let up. The thing shook. Liquid teeth gnashed.

Rainwater poured from the thing's body and splashed

on the rock. Disintegrating, it came stumbling toward Brandon, howling with thunder. Brandon finally got his feet beneath him and he was about to turn and sprint for the bridge.

But a claw came.

It broke upon his chest like a wave. Hard rain pelted his face. Sprayed all around. A hot slicing in his belly. The claw snatched Brandon's shirt and it flung him, hurling him toward the cliff.

Sliding on smooth, rain-slick rock, Brandon kicked his feet and flipped onto his belly. Clawed at the rock. Men ran toward him. Mike's huge shape sprinted and launched toward Brandon. Airborne, diving with his arm stretched out. Lighting flashed. Brandon reached. *Reached.* Mike slammed the ground on his chest, arm outstretched. Hand straining open. But his fingertips just barely brushed Brandon's.

Mike scrambled toward the edge.

Brandon slid. Flailed. Fingers scraped wet, naked rock. Grabbing for purchase. Fingernails dug, bent, broke. There was nothing to grab. Feet and legs went into air. Waist. Torso. Lighting flashed. White streaks reflected on the rain-soaked jungle canopy so far beneath him. Gravity reached up and took hold of Brandon's guts and pulled.

And there was the sound of meat slapping rock. A deep grunt. Fingernails gouged skin from the back of Brandon's neck. A fist snatched Brandon's collar and he stopped with a jerk.

And screaming. Like a wild animal trying to speak. It said, "I got him!"

The BDU shirt tightened around Brandon's neck, squeezed shut his carotid arteries. Blood pounded in his head. He hung, spun slowly like a wolf pup in its mother's jaws. His periphery blackened.

Above, in rain and dim light, Mike's teeth bared in a snarl. Face contorted in agony. Lighting flashed, and the fierce determination in Mike's eyes blazed. Screams and shouts and the wailing of different voices spilled over the cliff edge.

Mike's fist wrapped in the Brandon's shirt collar shook. He rolled his head back toward the shouting. "Someone help me!"

Darkness oozed into Brandon's vision. Trapped blood pounded in his forehead. Temples and eyes throbbing. He dug his fingers into his collar, tried to relieve the pressure. Shapes moved above Mike in the creeping blackness of unconsciousness. Man-shaped shadows congealed into one black bulk. Pulled apart into different heads and bodies. Brandon reached out to them. For hands that were just beyond his reach.

Up.

More hands on him. Grabbing handfuls of Brandon's shirt and sleeves and hair. They lifted him. The pressure in his head abated. They hauled him over the edge. Dropped him gasping and trembling on the gloriously hard ground.

Throat no longer constricted, the pressure in Brandon's head bled away, but the dark and dizziness of unconsciousness lingered. Sound beyond the creeping dark. A voice screaming. Screaming a name.

"George!"

Brandon's head lolled toward the voice.

A silhouette, a man sat and rocked in the rain. Cradling half of a man in his lap. "George!" The silhouette said. "Oh, God, George!"

"Secure that fucking bridge!" Someone shouted.

"What the *fuck* was that thing?" Another voice screamed. "Chris! What the fuck *was* that?"

"I don't know! Secure the fucking bridge!"

A smaller figure lay face down on the slick rock. Long dark hair splayed out. Jaran.

Was she hurt? Had that thing gotten her? Brandon tried to go to her. Tried to sit up. An acid burn ripped through his abdomen and he collapsed on his side. Hands going to his belly, his fingers poked through the frayed fabric of his uniform.

That thing. Its claws.

Brandon's fingers, sticky and warm when he rubbed them together.

"My guts…" Brandon wrapped his fingers around the bottom hem of his shirt. But hesitated. Images of George flaring in his mind, Brandon mumbled, "He said he'd rip out my guts."

He had to see. Had to make sure. He pulled his shirt up. Pressed his hand to his stomach. Pressed his fingers. Pressed them *in*. Into slick folds of warm jelly. Jerking his fingers away, he rolled onto his back. Tried not to think about what he had just felt. Tried to think of every first aid class the Army had given him. Tried to think of how to fix himself.

Have a pair of gloves ready…

But his mind was a numb with frenzied panic. "Help…" Brandon whimpered, hands hovering over his belly. He didn't want to touch it. Didn't want to make it real. He looked all around for help. Chris ran toward the bridge, rifle darting this way and that. George's head jerked in Terry's hands. Terry hugged him close. Mike knelt there with them, hands working. Dan sat on the ground with his hands in his hair, rocking back and forth. Mumbling, "Not real." Mumbling, "Can't be real."

Jaran hadn't moved.

Teeth chattering, Brandon shivered with chill as the warmth spilled from his stomach. He was losing consciousness. Losing blood. Gulping down giant, gasping breaths, Brandon screamed the only word he could think of to make help come.

"*Medic!*"

CHAPTER TWENTY-THREE

Sunlight dripped sparkling from tiny fingers. A wet, smiling face flinched as the boat—

Jaran snapped awake in the dark.

Chilly and damp. Millions of tiny bells rang in her ears.

Fingernails stuttering, scraping across wet, rough stone, she worked her hand into a fist. The coolness of complete physical exertion in her arms and legs.

Tired. Hungry. Cold.

Beyond the bells, voices. Short and sharp. Long and sad.

She propped herself up. Sat on the rock. Leaned on her hand. Dizzy. Shoulders aching, she fingered her soaked hair from her face.

In the rain, black shapes of men moving in the night. Too dark to see their faces.

Her eyes drifted.

By the cliff's edge, a smaller man lay on his back holding his belly. Screaming. Legs kicking. A much bigger man knelt over him.

Her head wobbled toward other voices. A man sat near her with his face in his hands. Rocking. Beyond him, by the wall of dark stone, a man lay on the ground. His legs were gone—

The projection!

Memories slapped her and she jerked upright.

The cave. The *wards*. She had to get to the cave. She'd be safe there.

She tried to stand. A cramp snatched her leg and she stumbled and fell to her knees. Grunting at the ache in her legs, she crawled, dragged herself into the cave. Stopped just inside. Gasping. She looked behind. Out into the night. The rain spattered outside. The projection, where had it gone? Pressing the wall she pushed herself to her feet. Fingers sliding along the familiar shallow grooves—the wards her ancestors had carved in the rock.

Touching those old markings summoned the memory of Grandmother holding Jaran's tiny hand. Together their fingers traced those markings over and over.

They keep us safe, Grandmother's soothing voice echoed from long ago. *The wards won't keep Erlik Khan's mortal bodies from crossing, but they will destroy a projection.*

With the memory also came grief. Jaran was safe here. But she was alone.

Safe.

Jaran's lingering terror of the projection compelled her deeper into the cave. Leaning against the wall, she limped down the passage.

Orange light flickered near the end. She went to it.

The crippled Vietnamese man, *Boing*, she had heard the men call him. Boing lay by a small flame.

Jaran fell against the wall beside the flame. Slid down and sat hard. Sleep pulled her down, but she fought it. Fought to keep her eyes open. She stared at the flame. A strange candle. A block of something, seemingly hand-molded to the size of a small rock, sat aflame upon a fat can from the men's food boxes.

The men.

She had left them. If Erlik Khan's projection came

back…

In that moment of terror upon waking her instinct had been to seek the safety of the cave. She had not even thought to warn the men. Had she left them to die?

The ache gnawing her muscles reminded her. She had *not* left them to die. She had sung the song. Just like Grandmother had taught her. The projection….

Had she banished it?

As a young girl, in her heroic fantasies before sleep, Jaran had saved the village by singing the song and banishing entire armies of Erlik Khan's Projections. She had stood proud and strong against that imagined evil. Such were the sunny fantasies of her youth.

Eyes fluttering, Jaran groaned and her head dropped. So tired. During Grandmother's lessons on the hill it was nothing for Jaran to sing the banishment song. Countless times Grandmother had made Jaran sing it. Once, Grandmother had caught Jaran singing it to a frog she had caught in the river.

Do not make games of our songs, Grandmother had said. *Would you be so careless with your sword by swinging it during play?*

"No, Grandmother," Jaran whispered to the past.

Sung at the right time, your songs can be just as deadly as your sword. Respect them. As wielding your sword in combat taxes your body, so it is to wield your song. To banish a projection, there will be a cost. Grandmother had looked down at her hands then. Turned them over and said, *I pray you never have to pay it.*

Jaran held up her hands. Turned them over—

She gasped. The skin over her knuckles and fingers, where it had once been smooth and soft was now shriveled and wrinkled. Thick blue veins stood prominent beneath the skin.

"My…" Jaran whimpered. "My *youth?*"

That was the cost?

Massaging the ache in her thighs, Jaran thought. The last thing she remembered before collapsing into sleep was the projection losing its form and pouring heavy on the rock.

Erlik Khan consumed his victim's life force to fuel his attacks. How cruel that mortals could only defend themselves by sacrificing pieces of their own lives.

How unfair that Erlik Khan's price for conjuring those unnatural things was not *his* price to pay.

Was that why he had never conjured a projection when he was imprisoned in the pit? Would the life-cost of conjuring a projection have killed that old body Erlik Khan inhabited for so long?

Erlik Khan's new victim, did he have enough life left to summon another projection?

Jaran muttered a prayer. Prayed that Erlik Khan's mortal body was too weak.

"Please," Jaran muttered. "Please be too weak."

Jaran couldn't sing again. Not yet. She had nothing left to give. If she had to sing again, if another projection came, the song would kill her.

The small man—Brandon. If Erlik Khan entered his mind again, would she have strength to push him out?

Jaran pulled her knees to her chest. Was Erlik Khan deliberately trying to weaken her? Forcing her to use up her strength to get to the men?

Jaran's prayers devolved into tear-soaked whimpers for Grandmother.

"I need you, Grandmother." Cupping her hands over her face, Jaran cried. "I can't do this alone."

But there was no one to answer. Grandmother was gone. She was never coming back.

Just days ago Jaran agreed to carry Grandmother's spirit in her dreams. She couldn't fight the image of Grandmother, burned and staring up from Jaran's lap in the field while those machines burned.

There had been no time to prepare. Erlik Khan was there. Trying to kill them. Grandmother had sung her song in that burned whisper. She had released her spirt for Jaran to take. But Jaran had been too afraid to sleep.

Erlik Khan had killed Mother and Father. He denied her Grandmother's spirit to guide her. He had slaughtered the villagers. There was no place left to call home. He had taken everything from her.

If there had been time, Grandmother's soul would be with her right now. Guiding her. Telling her what she needed to do. Jaran wiped her eyes.

Nothing had played out like it had in her stupid childhood dreams. Who could she turn to now for guidance? Who was left to protect her? Those men out there? They couldn't protect her from Erlik Khan. They couldn't even protect themselves!

She sat there hugging her legs. Thoughts of loss turned to thoughts of loneliness turned to thoughts of despair. Then the Projection. Then the men.

Those men can't protect themselves.

But they had tried. Tried to protect each other.

Brandon. Those claws had been meant for him. But another man intervened. She shook away the image of a man ripped in half. Saving Brandon's life had cost that man his own.

She was thinking about that when Boing coughed. She looked at him. He stared at her with drunken, heavy-lidded eyes. Eyes sunken in deep violet pockets. A silver tendril of saliva hung down from his bottom lip, glossy with spit. The fire's blood-red after-image hung above his head like an aura.

"It hurts," Boing moaned.

Down the passage, the men's faint shouts echoed. But no one came for Boing.

"It *hurts!*" Boing coughed. Wet and wheezing.

Everything about Boing seemed wrong. The way he spoke. The way one eye focused and the other did not. His breath as he groaned fouled the air with the dead-fish smell of sickness. Jaran pressed her hand over her mouth and nose against the stink.

More coughing. Boing hacked and spat a slimy black

gob into the fire.

Her eyes went to the dark green blanket covering him below the waist. To the tiny jagged lumps beneath the wool, like what a bird must see when it flies over the jungle-covered mountains.

The two large bulges at the end of the blanket, his feet, they were skewed. One of the bulges was too high on his leg. Jaran had some skill in basic medicine, setting small bone breaks and nursing the sickly back to health. But Jaran could only shake her head and guess at what destruction lay beneath that wool shroud. These injuries were beyond her. And whatever had broken this man, it was killing him. She didn't know whether to pray for his recovery or for the dignity of a quick death. So she didn't pray at all.

Jaran hugged her knees. She didn't like this. She didn't like the man's suffering. She didn't like how feeble he looked. How broken.

Boing groaned and twisted beneath his blanket. "It hurts!"

She put her hands over her ears. So much suffering. So much death. So much hurt. She couldn't block out the noise. Boing's painful cries got through. Tears spilled down the man's cheeks.

She couldn't stand it. She pulled out the vial hanging around her neck and popped out the cork and leaned over the trembling, sweating man. She grabbed his cheeks, his lips popped out like a fish's and she poured a few thick drops in his mouth.

Squeezing his eyes shut, Boing shook his head. Jaran palmed his mouth so he couldn't spit.

"I know it tastes bad," she said. "I'm sorry."

His throat worked up and down. Up and down.

"You'll sleep very soon." Jaran took her hand away from his mouth. Wiped the sweat from his brow with her sleeve. Felt the hot skin through the fabric. "Is there…"

She thought of entering Boing's dream to soothe him.

But would she have the strength for it? Would it drain her further? Dreamwalking had never drained her before, but now she couldn't be sure of anything.

She looked down the passage toward the exit. Would she be able to sense Erlik Khan lurking out there? Would he choose this moment to attack? So many things she didn't know.

"Is there what?" Boing asked, voice already heavy with coming sleep.

This man has suffered enough. It would only take a few moments to give him a pleasant dream. She could spare that much. "Is there anyone special you would like to dream of?"

Boing didn't question her. Didn't ask how Jaran could possibly influence his dreams. Boing said simply, "My family."

The look on Boing's face when he spoke stabbed Jaran's heart. The look of a man who knew he was going to die. And all he wanted was to see his family before his end. Fresh tears welled in Boing's eyes.

Jaran's own tears welled. She smiled. "I will find them." She dabbed a drop from her vial on her finger and swallowed it. Thick and earthy. Jaran inhaled... inhaled... exhaled.... "Sleep now."

Boing's eyes rolled and his eyelids closed.

She kept her hand on Boing's forehead. Only meeting him that day, finding his dream in the eternal would be difficult without some type of physical tether.

Ascending into the eternal shocked her so much she nearly lost concentration. So blank. Like someone had stolen all the stars from the night sky. Every time she had come here she had navigated a space exploding with vibrant colors: the dreams of everyone she loved. The villagers. Mother and Father. Grandmother. Now the black emptiness of it overwhelmed her with sadness. A reminder that everyone she had ever known and loved was gone.

Something materialized. A hazy yellow fog veined with throbbing rose cracks. Boing's dream—even his dream was filled with pain. She went to it.

Anxious to find any scrap of happiness, Jaran thrust her fingers into the whirl of Boing's memory. His mother was a strong presence, finding her was easy. A thin woman. Small. With kind eyes and a soothing voice. Boing's father was a dark presence, though not unkind. Not domineering, but he expected great things from Boing. His father had been disappointed to send his eldest son to war. Still, she found shared moments of joy between Boing and his father and took them.

Brothers, sisters, elders. She took them. Friends. Finding the people Boing had shared joy with pushed away Jaran's own melancholy.

Jaran populated the dream. She chose an open field bathed in sunshine and set for them a large meal. They talked and laughed and ate and celebrated their love for one another. Jaran did everything she could to help Boing forget his pain. To forget the reality of the place where his body lay.

Dream well, Boing.

It was difficult not to go to him. To join in his love. How wonderful it would be to spend an eternity in such joy. She stood there at the misty edge of dream and memory. Watched Boing sink into the warmth of smiles and laughter. But with her fingers still dangling in his memories, she saw other things. Other people.

She saw those other soldiers out there on the rock. She saw the faces of men she knew to be dead. And she saw Erlik Khan's most recent victim.

John.

That was his name. Strong emotions were attached to that name. She followed them. Learning something about the man might help her in her fight against him. Boing's emotions guided her to images of smoke and flashes and noise. She nearly abandoned that path of memory. She didn't need to see more war. Didn't want to.

But it was odd, the emotions Boing felt during the creation of these memories, they weren't like the Soup Soldiers. There was no horror here.

Here in Boing's memories, she felt happiness. She felt hope.

In one image, the man who had fired the gun near her head, *Chris*, he knelt protectively over Boing and shot his rifle into a green blur. At the same time, Mike stuffed big white bandages on Boing's stomach. And although fear was present, it was overshadowed by something else. Something good.

And there, another memory. A silhouette of a man through smoke and flame. John. Somewhere in Laos. As he emerged from some smeared inferno, he brought two children with him. One over each shoulder. And although a battle raged with the shadows around them, John had run into a burning mud and grass hut to rescue children he had never known, nor ever see again.

Love.

That was the emotion overpowering the fear.

Boing loved these men.

What madness had pulled Boing from his family and friends to join these men in war?

The thought spawned another question.

What had brought Boing to Jaran's home? What had brought these men?

This question pulled Jaran from her reverie. Reminded her of her duty. Fingers hovering over Boing's swirling memories, she hesitated. Memories were private things. It was one of Grandmother's first lessons when Jaran learned dreamwalking. Grandmother had caught Jaran in the Soup Soldier's dreams. She learned the punishment for rummaging in a dreamer's memory without their knowledge was severe. Jaran had the scars to prove it.

Invading the Vietnamese soldiers' dreams, that was a rare occasion. To violate a dreamer's memory against their will. Grandmother had only permitted it then because the First Oath demanded it.

And because of the dreams Jaran crafted, some of those soldiers had taken their own lives. Grandmother had seemed indifferent to that fact. She did not praise Jaran's actions, nor did she punish her for them.

The Second Oath permits the taking of life. If it is necessary.

That was all Grandmother had said about it.

A growing resentment for Boing and his friends outside the cave encroached on the joyous scene before her.

Jaran had killed some of those Vietnamese soldiers for the mere offense of thinking about going across the river.

Had Boing and his friends not committed a worse offense? Was it not their fault that Erlik Khan had escaped? Was it not their fault that her family was dead?

If all the fighting was so far south, what had been Boing's reason for coming this far north?

She wasn't sure how long she would have to search Boing's memory. She had to know what she was searching *for*.

There is power associated with Erlik Khan's name, Grandmother had said once. *Powerful names draw stupid men.*

Was that why they had come? Because they knew Erlik Khan's name?

She didn't have time to waste wondering *how* they knew his name. She had to focus on why these men came.

Only two of those men outside had spoken Erlik Khan's name in Jaran's presence. The small man, Brandon. And that tall man, Smith—the man who always seemed to stare at her.

Memories created by events were different than those by people. People left impressions on the dreamer and were easier to find. Events, though, things like specific conversations, those were difficult. Especially if those events were of little importance to the dreamer. Boing's memories, the images and voices and sounds, they swirled in a chaotic mess.

She looked.

CRACK.

Screaming.

Falling.

Jaran pulled her fingers from the memory, stunned by the intense fear Boing had experienced recently.

He fell from the sky. That's what broke this man....

She wouldn't have time to sort through the events. If Boing woke she wasn't sure when she would have this opportunity again. She'd have to narrow the focus to Brandon and Smith.

Brandon seemed to be their leader. He would most likely have the information she sought. She searched for him first.

She wasn't expecting to find what she did.

There was significant emotion attached to Brandon, but Jaran was surprised to see that the emotion attached to Brandon was the same Jaran had for the rest of those men.

Resentment.

The most prominent event attached to Brandon's face was a death. From Boing's perspective she saw a man lying bloody on the floor of one of those flying machines. Felt Boing's sadness and shock that his friend had been killed.

And when Boing's eyes turned to Brandon, arms crossed and staring out into the sky, a fiery anger flared in Boing's belly.

Later, Boing sat with his friends and drank. Jaran couldn't understand the language, but she felt the conversation stoking the fire in Boing.

Those men out there. They hated Brandon.

She searched further back. Found a memory from before Boing's friend was killed.

Boing and those other men laughed as they ate together in a large dim tent. Across the room, Brandon sat alone and ate. Occasionally looking over at Boing and his group. The hate was not there in Boing. Not yet. But the resentment was there.

Jaran found herself wondering what Brandon had done to anger these men so—

Boing's dream faltered. His pain must have been breaking through to the dream.

No time to pity Brandon. She needed answers.

She searched for Smith.

She found darkness and heat. Noise. Rumbling. A red light. Men sitting in the dark. A green light.

She sensed fear in Boing. A fear of falling.

Jaran watched in fascination. This was how they arrived. They flew here.

They had traveled a long time. Not talking much. Sleeping a little.

Erlik Khan.

Hearing the name nearly knocked Jaran from Boing's mind.

Smith.

It was Smith who had said the name.

Boing's fear of falling was so strong when Smith had said it. Finding any sort of emotional connection or sensation to the name was difficult.

Short bursts of information punched through Boing's fear.

Search. Find.

They came to search for Erlik Khan? How was that possible? How did they even know about him?

Friends, came another burst. *Dead.*

The group of soldiers Jaran and Grandmother found dead in the cave. Were Boing and his friends coming to rescue them?

Painful cracks split through Boing's dream. The pain was waking him. The pool of Boing's memories steamed. On the verge of evaporating.

She had to know more.

What else? She plunged her hands in. *What else?*

And just as Jaran was thrown from the dream and back

into the cave, she found what she was looking for.

She heard Smith speak.

"You fool," Jaran mumbled. Stunned that someone could be so stupid.

Powerful names draw stupid men.

She wished for anything else but this. She knew why Smith had sent these men. She knew why they were here. She knew why her family and friends were dead.

Capture.

That was what Smith had said.

She opened her eyes. In the cave, against the heat of the small fire, her skin was slick with sweat beneath her robes.

Smith was using these men to capture Erlik Khan. To what end, Jaran didn't know.

Nor did she care.

As long as Smith lived, he was a danger to this world.

Images of violence overwhelmed her. She embraced them for a moment. Picking up one of their rifles and shooting Smith. But shooting Smith was not an option. Those other men out there would kill her immediately.

Words pounded in her mind. Words she had learned and recited since she was nine years old.

The words of her Second Oath.

No. She would wait. She didn't need to pick up a rifle. She only needed Smith to fall asleep.

CHAPTER TWENTY-FOUR

"He said he'd rip out my guts," Brandon sobbed. Squeezing Mike's arms as he and Chris carried Brandon out of the rain. They set him down just inside the cave's opening. "Oh shit, Mike, my guts."

Chris ran back outside.

Mike swatted Brandon's hands away, but Brandon reached for his arms again. "Mike!"

"Stop!" Mike grabbed Brandon's hands and shoved them down. "I need my hands to fix you." And he undid the buttons of Brandon's top and pulled it open.

All Brandon could see was his brown undershirt. Dark, shiny blotches oozing in the shreds of fabric.

"Jesus, Mike how bad is it?" Brandon winced as Mike cut away the shirt with shears, the embedded fabric tugging out from folds and tears in his belly. "Am I gonna die?"

Mike's brilliant white flashlight hovered over Brandon's abdomen. Fingers prodding and moving things.

"Mike?"

Mike said nothing.

Brandon tried to lift his head to see.

"Don't look," Mike said.

But Brandon looked. And nearly fainted as Mike flicked his fingers and flopped a bulging yellowish roll over Brandon's bellybutton. His head dropped on the floor. "I'm gonna fucking die!"

"I told you not to look." Mike rummaged around in his kit. "Your abdominal wall is intact. But you have significant dermal damage."

"God, I knew it. I'm dead. I'm fucking dead!"

"Oh shut up. *Dermal* means *skin*. Your guts are fine. You're not going to die."

Mouth dry and mumbling with panic, Brandon said, "You're sure?"

"I'm sure." Mike poured canteen water over the wound and sponged it dry. "You'll be fine. You'll just have a hell of a scar."

Panic still laid eggs in Brandon's throat, but silently repeating what Mike had told him seemed to be enough to prevent them from hatching.

Men passed them in the tunnel. Chris and Terry carried a large bundle wrapped in a poncho. Beyond Mike's light, Brandon could see thick black liquid spilling from the poncho, spattering on the floor. They set the bundle down near Boing and went back out.

Brandon turned his head to the wall.

"I need to suture this," Mike said. "It'll take a while. You want some morphine?"

"No."

"You sure?"

"No morphine," he said to the wall. If that thing came back, Brandon didn't want to be asleep. What the hell was that thing? Where did it come from?

But he didn't have capacity for thought once Mike started his work. Brandon grunted as Mike tugged skin. Winched at the pinches of a needle poking through. Fought back vomit at the weird, cool pressure of Mike stuffing exposed rubbery fat back under Brandon's skin.

Chris and Smith stopped beside them as Mike worked. "How you feeling?" Chris asked.

"Been better," Brandon said. "How's everyone else?"

"Terry's alright. Dan is…" Chris looked down the passage toward the flickering light. "Well. He'll come around."

Chris didn't mention George. He didn't need to.

The pounding rain outside softened to static sizzle. The clip-clip and snip of Mike working the sutures echoed softly on the rock. In the lingering silence Brandon found himself mentally checking off the names of his men as Chris reported their status. He was waiting for Chris to finish. But then Brandon closed his eyes as he realized that there was nobody left to talk about. He looked at Chris and asked, "How are you holding up?"

Chris packed a can of chewing tobacco and fingered in a dip and tongued it into his cheek. "I'm alright." He looked thoughtfully out into the rain and said, "Before the sun went down I searched for John again with the binocs. I found him in the clearing laid out on his back. It was weird. He looked like a boxer grabbing for the ropes after waking up from a knock-out."

"I thought you missed your shot."

"I did."

"What do you think happened?"

"No idea."

Brandon looked over Chris's shoulder at Smith. "Any guesses?"

Smith shook his head. "We need to talk to the girl."

Brandon looked at Mike. "Any idea when Boing will be ready to talk?"

Setting his needle driver on Brandon's chest, Mike pulled out a large abdominal bandage from his kit. "Under normal circumstances I wouldn't wake him up at all." He tore the paper packaging from the bandage and tossed it aside. He paused with the cotton bandage hovering over Brandon's stomach. "But I guess these aren't particularly normal circumstances. I'll find a way to wake him up and keep him comfortable." He wrapped the bandage around Brandon's abdomen and tied it down. "Try not to do too much bending for a while. I don't want your stitches popping."

Mike closed up his kit and rose and Chris and Smith followed him down the softly lit passage to where Boing lay.

In the silence he tried to think. He went over everything that had happened. The insanity of it. But as Brandon laid there, Dan's ramblings drifted down the passage and cut into his thoughts.

"It wasn't real..." Over and over.

"Chris," Dan said. "It wasn't real, right?" As if mutual agreement could somehow make it so.

But Chris said nothing. Dan didn't seem to notice. He just went on. Whispers down the corridor. "It wasn't real. It wasn't real."

But for Brandon, hearing it said over and over that the thing was not real simply reminded him of how real the thing actually was. And he'd have the scar to prove it...

Brandon couldn't listen any longer. He avoided bending his midsection as much as possible and stood. Retrieved his poncho from the front pocket of his rucksack and put it on, then went outside.

He stood at the cliff edge in the night and the rain. The sound of heavy rain drops *pocking* and *ticking* on his poncho's hood downed out Dan's ramblings. Brandon welcomed the peace as he scanned the jungle below, trying to find the place where John had stood, but the night was too dark.

Earlier that day Brandon had thought that maybe he had used up all his fear. But looking into that jungle proved him wrong. Just knowing that John was waiting somewhere beneath that dark and gleaming-wet jungle canopy set the fear simmering in Brandon's belly.

Beneath his poncho Brandon ran his hand over the

bandages wrapped tight around his abdomen. Already heavy and soft with his blood.

The safety of this place on the mountain was dependent on its secrecy. Carelessly, Brandon had squandered that secrecy. He and his men were no longer safe here. New York had to leave. Fast. Before John found a way up. Before he alerted the NVA. Before another one of those *things* came. They had to get as far away from John as they could. Walking wasn't going to do the job. The boats were the only option. He had to make the team see that.

He was constructing his argument in favor of taking the boats when tiny lights sprouted from the village far across the river. Bouncing and circling like curious fireflies…

Of course.

Chewing his cheek, he mumbled, "Shit."

He almost laughed. It wasn't fear he felt at the sight of the NVA. The lantern lights conjured a queer kind of disappointment in him. The NVA's arrival simply made his life more difficult. Pushed him to move farther. Faster. Brandon and his men needed rest. But those lanterns, they were a sign that there would be no rest for a long time.

The lights circled the huts, eventually a few broke off and moved out into the field. Despite the dark and the rain, it would only be a few minutes before they discovered the helicopter wreckage and confirmed that there were Americans about. That would be exciting news to the NVA commander. If Brandon were in his position he would push his men to exhaustion until the Americans were found.

New York needed to move. Now. Brandon turned and went into the cave. He met Mike coming down the passage and asked if Boing was awake.

"The morphine has almost worn off. He's in pain, but he can talk, but I'm not sure for how long. Depends on his pain tolerance."

Brandon nodded. "Let's not waste time."

He couldn't imagine the pain Boing would have to endure without morphine. But the need to speak with Jaran, the need to escape, it outweighed Boing's discomfort. And it outweighed Brandon's fear of the team finding out how Boing ended up that way in the first place. He'd get this chat over with as fast as he could. After that, Boing could go back to sleep.

Echoing shouts from down the passage interrupted his thoughts. When he stepped into the light, Brandon saw the team gathered around Boing.

Terry shouted, "I don't give a shit about your HVT! We need to know what that fucking thing was!"

Smith leaned against the wall with his arms crossed. Dispassionately he said, "Finding the HVT is still priority."

Boing lay reclined against a rucksack. Skin sweaty and pallid in the orange firelight. Some kind of blotchy red rash covered his face and neck. Boing coughed, deep and wet, and spat. His sunken and dark eyes drifted lazily around the chamber.

"The immediate *threat* is the priority," Terry shouted back. "That's *John*! And that thing!"

Sitting near Boing against the wall, Jaran hugged her knees to her chest. Her long black hair hung down, covering her face. Two tiny points of light reflected behind her hanging-down hair like still-hot coals deep within a smoldering bonfire. Small and dark, she sat there like some unnoticed demon patiently waiting at a man's deathbed.

"Shut up," Brandon said. "All of you." The men looked at him. Smith with his hard eyes. Terry with a resentful sneer. "Start with the HVT. Then the thing. Then we'll ask her the quickest way out of here."

Terry stalked toward him.

Brandon didn't bother trying to stand up straight. He didn't bother clearing his throat to prevent a nervous crack. He watched Terry as he approached and said, "The NVA are in the village. How about you sit down so we can get this over with?"

Terry stopped short.

Chris nodded and sat, tonguing his chewing tobacco. He spat in the fire. "Well if that's the case, let's get started." He looked up at Smith and flicked his finger toward Boing.

Boing's eyes couldn't seem to focus on anything. He jerked as those deep, wet coughs rumbled way down in his chest.

"Boing," Smith said. "Ask the girl if Erlik Khan is here."

A line of drool spilled from Boing's mouth. His head lolled. Lethargic lips struggled to shape words. "Erlik *what?*"

Smith looked at Mike. "You said he'd be able to talk."

"I said the morphine is wearing off. He's gonna be a little loopy."

"Can't you give him something?"

"If I give him something to metabolize the morphine he'll be in too much pain to talk." Mike gestured at Boing. "This is what you get."

Smith let out an annoyed sigh. "Boing. Ask the girl where Erlik Khan is."

Boing coughed up something thick and chewed it back and swallowed it. His eyes slipped sadly to his ruined legs. "What are you *talking* about?"

Smith threw up his hands. "This is a complete waste of fucking time."

Chris moved around the fire and knelt beside Boing. He poured canteen water on a cravat and sponged Boing's face and neck. "Hey, Boing."

"Hey, Chris."

"How you feeling?"

"My legs hurt."

"I know it."

"Am I gonna die?"

"No." Chris spilled water on Boing's head. Combed his

fingers through the interpreter's wet hair. "No. You're not gonna die. But we might be in some trouble if we don't get these questions answered."

"Really?"

"Yeah."

"I'm sorry."

"Can you help us?"

"Yeah. I'm sorry."

"It's okay," Chris said. "This bad guy Erlik Khan, we're looking for him. Can you ask Jaran if he's here?"

"Who's Jaran?"

Chris flicked his chin. "That girl right there."

Boing's head followed Chris's eyes. "Oh." He waved to the girl. "Hi."

Jaran said nothing.

Wringing out the cravat, Chris folded it and laid it on Boing's head. "Can you ask her?"

Boing took a deep, labored breath and said, "Is Erlik Khan here?"

"Ask her in Vietnamese."

"Oh." And he spoke to the girl in Vietnamese.

Jaran looked at Boing. She sniffed and pulled her hair from her face. Her eyes puffy and red. When she spoke her voice was sticky with campfire phlegm.

"Yes," Boing said. "He's here."

"Good," Chris said. "Ask her where."

Boing spoke.

Jaran jutted her chin toward the exit and spoke.

"She says you saw him. He was the one shooting at you near the village."

"John?" Chris asked.

"What?"

"Ask her if she means John."

Boing spoke.

Jaran spoke.

"Yes. John is Erlik Khan."

"What?" Chris pinched his shirt. "You mean he's

dressed like us?"

Boing spoke.

Jaran shook her head and spoke.

"No," Boing said. "John *is* Erlik Khan."

"She's making shit up," Terry said. "John can't be two people. Spook's right. This is a waste of time."

"Quiet," Chris said.

Boing coughed. Winced. "My legs..." His face pulled tight in pain. "Can I have some morphine?"

"Yeah, buddy," Chris said. "All the morphine you want as soon as we figure this out, okay?"

"It really hurts."

"I know." Can you ask her where Erlik Khan came from?"

Boing spoke.

Jaran spoke.

"Hell."

Terry rolled his eyes.

"Ask her what she means," Chris said.

"No," Brandon said.

Chris looked at him.

Brandon came toward the fire. "Where he came from is irrelevant."

Conway. The cripple. John.

Brandon said, "Ask her *what* Erlik Khan is."

Chris watched him. Then turned to Boing. "Ask her."

Boing spoke.

Jaran spoke.

"Evil."

"Like a ghost?" Chris asked.

Boing spoke.

Jaran spoke.

"I don't really know the word she's trying to say. I think she means something like 'devil'."

It's warm here.

"There's a devil inside John?" Chris asked.

Boing spoke.

Jaran spoke.

"Yes."

"Come the fuck *on*, man," Terry said. "We don't have time for this shit."

"Shut the fuck up or wait outside," Chris said. "Ask her how we get Erlik Khan out of John."

Boing spoke.

Jaran spoke.

"You can't get him out. She says John's soul already belongs to him."

He made me kill them.

"Wait," Brandon said. He knelt beside Boing and Chris. "Conway survived. When I talked to him he told me the devil was inside him. He said the girl brought him back. I think he meant Jaran. Ask her how she brought Conway back."

Boing spoke.

Jaran spoke.

"She doesn't know who Conway is."

Brandon jumped up and grabbed Mike. "A man with skin like this." Brandon pointed to the back of the cave. "In the pit. Ask her how she brought him back."

Boing spoke, but a coughing fit overcame him and he jerked and grabbed for his legs.

Chris gripped Boing's hand. "Come on, Boing. Just a few more questions, okay?"

"My legs!"

"I know," Chris said. "We'll take care of you. Just ask."

Through gritted teeth, Boing spoke.

Jaran spoke.

"Con—" Boing gasped. "Conway died—"

"No," Brandon said. "He was alive. I talked to him. In the pit, I talked to him."

"—died in the river. Drowned. She brought him back."

"Who killed him?" But Brandon thought he already knew. *The cripple.* He just needed to hear the girl confirm it. "Who killed Conway?"

Boing tried to speak. His mouth moved but no words came out. Just an airy, high-pitched squeal. Tears spilled down his cheeks. "Mmmm… muh… morphine." And he coughed that terrible rumbling cough.

Mike pushed Brandon aside. "I'm stopping this."

Brandon grabbed him. "Last question, Mike. I swear."

But Mike shoved him aside.

"Please!" Brandon pleaded.

Head shaking back and forth, Boing let out a scream. And on that scream there were words.

Jaran hugged her knees tight against her chest. Eyes and cheeks wet in the firelight. Wiping her face, she spoke.

"Soup!" Boing screamed. "Soup Soldier!" He coughed and coughed. "She calls him Soup Soldier! Mike, please! It hurts!"

Mike dropped to his knees beside Boing and rummaged through his aid bag. Boing shook and screamed. And the scream devolved into terrible wet coughing.

Mike pulled out a morphine syrette.

"Wait!" Smith shouted, grabbing Mike's wrist. "Ask her how Erlik Khan enters a person."

"Get the fuck *off*!" Mike jerked his wrist, but Smith held tight.

"Ask her!"

Boing screamed. Tears spat from his lips.

Brandon watched Jaran. He walked around the mess of men screaming and shouting and struggling on the floor. He went to her. Knelt beside her. "Soup Solider," he said to her. He held out his arm. He made a chopping motion and brought his hand down on his elbow.

Jaran nodded.

That was it. That was why Jaran wouldn't let Chris or Mike shoot back on the river bank. That was what happened to John. The villagers, had they known? Is that why they ran? Is that why they didn't fight back?

Boing's screams echoed in the passageway.

"Give him the morphine," Brandon said. "We have what we need."

"I don't have what *I* need," Smith snarled.

"Chris!" Mike shouted. And he grabbed the syrette with his free hand and tossed it over his shoulder.

Chris snatched the syrette from the air and pulled the cap off with his teeth and spat it out. "Sleep tight, buddy." And he punched the needle into Boing's thigh.

"God damn you!" Smith shouted.

Boing's screaming quieted. Then stopped. He went lip. Mumbling.

In the settling quiet, Chris said to Smith, "You're kind of a dick, you know that?"

Smith looked at Brandon. Face dark with anger. "What did you gather from all that nonsense? What's so obvious to you that isn't apparent to the rest of us?"

Brandon ran his hands through his hair. Blew out a long breath. "You know those villagers we found in the jungle?"

"What about them?"

"I know why they were running."

CHAPTER TWENTY-FIVE

Brandon called Smith and the team to the cave mouth. Chris noticed Dan not moving and prodded him along. They left Jaran with Mike as he tended Boing. When they reached the cave mouth, Chris said, "What did you mean about the villagers? What were they running from?"

Brandon leaned back against the chilly wall, wondering how to put this madness into words? In the valley, through the rain, the NVA lanterns drifted south away from the village. There wasn't time to think about how to say it.

Brandon looked at Chris. "What if we were wrong about who attacked the village? What if it wasn't a group? What if it was just one attacker?"

"I wouldn't believe it," Chris said. "Someone would have stood up and fought back. None of those villagers did. They were slaughtered."

"That's what we think."

"No," Chris said. "That's what the evidence shows."

Brandon held up his finger and tapped it in the air. "Before today I would have agreed with you. But suppose we didn't see any evidence of resistance because the person who killed the attacker *became* the attacker himself."

"I don't follow."

God, this was frustrating.

Brandon told them what he found in the pit. "What reason would one of Florida's NCOs have for shooting a corpse? There's no reason, Chris." Brandon held up his palms, looking for words. "There's no logical reason for someone to shoot a corpse that old. Not unless something made him do it."

"Maybe someone shot him a long time ago," Terry said.

Brandon shook his head. "I found the spent casing. A forty-five. One of Florida's NCOs shot that old corpse. Now suppose that NCO attacked his team and Conway shot and killed him, and whatever had passed from the corpse to the NCO then passed to Conway."

"Doesn't make sense," Terry said. "The cripple attacked John, not Captain Conway."

Brandon flicked his head to the back of the cave. "Jaran said the cripple drowned Conway in the river."

Chris said, "So then whatever was in the pit passed from Conway to the cripple. And *then* the cripple attacked John?"

Brandon nodded. "And John smoked him."

"Bullshit," Terry said. "John just snapped. Happens to guys out here."

Chris shook his head. "The girl, I remember she pointed at John and screamed that name. Erlik Khan. When I tried to shoot back she wouldn't let me."

"Her grandma was in the way," Terry said. "The girl didn't want you zappin' her."

"Jaran tried to stop you on the cliff," Brandon said. "When you were trying for that long shot."

Chris leaned against the wall. "And I almost hit him."

"Yeah," Brandon said. "She was trying to stop you. Smith was holding her back."

Chris scowled at Smith.

Smith held up his hands. "I was trying to keep her from

getting shot. I'm learning everything at the same time you are."

Chris spat on the floor.

"So what are you saying?" Terry asked. "That we can't kill John?"

Brandon nodded. "That's exactly what I'm saying. If you kill John, whatever is in him will pass on to you." Brandon looked at Smith. "This is way beyond us. New York is a team of killers. They're not the right tool for this job."

"I disagree," Smith said. "Snatch and grab is right up their alley."

"This is *different*."

"How so?"

"Because you didn't tell me your HVT was a *devil*."

"A devil that's bound in the flesh of a man. The mission still stands. Snatch and grab."

Brandon's jaw fell open. "You can't be serious."

"I'm serious."

Brandon felt his mouth moving, but with his mind racing he couldn't make the words come out.

Chris shook his head. "Listen, I'm as freaked out as you are." He looked back down the passage toward Mike and Boing. "You said Jaran brought Captain Conway back." Chris sighed and said, "Maybe there's a way to help John."

"Help John?" Brandon said. "Help *John*?" Brandon paced in and out of the opening. Rain spattering above the opening spritzed his face. "Helping John means getting close enough to grab him. Look at how many people we lost—"

"Back then we weren't ready for him," Chris said. "Now we are."

"You're ready?" Brandon turned. "You're ready for shit to come out of the *rain* and cut you in half?" Brandon pulled his shirt up and pointed to the bandage around his stomach. "You have a plan for *this*?"

"I didn't say it would be easy." Chris stared down at Brandon. "But I ain't leaving a man behind if there's hope of saving him."

Brandon's fingers slipped from his shirt and he looked out through the cave opening. The lantern lights drifted from the Huey wreckage down to the riverbank. No doubt the NVA noticed the boats were missing. Had they noticed John's radio signals? Would they fall for New York's ruse and head south? Would they try to reach the far riverbank?

Would the NVA commander split his men and explore both options.

That's what Brandon would do.

Brandon rubbed his eyes. They needed to move. "If it hadn't been for Jaran and her grandmother, John would have wiped us out on the riverbank. We can't kill him. To capture him, first we have to track him. Then fight through whatever unnatural shit he throws at us. We can't..." He sighed. "We can't evade the NVA *and* track John."

"I'm open to suggestions," Chris said.

I'm open to running away.

That's what Brandon *wanted* to say. But—

Brandon laughed. "John tracked us here. God knows how he made it across the river, but he followed us. He knew right where we went."

"So?" Smith said.

"So," Brandon turned to the men. "We take the boats. We don't go far. Just far enough to put a few days between us and the NVA. John will follow us."

"Why's John gonna follow us?" Terry asked.

Brandon rubbed the bandages on his stomach. "Call it a gut feeling. Something tells me John isn't done with us."

It was a lie. Brandon had no idea if John would try to follow them or not. He just wanted to get in the boats and get the fuck out of there. But he was as surprised at how easy the lie had rolled off his tongue. Maybe he had unintentionally picked up the finer points of subterfuge from Smith.

Chris went to the opening and looked into the valley. He stood there a while and ran his thumb back and forth across his lip. Then he nodded. "I like it. We'll take the boats. We still have a few hours before sunrise. We can drift downriver a ways and then start the engines."

Relief poured over Brandon.

Thank God.

Chris turned to Dan and Terry. "Let's get the gear ready. We'll start down in ten minutes."

"Hold that thought," Mike said, coming out of the dark. Wiping his wet fingers with a cravat, he said, "I've got some bad news."

"Boing?" Chris asked.

Mike nodded. "I didn't recognize his condition right away because it's so rare. He's displaying a textbook classic triad of a fat embolism."

"You're gonna have to dumb that down for me."

"His legs," Mike said. "When they shattered they've been leaking bone marrow and fat into his bloodstream. In some cases the fat globules get in the blood and cause an embolism. The classic triad, three symptoms of a larger issue, the first is that rash he's got. It's called a petechial rash. The fat emboli are in his dermal capillaries.

"Two, respiratory changes. That cough. Hypoxia and dyspnea."

"It's in his lungs?" Brandon asked.

"Essentially, yeah. And three, his altered mental status. It would have been impossible to notice while he's doped up, I could've assumed it was the morphine. But right after you guys left he had a minor seizure."

"Jesus," Chris said. "Is he alright?"

Mike shook his head. "He won't be. The seizure, along with the other symptoms tell me the fat emboli are getting into his brain. I need to prevent any further damage. It might be too late already, but he'll die if I don't operate immediately. I need to remove the cause the embolism."

"Mike," Brandon said. "We have to get out of here. As in *right now*. Can it wait until we get down river?"

"Absolutely not. I'm not bullshitting you, sir. In a few hours Boing will be dead."

"What kind of operation?" Chris asked.

Mike stiffened. "Amputation. Both legs."

Chris rubbed his hand over his face. He breathed deep. "Okay. What do you need from us?"

Mike walked out into the rain. He let it fall on his hands and he rubbed them together. "My cutting instruments were destroyed with the Huey. I need to get back to the village and find—"

"The village is crawling with NVA," Brandon threw his arm out toward. "They know we're here. They're down there looking for us."

"I'll go," Terry said. "I'll take a boat downriver and walk up from the south."

"No!" Brandon shouted. "It's suicide."

"We need to do *something*."

"Then think of something *else*," Bandon fired back. "Nobody is going back to that village."

Dan rapped Terry on the shoulder. "I'll go with you. Come on."

Brandon's hands curled into fists. Why would no one listen—

"Hang on, boys," Chris said. "I have an idea." And he turned to Mike. "But you ain't gonna like it."

Mike turned to him. "Let's hear it."

Chris went to a rucksack and rummaged through it. He came back with what looked in the dark to be a coil of rope. He handed it to Mike.

Brandon switched on the red flashlight on his shoulder. When he saw the printing on the coil his breath caught in his throat.

PETN / 50 grain / Det Cord.

Mike's eyes went wide. "Are you fucking *insane*?

Absolutely not."

Chris looked at the det cord. "It'll do the job. It won't be clean."

"No shit it won't be clean!"

"Mike, it's what we have."

"I'm trying to save Boing's life you asshole! Not kill him faster!" Mike loomed over Chris. "Do you realize how much of my extremely limited resources I'll use up if I *blow* his fucking legs off?"

"I'm just trying to help."

"If *this*," and he shoved the cord in Chris's face. "If this is the kind of help you're going to offer then I don't want your fucking help!" Mike pointed at Brandon. "This motherfucker here talkin' 'bout not risking lives, then *you* tell me to blow someone's legs off. Fuck you guys." Cord still in hand, he stalked off toward the rope bridge and stood there in the rain.

Chris watched him go.

"Is there anything else we can do?" Brandon asked.

Watching Mike, Chris said, "He doesn't like hurting people. Doesn't like seeing people in pain. He knows there isn't any other option, he just needs to realize it. As soon as he does, he'll calmly explain how he can use the det cord and treat Boing's legs just like he would any other explosive injury."

Brandon looked at Mike. The rain spattered on his head and he ran his hand through his short hair. Mist sprayed up from his head and haloed in the red light.

And then, very calmly, Mike came back to them. He squeezed the bundle of cord in his hands. He looked up at the team. "I need someone to assist me. If I work fast enough, I'll be able to treat the wound just like any other explosive injury."

Chris winked at Brandon. "I know you'll make it work," Chris said to Mike. "I'm taking Dan and Terry down to make the boats ready for our trip. We'll haul as much gear as we can. As soon as you're able to move

Boing, get your asses down to us and we'll get the hell outta here. As for your assistant," Chris clapped Brandon on the shoulder. "I have the utmost faith in our commander."

CHAPTER TWENTY-SIX

Mike and Brandon went down the passage toward the flickering light. Jaran sat against the wall. As they approached, she looked up from the disgusting peaks and valleys of the wool blanket covering Boing's legs. Watched as Mike knelt beside Boing.

From his aid bag Mike pulled a clear plastic I.V. bag and laid it on Boing's chest. The liquid inside lapped with the rise and fall of Boing's weak breathing. Trembled with tiny heartbeat ripples. Mike found a vein in Boing's arm and inserted a needle. Slipped in the I.V. catheter.

Mike folded down the blanket from Boing's legs and with a pair of shears he cut away Boing's pant-legs and tossed them aside. Soaked with sweat, the pant-legs flopped in a heap like wet towels. With his bare skin exposed, Brandon fought the urge to recoil.

Everything below Boing's knees was pounded bread dough. Where skin should have been taught and stretched across shinbones, it was bent and dented and folded.

Mike pulled out a brown iodine bottle and some white cotton squares. From the bottle he poured the liquid over Boing's legs. The iodine in the firelight spilled like so much thin blood. Mike smeared it on the skin with the cotton.

After replacing some items into the bag, Mike stood and looked down at the det cord in Brandon's hands. "Chris says this is a low-yield cord. It doesn't pack as much of a punch." Mike took a length of the cord and slid it through his fingers. "I think if I apply this about three-quarters of the way up his calf, and have tourniquets immediately available, I should be able to treat the wound just as I would a landmine."

"What if…" Brandon's mouth went pre-vomit wet as images sparked in his mind. "What if it doesn't cut all the way through?"

Mike chewed his thumbnail. After a few seconds he said, "It should work. But I've got my combat knife and my sheers if it doesn't."

Brandon shook his head. "This is a stupid idea. And just… just fucking *cruel*."

Mike stared at the cord for a long time. Then said, "Help me move him."

"Where?"

"It'll have to be outside." Mike gestured around the cave. "The shockwave bouncing around in here might blow out our eardrums."

"But—"

"I know," Mike said. "The NVA might see the flash. As soon as I bandage him up we need to be moving." Mike pointed to Boing's feet. "Get the litter."

Smith came slowly down the passage. He stopped in the shadows and watched them.

"You want to give us a hand?" Brandon asked.

"No." And Smith shook a little bottle. A pill dropped into his hand and he popped it into his mouth.

Mike pointed to the litter. "Let's go."

"What are those pills he's taking?" Brandon whispered.

Mike glanced at Smith. Nodded. "Go pills."

"Go pills?"

"Yeah. Amphetamines. He won't sleep for days. Don't

go messing with that shit. I don't have any downers. Come on, grab the litter."

Brandon picked up the foot-end of the litter. Hands trembling so bad he nearly dropped it. Mike picked up the head-end and nodded down the corridor toward the exit. They emerged from the cave into a drizzle and set Boing down near the cliff edge and knelt on either side of him.

Mike fished a tourniquet out of his cargo pocket and handed it across to Brandon. "You know how to use that?"

"Yeah."

Mike fed the det cord beneath Boing's leg and looped it back over and slipped the end over to Brandon. "Loop it over his calf. No that's too high. Yeah, right there." Mike ripped a long piece of white medical tape and handed it to Brandon. "Secure the cord on his shin."

Pressing the tape, Brandon's fingers sank deep into soft flesh. In his fingertips the hollow scrape of broken things, like ice crunching. Brandon leaned back with a sudden dizziness. Jesus, they were going through with this. They were going to blow Boing's legs off.

Brandon grabbed Mike's wrist. "Stop."

Mike looked at him.

"Stop," Brandon said. "Fuck. Alright. We'll wait until the NVA clear out of the village. We'll go back there and look for something to cut with."

Mike shook his head. "They could be there for days. Even if they clear out by morning, Boing might be too far gone for me to do anything for him." He looked down at Boing and sighed. "We need to slide his legs over the edge so that his knees bend. That'll protect us from shrapnel."

"There's no shrapnel in det cord."

Mike looked at him. "The bone fragments…"

Wet chunks climbed up Brandon's throat and he chewed them back down. He and Mike slid Boing off the litter and lowered his legs delicately over the edge. Even in his drug-induced oblivion Boing groaned at the movement.

"Okay," Mike said. "That's good."

Any hint of the irritation and anger in Mike's voice was gone. Now it was an easy voice and calm hands as he checked that everything was in place. That everything was perfect.

Mike duck-walked up to Boing's shoulder. "Come up here. As soon as it detonates, we're gonna pull him back onto the litter. Then we pull the litter away from the edge so we can apply the tourniquets. You listening? As soon as he's clear of the edge we apply the tourniquets. Just below the knee. Right here. There's going to be a lot of blood. Wipe your hands on your pants if they get too slick."

All Brandon could do was nod. The nervous buzzing in his gut worked up to his throat and cut off his voice. He wondered how Mike could still speak.

"Hey," Mike said.

Brandon looked at him.

"You with me?"

Brandon swallowed hard. Croaked, "Yeah."

"Repeat back to me what we're going to do when it detonates."

Brandon said, "We apply the tourniquets—"

"Wrong," Mike said. "Take a deep breath and listen to me." Mike repeated the steps. He had Brandon repeat them back a few times. When Brandon could rattle them off, Mike nodded. Then he surveyed his patient one last time. He blew out a long breath. "Fuck, man." He looked at Brandon. "You ready?"

Brandon said nothing.

Mike took out the clacker from his cargo pocket and wiggled the rubber connector onto the det cord's end. "Close your eyes and look away. Boing's legs are essentially grenades now. I can't fix your eyes out here, so don't get them blown out."

Brandon turned his head away. The image he saw when he closed his eyes sickened him.

"Exhale hard and keep your mouth open," Mike said. "The blast wave will blow the air out of your lungs. That air needs a place to go. If it can't go out your mouth, it'll go out your ears. You pick."

Brandon yawned his mouth wide open and blew out with an airy *Haaaaaaa*....

"Here we go," Mike said. "Three, two..."

Brandon tensed.

"One."

It sounded like a pop-gun.

Bright pink flashed through Brandon's eyelids. The blast punched his insides, the skin in his throat rattled and snot ejected from his nose. When he opened his eyes the world was dark and spinning. Dizzied, Brandon could only react. Could only go through the steps Mike had outlined.

Grabbing Boing's shoulder, Brandon hauled him onto the litter. Took the litter handle and yanked. Dug his heels into the stone. Yanked again. Away from the cliff now, Brandon scrambled around to Boing's leg. Mike's moonlit outline did the same.

Jesus!

The legs were sheared completely off. Meaty tendrils dangled from the stump like wet yarn. Weak streams of blood heartbeat-spurted warm in Brandon's palms. Brandon reached down for the tourniquet—

"Fuck!" Brandon slapped around on the ground, looking, feeling for the tourniquet. He must have dropped it.

He swung his head back and forth. Searched. Couldn't find the fucking thing.

Mike's hand beat on Brandon's shoulder. His finger, gleaming with blood, pointed towards the cliff. The small black circlet sat there near the edge and Brandon grabbed it with sticky fingers.

Dark blood pumped from the amputation like a tipped-over a cola bottle. Brandon held up Boing's ruined leg and slipped the loop around the stump. Positioned it just below the knee and cranked on the stick. Immediately the blood slowed. *Crank*. The blood trickled. *Crank*. The blood stopped.

Mike's head shot up and he looked over Brandon's shoulder. Brandon turned. Jaran stood there, head titled and looking down at Boing. Her hand went to her mouth and she turned away and ran back into the cave.

"Tie it down!" Mike yelled, slapping Brandon's shoulder. Voice barely audible over the ringing.

Brandon tied down the tourniquet. He looked at Mike. "What now?"

Mike's head swiveled, his hands felt at the I.V. site at Boing's arm and his fingers slid along both tourniquets. With his bloody thumb, he tugged Boing's eyelids open and shined his flashlight in them. Mike checked and double-checked and triple-checked a mental list of things that only he knew. Hands touching everywhere. He leaned back on his knees, apparently satisfied with the scrutiny of his own work.

"Bring him back inside," Mike said. "I need to clean and dress these."

Brandon stood. Looked warily at Boing. Looked for anything that might have gone wrong. Adrenaline still surged through him. He felt like he should be doing something else. Something *more*. Felt like he had just run a marathon but had been told to stop right before the finish line. There must be something else that needed to be done.

He picked up the litter handles but they slipped out of his wet hands. He wiped his bloody palms on his trouser legs and picked up the handles and they took Boing back into the cave.

Mike jutted his chin. "Set him down by the fire."

They set him down and Brandon peeled his blood-sticky hands from the litter handles.

Jaran stood against the wall with her hand still pressed to her mouth. In the firelight her eyes were wide as she stared down at the carnage.

Smith stood near the pit gazing down. He looked up briefly at them with disinterest and looked back down into the pit.

Kneeling there, Mike took a bottle of clear liquid and squirted a stream onto the bloody stumps. Irrigated with saline, red-black liquid drained from the wounds and plopped on the ground. It didn't take long for Mike to dress Boing's wounds. The big white cotton bandages drank up the blood and drainage.

Mike looked up from his work. Brandon tried to hide the shock he felt splattered on his face.

"I have a few things to finish up before we can move," Mike said. "I can take it from here. Why don't you go outside and pull watch. See if there's any sign the NVA saw us."

"You sure?"

"I'm sure." He went back to his work.

Brandon wasn't sure what to do. What to say. They'd just done something incredibly stupid but—from appearances—incredibly successful. He felt they should celebrate. He felt like they should be ashamed of themselves. They'd saved a life. They'd taken a man's legs. He couldn't think of anything to say. He couldn't decide how he should feel. He backed out down the corridor, unable to take his eyes off of the mess they had made.

Slumping against the wall, Brandon slid down and sat behind the M60. He pulled his canteen from his hip and took a huge gulp of blood-warm water.

That's my fault.

He drank.

That kid lost his legs because of me.

He should tell Mike. Confess. When Boing wakes up and finds his legs gone, he's going to tell someone what Brandon did to him. How would New York view Brandon then? How would they be able to trust him after learning the truth?

He tried to turn his thoughts to something else, but

couldn't.

He and Mike had intentionally maimed that man. Was Boing even a man yet? He looked so young. Boing hadn't even had the chance to be a man and they—

No, not *they*: Brandon.

—had taken Boing's legs from him. He'd never walk again. When this war was over, what would Boing do? He could never work a farm. These people here, they didn't make their livings in office buildings. Sitting in chairs. They were farmers. They were fisherman. You needed legs for that work. Brandon didn't just take Boing's legs, he had killed him. He should have just thrown Boing from the plane without a parachute.

Compassion only lasted so long. Begging on the streets would only get Boing so far. People would only offer food and money for so long. After this war became a memory, after the children of this country grew up and forgot the war, how long would it take before their compassion for a maimed soldier turned to disgust for a begging cripple?

Brandon had killed him. Boing just had a few more years of suffering left before he finally died.

Mike appeared in the passage and he came and sat down next to Brandon. They looked out over the moonlit valley. They sat there for a moment not looking at each other. After a while, Mike asked, "Alright?"

Brandon had a difficult time figuring out how to respond to that.

Everything had been alright. Everything had gone so smoothly on the Laos mission aside from losing Phil. But here, God, everything had gone to hell so goddamned fast.

Alright? Brandon sighed. All he could say was, "I guess."

"Yeah." In the periphery, Mike nodded. "Well, I guess things could be worse."

Just wait until you find out why you had to blow Boing's legs off.

Brandon looked at his bloody hands in his lap. Just keep him on the morphine. In a few days Brandon will have twisted the truth enough to justify kicking Boing out of the plane. Would have made up some excuse. He always made excuses. He always—

BANG.

A sound like the world splitting open cut through the calm in the jungle below.

Mike and Brandon jumped to their feet and ran out to the cliff just as a rumble came up from the valley. The slick jungle canopy below rippled in the moonlight like some giant creature was waking up.

An explosion.

Brandon drew a sharp breath. Held it in. Listened. Heart throbbing in his throat.

In the moments that followed, in the time it might take for, say, three men to recover from an ambush, the faint popping of rifle fire came up from the valley.

"God *damnit!*" Mike grabbed Brandon's shoulder. "Come on! We gotta get down there!"

Brandon slipped his rifle from his back and ran toward the rope bridge. But as soon as he crossed the threshold of the cave, panic clawed his throat and he skidded to a halt on a slippery rock.

John.
John was down there.
Erlik Khan.

"We—"

Mike ran out of the cave with his rifle and his aid bag. "The boats!" Mike shouted. "We have to get to the boats!" He slung his aid bag across his shoulders.

The gashes in Brandon's belly pulsed as if stuffed with feeding maggots. Brandon took another step toward the bridge and froze. Stomach itching like bees stinging. Lightning strikes of panic streaked through his mind. He tried to follow Mike. Stumbled forward. Shook with the effort of trying to walk. But he couldn't force himself to go any further. He gasped and staggered back into the cave. "I…"

Come to me and die.

They couldn't go down there. They couldn't.

Brandon struggled with the words. With the excuses. "We can't leave. If the NVA are down there we have to secure this place."

John's dead-white eyes flashed in Brandon's mind. His belly squirmed. "The…" Brandon said.

It's warm here.

Brandon said, "The girl…" He couldn't move. "The girl needs us here. And. And Boing needs us."

"You gotta be shittin' me!" Mike screamed. "The whole team is down there in the shit! Probably wounded and fighting for their goddamn lives! They're just as fucking scared as you are! Get your shit and let's *go!*"

Clenching his fists, Brandon tried to move his feet toward the bridge. Willed them to move forward. But claws of fear reached out and slid in beneath his skin, sliced at the gash in his stomach.

"No," Brandon mumbled. Shook his head. "No! I can't risk losing you down there." If he lost Mike he would be absolutely alone. Smith would abandon Brandon. He couldn't lose Mike.

Mike snatched Brandon's shirt in both hands. The big medic yanked Brandon close and stared down with furious eyes. "You still don't get it," Mike growled. "You don't send men out unless you're willing to go in their place. You don't send men out unless you're willing to go out and bring them *back!*"

Mike watched Brandon. His grip loosened on Brandon's shirt and he said, "You've got three seconds to change your mind."

Brandon stared back at him. Fought the trembling in his body. Why wouldn't Mike listen to reason? If John was down there then the team had minutes—*minutes*—to live. If it was Counter Recon, maybe they would last a little longer. But the end would be the same. There wouldn't be anyone left to rescue—

Mike shoved Brandon and he stumbled back into the cave. The medic's face screwed up in anger. In disappointment. "You fucking coward." He turned and started toward the bridge.

"Stop!" Brandon called. "I said stop, Sergeant!" And he took a trembling step forward and shouted, voice quavering, "That's an order!"

But Mike kept going. He crossed the rope bridge and faded into the dark and rain. Then he was gone.

With fear streaming hot down his face, Brandon backed into the cave and slumped down behind the M60. The fighting down below popped staccato over his gasping breath. He grabbed the clacker. Thumbed off the little metal safety catch and watched the far side of the bridge. Ready to blow it the moment a silhouette appeared from the dark. He stared across the gap, praying that whoever was killing his men down there would not find the path leading up to him.

CHAPTER TWENTY-SEVEN

The gunfire in the jungle below had gone quiet. The drizzling rain outside the cave hardened to a downpour. And when it had quieted again to a soft patter, Brandon's panic softened with it.

Cowering there in the cave, the fiery itch in his guts burned less with each passing moment. Like a nest of angry wasps had been drugged or lulled and the only sensation left inside his belly was of tiny stick-feet probing for a place to sleep.

But across the river, a ball of lantern lights gathered, alive and pulsing with a vibrating activity at the edge of the river's black vastness.

Brandon pressed at his bandages. Dried blood flaked off and tumbled down his abdomen beneath the dressing. He looked out into the night, trying to make sense of that fear he had felt. That panic.

That hadn't been natural. It wasn't just a feeling. It was like something had crawled into his mind and crippled him. Just thinking of going down into the valley; hell, just thinking of stepping onto the rope bridge conjured images of his death.

Images of John.

The rain hissed on the rock outside.

Come to me and die.

So strange. Brandon was no stranger to fear. He had been afraid so many times in his life. He knew his mind's normal reactions to fear. And *this*...

He stared at the bridge and rubbed his stomach. *This* feeling was not normal. There had been no stimulus to trigger that absolute terror.

When that thing had come out of the rain, he had been terrified. But that thing was itself the reason for his terror.

But standing at the bridge, ready to go down. *Wanting* to go down, he just couldn't make his feet move.

He was still pressing his bandages and thinking about what had glued him in place when Jaran knelt beside him. She pulled his hand away from his stomach and put her hand on the bandages. Let it linger there as she spoke softly.

She nodded to him and stood and went out to stand by the cliff. She looked back at him with an odd sort of curiosity. As if remembering something. If whatever she was thinking was important, she didn't let on. She turned her eyes down to the valley.

Whatever she had done, Brandon felt no different. He switched the clacker's safety on and put it down by the M60 and went to stand beside the girl. Together they listened to the silence coming up from the jungle.

Were his men retreating? Were they still alive? Would they come back here?

Please let them come back.

A soft orange glow peaked out from the trees in the valley. Over long, wet minutes it grew and shined bright like a star being born.

A fire?

From atop the mountain the glow seemed small. It flared but did not spread through the rain-damp jungle.

The fire reflecting in Jaran's staring eyes showed her

confusion. She mumbled to herself as she watched it burn, as if trying to puzzle something out. Then her hands went to her mouth, capping the small gasp trying to escape.

Firelight trickled down over her fingertips and she turned away and stumbled into the cave. Echoes of her weeping diminished in the stone passage.

Whatever she had realized, whatever that fire was, for now it was her secret.

The fire below burned long. It was still burning when the rope bridge began to sway with the crossing of ghostly silhouettes.

Brandon's heart buzzed briefly, but only just. He knew those shapes.

"Tiny," Mike called.

"Bubbles," Brandon muttered. A deep shame kept his voice low.

One, two, three. Brandon counted the men as they reached the near side.

The men stumbled by him. Wet and tired and slumped-shouldered. They dropped their packs and their rifles near the cave mouth and took out their canteens and drank. The firelight below was enough for Brandon to get a good, up-close look at their ragged faces.

Chris went to his rucksack and opened it. He held the flap of it open and put something in it. After a long chug of his canteen, he said. "The boats are gone."

"What?" Brandon blurted. "What happened?"

No one spoke. Brandon looked around, waiting for one of the three men to say—

Oh shit.

Brandon counted them again. Then squeezed his eyes shut. "Where's Terry?"

But he could already guess. Their silence and grim faces said it all. And Brandon hadn't even thought to ask.

Brandon cleared his throat. "Chris—"

"Where were you?" Chris asked. His voice ghostly from exhaustion.

Brandon hesitated. "I was here."

"No shit you were *here*," Chris wheeled around, dropping his canteen on the ground and stalking toward Brandon. His face dark with shadow. Wet with rain and sweat. Eyes hellish black, spiked with dual pin-pricks of firelight. "Why the fuck weren't you *there*?" He pointed down to the valley.

Dan sat down and leaned back against the escarpment, pulled out his canteen and drank. Mike sat next to him. Dan passed the canteen to him. Mike drank. They looked at the ground.

Brandon's mouth went dry as Terry's voice echoed in his mind. *This is one of those things you don't see.*

"Nothing to say?" Chris asked.

Brandon took a breath. "What happen—"

Chris's fist caught Brandon on the jaw and he collapsed on his ass. Hand cupped over his buzzing face. Beyond his fingers he saw Mike and Dan. They were looking at him now. But the only movement was the canteen passing between them.

"Hey!" Chris turned. Smith emerged from the cave and shouted, "Knock that shit off! We've got—"

Chris punched him in the face. Smith stumbled back, but didn't go down. He sank into a low boxing stance.

"Go to your room," Chris spat at him. "Mommy and daddy are talking."

No, Brandon begged. *Don't leave.*

Smith was the only one who could stop Chris from stomping Brandon into the ground.

Smith passed the back of his hand across his lip. Looked at it. Then he spat and said, "Whatever you're going to do, do it quick." And he turned away and went into the cave.

No.

Chris turned back to him. Brandon raised his hands to block, but too late.

Chris's fist found a way in and Brandon's head filled

with cotton. His temple throbbed. Somehow he ended up on his back with Chris looming over him. Then the big man dropped to his knees, straddling him. Bodyweight crushing Brandon's belly. Beneath his bandages the sutured gashes *popped* open like knuckles cracking. A warm pudding oozed down his side.

"You wanna know what happened, *sir*?" It came out in a snarl. Chris punched his face. Soft lips split open beneath hard knuckles.

"We went down to prepare the boats like you asked, *sir!*"

Flash. Pain.

Brandon waved his hands to block.

"And Terry tried to drag one to the water, *sir!*"

Flash. Pain.

"And the boat blew up in his face, *sir!*"

Brandon choked. Spat out the bloody word, "Stop…"

Chris grabbed Brandon's shirt and pulled him in close. Whispered, "You know what happens to a man when a claymore explodes in his chest?"

Chris's right hook blasted Brandon's chin and knocked him to the edge of oblivion. The back of his skull rolled on the hard rock. He sucked in air and choked on slimy snot and blood. Hacked and coughed and spat out a wet, black wad that balled and jiggled on the ground.

Brandon's tongue worked around in his mouth. In the dizziness and confusion he almost laughed when he discovered all of his teeth were still in his head. Chris said something.

"I can't—" Brandon coughed. "What?"

"Mike came to help us." Chris took Brandon's chin and squeezed it hard. Forced Brandon to look up at him. "Where were *you*?"

Brandon's arms flopped around, buzzing numb like he had slept on them. One of his eyes swelling shut. Blood pooled in the back of his throat and he coughed it out and it ran warm down his chin. Down his neck. He rolled his eyes to look for help.

Mike handed the canteen to Dan.

They were going to let this happen. They were going to let Chris beat him to death. Terror fueled his arms. He punched at Chris, but it felt like punching through water. Broken and bleeding, Brandon fought for his life. But Chris didn't even grunt when Brandon's fists connected.

Another sledgehammer shot from Chris was probably all Brandon could take. If he got hit like that again he would probably stop breathing.

Please stop, Brandon tried to say.

Chris raised his fist high. Brandon pulled his languid hands in front of his face. A paper-thin defense. Brandon's eyes closed on their own. Anticipating a bashed skull. A swelling brain. A slow death of drowning in his own blood.

"Please," Brandon hacked. "I don't want to die…"

But this was how his life would end.

But when the *thwack* came, there was no pain. The sound was not from Chris's fist. Brandon cracked open an eye in time to see Chris's fist drop limp and thud harmless against Brandon's thigh. Chris's head drooped, and where his head went his body followed. He crashed down like a felled tree, his belly squishing Brandon's face. From Chris's mouth came the wet pig-snorts of unconsciousness.

Someone grunted. Then Chris's body wiggled and slid off.

Jaran stood over Brandon. She held one of their rifles. Still held it upright from the buttstroke she had delivered to the back of Chris' head.

Now Mike and Dan moved.

Fucking assholes.

The two men scrambled to their feet, but they froze when Jaran leveled the rifle at them. And when she clicked the safety off their hands went up.

Brandon tried to speak. Tried to say Jaran's name to get

her attention, but the sound that came out of his mouth was the sound of wet slop and she didn't look at him.

Her hands on the rifle were rock-solid and she stood as rigid as if she had been carved from the stone of the mountain. The only part of her that moved was her face. Her brow furrowed and relaxed. Her lips pulled back in a grimace.

Real quiet, Mike said, "Easy…" Then he said something in Vietnamese.

Jaran looked at the cave. She looked around at the men gathered there. She looked at the cave. She gasped like something hurt her and she looked down at Brandon and flicked her head for him to get up.

But he didn't want to move. He hurt all over. Mostly his face and head. He groaned as he rolled to his side and pushed himself to a sitting position. Dizziness rocked his head and he sat there and waited for it to pass.

Jaran flicked her head again but Brandon waved her off. He spat out blood and coughed. "Gimmie me a second, will ya?"

This kid was going out of her way to save lives. First she stopped Chris and Mike from shooting at John. Now here she was saving Brandon from fratricide. New York was accruing a large debt.

He looked at Mike and Dan. Neither of them spoke. And Brandon hurt too much to start a conversation.

Chris groaned. His hand crawled up to the back of his head. When he rubbed it he hissed. He took his hand away, fingers dark and slick. After a time, Chris rolled over and sat up beside Brandon. Looked around. Dazed. He saw the others watching Jaran and he tilted his head toward her. Saw the rifle still trained on Mike and Dan.

Lazily Chris's eyes went back and forth from the rifle to Mike and Dan. His eyes finally settled on the two men. "Next time someone's about to crack my skull open, will one of you warn me?"

CHAPTER TWENTY-EIGHT

With eyes locked on the raging fires, John stood in the dancing shadows encircling a field of monuments. Some sort of graveyard. The smell of gasoline on his hands.

It had been his hand that had set those tall timbers ablaze. Had been his hand that pulled the rifle's trigger, destroying the old carvings on the mammoth stones. It had been his hand, but he had not been the one in control.

The only things John could still control were his thoughts. And he used them to scream at the thing inside him.

You killed Terry!

John had watched. Helpless to do anything when his men, his friends, had arrived at the boats. Trapped in his own body John had screamed in the purest panic and fear he had ever felt. He knew the boats were booby-trapped, for it had been his hands that had done it.

But John's terror, it had simply aroused the thing inside him.

The graveyard burned. And John thought back in disgust. In despair. Remembered how his cock had stiffened when Terry had reached for one of the boats.

No! That wasn't me!

With his soul aching from the memory, he prayed.

But that thing let out a laugh through John's mouth.

"How dare you call me a *thing*?" John's voice said.

What else would I call you?

"A god."

I only know one God. You're not Him.

The thing chuckled. "I have *stolen* you. You are *mine*. Your fate will be the same as every soul I have stolen before. When I am finished with your body I will keep you. I will hide you away from your god. Know my name, mortal, for I am the only god who can hear you now.

The name came as if whispered in the flames of that burning graveyard.

Erlik Khan.

It wasn't using John's mouth to speak. It was inside him again.

Get out of my head.

In time, Erlik Khan said. *There's work to be done before this body of yours fails.*

Erlik Khan looked up to the mountaintop where New York was hiding.

No! John screamed. *Leave them alone!*

John. I couldn't do my miracles if you haven't gifted me such a strong body. You will watch as I consume these men. You will know that the things I do are your fault.

Erlik Khan's words were followed by tearing pain. Like acid seeped beneath his skin and ate away muscle and ligaments. John had felt this before when that thing—when *Erlik Khan*—had gone up to the mountain and whispered to Brandon.

John's soul ripped from his body and shot up into the night in a shaking blur.

And suddenly he was on the mountaintop. No body. Just a presence. Like he was made of the night. Erlik Khan was with him.

Fucking monster. Leave them alone.

I will not.

New York was there on the cliff, bathed in rain and moonlight piercing through gaps in the clouds. The girl was with them.

John had only seen her a few times. He had sensed something in her. Something *old*. But it was difficult to understand. Whatever it was, Erlik Khan sensed it, too. Erlik Khan didn't stick around long when she showed up. There was always some strange sensation bubbling up from the thing inside John when the girl showed her face. It had the taste of fear. Maybe it was—

Khan snarled, *You think I'm afraid of this girl?*

I know you are. I can feel it.

Although these sensations John felt were filtered through Erlik Khan, there was no denying that there was some kind of power radiating from her. So strong.

Chose, mortal. Which of your friends dies next?

Leave them alone!

Which of these men has confessed a weakness to you?

I'll tell you nothing.

Khan laughed. *You still think you have a choice.*

Something poked into John's mind. Then shoved. Images flashed. Memories. Every moment of his life jumbled together.

Ah. Which one is Dan?

No.

I'll find him myself.

In this strange spirt-world, Erlik Khan slipped between the men as if they were frozen in time. The girl, so small. Thin. Erlik Khan went closer to her. The danger of being so close to her was intoxicating to this devil. A thin leather cord hung around her neck. A glass vial. Erlik Khan stared as a fiery terror bloomed inside him. And when he could take no more, he recoiled from its black liquid.

You are *afraid of her.*

Erlik Khan ignored John's thoughts as he slithered among the men. The air. The rain. All was still as if John had stepped inside an oil painting. As if the people there were brushed onto a canvas of blue night and bare stone.

Chris and Brandon sat together on the ground. Brandon's face bloody and swollen.

Erlik Khan stopped beside Brandon and breathed him in.

John remembered this. How Erlik Khan had breathed in the men, searching for fear. Earlier he had found it in Brandon. But now John found himself looking on with an odd fascination. There was still a scent of fear emanating from Brandon, but it was buried beneath calluses of spite and determination. Pride welled in John. Brandon might have been a coward once. But no longer.

Don't be so sure, Erlik Khan said. *I have more horrors for this one.*

A steady hum. A vibration from Brandon's belly. Erlik Khan looked there. The hum was familiar to Erlik Khan somehow. Fear spurted from Brandon's calluses like blood from an opened jugular.

What is that? What did you do to him?

A perverted joy spread through Erlik Khan. *That is a surprise for later.*

Erlik Khan turned to Chris. John's soul ached at the scent of Chris's failing courage. His doubt. His shame. Like Brandon, Chris had calluses. A tough, opaque skin cocooning some secret that Erlik Khan seemed eager to poke at.

This isn't Dan, Khan said.

These men are going to kill you.

I hope they do. You won't last much longer. You have a tough body, but I'll need all of it. And you're leaking.

The bullet wound. John should have died hours ago. He could feel the filth spilling from his guts and poisoning his blood. He could feel the weakness of constant near-death. But he hadn't died.

After a while he began to feel other things. *Unnatural* things. He felt Erlik Khan's work and thought he had a vague understanding of what Erlik Khan was doing. Converting John's own life force into some unnatural energy. And somehow that energy was keeping John's body alive. Or at least slowing his inevitable death. How long Erlik Khan could keep him ali—

About two months, Khan said.

Get out of my head!

You asked.

Whatever scares you about that girl, New York is going to find out. I hope you're ready for an ass-kicking.

Blackness seized John like he had fallen into a crevasse. All around, burning, boiling.

Screaming.

This is what awaits your soul! Erlik Khan howled. *This is where I will hide you from your god after I have consumed your body. Cherish the time you have left on this earth.*

And the blackness vomited John back onto the mountain.

The horror lingered in John's mind. The sound of flesh boiling from bones.

So many people.

The absolute immensity of that place. Fractures jerked through John's mind.

God... help... me...

Something pulled him away from that void of madness. Screams faded and seeped into the rock and rain and the night on the mountaintop.

Welcome back, Khan said.

John was looking at faces he recognized from lifetimes ago. From the abyss came whispers of names in a voice that might have been his.

Mike.

Dan.

They stood against the escarpment with their hands raised. One of them smelled dark. Erlik Khan drew closer. Breathed it in. A familiar odor. John had smelled it in the place Erlik Khan had sent him.

It was not coming from Mike. Mike smelled of buttery spiced apples fresh from the pan. A warm and sweet smell of lingering hope. And…

John's soul soared when it struck him. The bright scent of faith. But not faith in God. An unwavering faith in the men around him. The team. Faith in New York.

Help them, Mike. John pleaded. *They need you.*
His faith is misplaced. One by one these men will crumble.
You don't know my men.
I know all men.

Khan slid closer to Dan. Embraced the dark stink of nightmare. The sulfur smell John had plunged into. The stink belching from legions of screaming mouths.

Despair.
Yes, Khan said. *Despair. This must be Dan.*

John sensed what Erlik Khan was preparing for Dan. The whispering he had tried on Brandon. Only by the miracle of that girl's intervention had Brandon escaped. But why wasn't she helping this time?

Because she's weak. She needs rest. Lucky for me.
Leave him alone! John begged. *Please!*
No.
Dan! John screamed. *Dan, run!*

Erlik Khan leaned in close. Stared into Dan's sorrowful eyes. He was about to whisper when he caught another scent. Excitement erupted in Khan as he searched the faces gathered there. But the man to whom this new smell belonged was not among them. The scent was dark. So dark it coated the stone like a film.

Desire, Erlik Khan cooed. *One of your friends has a dark soul.*

John tried not to think the name, but he couldn't help it.

Smith, Erlik Khan said.

A festering desire for power. John felt Erlik Khan's overwhelming need to find Smith. But Smith was hidden in a place where Erlik Khan could not reach.

Smith, Erlik Khan said again. As if savoring the taste. And he turned back to Dan. Eyes strained red from holding back tears. Eyes so full of despair. He had been through too much. So much had been taken from him.

You can't win this, Erlik Khan whispered to him. *There is no shame in giving up when all hope is lost.*

Fight, Dan! Fight!

A fresh sadness brushed across Dan's eyes.

Be at peace, the foul thing said to Dan. *Your suffering is needless. You can end it. You can!*

Something within Dan rumbled.

You can't win.

Yes, you can! Please, Dan! Please fight!

The foundations of strength and courage in Dan's soul fractured with the weight of such profound despair. He was crumbling from the inside. A long exhale, thick with the rotten stink of beaten-down faith and lost hope hissed from his mouth. That exhale was the most heartbreaking sound John had ever heard. The sound of a man giving up. The sound of faith collapsing.

A sudden icy pain ripped through John and Erlik Khan. The pain spoke to them. The sound of shattering ice forming the words.

I see you! The pain snarled.

Erlik Khan whirled. Came face to face with the girl.

The singing came again. Chants booming, crushing John's mind. Khan shrieked and turned and fled. Pursued by that piercing cold. Icy fingers reached for them. Just as they snapped closed, Khan dove off the cliff and sailed down, down into the warmth of the raging blaze so far below. Away from the cold. Away from the girl he feared.

CHAPTER TWENTY-NINE

So much noise. Brandon clapped his hands over his ears.

One of the men ran toward the cliff.

"Dan!"

But with Jaran's deep chanting reverberating in Brandon's skull, he wasn't sure who had called out.

Figures jolted into motion. Chris scrambling to his feet. Mike darting forward from the rock wall. But they had only closed half the distance when Dan put the pistol in his mouth and fired. There was a pop and a white flash.

Chris stopped dead. Mike skidded to a halt, arm reaching out, hand hovering in front of him.

Silhouetted blue, Dan went stiff and fell without sound over the edge. A spray of black hung for a moment in the moonlight before swirling down into the valley.

Mouth hanging open, a cool numbness spread through Brandon's chest. Breath held like he had just witnessed some macabre magic trick. Like suddenly Dan would reappear. Unharmed.

Chris and Mike perched there at the cliff edge like gargoyles, gray in the light of coming morning.

Something clattered on the rock and Brandon had to tear his eyes from the emptiness of where Dan once stood to see what had made the sound. When he did, he saw the rifle at Jaran's feet.

"Jaran!" He was only fast enough to croak out her name. He wasn't fast enough to catch her.

She collapsed on her hands and knees. Drooling. Frothy spit in the corners of her mouth. Eyes bulging, fixed on some singular point in the air. The skin of her face wiggled on the bone. Her whole body tense, trembling like she had grabbed hold of a live wire and every muscle in her body tightened with coursing electric current. She sucked a quick breath, a pneumatic hiss. Then grunted out a long, malformed word through a clenched throat. Another hissing inhale. Another squeezed-out word.

Unable to get his legs beneath him, Brandon scooted toward her.

"Who's shooting?" Smith shouted from the cave. "What happened?"

Jaran went limp just as Brandon reached her. He caught her and rolled her over in his lap. Her eyes darted, couldn't focus. The same look he had seen in her grandmother's eyes by the river.

"Hey," Brandon patted her face. "Hey, kid." Wiped sweaty hair from her face. "Jaran." She didn't respond. Her eyelids fluttered and shut and a croaking breath seeped out long from her mouth. Panic surged through his hands and he shook her. "Hey!" He pushed his fingers into her neck. Felt nothing. Adjusted his fingers. Shoved them deep into her neck. A weak pulse thump-thumped against his fingertips and he exhaled hard with relief. "Okay." A weak pulse was still a pulse. He rocked her, wincing but ignoring the agony in his back. "That's okay. Take a break."

God, what had happened to her? The things she was saying, it was like she was trying to sing again like she had in the night. Like when that thing—

"I asked a question," Smith barked. "Who the hell fired

that shot?"

Brandon ignored him. He put his ear to Jaran's nose. Still breathing.

"Captain?" Smith called. "Who fire—"

"Dan," Chris called, rubbing the back of his head. Staring into the valley. Nodding as if he had found an answer to some secret question in that gray mist below. He turned to Smith. And the next movement was so fast that when Brandon blinked, he missed it. Chris had drawn his pistol and aimed it at Smith's chest. Wiping his nose with the back of his hand, Chris said. "Dan fired that shot."

Smith raised his hands in a lazy, unconcerned show of surrender. Eyes wandering from Mike to Brandon to Jaran and back to Chris. "I see."

"Do you?" Chris's voice tight with agony. "Tell me what you see, Smith." The pistol wavered and Chris squeezed his eyes shut. When he opened them they were wet with tears. "Because I don't! I don't fucking see!"

Smith shook his head and shrugged. "I don't have any answers for you."

Chris's trigger-finger flexed. The numbness of imminent violence tingled in Brandon's arms. Breathing heavy, his face scrunched up in pain, Chris raised the 1911 skyward and pressed his forehead against the pistol grip.

Chris smacked himself on the forehead with the pistol, there was a thunk as metal hit skull. "Fuck...," he squeezed the word out through his gritted teeth. "Fuck..." Lips pulling down in a raging grimace, Chris slammed the pistol against his forehead. Again and again. Beating himself bloody, he screamed, "Fuck!"

"Hey!" Mike snatched the pistol away and threw his arms around Chris. Grabbing his head, he shoved Chris's face down into his shoulder. Mike hugged him tight. "I'm here, man." And he held Chris as the man screamed muffled wails into his shoulder.

At some point Chris' knees went weak and Mike helped him sit down on the rock. Mike held him as he shuddered.

Held him until Chris' uncontrollable shaking quieted to mournful sobs. Until the sunlight's yellow whispers warmed the gray world around them.

Wiping tears and snot on Mike's shirt, Chris whimpered. "It's my fault."

"That's bullshit, man." Mike rubbed his fingers through Chris's hair. "None of this is your fault."

"I couldn't save George. I couldn't save Terry. I couldn't save Dan. I…" Chris shuddered in Mike's arms. "I should've done something."

"You did all you could. We both did."

Chris shook his head.

"I can't get us out of this." Chris's arms squeezed Mike tight. "I'm so fucking scared."

"I know." Like a loving mother, Mike pressed his cheek on Chris's head. "You got my vote." Chris tried to look away but Mike took Chris' face in his hands, made Chris look him in the eye. "Listen. You'll get us out of this. You're the strongest guy I know. There's nobody better to lead this team. You got my vote, you hear? You got my vote."

"I can't—"

"Yes, you can!" Mike shook him. Took Chris' hand. Squeezed it. "We have everything we need to get out of here. We have maps, we have weapons, we have a plan, and we have the girl. You *can* do this."

The mention of the girl made Brandon look down in his lap. Jaran's eyes were open and she was looking at him. Brandon smiled at her, but her face was blank as if dreaming while awake. She looked older in the morning light. That youthful fullness had gone from her face. Like she had aged a decade overnight.

Chris' head dropped, chin pressed against his chest. He shook his head.

"You're in there somewhere." Putting his forehead to Chris', Mike whispered, "Where'd that hard motherfucker go?"

A long silence lingered. Then Chris mumbled something.

The hint of a smile appeared on Mike's lips. "I don't think I heard you."

Chris sniffed. When he looked up at Mike the fire of the rising sun shone in his eyes. Chris drew a long breath. "I said are you ready to take a walk?"

Mike stood and held out his hand. Chris took it and Mike pulled him to his feet. Smiled and slapped Chris on the shoulder. "There he is."

Chris spent the next few moments gazing out at the valley. Then he looked for a long while at Brandon. Chris said, "There's a difference between 'wouldn't' and 'couldn't'. So when you didn't come down with Mike, which was it?"

Brandon cleared his throat. "Couldn't."

Chris nodded.

A while later, they started down the mountain. Chris on point. Brandon took the rear and carried the M60, keeping near Jaran as she stumbled down the path. In the middle of the group, Mike and Smith carried Boing on the litter. Smith hadn't been happy about that, and he had voiced his displeasure on the mountaintop.

Throwing his rucksack on, Chris had nodded toward the path. "You go on if you want. But if you plan on stickin' with us, you pull your weight."

Smith had looked at Brandon.

"The fuck you lookin' at him for?" Chris had asked. "Commander was damn-near gutted and almost broke his back. He ain't carrying no fucking litter."

And that was all that was said about the litter.

They halted when they reached the river. The boats sat as they had when New York pulled them ashore and concealed them in the grass. Save one. The one Terry touched. A huge, black-edged chunk taken out of the bow. The chemical smell of gasoline and explosives.

The three rucksacks that Chris, Dan, and Terry had

brought down in the night lay in the grass as if being consumed by the jungle. Thick brown smears and droplets here and there on the boats, the palm fronds, the rucksacks. Like moles on an old man's skin.

Blood. Dried to a dull sheen.

A path, a slight wearing in the grass, skirted the river. Further along on that path there was a bigger, wetter blotch. Brandon followed it. A few more steps and there was another blotch. Two more steps there was another. And another. Like the blood had spurted to the rhythm of a heartbeat. Brandon followed them until there was no blood left to pump.

Followed it until the smell of voided bowels filled the stale air. And that was where Brandon found Terry. Facedown in the path. One arm cocked beneath his belly. One hand reaching out. Like he had been pulling himself away from something.

"Psst," Brandon hissed.

Mike set Boing down and dropped his pack. But when he started forward Chris held out his hand to stop him. "Don't touch him."

"He could still be alive." Mike tried to push his way by.

"He ain't. Even if he was, we haven't had eyes on him all night. I'm not risking you ending up the same as him." Chris looked at Terry. "Nobody touches him until I clear him."

"What?" Mike asked. "You think John booby-trapped him?"

Chris spat in the grass. "Dunno. He rigged the boats, didn't he?"

Mike stared at Terry. The look on his face said he might disregard Chris's warning. But ultimately he relented.

Chris dropped his rucksack by the litter. A small canvas tool kit was clipped to his LCE. Unzipping it, Chris pulled out some pliers, diagonal cutters, nippers, and some tool Brandon didn't recognize.

Turning to the group, Chris pointed at the abandoned rucksacks with a set of pliers. "Nobody touches anything that's been out of our possession until I clear it."

Brandon went back to the group and took a pair of binoculars from Chris's pack and went to the dock. Staying to the jungle shadows, he looked across the river. Vietnamese men on the far dock. One of those men was pointing across the river and up the mountain. He swept his hand at the water. A group of men nodded smartly and ran back toward the village.

Returning the binoculars to the pack, Brandon called to Chris, "NVA's still looking for a way over here."

Squatting beside Terry, poking slowly at his body, Chris called back, "We'll be moving shortly."

Jaran took Brandon around the arm. Apparently still weak, she leaned on him. She pointed south along the river path.

"What?" Brandon asked.

Jaran nodded and shooed him onward.

"Where are you going?" Smith asked.

"I don't know. She wants to show me something."

"Don't get spotted."

The path curled in on the mountain away from the river and opened up into a clearing. Jaran led him into a smoky blue haze and the smell of wet ash, like doused campfires.

Brandon pushed aside the foliage. Some distance away, a flat and jagged piece of rock maybe the size of a desk had toppled and lay askew on some other gray stone.

Black and greasy remains of burned wooden structures stood here and there in the clearing. In some places the wood was burned gray and flaking. In others, red eyes still glowed deep inside pillars. Something popped and hissed. Smoke crept out of everything and climbed skyward.

Maybe this smoke was what the NVA were looking at.

Jaran led Brandon from the line of shadow, the sun's warmth spread across his face. In the clearing, tiny pins of burned-black grass jutted from the ground and crunched beneath his boots like crusted snow. They pushed through low-hanging fronds, and when the clearing revealed itself in full Jaran's hand slipped from Brandon's shoulder, and she put it to her mouth to stifle the chirp of her soft weeping.

Jaran continued on as if drawn into the place. Brandon followed close behind.

Wooden pillars. Great slabs of smooth, polished stone. He didn't know what he was looking at, but through that blue haze of smoke, something seemed wrong.

There was an order to the place. Slabs were oriented in rings, the natural pathways between them all converged on one slab at the center of it all. Continuing on toward the center, Brandon put his hand on the smoothed edge of a slab. Wider than his hand was long. Looking up, he guessed this stone had to be about three men high. He brushed his fingertips against the sharp etchings on the stone's polished face. Two vertical columns of symbols. He couldn't understand the writing. Most likely Mongolian.

Jaran made her way slowly toward the center. Laying gentle fingers on wooden pillars and stones as she passed. Brandon followed her, gazing all around at the weavings of woodwork and huge slabs of stone. He didn't know what he was looking at.

But when he caught up to Jaran, when she looked at him and her eyes were full of sadness, he thought he understood.

A graveyard.

A *desecrated* graveyard.

There must have been thirty or forty headstones in all. Not able to understand the writing, Brandon could not say for certain which ones were older. Some didn't have etchings on them at all. But they all seemed to be cut from the same gray stone. Maybe the raw stone was brought down from the cave excavation. Fashioned later into these headstones. But how someone moved these monstrous things was beyond him.

This place couldn't have been the cemetery for the entire village. If the place was as old as Brandon thought it was, there would have been a lot more than forty headstones.

A wisp of smoke burned his nostrils as they passed a charred wood pillar. Nearing the center, Brandon glanced around the burned cemetery. Counted the headstones in their rings. So few for such a long time.

He looked at Jaran as she stopped at the headstone centered in the graveyard, set apart from the other graves by a circle of crushed stone.

Was this where they buried the shamans?

He went to her. She knelt down and touched pieces of what might have been pottery placed around the base of the headstone. It had all been shattered. The broken pieces ground nearly to dust. Jaran placed her hand upon the slab and mumbled something. Brandon followed her eyes.

Dread reached up and seized him as if it were the cold hands of the dead. Bringing up his rifle, Brandon put his back to the stone. Eyes darting between jungle shadows.

The fire in the night. This was the place he had seen glowing through the canopy. He swept his rifle back and forth. Peeked around the headstone. John. *Fuck*. John had drawn him here. This was an ambush. *Stupid*. Brandon was so stupid to come here. To expose himself in the open like this. He was—

Jaran gently pushed the rifle down. With a sad smile she shook her head and her eyes returned to the headstone.

Unwilling—maybe unable—to believe her, Brandon looked around once more. "He's not here?" Voice shaky. "You're sure?"

She ignored him. Bowed her head and murmured something.

Straightening, Brandon clicked the safety on. Turned

his attention back to what had caused his panic. The headstone.

The burned pillars were clear evidence that someone had been here, but this headstone's face screamed that it had been John.

Like the other stones, there were etchings there. And this particular slab was big enough that it featured a carved scene. But unlike the others, this one was scarred and chipped. Pockmarks and spider webbed cracks covered the smooth, gleaming surface. Brandon pressed his fingers to the stone. Slid them across the rough damage.

Bullet holes. A small-caliber rifle. Most definitely a CAR-15. The etchings, whatever name or words had been scribed there, they had been obliterated. Why would John take the time to do this? Why waste the ammo? But the ache in Brandon's gut reminded him that John didn't need ammo. He had other ways.

Brandon traced his fingers along the gouges. Following the frantic pathway to the carved scene. His fingers paused when they found a shallow bas relief. Even with the damage he could tell it had been a beautiful carving. But stepping back to see it, he noticed that only the heads of the two figures had been shot up. Maybe John hadn't had enough rounds left to erase the entire thing. But again, why even bother? It seemed so... *childish*.

Jaran whispered to the stone. Bowed her head.

Everyone needs their minute, someone had told Brandon once.

Stepping back, he turned away from the stone to look into the jungle where he had left the team. Maybe Chris would be done clearing the packs by now. Brandon could give Jaran another minute or two, but then they should start heading back. In his periphery, Jaran raised her head and put her hand on the carving. He glanced at her and his breath caught.

Jaran's walnut eyes were still red and wet with tears, but she had the look. He'd seen that look in other eyes before.

Men in his Infantry platoon, after Cox and Davis. In his own father's eyes on nights when he stood over Brandon with a belt, breath sharp and hazy with booze. People didn't do good things when they got that look. When their eyes showed the world what their soul wanted. What it needed. And Brandon could see in Jaran's soul that there was a wild need for violence.

She breathed hard as she stared at the carving. Brandon looked again. Cocked his head. Looked at it. Really looked at what the scene depicted. The faces had been destroyed by bullets, but there was still so much to see.

At the bottom there were faces. Swirling in some sort of giant cauldron in all attitudes of agony.

A thin line rose like steam or smoke from the faces. That line bulged out to become one of the prominent figures. To become its grotesque and contorted torso. Its hands... No. Brandon put his fingers to the sharp edges. Not hands.

Claws.

He looked at Jaran.

Solemnly, she nodded. "Erlik Khan." And she swept her hand to the other figure carved there.

The other figure was clearly human. Thin. With the head gone, Brandon couldn't tell if it was man or woman, but it was dressed in robes that were all-too familiar. The human figure was set higher than Erlik Khan, as if dominating him. Taking in the story presented there, Brandon saw something else that was familiar. He saw it in the human figure's raised hand as it prepared to strike down at that devil rising from Hell.

Laying his hand on the human figure, he said, "He defeated Erlik Khan?"

Jaran gestured to the grave at her feet. "Erlik Khan." She held her wrists close together in front of her. Miming shackles.

Images of the previous night sliced through his mind. The claws. The pure hate coming off that thing in the rain.

It had come when Brandon had insulted Erlik Khan. Brandon stepped back to regard the whole stone face and all the bullet holes. The damage done to this particular headstone.

Looking at the human figure, Brandon said, "I guess that explains why he came for this grave." He took Jaran gently by the arm. "Let's get back." But as he led her back to the team, his thoughts lingered on the destroyed carving.

Mike briefed him when he and Jaran returned. Terry and the packs were cleared. No booby-traps. Necessary gear and provisions were cross-loaded into rucks that the remaining members could carry.

Brandon nodded and went to the packs. It didn't take long for him to find what he was looking for. The hard leather scabbard was shoved in a rucksack's metal frame. He took it and turned to Jaran.

She looked at the sword. Brandon held it out to her. She looked around at the men.

"Hey," Brandon said. When she looked back, Brandon nodded for her to take it.

Warily she reached out and took it. Held it against her chest. The beginning of a smile forming at her lips. She nodded to him.

Brandon chuckled at an uplifting thought. For a moment he felt like he was living some fairytale. Where an unlikely hero draws a sword, maybe imbued with some ancient magic. Where she uses it to slay a monster.

But this was no fairytale. The sound of Smith stomping toward him through the grass grounded him firmly in this shitty reality.

Smith stopped in front of him. Looked at the sword in Jaran's hands. "What the hell are you doing?"

Brandon gestured to her. "We're going to have to fight to make it out of here alive."

Smith scowled and looked at Jaran. He turned back to Brandon. "So you're arming a prisoner?"

"No." Brandon watched Jaran wrap the leather sword belt around her tiny waist. Double the leather back and loop it and pull it tight. The scabbard hung along her leg. Just like the figure in the carving. "I'm arming a warrior."

CHAPTER THIRTY

Brandon took point. Jaran followed close behind him, guiding him west away from the graveyard. Away from the mountain and the river. Away from the village and their NVA pursuers. Out into that dense and wild jungle.

They walked for hours. Hacking and chopping through dense jungle with their black-painted Army-issued machetes. They stopped occasionally to rest their legs. To sip from their canteens. To let Mike and Smith massage their palms from carrying Boing's litter.

Then they moved on.

The jungle greedily absorbed the morning coolness. Before long, their uniforms turned dark and damp with sweat. Their faces sheened with wet. Casual sips from canteens during morning rest stops turned to sucking gulps in the afternoon.

Late in the day they stopped for food. Before Mike ate he tended to Boing. Switched out his I.V. bag. Wiped sweat and dirt from Boing's face with a wet cravat. He removed the blood-soaked bandages from Boing's legs and after irrigating the stumps Mike tightened the tourniquets and put on fresh bandages.

Picking through a C-ration, Jaran looked quizzically at the crackers and took a cautious nibble. She chewed, eyebrows going up in a look of pleasant surprise. She took her time eating the rest. After eating she stood and drew her sword. Every man there paused mid-bite to watch her—hands held stiff over pistol holsters like Wild West gunfighters.

But the only thing Jaran paid attention to was the gleaming metal in her hand. She sat down cross-legged in the grass, took out a cloth and wiped the blade. Picked at speckled spots of corrosion around the hilt.

Chris put down his food and walked over to her. Stared down at her. At the weapon across her lap. She looked up at him. Her hand running the cloth along the blade paused. Her other hand tightened on the grip.

Shit.

With everything that had happened, it was easy to forget that the last time Chris had spoken to Jaran was when he had shoved a gun in her face.

One good swipe and she'd be covered in Chris's guts.

Chris reached into his cargo pocket and pulled something out. Squatting down in front of her, he held that something out. Gestured with it up and down the length of the blade. A small bottle. Brandon relaxed.

Gun oil.

Reluctantly, she took it took it from him and nodded. Chris went back to his food.

Sitting apart from the team, Smith ate in silence, eyes far away. The conversation with Jaran in the cave had reignited his desire to capture Erlik Khan. Even the team had seemed eager to try and rescue John.

But after last night, after losing three more men, after they had seen what John was capable of…

Brandon set down his food. The memories spoiled his appetite.

Although it had not been specifically said aloud, the plan to capture *anyone* was unofficially aborted. The new and only objective was getting out of Dodge. But Brandon wasn't going to place any faith in the notion that Smith had any commitment to ensuring New York's survival.

If Smith still had plans of capturing his HVT, he kept them to himself. In fact, he had not said much to anyone as they marched. Fine by Brandon. If Smith didn't want to give any input, Brandon wasn't going to ask.

Chris ate and watched the group, knuckles still raw and split-skin red from the beating he gave Brandon on the mountain top. Brandon pulled out his canteen and sipped from it. Sloshed around the warm, stone-tasting water. Flakes of dried blood from his mending cheek swirled in his mouth. Water dribbled out between his swollen lips and ran down his chin. He swallowed and washed down the greasy phlegm coating his throat.

When Chris saw everyone had finished he stood and signaled for Brandon to get them moving. After a few minutes of collective groaning and stretching and putting on rucksacks, New York was moving again.

They hacked their way through that sweltering, humid hell. The sweat would not stop spilling from Brandon's skin. It soaked his clothes. Gathered between his shoulder blades and ran in a stream down his back into his trousers and into the crack of his ass and down his thigh and into his boots.

The M60's sling dug into Brandon's neck, sawing back and forth at his raw, sunburnt skin with each step. The machinegun slipped in his ever-sweating palms. No matter how many times he wiped his hands on his trouser leg, his palms poured another gallon of sweat between his hand and the M60's grip.

They walked on. Brandon thought he could dull the physical aches and pains of walking by retreating into his thoughts. But his thoughts produced their own kind of pain.

If the retrans aircraft reported negative contact with New York, SOG and the CIA would think New York was dead. If what Smith said about Mercury operations was true, no one would be coming to help. He thought about asking Smith if his director might authorize an *Icarus* mission, but thought better of it. Smith had stood by and let Chris beat Brandon nearly to death. In Brandon's book, that wasn't something that fostered a desire for conversation.

No. He wasn't going to talk to Smith unless it was absolutely necessary. Brandon kept his thoughts to himself and walked on. And, although he fought against it, his thoughts inevitably turned to John.

John was just one man, if he picked up New York's trail, he would move faster than them. He'd catch them. And if by some miracle John couldn't find them, Counter Recon wouldn't be far behind.

How was John even still alive? Mike saw him take a round to the gut. He should've died a long time ago. Or at least he should've been laid out somewhere dying.

But last night...

Images of claws. Images of blood. Images of a man standing by a cliff. They all assaulted Brandon as one.

He squeezed his eyes shut, forcing out the images, Brandon went on. He wasn't going to dwell on last night.

He focused on the here and now. He kept his eyes on the compass needle and kept it on his azimuth. Brandon led the team down a gentle decline until they came to a forked gulley. He stopped to study the arteries. Both paths glistened with damp.

Instinct told him to avoid this type of terrain altogether. The steep sides stood about a head taller than Brandon and a place like this was a good place for an ambush or to lay out anti-personnel mines.

A commander would only commit troops and anti-personnel devices to an ambush if he anticipated enemy troops coming that way. You didn't want to blow up your own men or civilian sympathizers. The overwhelming bulk of American troops were hundreds of kilometers to the south and, as far as Brandon knew, absolutely no fighting with U.S. troops had ever taken place this far north. Their NVA pursuers were still at the village and had yet to cross the river when New York had left that morning. There was no way the NVA could have gotten in front of them. Not this soon.

The shallower cut veered to the north and west, whereas the deeper cut continued south and west. He checked the map. Judging from the contour lines, either path would get them to the same place, but the northern cut went primarily uphill, dipping into steep cuts, whereas the southern cut descended gradually. Anything going downhill sounded pleasant.

Left it is.

Brandon took a step forward. The force that hit him was like a punch in the gut. So hard that his first terrified thought was that he had been shot.

But there had been no sound.

He pulled his shirt apart and looked. A dark and shiny stain blossomed in his crotch. Then he felt the familiar sting.

He was pissing himself.

Warmth squirted in his pants and he dropped the map on the ground. Stumbling back, he fumbled with his pants and pulled himself out and pissed in the dirt. Jaran gasped and backpedaled.

Mike and Smith walked up holding the litter.

"Come the fuck on, man," Mike said. "We have to walk through there."

Brandon's face flushed and he shifted to the side of the gulley and pissed. "Sorry," he said meekly. He emptied himself out into the grass and buttoned his pants. "Just really had to go."

He picked up the map. Droplets of piss were splattered across its plastic surface. He wiped the map on his trousers and scanned the file behind him. Everyone impatiently waiting for him to move out.

Except Jaran. Jaran watched him. Her head cocked and her eyes narrowed. Her eyes shifted to the southern cut and then back to him.

Brandon cleared his throat and turned back to the fork. He took a timid step toward the northern cut and—

Nothing.

He took another step. Body tense with the anticipation of the shock that would come. Just like the rope bridge. But after a few more steps, nothing came.

Brandon looked over his shoulder. Mike's eyebrows raised in disinterest.

"Just checking the footing is all," Brandon said.

Mike shrugged. "Okay to walk on?"

"Yeah. Seems fine. Seems okay."

Mike nodded. "Better get after it then."

Brandon continued on, eyeing the southern cut until it disappeared behind the gully's low wall. When it was out of view he let out a long, slow breath.

Just like last night. One moment, terror. The next moment, nothing.

They went on. Little vegetation grew in the gully. Moss on stones. Weeds here and there. The path inclined subtly. Barely enough to notice by sight alone. But enough that his leg muscles, just above his knees, burned. In the humid air, the wetness in his crotch did not dry.

When he had taken that first step down the southern path, it had been the same terror as last night on the mountain. On the mountain he'd at least had a reason to be scared. He had thought Counter Recon had been down there in the dark.

Don't lie to yourself. You thought John was down there.

True. That was who had scared him. Without knowing what was attacking Chris, Terry, and Dan, Brandon had assumed it was John. And it was that assumption that had turned his muscles to cement.

But at the gulley just then, out here in the jungle, in the daylight and with no reason to assume anything waited for them up ahead, what had scared him to the point of pissing himself?

On the mountain he had thought all of his men were dead. At the gulley he had neither seen nor heard anything to startle him. The trails, when Brandon had stood at the fork, looked almost exactly alike. There was nothing to be afraid of.

And yet.

Holding out the map, Brandon traced south from their approximate position to where the contour lines formed the southern trail. Stopping in his tracks, he turned to face the south and stepped forward.

He had only gone two steps before his heart quickened. Sensing the presence of that unknowable fear.

Turning to the east, he took a step and noticed nothing. Following the compass needle until he faced southwest, he took a step.

Blood thudded in his ears and he stopped dead. He looked up the hill. Stared into the dense jungle. Bit down on his teeth as he stared into jungle green and shadow. Sensing that fear gliding toward him through the—

"What's up?" Someone whispered.

Brandon held a hand out to silence the voice.

Sliding his foot forward, inching closer to the terror plowing toward him, the compass needle rattled beneath the glass in his shaking hand. Brandon forced himself to stand firm. Something was coming. Something was coming. Trembling. His empty bladder tried voiding itself. He stepped forward.

His heart pounded in his chest. The flashlight hanging on his LCE rocked with the beating. His body knew something his mind did not, but it would not give up its secret.

Only when he thought he might shit himself in fear did Brandon back away. With each backward step a cool relief ran through him until finally his heart slowed.

His eyelids felt heavy and his stomach ached. When he

turned back to see who had spoken to him, he saw the whole team had gathered around and were watching him quizzically.

Panting, Brandon wiped away the sweat on his face with the inside of his elbow. Looked at his watch. "How about we stop for dinner?"

They ate in silence. For that Brandon was thankful. He didn't feel like talking. Hopefully, no one would ask him why he'd pissed himself. Because, honestly, he was still trying to figure that out.

Sitting there eating, muscles finally relaxing, he dozed off and woke with a start when his head drooped and his C-ration spoon jammed the back of his throat. He was shaking his head against the fatigue when someone poked him on the shoulder. He turned.

Jaran. She beckoned him to follow.

"What is it?" Brandon asked.

She merely waved again.

He turned back to his food. Grunted. "I'm busy."

The sharp kick to his thigh made him yelp and he rubbed at the dull throbbing. Spoon held in his teeth, he mumbled, "What the hell is wrong with you?"

She looked down at him. Motioned for him to follow.

Brandon stared up at her. Rubbed the ache in his leg. She wasn't going to leave him alone. Brandon snorted, pushed himself to his feet and, picking up his rifle, followed her.

She sat down next to Boing and gently shook his shoulder. Brandon stopped short. So much for not talking.

Boing let out a soft groan and opened his eyes. They floated around and had difficulty focusing on any one thing. Jaran said something to him and he squinted and he said something back to her. She repeated herself and Boing's eyes drifted lazily up to Brandon.

Boing's voice was slow and heavy. As if speaking from underwater Boing said, "She says she saw you."

"Saw me do what?" It came out more defensively than

Brandon would have liked. But to Boing's sedated ears it probably went unnoticed.

Boing spoke.

Jaran spoke.

"At the fork," Boing said. "In the trail. She saw you at the fork and saw you just before we stopped to eat. You were afraid."

Face still numb and swollen with knuckle-shaped patterns, Brandon was a bit hesitant to discuss anything related to his fear.

Brandon kept his face tight and straight and avoided looking at Jaran to show any hint of recognition. "I had to piss at the fork and I got hungry here," Brandon said. "I don't understand what it is you're trying to tell me."

When Boing translated Jaran scowled up at Brandon. She spoke and drew claw-like fingers across her belly.

"Erlik Khan touched you," Boing said. "At the cave. The same thing happened to Jaran's ancestor. She says most people Erlik Khan has ever touched were not as lucky as you. There have only been two survivors of his touch. You and Jaran's ancestor. Jaran can feel Erlik Khan because of her ancestor's blood. But she can only feel him when he's close. But when he touched her ancestor..."

That's what that fear is? I'm feeling John?

Boing went on speaking but his voice devolved into an unintelligible buzzing. Brandon's mind swirled. Should he tell her? The sun glinted on the curved handle of Jaran's sword. In that flash he saw the bas relief. He saw the look in Jaran's eye as they crossed the river and fled her village. Her need for violence. Her need to find John.

Jaran didn't have to say anything more, Brandon knew how this would play out. If Brandon confirmed that he could feel John, she would want him to lead her directly to him.

Jesus, if Smith found out about this....

Jaran stared at him. Hard. She wasn't going to let this go.

The terror Brandon had felt on the mountain and at the fork had been the same. Is that why Brandon couldn't move? Because he could somehow sense that John was down there?

On the mountain Chris had said there was no sign of John when they went down. No sign of any enemy at all. If both what Chris said last night was true, and what Jaran was saying now was true, did that mean that just the thought of John would be enough to freeze Brandon in his tracks?

He tried it. Imagined himself fighting John. Looking into those dead eyes. Nothing happened. Not even a quickening of his pulse.

Maybe John just decided not to attack by the boats. Strange. John didn't seem like the type to squander a good opportunity for an ambush.

He's a different kind of mean. He'll take us apart. One by one...

"Shit," Brandon whispered. John hadn't *wasted* an ambush. He's wounded and fighting a bigger element. He's leveling the playing field.

Boing and Jaran spoke.

"What?" Brandon asked.

"She says if you can sense Erlik Khan," Boing said. "Then you need to lead her to him."

A smile tugged at Brandon's mouth, but he fought it. If this was true, if he could *sense* John, then he had a sure way of *avoiding* him.

Survival. That was the mission.

Not capturing an HVT. Not revenge.

Survival.

If he could sense John, he would avoid John. That was that. Nobody else had to die.

Jaran spoke.

"She..." Boing held up his palms. "She demands you lead her to him."

"Demands?" he growled. "*She* doesn't make demands.

She's a guide. That's all. If she wants to go off into the jungle and search for John on her own, fine. Tell her to be my guest. My mission is to get us out of here. Tell her if she doesn't like that then she's free to leave. We're heading south. She can come along or she can stay. I don't give a shit which."

After Boing translated, Jaran searched Brandon's eyes. Her eyes drifted down his body. A predator sizing up prey. She looked up into his eyes. She grinned. She spoke.

Boing said, "She says you're lying. You've been deliberately leading us north and west, not south and west. She knows you're avoiding something."

Despite the heat, Brandon went cold. "How does she know?" He said absently.

She spoke.

"She asks would it not have been faster to go downhill?" Boing said. "Why are we going up? The southwestern trail goes downhill. It's faster. Easier."

Footsteps brushed through the grass behind him and Brandon turned his head to the sound. Smith stood there, he said nothing. Just listened.

Brandon turned back to Boing and Jaran. "We're going uphill in case of heavy rain. I don't want to lose any of you in a flash flood."

Boing translated. Jaran spoke.

"Liar," Boing said.

"What's she talking about?" Smith asked.

"She thinks," Boing said. "That the commander can sense Erlik Khan."

"You seem a lot more coherent than you ought to be," Brandon grumbled at Boing. "And I can speak for myself." He turned away and said over his shoulder, "In any case, she's wrong." He went to his pack and hefted, winching at his throbbing back, and slid his arms in the shoulder straps, clenching his jaw to hide the pain it caused. "It looks like everyone's done eating," he called out. "Get up. We're moving out."

Brandon resumed his position at point, checking the map and verifying his azimuth. He walked and the team followed. The jungle thickened and he motioned for a five-meter spread in the file. The spacing and the thick vegetation hid him from the others every time he shook and shied away from the pangs of fear.

CHAPTER THIRTY-ONE

Only when Chris whispered Brandon's name did he emerge from his fatigued, dehydrated daze.

Brandon had walked on into the night, barely noticing the darkness that pooled from the shadows. It was the sound of Chris's voice that made Brandon realize that he could no longer see what was in front of him. Just blue-black shapes. Suggestions of things. The triple canopy jungle denied both star and moonlight. How long had he been walking like this?

He looked at the compass in his hand. Tiny luminescent green tick marks glowing in the night.

Is this even the right azimuth?

Squeezing his eyes shut against the fatigue he tried to remember how he had gotten here. But God, he was tired. He couldn't remember. He must have been walking on instinct, adjusting his path when his heart tightened in his chest.

When was the last time he had checked his compass? When was the last time they stopped for rest?

Dinner?

He remembered having dinner.

Did I?

"We should stop for the night," Chris said.

Brandon didn't argue.

They bivouacked where they halted. Chris took care of setting up security. Brandon could only grunt out *yes* or *no* to any given question. Decisions requiring thought were beyond him.

Chris set up the sleeping arrangements in a loose three-sixty. Throughout the night there was always one man pulling watch. Brandon woke to a soft nudging. When he opened his eyes Mike was kneeling over him. His face like a phantom's in the gray dawn. "Time to get moving," Mike whispered.

Brandon's legs, back, and shoulders—every muscle in him— had cemented overnight. His throat was raw and dry like he had slept all night beside a dying campfire and inhaled the wood smoke.

The headache hit him when he sat up. Forehead pulsing, he nearly vomited as he powdered his feet and changed his socks.

It took a few long, agonizing minutes for Brandon to get up from the ground. Eyes throbbing, he squinted at the team. Seeing they were ready, he moved them out.

After a while Brandon's legs loosened up and he fell back into his routine of walking and shying away from the slightest increase in his pulse. The tiniest buzz in his gut.

He led them like this for hours. Late in the afternoon Brandon pushed through some thick underbrush, like opening a thick door, and shoved his way into deep shadow that fell all around. He paused in the dark coolness. Gazed up at the earth, the *stone*, looming dark and gray above him like some biblical tidal wave: a massive natural wall of stone. Like the earth had ruptured and heaved this giant thing up. Gnarled roots snaked across the near vertical surface. So many wet streaks trickled and zigzagged across the face, converging and falling what looked like a hundred meters straight down to splash in a pool at the wall's base.

To the left and right the jutting escarpment stretched long and disappeared into the jungle.

Brandon pulled out his map. Traced his finger along the bunched-up contour lines, traced down through nearly two grid squares following the shape of a wide, upside-down 'U'. He looked left again. Looked right. He sighed. He was standing right in the middle of that 'U' shape. Adjusting his course based those feelings of fear had walked him straight into this wall. He studied the map. Looked for contour lines that might suggest a break in the wall or some natural steps that might allow them to pass. He looked for any way to get them out of this.

After a long look, he could see that there was no going over it. There was no going through. Brandon squeezed the map in his hands. Able-bodied men with ropes and climbing equipment would have a hard enough time negotiating this obstacle. Wounded men without climbing gear… The only way forward was going back the way they had come to get out of the 'U'. This was going to cost them.

All he could do in that moment was stare at the wall. Humbled at its sheer immensity.

"Shit," Brandon mumbled. He needed to think about this. He dropped his small rucksack on the ground, set his rifle on the pack and unfolded the map. He chewed his thumbnail as he considered their options.

Footsteps came through the damp grass behind him. "Why have we—"

The way Smith's voice cut off, it was the sound of someone's mind being confronted with too much bad information to process.

Brandon turned to Smith and gestured apologetically at the wall. He didn't know what to say. What was there to say that the giant obstacle could not convey on its own?

Smith whispered, "What have you done?"

Brandon said nothing.

Smith came and stood beside Brandon. His eyes turned skyward and climbed down the rock until they settled on Brandon. "What have you *done*?"

When Brandon didn't answer Smith snatched the map from his hand. Snapped it open. Traced with his finger. Looked up at Brandon. "*This* is where we are?" From the way Smith's hands curled into tight fists, crinkling the map, it looked like his tirade was going to be a rough one.

Brandon nodded, preparing for the ass chewing, imagining he must look like a dog when you catch him chewing your shoe. Brandon would wait out Smith's insults, then he'd tell Smith his plan. Then they'd move on. It was the only thing they could do.

Face going red, Smith whispered, "I fucking told them it was a bad idea to bring you six onboard." His hands shook, the map's edges flapping. "I expected incompetence, but Jesus, I didn't expect to get..." Smith held out a hand to the wall.

"Didn't expect to get what?"

Smith looked at him with shock. Like he hadn't expected Brandon to be so brave to actually speak. Face rattling with rage, Smith shouted, "I didn't expect to get a retarded *boy!*"

Brandon's eyes went to the ground. He nodded. Accepting responsibility. "It was a mistake. I'm sorr—"

"Your parents made the fucking *mistake*. Do you understand that?" Smith smacked Brandon's face with a stinging *whack*. Screamed, "Get that through your fucking skull. *You* are the mistake. You..." Smith spread his shaking hands at the wall. "Can't even read a fucking map!"

Chris and Mike pressed through the foliage. They looked up at the wall. Down at Brandon. Nothing about their demeanor changed. Chris simply nodded to the pool beneath the trickling water and said, "Fill your canteens and we'll start heading back. How far do we need to go to get around this thing?"

Smith whirled on Chris and shouted, "Eleven-*hundred* meters!"

Without even a flicker of emotion on their faces, Mike and Chris both nodded.

Smith turned to the wall. He let out his rage in an air-cracking roar. Hurled pure anger at the stone as if he expected it to crumble before him. When he had screamed himself hoarse, his eyes locked on Brandon's. Smith raised a trembling finger at him.

"Do you know why this man is here?" Smith called to Mike and Chris. "The agency wanted yes-men on these teams. Officers who would follow their handler's orders." Smith's nose scrunched up in disgust. "They gave me *him*. We interviewed his previous commander. Do you know what he said about this man?"

Brandon glanced at Mike and Chris. His gut buzzed, but he stood as firm as he could. "Don't."

Smith snarled, "He said, 'It's a wonder Doran's own platoon didn't frag him.'" Smith came closer. "He said, 'Doran can't even use foot-powder right.'" Closer. "He said, 'We lost some good men'. He said he'd trade *you* to have any one of them back. He said, 'It should've been *you*.'"

Brandon stared into Smith's eyes. Heat spread up his neck and burned in his face and he tried to suck back the pounding sting behind his eyes. These men would not see him break down. He wouldn't let them see how weak he was.

Mike waved a dismissive hand at the pool. "We can talk about this shit later. Let's get these canteens filled and get moving."

But Smith kept talking, telling Chris and Mike everything Brandon had wanted to keep hidden. And as Smith talked, they stared at Brandon.

"Private Davis," Smith said.

But anything said after that was lost to Brandon. A violent ring screamed in Brandon's ears. Embarrassment bulged in his head. He spun away from Smith and the men and he ran, bumping his shin on his rucksack, knocking his rifle to the ground.

Staggering, he left the things where they lay and plowed through the green.

Smith's hate followed through the underbrush. "That's good! Run off! Get fucking lost while you're—"

Fat leaves slapped Brandon's head and ears, swallowing Smith's voice. He ran until his breath wheezed in his head. Until his throat went raw. A lump of emotion ballooned in his throat.

It should've been you. Should've been you.

It repeated until Captain Goode's face appeared in his mind so vividly he almost thought the man was standing in front of him. Captain Goode's lips parted and whispered *It should've been you.* The words thumped Brandon like a claymore and he went down on his hands and knees. Vision going blurry as he fought to keep the warmth and wet from streaming down his face.

Brandon never meant to get anyone killed. He only wanted a reason to kick Davis and Cox out of his platoon. If they were sleeping on the line he could've punished them. Could've sent them somewhere else. He just wanted to catch them sleeping.

Captain Goode was wrong about Brandon. Smith was wrong.

Were they?

Black and sticky doubt flooded Brandon's mind.

Were they wrong? Or was it just too painful for Brandon to have his nose rubbed in his own life.

You got a lot of men killed. What gives you the right to live?

Brandon slapped his hands over his ears. Embarrassment and shame poured from his eyes. Smith was right. Brandon *was* a mistake. He never should've accepted this assignment. He should've quit after that first mission in Laos.

Smith knew every shitty secret Brandon had tried to

hide. Knew how horrible a leader he was. How poor of a soldier. And now Mike and Chris did, too.

The urge to give up was overwhelming. To just lay down right there and die.

There's no shame in giving up. Dan gave up. It was too much. Some people don't have the strength for this. You don't belong here...

Brandon curled up in the tall grass. Head nearly imploding with the crushing weight of shame and guilt and embarrassment. He had just wanted to be a staff officer. Work in an office. He hated, *hated* leading men in the field. He had done everything he could to get out of patrols. Everything short of shooting himself in the foot because he was too goddamned chicken-shit to even do that!

Give up. Rest.

Brandon rolled onto his side. The 1911 dug into his hip. He pulled his knees to his chest and buried his face in his hands. Cowards don't belong out here. And he was such a fucking coward.

Time passed not in minutes or hours, but in thoughts. His failures. His lies. Other thoughts tried to intrude. Dark thoughts. Deadly. But his mind was preoccupied with figuring out how he could even attempt to lead this team to safety. How he could face those men now that they knew why he was here.

These thoughts assaulted him until the jungle greens turned dark. Until the coolness of evening fell down around him.

Brandon stared into the jungle. He lay motionless and exhausted in the underbrush and watched the leaves hang still. Frozen.

It was peaceful. As if by laying so still and quiet that the jungle had forgotten he existed. If only it were so easy in the world.

Brandon lay curled like a stone, blanketed in a moss of contented peace. As if his fears had been purged.

He clung greedily to that peace. To move, he thought, would remind the jungle that he was still here. And the jungle would take his peace away. Like it took everything else away.

The thoughts that had poured from him left his mind clear. He could see the mistakes he had made. Mapped out and traced all the way back to his childhood. With his emotions out of the way he replayed his life leading up to this very moment. He watched it like he was observing from a reconnaissance plane. He could see what he should have done. Paths he should have taken. Decisions he should have made. Things he should have said. Things he should not have said. Most importantly, he could see how Smith had used him. He could see how Smith was still using him.

The agency wanted yes-men. Well, the agency had gotten a yes-man when they brought Brandon here.

That first briefing, when all the new captains were sitting on the plane from Okinawa, Smith had said they were brought on-board to keep the enlisted men honest. To make sure missions were accomplished to agency standards. Bullshit. All of it. Brandon had seen how New York conducted their reconnaissance in Laos. It was perfection. They gathered intelligence and avoided fighting at all costs.

Until Brandon had stepped in.

Now. *Now*, with his head clear, it was easy to see Brandon's actual purpose.

The recon teams were so good at their missions that they knew when someone was using bullshit as bait. They knew and they didn't bite. But bring in an outsider, dangle a carrot in front of them. Promise them a clean record and a prestigious assignment.

Yes, sir. Brandon had opened wide and taken that bait. Hook, line, and sinker.

John had known somewhere in his heart that this mission was bogus. He had only agreed to take it to rescue Florida. It was Brandon who refused to see the mission for what it was. And it had cost lives.

More *lives*.

Brandon's refusal to stand up against Davis and Cox had gotten men killed. His refusal to stand up to Smith had wiped out almost an entire recon team. Whatever Smith had dangled in front of Conway had sent Florida straight into a meat grinder.

No more.

No fucking more.

How long would John have let Smith string him along before scrubbing the mission and getting his team out of here? Probably not long. John might have humored Smith with a quick look around the village while the helicopters were inbound, but that would've been it.

Go up the mountain? No. John would have argued with Smith until the operative gave up out of pure frustration. Brandon knew the feeling.

A bittersweet smile tugged at Brandon's lips when he thought of John. Now that Brandon could see clearly he wanted nothing more than for John to come back. To guide Brandon. Teach him. John deserved to lead this team. And Brandon so desperately wanted to learn. John would not be helping Brandon any time soon. No. John was still a threat until they found a way to rescue him…

Still lying to yourself?

Brandon hugged himself. Made himself small.

There was no rescuing John. To get out of here, eventually they'd have to face John. And they'd have to kill him.

That time might be soon. Even though Brandon hadn't even seen John since yesterday evening, he knew the man was close. He could feel John out there somewhere. God, it was frustrating. All the random and sporadic gut-punches of fear during the long march. Veering off-course every time Brandon felt John's presence, choosing to take the worst possible route and wear out the team just to avoid that feeling. Instead of dealing with the problem, Brandon had run New York straight into a wall. Boxed them in—

...a whole different kind of mean...

Brandon squeezed his hands over his mouth and nose. Forced himself to take slow, deep breaths as the weight of what he had done crashed down on him. He focused on his body. Forced every muscle into complete stillness. The adrenaline pumping through him at that moment threatened to make him do something stupid.

Like move.

Terror plowed into him and for a flash of a moment he was back in Laos. In the dark. Sneaking around within arms-reach of a hundred NVA.

But it wasn't Brandon doing the sneaking now.

Laying there on his side, Brandon moved only his eyes.

He watched. Listened. Listened so hard. Nothing. But then—

But then something came.

Oh.

He could barely hear over his heartbeat.

Shit.

Deep breaths. Deep… Hold it. Out…

Between the pauses in his heartbeat, he heard the sound. The slow, slithering *swish*, like a snake shedding skin.

Brandon knew the sound. He had heard it nearly every moment of the last two days.

The sound of skin and hair sliding through the jungle.

Brandon strained his eyes toward the sound. Strained them until his eyes were about to tear themselves from their optic nerves.

He saw. So close.

Long black metal pushed through the grass. Then brown wooden fore-grips. Then a hand. The skin dark and sun-tanned. A bare chest glistening with sweat. Slung across a shoulder a green canvass strap. The strap hanging long to a bulging satchel charge at a man's waist.

Pressure crushed inside Brandon's skull. Eyes hyper-focused on the man. Then, beyond him, a mirror image of the man emerged. Then another. And more.

The fear that he had felt on the march. He hadn't been running away from John, he had been going right were John wanted.

John knew Brandon would do anything to avoid a fight. This rock wall was a trap. John had made it special for Brandon. And Brandon had willingly walked right into it.

And now New York was surrounded.

Counter Recon had come.

CHAPTER THIRTY-TWO

Too long.

Purple twilight trickled down the half-moon wall. Jaran knelt at the pool beneath it, dipping Boing's canteen. Cool water bubbling and sucking into the plastic mouth. Squinting into the jungle gloom, the way Brandon had gone, she wondered why none of the other men had gone to look for him. Or tried to stop him from running in the first place. She looked at the shadows crawling up the wall's face. It would be full dark soon.

She looked back to the jungle. Hoping to see some sign of Brandon's return. But there was none.

He's been gone too long.

She had not understood what was said between Smith and Brandon, but she knew the look of deep hurt on Brandon's face.

Stupid men.

Erlik Khan was out there somewhere and still they argued amongst themselves.

She shook her head.

Shortly after Brandon had run off she felt a weak sensation. Not the full terror signaling Erlik Khan's presence. More like a whisper from across an angry river, drowned out by the hiss of furious emotion. Something had been there, and then it had not.

She tried to relax. If Erlik Khan was near, she would feel it.

Can Brandon feel him?

The way Brandon had walked, starting and stopping. Shifting his course. Ignoring Jaran as she attempted to guide him. Everything about his behavior was so familiar. Like she was watching Grandmother's story unfold. In the story, the projection had tried to take her ancestor's head, but the other shamans had sung together and banished it. But not before a disintegrating wet claw had swung out and slashed her ancestor's eyes.

Brandon's fear. His erratic walking. Grandmother had said her ancestor suffered a similar affliction. Walking in a certain direction paralyzed her ancestor with some inexplicable terror. But stepping any other way had no such effect. It didn't take long for the shamans to discover Erlik Khan's unintentional gift. The gift of awareness. And they had exploited it, tracking Erlik Khan to the river where her village now stood. The hardest part was figuring out how to shield the blind shaman's mind from the fear.

Jaran fingered the vial at her neck.

Brandon denied having feelings similar to her ancestor's. Maybe Jaran was mistaken. There were differences in Grandmother's story and what Jaran had seen. If Brandon had felt Erlik Khan he should have been paralyzed. But he hadn't been. He never stopped walking, just altered his course.

Jaran stood and twisted on the canteen's cap. When Mike had woken Boing to eat, Boing had said the wall was too wide to go around. Said they had to prepare to walk back the way they had come when Brandon finally returned.

She looked at the wall. This must be the place the Soup Soldier had found when he abandoned his army. The place she had seen in his peaceful dreams.

All the water I could drink... she heard the Soup Soldier say.

Strange. Jaran remembered wanting nothing more than to see this place one day. Now all she wanted to do was leave.

It was painful to think of the Soup Soldier. He had been so kind to her. When Erlik Khan had escaped, the Soup Soldier had kept his word and tried to protect Jaran's village. Thinking back on everything that had happened, maybe Jaran should have told the Soup Soldier that, despite the peaceful appearance, her village was not a safe place. Maybe she should have told him to leave.

She'd never thought Erlik Khan would escape. What reason had there been to even consider such madness? In her naïve mind Mother and Father were infallible. Because of her foolish youth, she knew, she *knew*, that Mother and Father would keep Erlik Khan trapped forever.

Jaran wiped her eyes. Forced the painful thoughts of her parents from her mind. She didn't have the strength to grieve them now.

She thought back on the Soup Soldier and how he had tried to protect her people. He was a soldier, yes. But he was still a man. He hadn't known what type of foe he faced. If he would have known, he would have run like all the other villagers.

Regret cracked Jaran's heart, wishing she could have told him the secret she was sworn to protect. That killing Erlik Khan's mortal body would unlock the door to his own soul. And because of her oaths, Erlik Khan had flung that door wide and stepped inside the Soup Soldier's body. Worn his skin. Knew—

Jaran spun toward the wall. Nearly covered now in the coming dark. Her eyes jerked up and down its pocked face. Fear creaked in her voice. "He knows what he knew."

Jaran held up the canteen. *All the water I could drink.*

Images of Brandon slammed in her mind. At the fork.

Afraid to take the easier trail. Then all day walking, shifting, changing course with no reason at all.

He hadn't even been using his compass.

If Erlik Khan knew this place from the Soup Soldier's memories…

Jaran had to warn Boing. Tell him to get these men moving. Tell them they were in danger. She never got the chance.

Gunshots.

Jaran dove into the short grass with a yelp. Eyes darting everywhere, trying to see from where the attack was coming.

Everywhere.

Pops of light sparked in the gathering dark. Men screamed from the shadows. Long wails. Battle cries.

The gunshots stopped almost as soon as they began. She pulled herself forward in the grass. Pushed the blades aside to see.

Mike and Chris had been sitting together and looking at a map when she had gone to fill the canteen. Now they lay on their backs with their hands raised. Short, shirtless men emerged from the jungle and stood over them, rifles pointed at their heads. The shirtless men screamed, "Don't move! Don't move!"

Boing and Smith were lost somewhere in the grass. But farther off, two other shirtless men stood with their rifles pointed down and screamed, "Don't move!"

Jaran counted six attackers in the tiny clearing. There could have been more hiding in the dark. She didn't know what to do. She was defenseless. She had been cleaning her sword when Boing asked her for some water. It was lying unsheathed by the men's packs.

What could she do?

She had not heard any gunshots out in the jungle before these men had come. If Brandon was still out there, he wouldn't come running to the sound of gunfire. She had seen him cowering in the cave when the other men were fighting down in the valley.

And Erlik Khan controlled Brandon's friend. If these Vietnamese men had seen Erlik Khan out there, they would have most certainly tried to capture him or kill him.

"No," she whispered. "Not now."

If Erlik Khan showed himself now, if these Vietnamese men killed him, she'd have to fight through at least five men to restrain him before he took control of the new body. But none of these men would believe what she was trying to do. She wouldn't have time to explain. She swallowed hard. She'd have to kill them.

Kill them *now*.

Even if she surprised them she would be shot down. If she could get to a gun—

"You!"

Jaran looked up. One of the Vietnamese men spotted her. Through the grass he raised his rifle at her. "Come here!"

The other men aimed their rifles at her.

They were so close. If she ran she'd be shot in the back. There was no way those men would miss her at such close range.

She got to her knees. Looked all around. Reached out with her mind, feeling for Erlik Khan lurking somewhere out—

"Now!" the man barked.

Feeling nothing out in the shadows, she obeyed his commands. Standing slowly, she kept her hands raised.

"I said come here!" The man stood at least two heads taller than the others. She approached him. The whole time thinking of a way to warn them. Explain that they were in danger. When she got close enough, the Tall Man grabbed her arm and shoved her to the ground next to Boing.

The Tall Man spoke quickly. "What are you doing with these men?"

Jaran craned her neck to look up at the man.

He kicked her in the mouth. Jaran's jaw snapped closed. "Don't fucking look at me! What are you doing with them?" He nudged her shoulder with his foot. "Speak!"

She grabbed her chin and groaned. "Traveling," she spat around her swelling lip. "For my protection." It was the quickest half-truth she could think of.

"Liar!"

"No."

The Tall Man spun his rifle barrel-up. He screamed, "What are you doing with these men?" The rifle-butt hammered down, smashing Jaran's outstretched hand.

She felt nothing in that first bewildered moment. When she took her first breath, that was when the pain came.

The Tall Man hooked his foot under her belly and shoved, rolling her onto her back. Her shrieks rattled the air as the Tall Man stomped her belly and screamed, "Speak! *Speak!*"

"My—" Stomp. "My—" Stomp. "My village!"

The stomping quit. She seized the moment to suck in air to fuel her screams. She grabbed her hand to try and stop the pain, but her palm closed around a destroyed finger and the bone sliced inside the skin and she howled and let go. Grabbed her wrist and squeezed it tight. Tried squeezing the pain out. It didn't work.

Breathe.

"What village?" The Tall Man asked.

Inhale...

Embrace this pain.

Jaran's breath stuttered. "My village was destroyed." *Inhale...* "Everyone is dead." *Exhale...* "These men," *Inhale...* "forced me to lead them away."

Inhale...

The Tall Man watched her. In the near darkness Jaran breathed. Retreated into her mind.

Embrace this pain.

The Tall Man turned to the other shirtless men. "You

see, men? You've captured murderers! The girl says they murdered her whole village. Expect great rewards."

The shirtless men said nothing. This Tall Man, then. He was their leader.

The Tall Man turned back to her. "Americans?"

Cradling her hand, Jaran said, "I don't know what that means."

There was just enough light left to see the confusion on the Tall Man's face. "You don't know about the invaders? The war?"

"I know about the war," *Inhale*... "I don't know who you're fighting."

The Tall Man gestured at Mike and Chris. "We're fighting them." He squatted beside her and brushed the hair from her face. He spoke kindly, "Where is your village?"

She got her breath under control and told him. The Tall Man's eyes lingered on hers.

"Mong-Co?" The Tall Man whispered.

She nodded.

He watched her as if examining some animal he'd never seen. "I've heard of your village. We're forbidden from going there. No one ever explained why."

Jaran lay there and clutched her wrist as he studied her.

He stood. Without taking his eyes from her, he said to his men, "Tie up the Americans and take their weapons. Light a fire and make rice. Post a guard. We camp here, tonight."

Relief descended on her. If they went to sleep she might be able to work something out. Maybe free one of the Americans.

The shirtless men rounded up Chris, Mike, and Smith and bound their ankles with crude rope. Tied their hands behind their backs and laid the men on their bellies.

One of the shirtless men took Chris's pistol with the long, black tube on the end and pointed it to the sky. When he pulled the trigger it did not make the barking sound most guns make. It hissed and made a metallic ka-chink. The man smiled a toothless smile and stuffed the pistol in his shorts.

The shirtless men lit a small fire and Jaran looked around the clearing. Searched the flickering jungle shadows for any sign of Brandon. Still there was none.

If these shirtless men had not killed him, if he had been on his way back to rejoin the group, the gunfire would have scared him away. She squeezed her wrist tighter. She'd have to get these men on her side. Convince them to release her. If she could get away, maybe she could find Brandon. She regretted thinking about abandoning these Americans, but if she could not find a way to stop Erlik Khan, they would lose so much more than their lives.

The shirtless men went about their duties in silence. The Tall Man walked around, moving pieces of equipment and packs about with his foot.

They left Jaran lying there, didn't tie her up. The Tall Man knelt next to the packs and lifted her sword. Looked at her. His eyes flicked to the empty scabbard along her leg, then back to the sword. He dropped it on the ground and motioned for her to come to him. She stood, careful to avoid pushing herself up with her shattered hand.

When she went to the Tall Man he pointed at Boing and said, "What happened to that one?"

Boing looked up with lazy eyes.

"He was injured," Jaran said. "Fell, I think. They cut off his legs. They didn't tell me why."

The Tall Man nodded. Snapped his fingers at the closest shirtless man. The one with Chris's pistol came running.

"Yes, sir?" The shirtless man said.

"His moaning will give away our position on the march back. We'll collect the live-bounty on those three. Shoot this one."

"Yes, sir."

"No!" Jaran cried. The shirtless man stopped.

The Tall Man looked at her. "No? Why?"

Think of something.

She needed Boing to talk to Brandon. To find Erlik Khan. But she couldn't tell the Tall Man that. Not yet.

"He speaks their language," Jaran said.

The Tall Man shrugged. "These dogs understand 'stop' and 'go' when there is a gun at their back." He nodded to the shirtless man. "Shoot him."

"Wait!" Jaran said. "There are others out there. Other *Americans*. They speak to each other with that green box. If you let him live he can convince them to come here. You said there is a bounty for those men. Maybe…maybe you can get a bigger bounty."

The Tall Man's eyes narrowed in the firelight. Drifted around the small pocket beneath the half-moon wall. His eyes lingered on each American in turn. Jaran followed his gaze as it moved. His eyes swept from the sword to the packs and then back to her. His voice dangerously calm when he asked, "Do you think I am a fool?"

Jaran was about to shake her head, but the Tall Man snatched her hair and dragged her screaming away from the fire. Away from the Americans. He held the sword up to her face.

"Even Americans aren't stupid enough to let their prisoners carry weapons," the Tall Man said. "I would've believed you if you told me they forced you to carry one of their packs. But this," and he shoved the sword's edge hard against her throat. "*This* tells the *truth,* girl!" He snarled at her, teeth flickering orange and black. He spoke the next words slow. "A prisoner wouldn't beg her savior to spare the lives of her captors.

"There's one too many packs. One too many rifles." His face came close and there was murder in his voice when he said, "I'll give you a chance to save your own life. There is a man missing. Tell me where he is." He pressed the blade harder. "Tell the truth."

The truth.

She shut her eyes. Inhaled.
What would Mother and Father say?
Exhaled.
What would Grandmother say?

Her eyes flicked open. She stared into the Tall Man's eyes as he pressed sharp metal into her throat. When she spoke she didn't recognize her own voice. "Listen carefully, fool."

The Tall Man's eyes went wide. The sword eased off her neck.

"The missing one and the cripple," Jaran said. "*I* need them." She pushed her face forward. Throat skin pushing into the blade. "Take the others and go collect your bounty. I don't need them."

The Tall Man's eyes narrowed. Through the metal pressed at her throat she felt his hand tense on the handle. "Who—"

"*Fool!*" Jaran roared. "Your superiors forbid you from entering my village because of the secret my family keeps. Because we *protect* you." Her shattered hand throbbed. She fought to keep her voice from faltering. "Your coming has ruined *everything* I had planned. Take those three and go. They're nothing but meat to me. Meat to lure a beast. Leave me the cripple and *leave!*"

"How dare you speak to me as—"

She roared at the pain in her mangled hand. "When I'm done with the two I need I'll kill them myself! My family is dead because of them!" Spit popped from her lips. "Take those three and go!" She pushed her neck against the blade. "Leave!" Tears of rage went hot down her cheeks. "Leave while you still—"

The punch to her mouth knocked her dizzy. She bit down against the sudden swelling and pain. He had hit her with the hand that held the sword, his fist wrapped tight around the grip.

She raised her head to look at the Tall Man. With blood filling her mouth, with warmth dribbling down her chin, she coughed, "Take them and go."

He drew his sword hand back. His fist flashed and the back of her head slammed against a tree. The Tall Man said something beyond the blur. Jaran was trying to get her mouth to form words, but he punched.

When she lifted her head again, the jungle was completely dark save for the firelight behind her. She must have been unconscious. Her back was to a tree. Her wrists were bound above her head.

The Tall Man said something.

"What?"

"I said there is no bounty for filthy Mongol girls. You admitted to leading these men. You have aided an enemy of the people. As the senior commander in the field, I sentence you to death."

Inhale...

Her head ached from the beating. With the fuzz in her mind it took a moment to understand what the Tall Man had just said.

Beyond the immediate fear of death, there was a flicker of bittersweet happiness. She would not die by Erlik Khan's hand. She would be safe in the afterlife. She would be safe from Erlik Khan's Hell.

Still...

She had failed this world. Failed her family. She was the last. After the Tall Man murdered her there would be no one left to defeat Erlik Khan when he came.

And he would come. And he would do horrible things to this man. She almost felt sadness for the Tall Man. Almost.

If this was her end. So be it. She had been born to sacrifice herself. To die.

Still, a hole of sadness opened up inside her. To die like this felt like such a waste of her life. To be cut down by some nameless man for the crime of helping other men.

Such is war.

She felt tears coming. She dropped her chin on her

chest and she let them come. She said to the Tall Man, "You are the enemy of the people for not letting me go." Her lips trembled with fierce anger. "Fucking dog." And she spat blood on the Tall Man's feet.

The Tall Man's rough and calloused hand squeezed her chin and he pulled her face up to look at him. "Say that again."

Jaran's legs wobbled and she sagged against the tree. "Fucking. Dog."

She heard the squeezing creaks of leather as he tightened his fist on the sword's grip. The fist came. Bashed her lips. Something broke in her mouth, a sharp edge cut into her tongue. Her teeth. He broke her teeth. Warmth bubbled up from the holes in her mouth.

"Are you all right, sir?" A man asked.

"Leave me!" The Tall Man growled.

Footsteps went away through grass.

The Tall Man squeezed Jaran's broken-open chin and said, "I was going to make it a quick death. But for the insult," the Tall Man Growled. "For the insult I'm going to fuck you."

Jaran tried to kick at him but she forgot how to use her legs.

He pulled Jaran's robe tight. With her sword he slashed the fabric from breast to thigh. Grabbed the cut-open fabric and ripped it aside. He grabbed her breast and squeezed. He laughed at her body. "The tigers will be disappointed to find such *little* meat."

Around a mouthful of blood Jaran said, "The tigers would say the same of your cock."

Shadow and light played on the Tall Man's face. He chuckled in the dark. "I *do* wonder what they would say about that." The sword point traced a scraping line down Jaran's chest. Down her belly. "We should find out what the tigers think. You can ask them when they come. I'm sure they'd prefer live prey..."

An image of Erlik Khan came and terror screamed up

from inside her. "Not alive," she gasped.

The Tall Man laughed.

"Not alive."

She couldn't be left alive. If Erlik Khan found her…

She had to make the Tall Man kill her. But she couldn't move. She could barely speak.

The Tall Man dropped the sword in the grass. He reached into his shorts and pulled himself out.

Jaran spat a thick stream of the blood pooling in her mouth in the Tall Man's face. It spattered in his eyes and slid down his cheeks and chin. A white fleck, her tooth, pinged off his cheek and dropped into the dark.

"Fucking dog," she tried to say.

The Tall Man squeezed his eyes shut and he wiped away her blood and spit with his wrist. Smeared it across his face. The light of the campfire burned in his dark eyes.

The next punch slammed her head against the tree. Cheek and head stinging. Swelling. Darkness squeezed in all around her. Dizzy. The soft edges of firelight spun around her. Pain dulled with her other senses. Only by the jerking of the world around her did she know he was still beating her.

Jaran sank down, arms pulling tight above her. Darkness crept in. Her head. There was something wrong with it. All her pain was slowly draining into the night. She was on the verge of something more than unconsciousness. She barely felt the Tall Man push her legs apart. He pressed his sweat-slick body against hers. The sharp stink of his armpits. His knuckles against her thigh, he searched for her with his cock. Something out there beyond the dark hissed like a viper. The soft mechanical *ka-chink*. The Tall Man stiffened. In her ear his groans of painful ecstasy turned to wet, vomiting gurgles.

CHAPTER THIRTY-THREE

Brandon exhaled, pistol smoke bulging and rolling from the 1911's fat suppressor.

He lay prone in the foliage. Paces away, the Counter Recon man lay in the shadow of the tree prostrated at Jaran's feet as if praying at the feet of a God.

Neither Jaran nor the man moved. The other Counter Recon men sat around their fire, talking and eating. They must not have heard the shot.

Steadying the black pistol sights on the Counter Recon man, Brandon fingered the trigger. Ready to shoot again if the man moved. He never did.

It had been a risky shot. So many things could have gone wrong. Brandon had aimed for the back of the man's head, but in the dark it was difficult to line up the sights against that shadowy silhouette. At least Brandon knew he hit the man, he just didn't know where.

He should have waited until the man stepped away from Jaran before firing, but the way he had been beating the poor girl's face. And what he was doing to her after…

Wincing, Brandon shoved the thoughts aside and focused on the girl.

Jaran hung there. Her shadowed face looking down on the dead man as if in pity. She didn't move.

Had he been too late?

"Come on," he whispered. "Move."

If she was dead there was no reason to risk cutting her down. He could get her down as soon as the rest of the men had been dealt with.

But how was he going to deal with them? He only had a pistol. And he still wasn't sure if the man he had shot was dead. It was a stretch, but he could be playing possum.

Brandon watched from the grass. The longer he watched, the more time he had to think. Maybe that wasn't such a good thing. An electric numbness crept into his muscles, the feeling that he had just set irreversible events into motion. That he would have no choice but to play these things out. He couldn't run. Not anymore. As soon as those other men discovered their dead comrade, the hunt would be on. And they were far better at hunting than Brandon was at running.

He aimed the pistol. He thought of putting one in the man's back. Just to make sure.

It was too quiet now, though. Before, the man had been yelling and beating the girl. His own fury had masked the sound of his death, the gas spitting from Brandon's suppressor. Without the yelling to mask another shot, the others would hear.

The outline of the man at Jaran's feet flickered in an orange line of firelight. His shoulder and leg. The AK-47 slung across his back.

Well that could certainly even things out a bit.

Brandon let out a long breath and shifted his eyes to the men gathered around the fire. Such minimal security for such elite soldiers. Maybe they thought they had captured all of the Americans.

They almost had.

There were still two out here.

The sudden thought of John coming set Brandon

hands to shaking.

Please don't come. Please, please.

If John showed up in the middle of this, it would be chaos. It almost seemed moot to think about what to do if John came. If John came, everyone in this little patch of jungle would die. The best way to avoid that was to get moving. Whatever Brandon was going to do, he had to do it before someone found that body.

Even with relaxed security, there were still four Counter Recon men to deal with. And they had AKs and all of New York's weapons.

And a campfire? That was pretty brazen of them. They really did think they'd caught the whole team.

He couldn't overthink this. Couldn't try to control it. He lost control of everything as soon as he fired that first shot. For now, he could only control his own actions. So, what could he do?

Put guns in the hands of the Green Berets over there. That would help. Things would just kind of sort themselves out after that.

First, he'd have to get past the four Counter Recon men guarding them.

Okay, so Mike and Chris weren't an option. Not yet.

He looked at Jaran hanging there and shook his head. Regret stinging in his neck. If he made it through this, he'd at least give her a proper burial. That much he could still do for her.

He looked at Boing. Boing wasn't an option either. Crippled like he was he couldn't even—

Wait. Nobody was watching Boing. He lay on his litter in the grass close to Jaran. They hadn't even tied him up.

Brandon looked back to the dead man. And his AK-47. The ghost of a plan formed in Brandon's mind and he pulled himself to his knees. Kept his eyes on the enemy by the fire as he crept to Jaran, keeping his pistol handy in case the men by the fire saw him.

He kept low and to the shadows, and when he reached the base of the tree, he looked at the man he had shot. In the fire's glow, shiny bone and slick gore protruded from the man's temple.

Dead.

Brandon looked up at Jaran. The ambient firelight shivering on her face showed what the man had done to her.

"God," he breathed.

Blood streaked down from all over her destroyed face. Her mouth hung open. Her jaw crooked.

She hung forward. Legs loose and knees buckled beneath her. Her robe was cut open and shadow shrouded her bare skin. Her arms wrenched up awkwardly above her and tied to the tree.

Dead.

Brandon bit down hard and looked away from her face. He owed his life to this girl. She had made a habit out of saving his ass. He had been too late to return the favor.

Down on the ground, the dead man's AK was slung across his back. To roll him and slip it off would risk making noise. Brandon put his pistol down in the grass and took out his knife, grabbed the rifle's sling and sawed through it. When it was cut, he took the rifle and held the barrel into the firelight and pulled the bolt open just enough to see if there was a round chambered.

There was.

Good. One less noise.

He looked at Boing. If he could get the rifle in Boing's hands it would be one hell of a surprise for Counter Recon. As Brandon was getting to his belly to crawl something moved above him. He jerked his pistol toward the sound.

Jaran lifted her head.

"Holy shit," Brandon breathed. He stood slowly in the tree's shadow and put a gentle hand over Jaran's mouth. Whispered, "Shh. It's okay. It's me. I'm here."

Her swollen eye cracked open.

"It's me," he said. "Brandon."

Her lips moved. Thick blood stuck to them in strings. She made no sound.

Brandon holstered his pistol, wrapped his arm around Jaran's waist, then took his knife and sawed through the rope at her wrists. When she dropped he caught her tiny weight and lowered her to the ground.

"Stay here," he said. "I'll come back. Okay? Stay here."

He laid her gently in the shadowed grass. Moving away, he stepped on something hard. Jaran's sword. He picked it up and laid it in her lap. Brushing her hair from her face, he said, "Stay here."

A weak hand caught his neck and she pulled him to her, touching his forehead to hers. She held him only for a moment. She laid back, her hand falling softly against her chest.

Brandon smiled. He might get that chance to repay her after all.

He peeked around the tree. They still sat around the fire, eating rice from small bowls.

He grabbed some extra AK magazines from the dead man's bandolier. Staying at the edge of the firelight, he crawled on his belly with the rifle cradled in his forearms. Beside the litter, he whispered, "Boing."

Boing went stiff but kept silent. After a moment he rolled his head toward the sound of Brandon's voice. When he saw Brandon he mouthed, *Took my gun.*

Brandon nodded at the AK-47 in his arms and slipped it to Boing by the barrel. Brandon mouthed, *Loaded.*

Boing nodded and spared a glance at the Counter Recon team. He reached out and took the rifle and laid it beside him.

Boing mouthed, *Roving guard.* He motioned to the jungle with his eyes. Mouthed, *twelve to nine o'clock. You. Go six to nine. Neutralize.*

Brandon nodded. Mouthed, *Ten minutes. You. Make noise.*

Boing checked his watch. He patted the AK's wooden

foregrips and an evil grin split his face.

Brandon pushed himself back into the shadows far outside the fire's light. He worked his way on his belly to the six o'clock position of the clearing. When he reached the near absolute darkness, he pushed himself up into a low crouch and very slowly, very deliberately, pushed through the jungle from six to seven. Seven to eight. He didn't look directly at the fire, he didn't want to ruin his night vision. He was looking for a roving sentry on the periphery. He would need every bit of night vision he could get.

As he picked his way from eight o'clock to nine he saw Smith, Mike, and Chris lying on their stomachs. Hands tied behind their backs and ankles bound. A sentry, having finished his meal of rice, stood between Brandon and the other Americans and watched them, his AK-47 at the low ready.

Brandon inched further through the underbrush and the jungle rustled in front of him. Brandon froze. A low, coughing grunt came from the dark. Then came the sound of piss hitting ground and leaves.

The sentry by the fire called out, and the pissing man somewhere out in front of Brandon called back and the two men laughed.

Brandon brought up the pistol and pointed it into the dark. Toward where he thought the sound was coming from. He flicked his eyes to the sentry in the clearing. Gauged the distance.

Too close. If Brandon shot into the dark, the sentry by the fire would hear the gun working. And if Brandon missed the man out there in the dark—

You. Can. Not. Miss.

"Hey!"

Brandon flinched, nearly jerking the trigger.

"Hey!" Boing called again.

More rustling in the jungle beyond Brandon's suppressor, but no sign of his target.

Boing called again, "Any of you guys speak English?"

Had it been ten minutes already?

Brandon peeked through the leaves at the fire. One man put his bowl down and stood and pulled a suppressed 1911 from his waistband. Turned to Boing some distance away.

"Nobody speaks English?" Boing said. "That's too bad. If you could I'd be able to tell you I have one of your rifles and my captain is in the treeline. He already killed your commander."

The man with the pistol yelled something quick and sharp at Boing. Boing responded in Vietnamese.

"That all true, Boing?" Chris called.

"Yep."

"Things about to get loud?"

"Oh yeah."

Chris laughed. "How 'bout that." Brandon could hear the smile in that crazy fucker's voice.

The sentry standing over the Americans stepped forward and kicked Chris in the side and shouted something.

"Bad guy coming to you, Boing," Mike said. "Pistol."

Boing called, "Get ready, sir. I hope you found that guard."

Shit.

This was going sideways fast. Brandon still couldn't see the man through the trees. The men around the fire had to die, but before Brandon could kill them, he had to find the roving guard. If he didn't, he might start killing the prisoners once Boing started shooting.

Chris said, "I haven't heard anything out there, Boing." And the sentry kicked him. Chris groaned, "Gah! I think we kicked this off a little too early."

"Cap!" Mike yelled. "You gotta take out this guy watching us. And there's two guys on the other side of the fire."

Shit!

The sentry stepped over Chris and slammed the butt of his rifle in Mike's back.

Chris yelled. "Any fucking time, Brandon!"

I can't, asshole!

The pistol-slinger was almost to Boing.

Behind the sentry, Chris rolled to his side and pulled his knees to his chest and grunted as he dug his head in the dirt and got his feet under him. He said, "Looks like we're starting this party, Mike."

"First round's on you," Mike said.

Smith rolled onto his side and curled himself into a ball.

Chris launched himself low and slammed his shoulder into the back of the sentry's knees. The sentry snapped back hard and flopped in the dirt.

Mike rolled on the sentry's chest, growling and biting his face. The sentry screamed and his hands flailed, searching the ground for his rifle.

The jungle rustled in front of Brandon as the roving guard burst into the clearing, his glossy, sweaty back completely exposed to Brandon. He raised his rifle at the mess of men in the grass.

Three or four rounds of automatic rifle fire erupted and everyone, American and Vietnamese alike, jerked and stopped in a queer moment of confused silence. All heads turning to the sound.

The pistol-slinger standing in front of Boing stumbled. Took a few confused steps. Angry black holes blossomed from the man's back. He turned and put his hand to his chest, right where his heart might have been if giant pieces of it hadn't just been blown out his back. His fingers curled into claws. His face stretched in a painful grimace.

Then he collapsed.

A collective scream went up and the clearing came alive with movement. The roving guard shook off his daze and ran toward Chris and Mike. Brandon raised his pistol and shot him in the back.

Twice.

The guard yelped and jumped and whirled around and brought his rifle to his hip.

Why wasn't he dead?

The guard made weird sucking snorts and searched the jungle. Brandon wasn't sure if the guard had seen him or not, but it didn't seem to matter. With a wet, vomiting scream, the guard hosed the jungle with light and noise.

Brandon went prone, flinching as his ears rattled with the AK's flashing.

Shredded leaves and heat fell down on Brandon and he reached out his pistol and squinted in the noise. Saw the guard's quaking silhouette in the firelight and pulled the trigger. The guard's chest twitched and as the AK went silent the guard's knees knocked together and he fell down in the grass, hiccupping violently.

The two men left across the fire were on their feet and Brandon shifted his pistol sights and shot through the fire. The pistol rocked quiet in his hand, but neither of the men reacted.

He missed.

"Ah fuck," Brandon hissed. And he got up in a crouch and darted toward the fire, staying low so it would mask him coming out of the dark.

When he got closer, Brandon stood and planted his feet, aimed and fired. And fired. A man beyond the orange light went down and Brandon transitioned his sights to the next man and pulled the trigger.

But the trigger stuck. Brandon flicked the pistol sideways. Silhouetted black in the firelight, the 1911's slide was locked to the rear.

Brandon thumbed the magazine release and the man standing beyond the fire looked right into his eyes. Brandon stripped the magazine from his pistol and yanked a fresh one from his waist. The other man aimed his rifle and just as Brandon rammed the mag home, the air rocked with full-auto thumping.

The man fell down behind the fire and Brandon let the slide go forward and aimed at where the man had fallen.

Brandon stood there. Scanned for his target, confused.

"You're welcome!" Boing yelled.

Brandon looked over at him. Boing had dragged himself through the grass toward the fire and lay prone behind his AK-47.

"Brandon!" a voice called from behind.

Boing yanked up his rifle. Aimed beyond Brandon.

Brandon spun, brought up his pistol.

But there was no target. Just Chris standing there, hands still behind his back. Ankles still tied together. Brandon squinted. Then he noticed the skinny arm wrapped around Chris's waist. A black-haired head poked out from behind Chris's back. The sentry Mike and Chris had attacked. Brandon had forgotten about him.

"He's got a rifle," Chris said.

"Hey, Chris," Boing called. "You make a really good human shield."

"Fuck you, Boing."

The Counter Recon man shouted something and drew his head back behind Chris.

Boing said, "He says to drop your weapon, sir."

"Yeah," Brandon said. "That's not happening."

Chris said, "You think if I just fall down you can shoot him real quick?"

Brandon shrugged. "Maybe?"

"Okay, never mind."

Brandon kept his pistol trained just to the side of Chris's belly where the head might poke out. He only had inches to play with and had already missed his intended targets a few times. He doubted he could take the shot without hitting Chris. He had to think of something else. He breathed slow. Relaxing.

"Tell him he's outnumbered," Brandon said. "Tell him we'll let him live. We won't even take him prisoner."

Boing spoke.

There was a brief pause before the man spoke from behind Chris.

"He says he knows what Americans do to the people they capture. He says he doesn't believe you."

Fair enough.

Given what was said about Americans, this guy probably thought Brandon would shoot *through* Chris just to kill him. Brandon lowered his pistol and holstered it.

"Tell him I holstered my weapon. Tell him he's free to go."

"Don't let him leave," Smith said. "He'll tell every NVA soldier where we are."

"Shut up," Brandon said. "Tell him if he drops his rifle he can leave."

Boing spoke to the man. "He doesn't believe you."

"Well—"

A black pain slashed in Brandon's skull. Pressure blossomed in his brain and pulsed beneath the bandages on his belly.

"Oh," Brandon croaked. "Shit."

"What?" Mike asked.

"John. John is coming..." but it came out in a clenched-throat whisper.

They didn't have time for this. "Tell..." Brandon said. "Tell him—" Brandon collapsed on hands and knees. Puked water and C-rations, hot and slimy on the backs of his hands. "Go!" He roared through the vomiting. "Tell him to go!"

This was worse than the mountain. Brandon was worthless here. He needed to get the men untied. His vision blurred with tremors. The Counter Recon man peaked out from behind Chris, saw Brandon on the ground and he bolted. Jumped through the fire and ran beside the pool and on toward the dark tree-line.

Brandon clawed in the chunked dirt toward Chris. Waved Chris to him. Throat seized tight in fear, Brandon couldn't call out. He'd have to cut someone loose if they were going to survive a fight with John.

Chris saw him waving and hopped toward him. "What the hell is wrong with you?"

"Chris," Brandon gasped.

Chris and Brandon inched toward each other. The running Counter Recon man slammed into some invisible wall and stopped dead. Stood stiff in the shadows. His sweating skin glistened in the firelight.

The tremors in Brandon's belly ripped at his guts.

"Chris!" he tried to scream.

The Counter Recon man fell over, but in his place stood a shadow. Its white eyes glowing in the dark.

Chris followed Brandon's eyes. Then he saw. He bunny-hopped furiously toward Bandon. Gasping, "Oh shit, oh shit, oh shit!"

John knelt and yanked his knife out of the man's chest. Then took the man's AK-47.

"What do I do?" Boing screamed.

"We can't shoot him!" Mike yelled.

"Oh shit, oh shit, oh shit!"

John stepped smiling into the firelight. "Figured it out, have you?" He gestured around at the dead men. "I was hoping to get one of these bodies. Good and rugged. This one's getting a little slow." He shrugged. "No worries. Your souls will give this one some more mileage."

Boing aimed his rifle at him. John looked down his nose at him. "No, thank you. I still have some walking to do."

Chris came hopping to Brandon. Brandon raised his pistol at John.

When John saw that he stopped. Cocked his head. "Now that would be fun. I'd like to get in there and see what happened in your life to make you so afraid." He raised his arms wide. "Fire away."

"Shoot him!" Smith screamed. "For God's sake, shoot him!"

Brandon's finger trembled. He tried. But all the

strength went out of him and the pistol fell from his hand and dropped in the grass.

"Such a disappointment," John said. He raised his rifle, muzzle aimed between Brandon's eyes. "No courageous act before you die?"

Brandon stared down the barrel. He wasn't going to look away. Not anymore.

A tiny shadow broke from the jungle behind John—trailing a sliding glimmer of long, curved light.

The sword flashed up and Jaran brought it down hard.

John's rifle fell to the ground. And with it, John's hand. Severed at the wrist, it still clung to the AK's pistol grip.

Jaran spoke, muffled through her ruined mouth.

John shrieked and went for the rifle, but Jaran, lumbering on her feet, kicked him hard in the belly and he tumbled backward. When he hit the ground, Jaran leapt on him.

Chris dove to his belly next to Brandon. "Untie me for fuck sake! Cut me loose!"

Brandon wrenched his knife free from his belt and sawed with shaking hands through the ropes at Chris's wrists.

When his hands snapped free, Chris grabbed the knife. "I need to borrow this." He cut through the ropes on his ankles in a fraction of the time.

Chris was up and running to Mike. In moments Mike and Smith were free and grabbing whatever weapons they could find.

The three of them ran to Jaran. Mike pulled the girl off of John. When she was clear, Mike and Chris stood over John, looking down at him. They looked at each other for the briefest of moments.

And then they beat the absolute shit out of John.

Stomping and punching and stomping some more.

All the while, John howled.

Stop! Brandon tried to say.

He sucked in air. Held it. Then forced it all out in a

scream. "Stop!"

Mike and Chris paused with feet raised.

Brandon waved them off. "Don't. Don't kill..." and he flopped on the ground and shivered.

"If he bleeds to death," Mike asked. "Will he take over the girl?"

Brandon didn't know.

Chris and Mike looked at each other. Looked at Jaran. Looked down at John. Whether they believed any of this madness or not, they went to work.

Chris dropped down and straddled John and kept him subdued. Mike ran to the pile of gear and returned with his aid bag. After applying a tourniquet to John's forearm and bandaging his wrist, they dragged him to the fire and tied him up.

John's demonic wailing shook the air.

Mike took John's uninjured arm and tried to insert an I.V.

John shook violently. "Don't touch me you fucking nig—"

Mike punched him in the mouth. Pulled two cloths from his kit and handed them to Chris. "Gag him."

Chris balled one up but John refused to open his mouth. Chris punched him in the throat, when John gagged Chris shoved it in his mouth. The other he wrapped around John's head between his teeth.

When the I.V. was running and John was tied and seated by the fire, Mike went to Jaran and helped her up. Brought her to the fire. In the light, Brandon could see the true extent of her injuries.

It wasn't just a wonder she was alive. It was a miracle. She should have been brain-damaged. Or blind.

Chris came over to Brandon. "What the fuck is with you, man?"

Brandon pointed at John. "Cuh-cuh-can't muh-muh-move—"

Chris looked at John. "What? Like when John's

around?"

Brandon grabbed his belly. "He tuh-tuh-touched muh-me."

"Aww." Chris knelt and helped Brandon to his feet. "Did the bad man tuh-tuh-touch you?" He draped Brandon's arm over his shoulder and supported him.

Chris dragged Brandon over to the fire, sat him down and handed him a canteen. Brandon took it and sucked down the water.

"Hey, sir," Chris said.

Brandon looked up at him.

Chris looked around at the carnage in the clearing. He looked down at Brandon and smiled. "Boy, I'm fucking glad you came back."

"Th-thanks."

"Hey…" Chris rubbed the back of his neck and knelt next to Brandon. "Listen. No offense, but it's really annoying when you talk like that."

Chris stared at him.

Brandon stared back. He lowered the canteen from his lips and said, "Fuh-fuh-"

Chris threw his head back and howled with laughter and slapped Brandon on the shoulder. After a moment, Brandon laughed, too.

CHAPTER THIRTY-FOUR

Darkness pressed in hard against the dying campfire. John stared at Brandon across the low flames. Every time Brandon closed his eyes those two white orbs haunted the dark behind his lids.

Shivering as if he lay naked in some arctic wasteland, Brandon leaned back against a rucksack. Hugged himself. The constant urge to vomit pulsed in his raw throat. Everything ached. So thirsty. Any water he succeeded in drinking he almost instantly puked up.

"Man," Chris said. "You don't look too good."

"Yeah," Mike knelt beside Brandon. "Can you tell me what's wrong? Did you eat something bad? Have you been purifying your water?"

Brandon couldn't answer. His teeth clenched so tight they threatened to shatter in his gums.

It had to be the proximity to John. Had to be. Maybe some distance would help. Just get away from him for a minute. Brandon rolled onto his side, tried to push himself up. His legs seized. The only progress he made in the way of standing was kicking dirt into the fire. The fire hissed angrily. The pulsing orange glow in the trees above dimmed a little more. The thought of lying helpless in the dark with John so close would have made Brandon piss himself if he'd had any piss left. He tried to stand again.

"Easy," Mike said.

Head in the grass, inhaling the smell of damp earth, Brandon watched Jaran.

Watched her watching John.

Frail, she leaned on her sword like a cane. Fingers of one hand curled around the grip, point stuck in the dirt. Hunched over, she stood there as if at any moment she might topple.

Such a vast difference from when he had first met her. That sword was probably the only thing keeping her on her feet. Despite her broken appearance, she stared at John with a hardness that suggested she would fight him again if she had to. Suggested that she might be *eager* to.

With some trepidation, Brandon hazarded a glance at John. His white eyes now scowled fiercely at Jaran.

Images of filth assaulted Brandon's mind and he retched. Thick yellow froth oozed from his mouth. The sound must have broken whatever spell Jaran was under.

Caked in blood and dirt, oblivious or uncaring of her torn robe and her nakedness, she limped toward him like she was clawing her way out of Hell. The point of her sword dragged behind her in the dirt.

Mike held Brandon as he trembled. Jaran came and her sword fell from her hand and it thumped in the grass. She took the vial from around her neck and bit out the stopper. Plucking a long, thin piece of grass from the ground, she dipped it inside the glass. When she withdrew it, a thick black ichor coated the grass. She held it to Brandon's lips.

Brandon tried to ask what the liquid was, but his words came out a stuttering mess.

Jaran spoke. Boing translated. "She says it will calm your fear."

Whatever it was congealed on the tip of the grass in a

heavy black bead. Brandon didn't trust the look of it. But he was at the point where he'd try anything to stop those terrible shakes. He parted his lips. Jaran put the grass on his tongue and she pressed her hand over his mouth, apparently anticipating his immediate gagging on the bitter and earthy taste of a tree root slick with wet dog shit.

When he gulped Jaran put her hand on his stomach. Some sound came from her swollen and slack mouth.

The shaking stopped. He looked down at her hand on his belly, amazed.

Suddenly able to think clearly, Brandon said, "Someone get her some fucking clothes."

Mike and Chris watched him for a moment, stunned. Then Chris went to Boing's pack—they were about the same size—and came back with trousers, a belt, a fatigue jacket, a pair of socks, and a pair of boots.

"What the hell did she give you?" Mike asked.

"No idea." Brandon tongued his teeth and spat in the grass. "Tastes awful."

Mike looked at Jaran quizzically. Then picked up his aid bag and took Jaran by the elbow and guided her to the fire. He sat her down and inspected her face.

Fix her good. God knows we might need her again.

Brandon stood, still anxious to get away from John. His muscles ached, but he felt surprisingly refreshed.

Chris mimed disrobing, and Jaran looked down at her cut-open robes. She wasn't shy. Chris helped her stand and she shed her robe like old skin.

Brandon gasped at the sight of her naked body. She looked like she'd been mauled by an animal. Her back, from neck to waist, was crisscrossed with long raised scars. Many of those scars were split open with new gashes.

Mike saw. "Jesus…" He rummaged in his kit for bandages.

Jaran went on without wincing, without notice. She slipped her leg into the trousers Chris held out.

John stared at her. His smiling eyes igniting some

forgotten anger deep in Brandon. An anger he had not felt since climbing out of that pit and nearly executing Jaran. An anger that, until recently, had nearly been snuffed out by pure fear and anxiety. But now…

Now it had the room it needed to burn.

He took a cautious step toward John. Hesitated. He tightened his gut muscles, anticipating the ice-water shock of fear. It did not come. He circled around behind John, avoiding his eyes. When he was behind him, Brandon pulled his bandana from his first aid pouch and tied it around John's eyes. John let out a deep and muffled chuckle from behind his gag.

Brandon had never wanted to kill anyone. Hadn't even wanted to kill the Counter Recon men. Right then? He *wanted* to kill John.

Chris buttoned Jaran's jacket and tightened her boot laces. The clothes were somewhat baggy on her small frame, but it was better than being naked.

Mike cleaned the blood from her face with a brown washcloth soaked in the pool's water. The damage and swelling was far worse than Brandon had thought. When he had cut her down from the tree her nose had been beaten flat. Now it had swollen shiny and round like a puss-filled blister. Her mouth still hung open like she had just run a marathon. At first, Brandon had thought it was from the exertion of swinging the sword. That was not the case. Her mouth hung open because she could not close it. That motherfucker had broken her jaw.

Smith came to the fire and said to Boing, "What did the girl tell the Counter Recon commander?"

Boing hesitated, looking at Chris and Mike. Then Brandon.

Smith cocked his head. He didn't bother disguising his anger. "Don't make me ask again."

"She said something about only needing me and the commander. She said she was using us the whole time. As bait."

"Bait for what?" Smith asked.

Boing jutted his chin toward John.

Brandon waved dismissively at her. "Probably bullshitting him."

Boing shook his head. "She wasn't afraid. She was *angry*. She told him he was ruining her plans."

"I *saw* what he was doing to her." Brandon pointed to the tree where she had been tied. "He was beating her to death. He was *raping* her. If it had been me hanging there, I would have told him anything just to make him stop."

Boing's eyes drifted to Jaran.

"Seems odd," Smith said. "That she would only barter for *your* life and leave the rest of us to Counter Recon. I can see why she wanted to spare the interpreter. She needs him to communicate with you. What I can't figure out is why *you* are worth saving."

"I have no idea." Brandon doubted Smith thought any of the men were worth saving.

"I believe it has something to do with that stomach wound of yours."

Brandon's hand flinched, about to press itself against the gashes in his belly, but he stopped it.

Brandon looked at the thin slice of wall still illuminated by the fire. When Brandon denied having those feelings, Jaran hadn't pressed him. She let Brandon wander. She had let him walk right into this trap.

Jaran cradled her mangled hand in her lap.

He remembered the graveyard. The carving.

If she was a warrior, it only made sense that she needed an enemy to fight. John certainly fit that description. Was New York somehow standing in her way?

"That true, princess?" Chris spat in the fire. Knelt down and stuck his face into Jaran's. "You thinking of fuckin' us over?"

Jaran scowled up at him.

"Hey," Brandon snapped his fingers angrily at Chris.

Chris looked at him.

"We treat her like one of our own until we figure this out."

"What's left to figure out?" Chris stood and held out his arms to the wall. "She walked us into an *ambush!*"

"*I* walked us into an ambush!" Brandon planted himself between Chris and Jaran. He looked up at Chris. "The only reason we're able to have this conversation is because she got the drop on John. We're not going treat her like an animal."

There wasn't much empathy on those faces in the firelight.

"She saved our lives," Brandon said. "She deserves the chance to explain herself." He looked at Chris and Mike. "Everyone gets a voice."

Chris watched him. Tongued the wad of tobacco in his lip. Spat in the grass. "Fine."

Brandon turned and knelt in front of Jaran. He looked over his shoulder at Boing. "Let her talk."

Boing wrinkled his face. "What if she lies?"

"Then she lies!" Brandon held up an apologetic hand to Boing. He needed a nap. Just thirty minutes would restore some of his sanity. "Translate for me."

Jaran looked up at him with her one good eye. Brandon said, "Help me understand what's going on. Tell me how we can help."

Boing spoke.

Jaran's eye drifted lethargically. Some kind of wet clicking, a grinding sound spilled out of her mouth. She lifted her palm to her mouth. She whimpered. Brushed her fingertips across her chin. Her head drooped and when she shut that bruised eye, a tear fell in her lap.

"Her jaw's broken," Mike said. "Talking won't be pleasant for her."

"Can you give her some morphine?" Brandon asked.

"All gone."

Brandon shook his head. "Boing, tell her we don't have any pain killers left."

Boing did so.

Jaran nodded and pushed her hand trembling into the grass. She plucked a piece and dipped it into the vial around her neck and tongued the liquid. This she repeated twice more. She held the little vial in her broken and crooked fingers and tried to put the stopper in it with her good hand but kept missing. Brandon took her hand and held it firm and she pushed in the stopper.

She nodded to him and let the vial hang. Putting her hands in her lap, she inhaled deep, hissing through her broken nose, inhaled again and let out a long exhale.

Her hands relaxed in her lap, fingers spilling open. Her eye opened just a little. She sat for a long time and breathed with that odd *in, in, out* rhythm. Her eye focused on nothing. She did not blink. Soon, as if with no pain, she spoke in garbled, malformed words.

"Can you understand her?" Brandon asked.

"Barely."

She spoke and then she paused long enough for Boing to translate. Then spoke again. The men listened. Soon they were sitting before her and leaning in to hear every word she said and every word Boing translated.

Jaran spoke of an ancient deception and how Erlik Khan first came to this world. She spoke of the hunt her ancestors led, over years and thousands of miles. She told of Erlik Khan's capture where her village now stood. She told of her family's secret. Their oaths. She told of the lives she and her family had taken to protect that secret.

She told them that she was the last person left who could stand between Erlik Khan and this world.

And by the time the fire had died considerably and the black jungle turned the steel color of a new day, she spoke of the price she must pay to stop Erlik Khan. And she spoke of her willingness to pay it.

No one spoke when Jaran finished. The silence lingered. Brandon, and perhaps each man, reflected on the things she had said.

The longer Brandon thought, the more sure he became that they couldn't hide Erlik Khan away again. Not the way Jaran's family had done. Not in the pit. There was no way Smith would let something this extraordinary slip away.

Brandon shoved his palms into his eyes. "Ask her how we can help." He wasn't sure he was ready to hear the answer. "What does she need?"

Boing spoke.

Jaran spoke.

"Her sword," Boing said.

Raising her head, she looked at John. Pure hate glowed in her eye. And she spoke again.

Boing's mouth dropped open.

"What did she say?" Brandon asked.

"She said…" The look of shock plain on his face. "She said she needs John's head."

CHAPTER THIRTY-FIVE

The shock of Jaran's last words left Brandon dumbfounded and slack-jawed. Harsh, angry voices shouted around him but he had no idea what they were saying.

Jaran sat motionless. Gazing disinterested and unblinking into some great beyond.

"I ain't letting her kill John," Chris said. "No way. We have him now. We can figure out a way to help him."

"I agree," Mike said. "Last time I checked we don't execute prisoners of war."

Brandon looked at Smith, expecting his opinion to be the same as the others', but for different reasons. But Smith was looking at John with such intensity he noticed neither the team's eyes on him, nor the sudden quiet.

Brandon left Smith to his thoughts and turned back to Jaran. He watched her for a long time, thinking about her story.

"Ask her how killing John will stop Erlik Khan," Brandon said. "I thought killing him was the worst thing to do."

Boing spoke.

Jaran closed her swollen eye. She replied.

"She says she won't give him the chance to take her body."

After Boing spoke Jaran held up her hand. She slid a finger across her wrist and repeated the gesture on the other wrist. She gestured at John and drew her finger across her throat.

Brandon exhaled, the weight of her implication pressing down on him. "I see."

"So do I," Chris said. "And there's no fucking way I'm letting her kill my friend. He's tied up and he ain't going anywhere. We have time to figure out how to help him."

Massaging his wrist with his thumb, Brandon said, "You study much shamanism, Chris?"

"What?"

"I'm curious to hear your plan for pulling the Devil out of John."

A brief silence. Then from behind there came the familiar click and zip of gunmetal sliding from a nylon holster. Chris came around and stood between Brandon and Jaran, holding his 1911 alongside his thigh. "How about I end this little discussion right now?"

Jaran didn't move.

The pistol twitched in Chris's hand.

"Put that up." Brandon looked up at Chris. Then back to Jaran, or what little of her he could see between Chris's legs. "You were bluffing the first time you pulled it on her. You're bluffing now."

"I ain't bluffing."

"Mmm," Brandon muttered. Too lost in thought to give Chris much consideration. Eventually Chris holstered his pistol and walked away. As he watched Jaran, a whisper of a memory kept calling to Brandon. Conway's voice. *She brought me back... She brought me back...*

"Ask her again about Conway," Brandon said. "I need details."

Boing asked her. After some back and forth Boing said,

"She says the Soup Soldier drowned Captain Conway in the river. He must have been dead long enough for the transfer to occur. She and her grandmother resuscitated Conway and put him in the pit in case they figured out a way to capture Erlik Khan without sacrificing themselves."

"Did they figure anything out?"

"No."

Brandon thought about that. "Can Erlik Khan re-enter someone once he has left their body?"

Boing spoke.

Jaran spoke.

"She doesn't know."

Brandon chewed his fingernails. This was such an abstract problem. Erlik Khan would take possession of whoever killed John. Jaran's solution was murder-suicide. Well, now that Brandon thought about it, the problem was actually pretty simple. It was the *solution* that was abstract: how could they defeat Khan, but save John *and* Jaran? This needed more thought, and he was thankful Chris had shut up and given him some quiet in which to think. But in that quiet, the hiss of water falling in the pool behind them grew loud and just as annoying as Chris's mouth—

She brought me back.

Clinging to a hope, Brandon pointed at the pool. "Ask her if that will work."

Chris knelt beside him.

Brandon kept his eyes on Boing as he and Jaran spoke. Searched Boing's eyes for the slightest hint of disappointment. Hopeful that it would not come.

But it did.

Boing looked at Brandon and shook his head. "She won't sacrifice herself if there is a chance that Erlik Khan will return."

"He didn't return to Conway."

"I told her that. She said Khan never had the need to return to Conway's body."

Brandon was about to protest but he looked at Jaran

sitting there. Broken and traumatized. She was volunteering to end this nightmare. Volunteering to kill herself so that Brandon and his men could have a chance to live. Arguing with her about *how* she should kill herself made her sacrifice seem egregiously trivial.

It was quiet while Brandon thought. Maybe the others were having the same thoughts Brandon was having. Jaran spoke first.

Disgust tightened upon Boing's face and he shook his head, angrily muttering something to himself.

Brandon flicked up his palm impatiently. "What'd she say?"

"Nothing, sir," Boing said. "It's stupid."

"Let me decide what's stupid."

Boing rolled his eyes. "She says if one of us wants to test your idea of drowning John, she'll instruct us how to do it. But she says having Erlik Khan inside you won't be pleasant."

It was hard not to recoil from that.

Go back to the beginnings of war itself and you'll find soldiers who have said they would gladly lay down their lives so that their friends might live. But in that little piece of jungle, as the air around them turned pre-dawn blue, not one man raised his voice to volunteer.

"Okay," Brandon mumbled. He rubbed his face. Ran his hand through his hair. The insanity of what he wanted to say gnawed at him. He nodded. "Okay. We're gonna let her do it."

The sound that came next was like a gunshot as, in unison, the four men around him shouted, "*What?*"

Brandon turned to see mouths hanging open. Hard eyes full of disbelief. Shock. Anger.

Chris squinted at him, "Let me make sure I heard you cor—"

"You heard me," Brandon said. "I'm going to let her do what she needs to do. This…" Brandon held up his palms, motioned toward John. "Whatever the hell is going on here, it needs to end. *Now*. You've seen. You've *all* seen what he's capable of." Brandon pointed at Jaran. "She is the *only* weapon we have against him. Without Jaran, he's unstoppable."

"We can *help* him!" Mike said.

Brandon shouted back the only question that seemed relevant. "How?"

Mike's face curled back in anger. "We can figure that out when we get him home!"

Brandon's own calmness with this was starting to concern him. "You mean *if* we make it home." Brandon nearly laughed when he said, "What do you think will happen if we make it back?" He gestured at Smith. "He knows what's inside John now. You think he'll let John ever see the light of day again?"

Smith bristled with a quiet anger.

Brandon ignored him. "John will spend the rest of his life plugged into machines until they think he's ready to go on a U.S. sponsored killing spree." He nodded at Mike and Chris. "I remember each one of you telling me," Brandon tapped his fingers and listed off names of dead men. "Terry, Dan, Howard." He pointed at John. "Even *John* told me not to trust Smith. Now all the sudden you trust him to protect your friend? To help him? Guys, John is a walking plague. He's a human nuke. Give him six months and he could wipe out half of Europe. Maybe more. You *actually* believe the government will throw that kind of power away to save one man's life?"

Mike and Chris said nothing. Smith said nothing.

Brandon sighed. "Listen. It's a shitty situation, but…" Brandon looked around the jungle, searched for the right words. He looked at Smith. The operative's eyes dark and sunken like a skull's in the near-dead firelight. Then his eyes fell on John. Brandon gestured at him with a weak flick of his finger. "John. John told me the burden of command is heavy here. Well, shit he was right. So I'll share it with you. You can either hate *me* for letting Jaran kill him now; or you can hate *yourselves* for letting the government kill him later."

Brandon watched Chris and Mike in the blue quiet. When their faces did not change, when they said nothing, Brandon said, "I'll give you some time to make your peace with this." He stood. "Say your goodbyes."

Brandon looked at Smith briefly before turning away and slipping slowly into the jungle. Smith didn't look happy. Brandon walked until the sound of water splashing in the pool was lost behind the wall of vegetation, until there was nothing but peaceful quiet. Then he sat down. With a big sigh all the tension went out of him and he sank tiredly forward until the pain in his back made him tighten again.

He wished there was another way. Wished Jaran would just try what had worked for Conway. Drown John and—

What an absolutely selfish thought to have.

To think it was too bad that Jaran wouldn't kill herself the way Brandon wanted her to. He should've been thinking it was too bad she had to kill herself in the first place. Should've been thinking about the suffering she would endure in that Hell. For eternity.

Eternity.

He had said the word before. He knew the definition. But it was a concept Brandon had never seriously considered. Never really had to. Eternity in Hell. Suffering forever. Just trying to think about time on such a large scale hurt his mind.

Brandon combed his fingers through his hair. "Brave kid…"

Well. At least with her sacrifice Smith wouldn't get the chance to unleash Erlik Khan on the world.

The underbrush rustled behind him with the sound of someone stepping through. Brandon cocked his head. He sighed in anticipation. Like when his father stumbled drunk through Brandon's bedroom door. Leaned against the doorframe and gazed in disgust as his son wrote or painted. Words slurring as he wondered aloud how his son turned out to be such a faggot.

"I figured you'd be right behind me," Brandon said. "Did you need a minute to calm down?"

"Oh," Smith said. "Quite the opposite."

When Brandon turned to face whatever hateful tirade Smith had prepared, Brandon got a facefull of the *opposite*.

The hard leather toe of Smith's boot cracked him in the jaw and Brandon's teeth clacked shut. When he opened his eyes he was on his back in the grass and looking up at Smith towering over him.

Smith glared at him. "I had to decide if I was going to kill you or not." His fingers worked into fists and relaxed and worked into fists again. "I'm still undecided."

CHAPTER THIRTY-SIX

Smith grabbed Brandon's wrist and yanked, twisted, flopping Brandon over on his stomach. Face in the dirt, Smith's boot thudded on the back of Brandon's head. Brandon drew in air to cry out but he inhaled sharp grass that poked the roof of his mouth and he went into a coughing fit. He spat out dirt. He spat out blood. He tried to push himself up, but Smith wrenched his wrist and pushed him back down.

"We need to have a talk," Smith growled.

Rolling his head in the wet mash of blood and dirt, Brandon looked up at Smith. He stared back as calmly as if reading a newspaper.

Blood and drool dribbling down Brandon's chin, he said, "I'm not going to let anyone else die. I don't—"

Smith wrenched his wrist and Brandon cried out. "You're going to do what I *tell* you to do."

Kneeling on Brandon's back, Smith pulled Brandon's elbow against his leg. "I won't have my operators going rogue." Smith pulled, Brandon's forearm bending the wrong way over Smith's thigh. Elbow straining. "We're all going to get back on the same page, do you understand me?" He pulled Brandon's arm. "One team." He pulled. "One." Pulled. "Fight."

The tendons in Brandon's arm strained and something rippled under his skin. Down his arm. Down in his shoulder. Down in his neck. Brandon flexed his arm hard, so hard it shook, fighting the strain, but his arm was giving—

God.

—it was giving. The inside of Brandon's elbow bulged under his shirt sleeve and he bit down hard. The scream in his throat leaked out through his clenched teeth.

"*Understand?*" Smith said.

Brandon wanted to say *yes*. So bad. Wanted to give in and get his arm back. To stop the hurt. Snot blew out his nose in quick, panicked exhales. Things popped and plucked beneath the skin. He wanted to say *yes*.

Instead he spat blood and said, "That girl's whole family is dead." Something crackled in his arm and Brandon winced, inhaled sharply. "We're responsible. Us! I'm letting her finish this."

Smith leaned on Brandon's arm. "Is that what you think is going to happen?"

"I know it is. I'm the fucking commander."

Smith let out a snarl and pushed his face toward Brandon's. "You're not in command of a Goddamned thing. The CIA *created* SOG. This might be your pie, but my fingers are buried knuckle-deep in it."

Smith kept hold of Brandon's arm with one hand and with the other reached for his hip. There was a *snap* and the whisper of gunmetal.

Smith said, "Erlik Khan will be turned over to American hands. With or without your team."

Through Smith's legs, the jungle moved. A shadow materialized and stalked toward them. Rifle at the low-ready. The shadow made no sound. No sound at all. Not until it was nearly on top of Smith.

Then the shadow whispered, "Ssssmith…"

Smith jerked his head around as the rifle butt swung.

The sound Smith's face made was disgustingly similar to when Brandon accidently dropped one of his mother's watermelons in the driveway. The hollow crack when it broke apart, the slap when its red guts blew out onto the pavement.

Smith's legs newborn-calf wobbled. Then buckled. He released Brandon's arm. Smith collapsed and dropped the pistol and shoved his face into his hands. Dark blood leaked out from the sides of his palms and poured in fat lines down his cheeks like tears. His head lolled and his eyes moved about haphazardly as if the blow had knocked his brain loose.

"You okay?" Chris asked.

Brandon rubbed his elbow. "Yeah."

Chris slung his rifle and stooped and grabbed Smith's pistol from the ground. From over the barrel he looked at Smith and said, "Boys who misbehave get their toys taken away."

Inspecting the 1911, Chris clicked out the magazine, looked at the rounds, slipped the magazine back into place. Pinch-checked the slide and clicked on the safety. Then he took the pistol by the suppressor and held the grip out to Brandon. "There's one in the chamber. Gun's a little dirty. Needs a cleaning."

Brandon stared up at the 1911.

Chris shook the pistol grip at him.

Blood ran from Smith's hands down his neck and onto his shirt. When Smith took his hands away a ball of blood dropped in his lap. He put his hands back over his nose.

"Hey," Chris said, shaking the pistol at him.

"I already have one," Brandon said.

"Yeah..." Chris rolled his eyes. "But I'll bet it'll piss him off a lot more if *you* hang on to his gun."

Brandon shook off the shock of what just happened. He pushed himself up and straightened out his shirt and he took the pistol. "Thank you."

Chris daintily put a hand on his chest and mockingly gasped. "Why, you are *so* welcome." He turned to Smith. "See, Smith? Good boys use their *manners*. Remember—"

"You bwoke my fucking nothe!" Smith screamed. Voice muffled and nasally through clasped hands.

A grin spread across Chris's face. He cocked his head at the man. "Well, that was pretty much my intention. Just count yourself lucky you didn't raise that pistol any higher." Chris slid his rifle off his shoulder and bounced it in his hands. "I'd have blown that *nothe* of yours through the back of your *thkull*."

Wet growls bubbled from behind Smith's hands.

Chris leaned down and gave Smith a friendly pat on the shoulder. "That's your first and only warning. I still have some things in my pack that go boom. If you ever think about gettin' froggy again, there won't be much of you left to bury." Chris pressed in close over the operative and said, "*Understand?*"

Smith shrugged him off, staring hard at him from behind his bloody hands.

"I'll take silence as compliance." Chris turned and went back the way he had come. Then he paused. He didn't look back when he said, "I came over here to tell you that Mike and I agree with you. Come on back and let's get this over with. Before we change our minds."

Brandon stared a moment. Stunned. Doubting he'd ever get used to the way Chris shifted gears from peace to violence.

"Be right there," Brandon said.

Chris hesitated. Then he went on.

Smith stood. Stumbled a bit toward Brandon, one hand still covering his face and the other pulling out the O.D. green cravat from the first aid pouch on his shoulder. "Stop that man, Captain."

Brandon watched him. Seeing Smith look so weak was odd. Alien. "That's not gonna happen."

Smith stopped dead. Eyes working back and forth

between Brandon's. He was slow in putting the cravat over his nose. As if he had just realized something profound but could not put it into words.

"Your..." Smith said. Then paused. "Your *Colonel* will hear about this! This *insubordination*! He'll hear about what that man did to me!"

What *Chris* had done?

He looked at Smith. "*I* did that to you." Brandon was a little surprised at the words that had come out. It had just seemed like the right thing to say. It certainly shut Smith up for the moment.

"*I* did that..." Brandon repeated. And he made an effort to stand a little straighter despite the pain in his back. He remembered John. How he had been quick to plant himself firmly between his men and whatever antagonized them. Brandon's heart sank a little at the thought. During Brandon's short time here, John had usually been planted between *Brandon* and the team. All of John's arguing and questioning, John wasn't being insubordinate, he was simply doing the best he could to protect New York. Now Chris had just done the same for Brandon. How long ago was it that Chris had nearly beaten Brandon to death? And now he had just saved his life. Brandon almost laughed.

That's Chris for you...

But what changed?

"Are you listening?" Smith said. "That man is finished. *You* are finished!"

Brandon had been gazing off into the jungle, but when Smith spoke his eyes snapped back to the man. "I was finished way before you brought me here. Maybe it's time I made up for some things." Brandon squared his shoulders. "*I* did that to you. I *ordered* Chris to hit you."

"What—"

"My report," Brandon said. "Will include an account of how you broke under pressure. In the face of the enemy. And when you became a danger to the team, my report will say, you had to be restrained." Brandon's voice was flat and even and far away, as if he were listening to someone else speak. Imagining sitting before the staff officers and the Colonel in his debriefing.

Brandon chewed his thumbnail. Almost hearing the letters of his statement on the typewriter. "When our handler became combative and turned his weapon on the team, I ordered my NCOIC to subdue him. Our handler was injured..." Brandon glanced at Smith's face. "...*significantly*, in the process."

Smith. Hunched over. Small. His eyes narrowed at Brandon behind the blood-soaked cravat. "All of a sudden you're a compassionate commander? Looking out for your men? Stop lying to yourself. I *know* about you, Captain. You're an incompetent fucking coward and you always will be. The only thing you're good at is getting men killed. Getting *better* men killed."

Brandon tensed like he'd been kneed in the gut, but he forced himself to stand tall. He swallowed. When he was sure his voice wouldn't crack, he tossed his hand in a dismissive wave and said, "My guys are going to report whatever I tell them to report. You won't win this one."

That must not have been the reaction Smith had wanted. His demeanor changed so rapidly it was like a different person was speaking. "Brandon," Smith said softly. "Don't you understand what that man is? Don't you understand what we could *do* with him? We could win this entire war with one man. *One man!* This is so much bigger than us."

Brandon nodded. "For once I agree with you. It *is* bigger than us."

Smith's eyes softened.

Brandon shook his head. "So much bigger. And you kept throwing men at a thing we never stood a fucking chance against."

The look in Smith's eyes went murderous. Heavy, wet breaths blew out behind the cravat.

Brandon stuffed Smith's pistol in his belt. "If you think you can control something like that, you're the one who's lying to yourself." Brandon shouldered by Smith on his way back to his men. He said over his shoulder, "John dies. Right now. End of story. Then we get the fuck out of here."

Brandon left Smith where he stood and backtracked through the foliage. He found Mike and Chris standing around Boing. He joined them. Chris had collected Smith's rifle.

Boing sat with his back leaned against a rucksack. His ruined legs—

Fuck.

How do you even begin to apologize to a man for something like that?

Jaran sat by the smoldering fire. Eyes closed. Her lips moved silently. She had taken off the camouflage jacket and wore only a baggy brown undershirt.

"Praying," Boing said softly.

Brandon nodded. He should probably do that too. Just in case. In his fuzzy exhaustion, he tried to remember how. How had his mother done it? He could only remember looking out the dark window above his bed before sleep and the simple prayers of the child who knelt there.

God bless Mommy and Daddy and my teacher Mrs. Crary and I would really like a fire truck like the one Tim has.

"She won't be long," Boing said.

Brandon cocked his head to look at Jaran's arms, there was something—

"I.V. tubes," Mike said.

Brandon could see that. Short little stubs of clear plastic tubing taped to her arms. Pinched off with tiny blue crimps.

"Why are they cut?" Brandon asked.

"It'll have the same effect as opening up her wrists," Mike said. "But it's slower. More controlled."

"It'll give her more chances at bat," Chris said. "In case

something goes wrong."

"*Or*," Mike said, "If we think of something better at the last minute. Just because I agreed to this doesn't mean I've given up on John. I just wanted more time to think."

Brandon nodded at all this. Blinked. And blinked again at the fatigue crawling up his neck and burrowing into his skull. "Good thinking, Mike. Good thinking." He looked down at Boing. "You mind if I join you?"

Boing's eyebrows went up. "No. No, not at all."

Brandon sat down behind Boing and leaned up against his rucksack. "Wake me when she's ready."

"Uh. Sure," Boing said. "Okay."

Brandon closed his eyes. He was so tired it was making him dizzy. He felt sleep coming fast.

"Sir?" Boing said.

"Hmm?"

"Good job today."

Brandon pulled open his eyes. The light was coming through the thin parts of the jungle canopy. They had made it through a whole day without losing anyone. He was thinking that maybe things were beginning to turn in their favor. That maybe they could make it through this coming day without losing anyone else.

Then a pang of sadness hit him and he rolled his head on the canvass pack to look at Jaran. If everything went right in that coming day, he would lose two more.

"Thanks," Brandon said. "Couldn't have done it without you." And he closed his eyes.

And there on the ground, exhausted and swirling into dark, Brandon tried to pray before the sleep pulled him all the way down.

God bless Chris and Mike and Boing. And John and Jaran. Especially those two.

And Smith...

Brandon grunted softly.

Smith can go to Hell.

CHAPTER THIRTY-SEVEN

John felt his soul ripping again from his body.
Just let me die!
His body was so weak. These things this demon did, the things he conjured, the tearing of John's soul to travel beyond his flesh, they were killing him.
Yes, Erlik Khan said. *You're all used up. But you'll have to last long enough for me to find another. Even I can't fight death forever.*
Mike, Chris, and Boing sat around the girl, but Erlik Khan avoided them. He drifted toward Smith.
Smith sat apart from the others, holding a cloth over his bloodied face. He smelled of charred anger, but cruel determination pooled around him like smoke.
John recognized this scent on the mountaintop. When Erlik Khan had whispered to Dan.
You're going to kill Smith, too?
Oh no. Can you not feel what's in this man's heart? Oh, but the poor man's conflicted. He won't do what he desires. There still seems to be some humanity left in there. I'll need to fix that.
What are you going to do?
This man needs permission. Rank laughter rumbled. *I'm going to give it to him.*

John's soul cried out as Erlik Khan willed some kind of spiritual hands into existence. With these hands Khan reached out and placed them on Smith's shoulders. A tremor rippled across Smith's blood-blackened face, like some force tore at his mind.

I know what you want, Erlik Khan said to Smith. *But they won't let you have it. You must take it. So many lives will be spared if you do. Good lives.*

On and on Erlik Khan whispered. And with each word whispered to Smith, John felt his life force spilling out into that eternal nothingness around him.

Smith's soul did not crack or crumble like Dan's. For Smith, bright rays of a pure joy pierced his eyes and shot out into that dull spirt world.

Good.

Erlik Khan's phantasmal hand took Smith's and brought it down. Slowly down to Smith's leg. Slowly down to his boot. Together, their fingers closed around the knife's handle.

Good…

CHAPTER THIRTY-EIGHT

Through a heavy warm haze a voice said, "Brandon…"

Someone shook him. Though the blurriness of sleep, he saw dark skin. He closed his eyes again.

"Brandon," the voice said again. Brandon swatted at the sound like a nat. Soothing warmth and the promise of dreams held him firm.

But then someone had a hold of Brandon's shirt and pulled him up. He sat there, dazed, and slowly came into wakefulness. Slowly remembered where he was.

Brandon dropped his face in his hands. "Shit."

Mike was kneeling beside him. "You awake."

Rubbing his face, Brandon grumbled, "Yeah." He pushed himself sleepily to his feet. "But I don't want to be."

"Yeah, I hear you."

He had never felt such a strong desire for sleep.

No. Not a desire. Brandon had never felt such a strong *need* for sleep. Never felt it pull so hard.

But his silent whining and wish for sleep dulled when he stumbled over to join Mike, Chris, and Boing around Jaran. Chris carried her sword. Unsheathed. No doubt standing ready to hand it off to her.

She had not moved from where she sat cross-legged when Brandon laid down for his catnap.

Boing looked up at him. "She's ready."

And with the bump of adrenaline from hearing those words, Brandon was awake.

Chris turned the sword upside down, held it high and drove the blade into the ground beside Jaran.

She didn't flinch.

In the most unceremonious of fashions, Mike reached down and turned the little blue plastic valves on the I.V. tubes protruding from Jaran's forearms.

She sat with her hands on her knees. Two streams of blood criss-crossed in a dark X and splattered on her pants. The sound of rain on tarpaper.

Jaran's eye, shot red from a burst capillary, dipped down to look. When she saw her life draining from her she hissed through gritted teeth and squeezed her eye shut. Tightened her hands into fists. The blood streams shuddered and she let out the tiniest of whimpers.

"This is fucked," Chris whispered.

"My thoughts exactly." Mike pushed forward. "I'm stopping this." And he dropped to his knees before the girl and took her forearm in his huge hand and turned it up and reached for the valve.

Jaran slapped his hand away, flinging blood in a wide S and spraying Mike's uniform.

Brandon crossed his arms and rubbed his forearms with his thumbs. Skin tingling with phantom pain as if his own blood was draining.

With Jaran's blood dripping down his chest, Mike watched her settle. Watched her breathe. Inhale. Inhale. Exhale. Watched her calm herself.

Brandon's chest rose and fell in hyperventilating rhythm. How the hell could she be so calm about this?

Mike brought up his hands and looked at them. Blood spilled from his palms and ran down into his shirt sleeves.

He took Jaran's hand in his own and held it tight.

Chris knelt down and took her other hand. Her blood ran down her arm and spilled over their joined fingers. "We're here, kid."

A sad smile pulled at her eyes. As if she understood just by the tone of Chris's voice. The blood ran. The smile vanished. She fell deeper into the rhythm of her breathing. Inhale. Inhale. Exhale.

"How long…" Brandon whispered. He cut off his words, unsure of how to phrase the question without sounding callous.

"She's almost done," Mike said without taking his eyes off her. "She said she wants to be right on the edge when she…" Mike shook his head.

"When she opens John's throat," Chris said. "She thinks if she's gone before he dies then there might be a chance for her to escape. Go to Heaven. Or wherever she goes."

The blood streams stuttered, and though they still poured from her, the force behind them lessened. Jaran's eye fluttered. She waivered where she sat. Her eye tried to focus on something. Something behind the men. Then her eye snapped open. The terror on her face shot through Brandon and he spun.

"Smith!" Brandon screamed, because screaming was the only thing he could think to do after seeing something so insanely wrong. The image of Smith in profile standing over John, his combat knife raised in both hands, body tensed with the anticipation of a hard, downward blow. Straight through John's heart. He was too far away. Even if any of the men wanted to reach Smith before that knife fell, it would be too late. The insanity of it, Brandon couldn't think of anything else to do but scream.

Then Chris shot him.

The side of Smith's uniform popped and he bent sideways and he tucked his elbows into his belly. His knees buckled. As he collapsed he reached out with the blade, tried to stab John on his way down, but the knife only snagged part of the cravat around John's eyes. It peeled down revealing one white orb.

Brandon whipped his head to Chris. Shouted, "What the *fuck?*"

Chris shouted back, "What do you mean what the fuck? What the fuck was I supposed to do?"

Brandon shot his hands up, trying to pull answers or logic or reason out of the damp jungle air. "You shot a fucking *American!*"

"Did you see what—"

"Guys!" Mike shouted. And they looked at him. But he was watching John.

And when they looked, Smith was still moving. He had already cut through the paracord around John's feet and was working on the cord around John's arms.

"Shoot him!" Brandon screamed.

Chris fired. And fired.

Both rounds tore fabric from Smith's pants, but Smith didn't even flinch.

"His legs are paralyzed!" Mike shouted. He grabbed Jaran and pulled her up to her feet. "Shoot him in the head!"

John watched them. Even with cravats covering most of his face Brandon could see the eager smile on John's face.

"Come on, sweetheart," Mike said, lifting Jaran. He stood behind her. Braced her with his chest. He lifted her arms. Put his own 1911 in her lethargic hands. Her limp fingers slid over the trigger. "You can do this." Desperately, he said, "Come on, now."

Insane laughter erupted in the jungle. Smith rolled onto his back, bellowing incoherent sounds of triumph. Knife held aloft as if he had pulled it from a stone. His gleeful cackles went on as John stood and reached up and pulled the cravats from his face.

"*Come on*, Jaran," Mike pleaded. "It's showtime."

"It certainly is," John said.

John held out his hand to Smith. And the way Smith's face brightened upon seeing John reach out to him, the way his eyes widened, Smith looked to be in pure ecstasy. He reached up to take John's hand.

But when Smith's fingers touched John's they were slapped away. "The knife!" John shouted. "Give me the *knife* you wretched thing."

Smith's face drained, but he handed up the knife just the same.

John took the knife. Looked at it. Looked back at Smith. "You..." John growled. "You *touched* me."

And John brought up his knee and stomped down on Smith's throat. Grinded his dirty black boot into Smith's windpipe.

Smith's face contorted and he bared his teeth. Opened his mouth wide. But if he was screaming, there was no sound.

"Jaran!" Mike shouted. Still helping her stand. "Come on, honey. Come on!"

Jaran's head slumped and she fumbled the pistol and it thumped heavy in the grass.

Mike bent and snatched up the 1911 and the moment he let go of Jaran she slid down and collapsed in the grass.

The jungle writhed with John's dark, mocking laughter. "You were so close!"

Chris jerked his pistol toward John. John paused in his tracks, pure disgust smearing across his face. "Don't you *dare*," John growled, stalking forward. "I refuse to wear a faggot's skin."

Chris's finger trembled on the trigger.

"Disgusting..." John said. "Isn't that what Daddy called you?" John cocked his head. "Mmm. No... it was *Mommy*."

"Shut up," Chris croaked.

Inching forward like a stalking tiger, John grinned at Chris. "Mommy was so disgusted when she found out

In Human

about little Chrissy. He was so hurt he ran away. Volunteered for Vietnam. But all those slick cocks in the showers made him forget about the hurt."

Chris's face reddened and his lips stretched back in a snarl. "You shut your fucking mouth."

Brandon's eyes darted between John and Chris. The 1911 and John's face. If John had been worried about getting shot he'd have made some sort of move already.

"Chris," Brandon said. "He's baiting you."

Chris's head sunk down, eye-level with the pistol's rear sight.

"I've seen your dreams, Chrissy." John rubbed the flat of the knife in a circle around his crotch. "Filthy dreams of this cock on your lips." He slid the blade into the fly of his trousers. Jerked. Out came a button. "Do you still want it?" John purred. "Open wide…"

"For fuck sake, Chris," Brandon pleaded. "He *wants* you to shoot him."

Chris's trembling brow relaxed. "Good."

The calmness in Chris's voice chilled Brandon to the core. "Don't…"

But the next sound that came was the gas spraying from Chris's suppressor.

Mike's head jerked up. Brandon's hands shot to his mouth.

John howled. He dropped the knife to the ground and grabbed his knee. He shifted his weight and stood heavily on his good leg. The one without the bullet in it. John's furious eyes locked on Brandon's.

Exhaling with pure relief, Brandon said, "Jeez…"

"Don't go running off, John," Chris said. "The girl ain't done with you." The slide of his pistol was locked to the rear and he dropped the empty magazine and took out a fresh one. As he inserted it he mumbled something about knives and gun fights.

Out of the corner of his eye, Brandon saw movement. A blur. He barely had his head turned in time to see John drop to his knee and reach into the grass and raise his hand and fling his arm. In the space between Brandon and John's empty hand there was a glimmer of light. If he had blinked he would have missed it.

He was still wondering what that glimmer was when a weight punched his chest.

Instantly something didn't feel right. Brandon grunted. Something inside Brandon... something *shriveled*. Deflated. The very next breath he took bent him over sideways, from his armpit to his waist there was a pressure ballooning inside him. Brandon sucked in air. Then screamed. Feeling as though his chest might blow itself wide open.

"Brandon?" Chris said. Then Chris's hands were all over him. "Brandon!"

Brandon's hands went up to his chest. To where the pain was. His fingers curled around thick, cylindrical metal. Fingernails scraped and *zipped* on the knurling.

"Oh no," Brandon groaned. "Oh no." He slumped in Chris's arms.

Grabbing him, Chris turned him and guided him down to the ground and laid him on his back.

"It's okay!" Chris said. But his voice was trembling, his face was wide and pale with creeping shock. "I'm here." Chris's eyes darted down and up and down again. Then squeezed shut. "Oh fuck." And his eyes popped open and he looked at Brandon and he said, "I got you." He said, "We can fix this." He turned his head over his shoulder and the air vibrated with his terror when he screamed, "MIIIIKE!" When he inhaled long and screamed, "*MEDIC!*"

Someone yelled, "He's running!" Then there were gunshots. From where Brandon lay on the ground, through flashes and throbs of pain, he saw a big dark shape limping off into the jungle.

Someone yelled, "Goddamnit!"

Someone yelled, "Boing, watch our backs!"

Someone yelled, "Mike!"

And Mike was there with Jaran limp in his arms and he laid her on the ground. Thank God for Mike. He'd have something for the pain.

"M-morph..." Brandon said. A crack inside his chest snatched away his words.

Mike shoved Chris out of the way and knelt over Brandon. When he looked at Brandon's chest his eyes went wide. But only for a second. When he looked into Brandon's eyes his face went flat. Clinical. Calmly, Mike said, "Morphine's all gone, Brandon. But you're tough, right?" Mike nodded to him. "You won't need it, right? I'll fix you up good, you just need to tough this out for me, okay? Stick with me, okay?"

Brandon shook. The pain in his chest was too much. Mike grabbed the knife handle and Brandon let out a wail like an infant and he kicked his legs and flailed his arms.

Mike grabbed Brandon's arms and pinned them against his belly. "Stop! Stop it!" He turned to Chris. "Get his legs!"

And a giant weight fell on Brandon's legs. Arms snaked in under his calves and constricted.

All Brandon could move was his head and he shook it furiously. Screaming. Sobbing. Spittle flew from Brandon's mouth. The pain hammered his chest. Tears poured down the sides of his head.

He just wanted to die. Just wanted the pain to go away. Defeated. Wishing for death, Brandon let his head fall. He cried. Cried so hard. Rolling his head he saw Jaran lying beside him. Her good eye looking at him. Her head lay on her arm, her bloody hand stretched out to him, fingers curled just slightly, like she had been holding out a piece of paper to him or maybe a flower but had dropped it somewhere.

"Kill that fucker," Brandon croaked to her. His dying wish. If he was going to die, he'd die cursing Erlik Khan's name. Brandon gritted his teeth and growled "*Kill—*"

But through his agony, a cold realization floated up. Jaran wasn't blinking. She wasn't even really looking at him. That fire, that bright rage that had once occupied her dark eyes, it was gone. Replaced entirely now by a waxy, heartbreaking dullness.

"No..." Brandon said. He closed his eyes. Overcome with fear, he screamed, tried to scream, "Don't let me die! Fuck, Mike, don't let me die!"

"I won't," Mike said. "I'm here. We're all here."

Brandon lay there in fear and pain and listened to Mike trying to save his life. Heard only bits of the things Mike said.

"Tension pneumothorax..."

"...hyper resonance..."

"...pleural space..."

The pain swelled and pushed inside his chest.

No morphine!

What had Jaran given him for his fear? That awful tasting stuff?

The vial.

Brandon rolled his eyes to Jaran. He saw the cord around her neck.

"Mike," Brandon said. "The vial. Jaran's neck. For... For the pain."

Mike dug around his aid bag. Clinking of glass. Tearing of paper. "I don't know what that shit will do to you."

"PLEASE!"

Mike sat back on his heels. Looked Brandon in the eye. His eyes flitted down to the knife buried in Brandon's chest. He sighed. Then reached over and gently raised Jaran's head and slipped the cord from around her neck. Popped out the stopper and held the vial to Brandon's lips.

The thick, filthy liquid oozed to the back of his throat, but Brandon sucked it down greedily. Swallowed it all.

Brandon lay his head back and Mike went back to work. Slowly, gradually, the voices around him dulled. He took shallow breaths. The way he had seen Jaran do it.

Inhale, inhale, exhale.

The pain dulled. The light drained from the world. Brandon slipped into warmth and into darkness and he left behind the fading memories of exhaustion and fear and pain.

But somewhere out in that dark, he thought he heard someone calling his name.

CHAPTER THIRTY-NINE

Click.
Click.
Green. Bright white slashes. Maybe blue. Colors bled into the blackness and gelled into shapes.
Click.
Click.
Brandon was on his back looking at sunlight through the jungle canopy. He inhaled. A pneumatic *hiss*.
Click.
He rolled his head to the clicking sound. Chris sat cross-legged on the ground beside him. Loading pistol magazines. Thumbing in the rounds. The squeak of the spring. The click of brass on brass.
"Good afternoon," Chris said.
Brandon rubbed his face. "How long was I out?"
Chris looked at his watch. "About six hours."
Brandon forced his eyes open wide. Squinted. Rubbed his eyelids. Tried to rub away the tiredness.
"Remember much?" Chris asked.
Brandon rolled his head back to the sky. He breathed heavy and slow. Swallowed the wet and coppery taste in

his mouth. "Yeah." Rubbing his face, he groaned, "Where's Smith?"

"Buried."

Dropping his hands from his face, Brandon tried to sit up. Chris put his hand on Brandon's chest and pushed him back down. "Not yet. Mike doesn't want you moving for a bit."

"Why?"

"Mike stuck a chest tube in you. And he took a whole bunch of your blood."

"My *blood*? For what?"

"For Jaran. You're O negative, right?"

"Yeah…" Brandon lifted his head. Some distance away Jaran lay on her back. Mike knelt over her, tilting and seesawing a bag of blood. Crimson ran in clear plastic tubes stuck in her arms. "She's alive?"

"That's what Mike says."

"She'll be alright?"

Click.

Click.

"Mike," Chris called. "He's awake."

Mike looked over. Jaran's sword was stuck in the ground and he hooked the blood bag on the hilt. He stood and came over, wiping his hands on his trousers. He pulled a stethoscope from his cargo pocket and put it to his ears and put it to Brandon's chest. On his belly. On his arms. Pulling the stethoscope from his ears and letting it hang around his neck, he said, "How are you feeling?"

"Alright, I guess. My side itches like a son-of-a-bitch. How's Jaran?"

Mike pointed to Brandon's side. "Yeah, well don't scratch at it. That itching is probably from the sutures. They're keeping the chest tube in place."

"How's Jaran?"

Clearing his throat, Mike said, "That knife caused your lung to swell. I put a chest tube in to relieve the pressure. There's a suture on either side of the incision to keep the chest tube in place."

"You gave her my blood," Brandon said. "Is she going to live?"

Mike looked over his shoulder at Jaran. Then he sat down beside Brandon. Brandon didn't like the way he kept clearing his throat. Stalling.

"Blood's mostly water," Mike said. "Blood loss wasn't her problem. Not entirely. The problem was she didn't have enough red blood cells carrying oxygen to her brain. That's why she got all droopy. Her brain was starved of oxygen."

"So with more blood she'll be alright?"

Mike said nothing for a long time. When he finally spoke his voice was clinical and cold, as if reciting from memory a fact from some medical book.

"Due to blood loss, she's experiencing cerebral hypoxia. Damage to the brain can be immediate. The body has a kind of failsafe, it will double the blood flow and direct the blood to the brain, but…" and he spread his hands out before him. As if over an imagined pool of blood.

"I knew a guy," Mike said. "He drowned in a pool. Lifeguards pulled him out after about ninety seconds or so. They did CPR. I remember everyone cheering when the guy's heart started back up. Lots of pats on backs.

"Except the guy never woke up. Not really. He was *alive* in the very basic sense of the word. His heart was beating. He was breathing." Mike put a crooked finger to his temple. "But up here…" He shook his head. "Breathing and pissing was pretty much all he could do after that. After about a week in the hospital, he died."

Jaran's chest rose almost imperceptibly. Her eyes half open. Her mouth hanging slack.

Mike stood. "I'll do what I can for her. Get something to eat and rest." And with that, he stood and went back to sit beside Jaran.

"She's in good hands," Chris said.

Brandon laid his head back. "I know."

"Can I ask you something?"

Brandon looked at him. "Depends on what it is, I guess."

Chris nodded and looked down at the magazine in his hand. Pushed in another round. "What was Smith dangling over you?"

Brandon chuckled and looked out at the jungle. "An assignment at the Pentagon."

"No," Chris said. "Not dangling in front of you. *Over* you. What kind of dirt did he have on you? Was all that shit about your former commander true?"

"Mmm..." And Brandon went very cold. "Not sure I want to talk about that."

Chris nodded and clicked the last round into a magazine and set it aside and started loading the next. "You ever wonder why the rest of us never trusted Smith? Or guys *like* him?"

"Figured you were just arrogant pricks to be honest."

"Fair enough. My point is, you're not the only one with secrets. The team, these guys here, you can talk about your shit with us. You can trust us. Just like we hope we can trust you." Chris patted the magazine in his palm. "A lot of people are gonna want to know what happened out here. Every little detail. A lot of those details are better left out here where no one can find them. That make sense?"

It didn't make sense at all until Brandon thought about it. "Oh," Brandon said. "No. Hey man, I'm not gonna tell anyone about what John said. It's none of my business."

Mouth open, Chris stared at him. Then he laughed, "Well I appreciate that, but that's not what I meant."

Chris thumbed in the last round and set the magazine aside and picked up the next, but this one he held onto with both hands and folded his hands in his lap and looked at the magazine as if he had never seen one before.

"John and I met about two tours ago. We ended up in SOG when the agency was transitioning operational control to the Army. But the agency had some loose ends to tie-up before they'd hand over the keys to the kingdom.

"They had this team of indigenous guys. Guys like Boing. All trained up in tactics and intelligence gathering and whatnot. But they were a little lazy. Didn't like to go out on operations. One day their honcho come up and told their handler they wanted to transfer back to the regulars. Said the work was too dangerous. Can't say I blame 'em.

"Anyway, helicopter insertions became the preferred method of getting troops on the ground and these mandatory training requirements got published. These indigs, all ten of them, they had to load up on some birds and complete a training insertion.

"Our first mission together, me and John, we had to supervise that training. See how the indigs handled themselves on the bird. How they moved on the ground. I was on one Huey, John was on the other.

"'Every swinging dick gets off those birds.' Those were our instructions. And we made sure they all got off. All ten. We were supposed to circle overhead and pick them back up and fly them back to base.

"Funny thing, though. The helicopters didn't circle. We just lifted up, went straight back to base and landed. And it was a *long* flight. John made a huge stink about leaving them boys out there. One of the pilots said the mission changed in the air. Said John didn't hear about it because he wasn't wearing a headset. Said the indigs were going to run an overnight exercise. The pilot said that happens sometimes. Things changing in the air. These weren't Army pilots by the way. After we landed at the base, we never saw those pilots again. So we asked around about the indigs we left. Eventually someone told us that another set of Hueys would be dispatched the next morning to pick up the indigs.

"And you better believe that me and John set right there at the flight line looking at maps and figuring out where we had set those boys down. You know what the symbol for enemy-held territory looks like on a map?"

"Yeah."

"Yeah. So we watched the birds for a long time, waiting for them to take off and go collect those men." Turning the magazine in his hand, seeing that it was full, he put it aside and picked up the next. "I'll give you one guess how many birds took off."

Click.

Click.

Click.

The rounds seating in the magazine seemed almost as loud as if they were being fired.

"Jesus," Brandon said.

"I doubt Jesus found them boys before the NVA did." Chris let out a sardonic laugh. "So that's mine and John's little secret. One of them, anyway. I guess that's how we ended up getting so close. Sharing shame." He shrugged. "Or whatever you wanna call it."

Chris looked to the canopy above. Brandon searched his face. Chris sighed. A long, lonesome exhale. Brandon expected there to be sadness pouring from the man's face. But sadness was not what he found there. In fact, there wasn't really *any* emotion showing. It was more like there was an absence of something. And when the sun strayed and caught Chris's eye, that's when Brandon noticed.

That shine that Brandon had hated ever since he had noticed it in Laos. The one that had flashed as Chris slid from the jungle and rescued Brandon from Smith's beating. That ever-present mischievous gleam.

It was gone.

"Anyway," Chris said, whirling the magazine slowly around at the jungle surrounding them. "Everything that happened here. Everything that will happen. You share that with us. There ain't many of us left. Hell, the few of us that *are* left might not make it. But we're gonna give it our best shot."

Chris put the magazine down and looked at Brandon. "You had the chance to run out on us but you came back and pulled us out of the fire. That meant a lot to me. And I ain't one for forgetting something like that. None of us are. From here on out, I want you right there with us if shit goes south. I want you there because I know I can count on you. That goes for all of us. Whatever happened in your last unit doesn't matter to us. We want you here."

There were a lot of things Brandon wanted to say just then, but he doubted he would have gotten the words out. As soon as Chris had said he wanted Brandon on the team his throat had tightened.

Chris stood. He looked down at Brandon and chuckled. "You're gonna need all new parts when we make it back."

"*If* we make it," Brandon choked out.

Chris shook his head. "*When.*" And he tossed five of the pistol magazines he had loaded between Brandon's legs. "Oh, I almost forgot." He pointed to Brandon's chest. "I found that in your pocket. Figured you might want to keep it out. All things considered."

Flopping his hand up to his chest, Brandon's tired fingers found the tiny metal chain. He lifted it.

John's cross.

He shook his head. "Not mine."

Chris looked at him. "John's?"

"Yeah."

"Well," Chris shrugged. "Couldn't hurt."

Brandon thought about that. He looked up at Chris. "Do you believe?"

"Nah. But John did. *Does.*" He shook his head. "I'm talking like he's already dead. John believed God told him things. He'd get these gut feelings you know? He'd call a halt for no particular reason. Most times nothing would happen. I remember one night something was bugging him about a place we were dug in and he told us to move. Sure as shit, here comes Charlie. Stepping right where we would've been sleeping. I've seen other guys do stuff like that once or twice. You play it off as luck. But with John, man. I just *kept* seeing it. The other guys kept seeing it."

"That's funny," Brandon said. "I never heard him mention anything about God."

"Yeah, that's John." Chris nodded. "He'll be the first to tell you he ain't no preacher. He's just a guy who believes. Tell you what, though. If you don't get a chance to give that back to John, make sure his wife gets it. Don't send it in no envelope. You deliver it in person. She deserves that."

Brandon looked at the cross in his hand. Then he held it out for Chris to take.

"What?" Chris asked.

"Sounds like you know her better."

Chris held up his hand. "With all the shit you've survived since you started carrying that thing around, I'm starting to think it works."

"All the more reason for you to carry it. Doesn't seem right for me to have all the luck."

Chris shook his head. "Somebody told me once it don't work for guys like me." Then with a sigh, Chris said, "How about we take a look at the maps and figure out a way out of here?"

The jigsaw sky beyond the canopy darkened, and another winter rain tapped the palm fronds. The jungle foliage turned damp and luminous in the drizzle. Brandon tugged his poncho out of his rucksack and slipped it on over his head.

A few minutes later Brandon sat beside Boing and spilled everything from the manila envelope Smith had given him and laid it all out. Maps. Aerial reconnaissance photographs. Clear plastic overlays. Chris and Mike knelt on either side of him and slid the papers around until they were looking at a collage of Vietnam. Brandon took out the map of the Ho Chi Minh Trail John had given him sometime in the distant past.

They studied the known parts of the Trail. They looked at terrain features. Tried to discern where the Trail might begin.

"If I had to guess," Mike said. "I'd say Charlie wouldn't bother running a supply line along the Laotian border this far north."

"Why not?" Chris said. "Dien Bien Phu is right on the border. It's still an active air strip. They still need to get supplies out that way."

Mike scratched his chin. "No. Look here." He pointed and slid his finger along the swerving black lines on the map. "Established roadways. The NVA controls that territory. They can use the roads between Hanoi and Dien Bien Phu for resupply. I doubt they would bother running the Trail all the way out west."

"You don't think they're worried about us bombing the roads?"

Mike shrugged. "We bomb the hell out of the Ho Chi Minh Trail, it's repaired by the next day like nothing happened. All I'm saying is that if supplies come in from China, the NVA aren't gonna go three-hundred kliks west just to get on the Trail and turn south. Most of the stuff they carry is transported by foot or bicycle. The NVA leadership won't burn out their guys like that. No. Look here at Khe Sanh." Mike pointed to the American combat base and traced his finger north across the DMZ. "Look at how the Trail runs just on the inside of Laos."

The penciled-in line marking the Ho Chi Minh Trail skirted the border of Laos and Vietnam, nearly a mirror image of the border.

But the pencil marking ended abruptly about twenty miles north of the DMZ. None of the Recon Teams had yet to make it any farther north than that during their recons. Brandon's heart sank a bit when he looked at all that green space between the Trail and where they currently sat in the rain.

Brandon glanced at the scale on the lower edge of a

map and he did the estimate in his head. The numbers pounded in his mind like dropped concrete blocks. He would have laughed if he didn't have a chest tube punched between his ribs.

New York's current position was approximately three-hundred fifty kilometers north of the Trail's closest known location. Three-hundred fifty kliks of jungle and mountains and God only knew how many NVA and villages sympathetic to them.

Brandon asked, "Can we make it?"

Mike laughed. "To the known parts? Doubtful. We'll definitely run out of food by then. And we'll most likely get caught. No. We'll have to find a way to get a message to some friendlies and request extraction."

Brandon nodded. "Smith mentioned a CIA base somewhere. Is that what you're talking about?"

Mike shook his head. "Smith never told us where that base was."

"So…" Chris said. "There's little depots spaced out along the Trail. Places where trucks can refuel and the troops can rest." Chris looked at him gravely. "We'll have to find a compound and hijack their radio equipment."

"What?" Brandon's mouth dropped open. "We have to…" Brandon put his head in his hands at the thought of deliberately walking into a hornets' nest.

"Yeah," Chris said. "I'm thinking the same thing you are."

"We won't make it to the DMZ," Mike said. "But our chances will be better if we can locate a northern artery of the Trail." Mike stared at the maps for a long time. Then he planted his finger on Hanoi. "The NVA can move freely from here," and he traced his finger south to where the bulbous North Vietnam slimmed abruptly between Laos and the South China Sea. "To about here." Mike planted his finger about one-hundred fifty kilometers north of the DMZ and slid it over to the Laotian border and tapped it. "Here. My guess is that around here, that's where the Trail starts. That's where we need to go."

"You sure?" Chris asked.

"It's my best guess."

Chris shrugged. "Good enough for me."

"Two-hundred kilometers," Brandon whispered.

"Yeah," Mike said. "It's a hike. We'll shoot for twenty miles per day. Doubtful we'll hit that, but it'll probably average out."

Brandon pulled the maps toward him and looked at where Mike had pointed.

Avoiding Hanoi and Dien Bien Phu was the easy part. The eye of that needle was three-hundred kilometers wide. From New York's current position to where Mike had indicated on the map, the course was essentially due south. A straight line. Not difficult at all. At least on a map. On the ground, however…

The terrain in the pieced-together collage of aerial surveillance photographs was like a thick towel that someone had pulled dripping from a pool, wrung out, scrunched and let sit in the sun. Looking down on all those creases and folds, God, it was some of the roughest terrain Brandon had ever seen.

"That's a long way for a guess," Brandon said.

The men were silent for a while. Then Chris rose and walked over to the pile of rucksacks. "Moving on to the next topic of discussion." Kicking a pack, he said, "What we're taking and what we're leaving behind. I vote for taking ammo and food."

"Socks," Mike said. "All the socks you can find. We'll need them."

"Why are we leaving anything behind?" Brandon asked.

"Because *you* can't carry a pack," Mike said. "And Chris and I can't each haul two-hundred pounds of stuff."

"I'll be fine," Brandon said. "I can carry—"

"No, you can't. If that chest tube gets snagged in a shoulder strap it'll rip out from between your ribs."

"Yeah," Chris said, and put his fist against his side and

made a crowbar motion. "That probably won't feel too nice."

Brandon cringed and placed a protective hand over his incision.

"Food and ammo, probably one radio and socks," Chris said. "Not too bad. Me and Mike will carry the rucks." He looked at Brandon and smiled. "You get the sixty."

Brandon sighed and looked around. The Counter Recon men stacked neatly in a pile and covered with ripped-out foliage. "You want to grab their weapons? Their satchel charges?"

Chris shook his head. "Those little posters you see around the bases telling you to never fire an enemy's weapon, they were made because of all the bad ammo the SOG teams slip into NVA ammo dumps. You fire Charlie's weapon, you run the risk of blowing off your hand."

"Or worse," Mike said.

"Yeah!" Chris cackled. "It's always worse."

"Are you serious?" Brandon asked.

"We weren't anticipating finding ammo dumps on a rescue mission, so we didn't bring any. But John always has a few mags of bad ammo in his pack." Chris smiled and gestured at the AK-47s. "Try your luck?"

The sun went down and the jungle darkened and Mike cleaned Brandon's chest tube and placed a small dressing over the incision. "Get some rest," Mike said.

"I want to help get ready for tomorrow."

"And I want you to heal so you can eventually carry some of this stuff. Chris and I will take care of it."

Reluctantly, Brandon nodded and went and lay down next to Boing.

Sleep did not come to Brandon. The long walk ahead of them played itself out in his mind. A slow, south-panning bird's eye view of the terrain. He thought about how long they would walk before stopping for a breather.

Thought about where they would find fresh water and where they would rest. He thought of everything. Everything that could go right. Everything that could go wrong.

Thought about the NVA still out there looking for them. And Counter Recon. He shivered. They needed to move fast. But carrying wounded and heavy packs, they wouldn't cover ground quickly. If they couldn't be fast, hopefully they could be consistent.

Twenty miles a day.

God, that would be hard over that terrain.

Once they made it to the start of the Ho Chi Minh Trail—*if they could even find it*—they'd have to move in the dark. But only if nothing happened between here and the trailhead. Only if John didn't take another shot at them—

Instinctively, Brandon scoffed at the thought. Told himself to just prepare for when John did come back.

He rubbed a hand over his belly and the gashes there. Ever since Jaran had put her hand there and muttered whatever spell or prayer, he only felt a weak sensation. An awareness. The crippling terror had all but vanished.

Maybe John was finally done with them. Maybe New York proved too much of a hassle. Maybe John was afraid. It was an odd thing to consider. But New York knew how to stop him now. Maybe that knowledge made New York a harder target in John's mind.

Brandon's instinct was to anticipate John attacking, but something just felt...

Different.

Staring into the gathering dark, he spent the next hours thinking. Then worrying. Thinking some more. And then just listening to the pops and buzzes of life and the sound of things crawling in the jungle.

He thought of Jaran. Thought of how much had been taken from her. Thought about how she wouldn't get the chance to avenge her family.

Brandon curled his hands into fists, scolding himself

for thinking of her as though she were already gone.

Mike would fix her. He would make her well again. Tomorrow she would come around and they would walk out of here together.

Late into the night and his wandering thoughts, Brandon heard Boing shuffling on his back. Swatting at some insect. Brandon lay there and listened for a time before asking softly, "Still awake?"

Boing cleared his throat and from the dark he answered, "I have trouble sleeping before missions."

Brandon ran his fingers along his scared belly and stared up into the dark.

They lay in silence a while. Brandon replayed the jump in his mind and winced at the repeating *crack* of Boing's legs as he slammed the earth. He was overcome with a solemn regret for having played a part in what had happened to the kid. But he also felt an uneasy wariness. Boing had been off the constant morphine for some time, but he had not told anyone about what happened in the plane. Or if he had, no one had confronted Brandon about it. The question gnawing at Brandon's mind was why Boing had kept silent.

It gnawed at him until Brandon blurted, "Why haven't you told anyone?"

Boing's neck skin shuffled against his shirt collar. "Told anyone about what?"

Brandon's heart flared beneath his hands. "About the jump. About what I did."

Just voicing the question took a toll on Brandon's sudden burst of courage. He didn't have enough left to even turn his head toward the interpreter. Not even in the dark.

After a time, Boing said, "I couldn't."

"Why not?"

"Have you ever tried to talk on morphine?"

The shock of what Boing said pulled Brandon's mouth open. He could think of nothing to say.

Boing fell into a fit of quiet laughter and Brandon could hardly believe what he was hearing. Soon the absurdity of it infected Brandon and it wasn't long before Brandon was grabbing his sides and aching from laughter.

"You two," Chris whispered from the night. "Shut the fuck up."

They paused a moment. But Brandon's guts were jackhammering and he was helpless to hold it in.

Snorting laughter and snot burst from his nose and he cupped his hands over his face but he couldn't shove the sound back down.

Laughing. It felt incredible. It had been easy to forget about joy out there. Maybe that's why it made Brandon feel so good. It made him forget, if only briefly, about everything.

But the jungle would not permit them to keep their joy for long, and when the laughter between them died, Brandon said, "I'd like to know. Truly. I can't figure out what I did to deserve your silence."

Boing was quiet for a time. From the dark there came a long sigh. Brandon couldn't begin to imagine what he was thinking. Boing said, "I guess I know what would have changed if I told them."

Brandon nodded. "Not much, I guess."

"That's not what I meant. I meant that the rest of the team would have hated you. Chris might have even killed you. Or at least he wouldn't make any effort to save you if he had to. I've worked with these guys a long time. We know we can't survive out here alone. We need each other. Each man needs the team. Every time one of us goes down, we know it just gets harder and harder for the rest of us to get back home. I think you understand that already."

"What do you mean?"

"Why did you come back when Counter Recon attacked us? You could have run."

Brandon lay quietly and thought about that. "I

wouldn't have made it very far."

"Right," Boing said. "We need each other. Mike and Chris, if I told them what happened, they would blame you. Blaming others just drives a team apart. That's what I meant. That's what telling them would have changed." Boing chuckled. "Besides, you already make it so hard to like you. You don't need my help."

They laughed.

Brandon thought about the insightful things Boing had said. In the Infantry Brandon had competed with his peers for notoriety for so long that assigning blame for any given mistake had become second nature. To highlight someone else's fuck-up just to make himself look better.

Boing had a conspicuously level head about what had happened to him. Brandon doubted he could have handled it as well as Boing if Brandon was the one to lose his legs.

No. If it were Brandon who had lost his legs he would have slipped into a callous bitterness. Blamed everyone for his loss except himself. What a blessing it would be to be free of resentment.

These men. This team. They worked together not because they were ordered to, not because the Army happened to throw them together and call them a team. But because they cared about each other. Recon teams were voluntary, one of the few positions in the Army that a man could quit if he wanted.

"You guys don't quit," Brandon said.

"New York?" Boing let out a gentle chuckle. "Never."

CHAPTER FORTY

Brandon dreamt. Jaran appeared as a black silhouette in bright halo of sunlight. In the way of dreams, Brandon knew her without having to see her face.

She spoke. And though her words were not English, Brandon understood her. Nor were her words Vietnamese. A long time ago, a neighbor had hung a wind chime on their porch. Long metal tubes. Autumn nights as a boy, Brandon had lain in bed, window cracked open. The scent of fallen maple leaves. On passing breezes came the long, low tolling of the wind chime. That tolling. *That* was Jaran's voice as she said, "I wasn't expecting this."

"What were you expecting?"

"I'm not sure." She turned to him.

The damage inflicted by the Counter Recon commander was gone. Her face was perfect. She held out a hand to him. "Come."

He reached out and took it.

She led him into the daylight. Into the sky. Crossing miles with each step. Below, passing lazily, there were hills covered with thick trees. Dark shadowy folds. Bright mountain peaks and hilltops washed white in sunlight.

The sun streaked across the sky as she guided him. When the sun dipped below the horizon the mountains and valleys turned dark blue. Then black. In a few moments the sun rose again, breathing green back into the landscape.

They went on.

When the sun set again Brandon gazed down upon a crimson light flaring from the trees beneath him. Like a star had formed on the surface of the earth. Infernal rays pierced the jungle mist and shot skyward, painting the clouds above in hues of red. Red like malice. Red like hate. Brandon thought he knew what the source of that light was. Jaran confirmed it.

"He is weaker now," Jaran said. "Erlik Khan has used up much of your friend's body. I think he'll exhaust what's left to move quickly."

"Where is he going?"

"I think I know. Come."

They overtook the flare and sped on, leaving the crimson light far behind. But over the mountains Erlik Khan's hellfire glow pulsed and reaching up to the sky.

When the sun rose again, the flare was gone. The sun arced and set and rose again.

Jaran led him down into the jungle. A river flowed there. Very shallow. Beyond the river, some distance through the trees, they came to a roadway made of red clay. Jaran walked with him along the road until they came to a bamboo fence. Inside the fence were huts similar to the ones in Jaran's village. Smaller gray shapes moved inside the compound. Blurry shades of people, leaving ghostly white trails as they moved. Like they existed only in the memory of a dream.

Phantom cargo trucks drove in through the gate. Men scurried, loading and unloading wooden crates from the trucks. Loading small metal cases. Large sacks of rice.

The sun went down.

When their work was done and the trucks had left, the

shadow people gathered around tables in the muggy night. Pots hung over cook fires and aromatic steam drifted above the tables. Bowls were placed in front of men and they ate. Smiling and laughing and praising the food prepared by a one-armed cook.

Here and there the shapes would pause long enough for Brandon to see clear snapshots of their faces. Those men were barely men at all. So young.

The sun rose. The men worked. The sun set.

Beyond the mountainous jungle rising beyond the compound, Erlik Khan's red glow came. Encroaching like the blaze of a forest fire, illuminating the jagged ridgeline.

"Is this happening now?" Brandon asked.

"It's one of the Soup Soldier's dreams," Jaran said. "I've seen this dream before." She lifted her hand to the hideous glow. "Erlik Khan has seen this dream. This is where Erlik Khan is going."

"How do you know?"

"He took the Soup Soldier's body. He knows everything the Soup Soldier knew."

"Why come *here*?"

"You and your men know how to stop him," Jaran said. "I believe he's coming here to claim a new body."

"He's going to get himself killed?"

"That is his only way to survive."

"What about the soldiers following us? Why won't he just run to them?"

"He knows there are people here. And he knows they will be hostile to the skin he wears."

Brandon watched the dream-men slurp long noodles from steaming bowls. "Are those men still here?"

"Perhaps."

One.

Two.

Three.

Beyond the borders of Brandon's dream, someone grunted, *six, seven.*

"You must reach this place before Erlik Khan," Jaran said.

"How? I don't know where it is."

Ten.

Eleven.

"I will guide you."

Twelve.

Brandon smiled at that. "I thought we were going to lose you."

Jaran turned to him. A smile appeared on her perfect face. But in her eyes there was a sadness. "Trust me." She placed her hand on Brandon's stomach. "Trust *this*."

Brandon looked at the men as the red flare crested the mountaintop. Its terrible radiance flooded the valley, consuming the trees and bamboo huts and gray people at their tables. He looked at Jaran as her skin turned the color of flame. He asked her, "What do we do when we get here?"

Her sad eyes turned and lingered on the young men gathered at the table. As the light came screaming into the valley, she closed her eyes and bowed her head.

"What you must."

Brandon opened his eyes. Dull gray morning mist. Familiar pain. He pushed himself up and rubbed his face. Clinging to the fleeting words said to him in a dream. Pulling his hands down his face, pulling his eyelids down, over his fingertips he saw the jungle.

Something out there drew his gaze. Not movement. Not a specific color. Neither tangible nor observable. It was more like a feeling. Something out there beckoned him. Or something waited for him. His eyes drifted and settled on a single point on the rock wall. Then his stomach buzzed—

Mike's panting voice shouted, "Breathe!"

Brandon turned to the sound. Mike and Chris knelt over Jaran. Mike's hands on her chest, Chris's mouth on Jaran's—

Brandon scrambled to his feet and darted over to them. "What happened?"

Mike pressed Jaran's chest. Counted, "One." Pressed. Counted, "Two." "Her heart stopped... four, five, six..."

Brandon fell to his knees beside them. "How long?"

"We've been doing CPR about fifteen minutes," Chris said.

"What can I do?"

"Mike needs a break. Can you do compressions?"

Brandon knew CPR from basic combat casualty care, but he'd never had to do it before. "I can."

"Then take over."

"Twenty-nine, thirty," Mike said. "Breathe."

Chris grabbed Jaran's mouth and blew. Her chest expanded and deflated. He blew again.

"Compressions," Mike said.

Brandon leaned forward. Put his hands on Jaran's sternum. Something shifted beneath her skin. Like the shattered bones in Boing's legs...

"Let's *go!*" Mike yelled.

Gritting his teeth, Brandon pushed. Her chest was soft, like no bones were there at all. Every time he pushed there was a *crunch*.

Brandon pressed. "What the fuck happened to her chest?"

"The ribcage breaks during compressions," Mike said. "Completely normal. Calm down and keep going."

Brandon pressed. And pressed.

"Keep count," Mike said.

"Thirteen, fourteen, fifteen..."

Jaran's head rocked with each compression. Her waxy brown eyes stared up into the nothing beyond the jungle canopy.

"Twenty-eight, twenty-nine, thirty, breathe!"

Chris breathed. And breathed.

"Compressions," Mike said.

"One, two, three..."

They went on and on. Beads of sweat fell from the tip of Brandon's nose with each downward thrust. The constant panic in the periphery of his mind held in check only by his determination to keep Jaran alive.

The men rotated positions. Soon Jaran's chest was so soft and broken that the men put hardly any force into the compressions. Like all that was left beneath her skin was her heart.

How would she be able to walk after this?

How could Mike fix her ribcage?

How would she be able to fight John?

Mike looked at his watch and shook his head. And with four words, Mike answered the questions swirling in Brandon's frantic mind. "That's enough," Mike said. "She's gone."

Brandon looked up from his compressions. "What?"

Mike looked at him. Shook his head. "It's been an hour. She's not coming back."

Brandon looked down at her. "No…"

And he pressed her chest. "I'm not giving up on her." With every compression air hiccupped from Jaran's mouth. He pressed and pressed.

"Brandon," Mike said softly.

"Eighteen, nineteen, twenty…"

"Brandon…"

"We *need* her!" Brandon wheezed through his tight throat. "Twenty-nine, thirty, breathe!"

Mike and Chris knelt there. Their solemn eyes cast down at the girl on the ground.

"Breathe!" Brandon begged them. "*Please!*"

And when neither of them moved, he shoved Mike aside and put his mouth on Jaran's and blew. Her chest rose. He blew again.

He shifted back to her chest to start compressions, but big arms wrapped around him from behind and pulled him back. Pulled him away.

"She's gone," Chris said in his ear. He held Brandon

tight. "She's gone, man."

"No!"

Chris's arms squeezed. Bricks of muscle holding Brandon back. "She's gone."

"No!" Brandon reached out for her. "She said she'd lead us out of here!" He beat his fists against Chris's thighs. "She's not dead!"

"Let her go, Brandon."

"Goddamnit, she's not *dead!*"

Arms squeezing, Chris said, "She's gone."

"No!" Brandon sucked in air. His words devolved into wails. Chris held him tight. Held him until Brandon's screams drained all the fight from him. And long after, when Brandon was a limp, sobbing mess, Chris still held him.

CHAPTER FORTY-ONE

No one spoke as they dug. Only the rattle of loose dirt spilling into a grave. Somewhere in the jungle, a bird called.

Jaran lay beside the hole. In the air was the chemical smell of the nylon poncho the men had wrapped around her. An OD green shroud. Para cord around her ankles, waist, and shoulders. The hood pulled up over her head and the drawstrings pulled tight. Her sword lay sheathed on her chest.

Brandon spilled a shovelful of earth on the growing pile and straightened, stretching his back. Wiping sweat from his face, his eyes wandered. And stopped at an unremarkable spot on the rock wall. The same unremarkable spot on which his eyes had settled the past ten times he had done this. He pulled his compass from his cargo pocket. Same azimuth. He clicked shut the compass and put it back in his pocket. Jammed the e-tool into the earth and scooped.

The mindlessness of shoveling and dumping allowed his mind the freedom to curate snapshots of the previous night's dream. The NVA in some far-away compound. The red flash of Erlik Khan.

When the grave was ready, Brandon let his eyes wander again. Pulled out his compass again. Looked at Jaran's body. Clicked his compass shut.

I will guide you.

"You keep pulling that compass out." Chris folded up his shovel and sat on the edge of the grave. "You gonna tell us why?"

Brandon was about to shake his head. And why wouldn't he? His whole life he had been conditioned to dismiss anything unnatural as fantasy. As insanity. But looking at Mike and Chris, they looked eager to hear what he had to say.

"I'm going to run this by you," Brandon said. "If you think it sounds just as crazy as I do, you don't have to do it."

Chris wiped his dirty hands on his trousers and pulled out a can of snuff. "Crazy sounds right up my alley."

"To get home…" Brandon gestured at Jaran and paused, searching for the right place to start. "You said we need to find an NVA compound and hijack their radios, right?"

"That would be ideal," Mike said skeptically.

Brandon pulled out his compass and let his eyes roam. When he found the place on the wall his gut fluttered. He motioned with his compass. "That way. If we march hard for five days, we'll find a small NVA compound. I think it's a depot of some kind. They store rice and ammo there."

Chris stuffed a pinch of tobacco in his lip. "That's pretty precise. Mind telling us how you found that out?"

Lies were the first thing to creep up in Brandon's head. But he shook his head and said, "I had this dream last night…"

And he told them. Told them everything that he had seen and heard in the dream. He expected apprehension. He expected an outright refusal to believe from Mike and Chris.

But Chris said, "I don't know, man. If John's heading there, then isn't that the one place we *don't* wanna be?"

"Chris is right," Mike said. "We have a good chance of escaping if we just leave him alone."

Brandon couldn't argue with their hesitation. They wanted to live. Going up against John *and* the NVA dropped their chances of survival to near zero. Maybe they should just continue with their original plan.

The burn in his stomach flared. He grabbed his stomach and glanced at the wall.

"That's John you're feeling?" Chris asked.

"I don't think so. Jaran did something to me in the dream. She said to trust her." And Brandon put patted his stomach. "She said trust *this*."

Chris laughed. "Trust your gut, huh?" Chris looked up at Mike. An awkward silence between them.

Mike flicked his finger at Brandon's stomach. "That gut of yours caused us some trouble with Counter Recon. What if it's another trap?"

Brandon chewed an already bit-down finger nail and thought about that. "Pull out your map."

Chris took out his map and unfolded it. Mike sat beside him and said, "What are we looking for?"

Without looking at the map, Brandon recited every terrain feature he had seen in his dream. From the wall all the way to the compound. When they looked up at him, Brandon said, "Accurate?"

Clapping softly, Chris said, "Neat trick. Now tell me what number I'm thinking of."

"Memorizing the map doesn't mean we won't be ambushed," Mike said.

"I didn't memorize anything. Jaran showed me."

"Or *John* showed you." Mike said. "We know he can get in our heads."

"How many times have you showed your enemy where you were going when you were trying to escape?"

Chris made an exaggeration of thinking and ticking off

his fingers. "At least four times. And they walked right into our ambush."

Brandon's mouth dropped open to speak, but the words he needed to make Chris and Mike understand, they just were not there. The only words that came were, "It's not a trap."

"Brandon." Mike held up his palms. "How do you *know?*"

"Because..." Confused, Brandon sat on the bench of earth. Both feet in the grave. He put his hand on his stomach. He sighed. "Because I'm not afraid."

"What's being afraid have to do with anything?" Chris asked.

Gesturing around at the wall and the jungle, Brandon said, "The whole time we were walking, Erlik Khan used fear to nudge me. Even though I knew it was the wrong way to go, I kept letting the fear push me because I was too afraid not to. I was too afraid to face him. That's how he trapped us here. With fear." Brandon looked at them. "That fear is gone now."

"What do you feel now?" Mike asked.

Brandon looked at Jaran. "Anger. I think it's *her* anger. I think she gave it to me."

"That doesn't make any sense."

Brandon shook his head. "Nothing has made sense to me out here. But here's what I know. If I continue on with you, even if we were to make it home, I don't think I would survive." Brandon looked at the wall. "This *rage* inside me, I wish you could feel it. It's like I know that if I don't go after him, if I don't try and stop Erlik Khan from reaching that compound, I won't be able to live with myself. I think running away will kill me."

Brandon looked up at them. "Like I said, you guys don't have to come. But I'm going. I have to try. If this is where we part ways, I understand. You've done more than enough. I won't hold it against you if you leave."

Mike put his chin in his hand and watched Brandon.

His eyes flicking between Brandon's stomach and his eyes. He shook his head and looked at Chris. "I think I liked him better before he grew a set of balls."

"Mmm…" Tonguing the tobacco in his lip, Chris eyed Mike sidelong. "Tell me about it." Chris stood and went to Jaran. "Help me."

Together the three of them lowered Jaran into her grave. They scooped shovels of earth from the pile. They hesitated. All looking at her.

Chris nodded to Brandon. "Go ahead."

Brandon exhaled. Then he dumped his shovel. Mike and Chris dumped theirs. They filled the edges. The bronze sword handle gleamed through the earth like a shining river seen from the sky. And with one final shovel of earth, it was gone.

When the grave was covered, Brandon turned to his men. "Ready?"

They nodded.

CHAPTER FORTY-TWO

The last thing they did before they left was drink their fill from the pool at the base of the wall. Mike and Chris carried Boing. Brandon led them. As they backtracked away from the wall, a quiet mist grew. It followed them. Tumbling over their shoulders like sentinel spirits of the newly buried. Somberly escorting the living from that hidden place of the dead. As quietly as it had come, the mist returned to the earth.

They walked. They sweated. Cut through thick vegetation with machetes. They complained of muscle aches and blisters on their feet. Of the fatigue gripping their legs over the tough terrain. But they pressed on.

Brandon led them without map or compass. He followed the burn in his gut. Focusing on the ache kept him sharp. Alert. Throughout the day Brandon caught himself daydreaming. He had to remind himself constantly to watch his surroundings. Remind himself where he was. And who was out there.

Still, the longer they walked, the easier it was for Brandon to get caught in the comforting traps of his thoughts. He thought about Mike, Chris, and Boing. He owed them a chance at survival. He was in debt to each of them. To Chris for saving him from Smith. To Boing for keeping his secret. To Mike for fighting off death itself to give Brandon a second chance. Brandon couldn't fail. To repay these men he would have to endure these five days. He had to get them to the compound. To the radios. And then…

That infernal crimson glow encroached on his thoughts.

And then I'll do what I must.

Stop Erlik Khan. Defeat John.

He had no idea *how* he was going to accomplish either of those things. The words *stop* and *defeat* were still abstractions that had yet to form themselves into concrete plans.

I'll do what I must.

It became his mantra. Repeating it and clinging to it as he led his men through valleys and across rivers. Up hills and down. As the sun arced overhead and as they hacked through dense jungle and sprinted across small open fields. Sloshed through wet paddies and muck.

They marched hard. Hardly stopping. But when the sky had deepened to a blue, near-dark, Chris asked Brandon to stop for the night. Brandon was hesitant. He knew John was weak, but he might keep moving in the dark. That was John's advantage, he could keep moving. These men were still human. They needed rest.

They made their sleeping places by the red glow of their flashlights. Brandon pulled off his boots and peeled off his stinking socks. Limp with sweat and gritty with dirt. A giant blister had formed and burst on one of his heels and the exposed flesh was wet and pink. The rubbing boot leather had torn back a flap of grayish opaque skin.

Mike rummaged in his kit and cut a few strips of gauze and handed them to Brandon. "Clean and powder your feet. Then put this on and swap out your socks."

Brandon did as he was told, sparing a little water from

his canteen to spill over the stinging flesh

They pulled two-hour watch shifts.

"You should take the first shift," Mike said. "Get a solid six hours of sleep. Let those wounds get some recovery time."

"You sure?" Brandon asked.

Mike nodded. "And maybe Jaran will have something more to say."

Brandon nodded, returning his gaze to the jungle. "Maybe."

He leaned against his pack, picking at his fingernails and stared at the jungle. Soon, the soft snoring of his men gave way to the haunting laughter of the young men from his dream. He stared into the jungle, not needing light to see where they were going. He stared so hard that he was late waking Mike up for his shift by almost an hour.

Brandon had thought that sleep might be difficult, but when he laid down his exhaustion proved too much for the voices in his head. Not long after he put his head on the ground, he was out.

And he did dream. Jaran was there waiting, hand extended in welcome. He took it and they glided over darkness as shards of starlight fell behind them. Twinkling and dimming and disappearing.

He saw Erlik Khan's red flare in the jungle. Radiant and yet somehow weaker. Less vibrant. Slowly Brandon overtook it. And soon he drifted down once again into the jungle. Into another man's dream. Into the midst of the NVA.

Oil lamps hung on posts. Mosquitos buzzed. Food was served to young men, shirtless on a hot night. Chests and shoulders shining with sweat. They smoked cigarettes and laughed. He looked beyond the tables and lamplight into the dark. Near the rear of the compound a clump of three huts. Thick wires ran between them. Beneath the laughter and chatter, a rumbling like an engine.

Chris woke him with a gentle shake. "Morning."

Brandon rubbed his face. "Good morning."

They studied the maps as they ate a small breakfast of C-ration crackers and fruit cups.

Chris slurped down the sugary fruit cup syrup. "Learn anything last night?"

Brandon pulled his eyes back from where they were fixed on the jungle. "I think so." He swallowed a spoonful of canned fruit. "I think I found the radios."

The men's eyebrows went up in surprise. "You can see all that?" Mike asked.

Brandon shrugged. "The things Jaran shows me, they're from someone else's dream. Or a memory. Maybe both."

The men nodded, seemingly accepting this as the truth. Chris looked down at the map. "I don't see any rivers or anything too big in our way. We should get some good distance in."

And they did. The terrain was kind to them. They found small streams and filled their canteens. Purified the water with iodine tablets.

Late in the day when the sun was setting Chris asked Mike to set down Boing's litter. Chris raised his hands in front of his face. The thick callouses at the base of his fingers were torn. Little folded flaps of skin. Dried blood in the creases of his palms as if his hands had rusted. He worked his stiff fingers into fists, hissing at the torn-open meat in his hands.

"Wash those," Mike said. "I'll get some gauze."

"I can help," Brandon said. "Let me carry him a while."

"I'm fine." Chris poured canteen water on his hands. "You just worry about getting us to where we need to be."

"You're sure?"

"I'm sure." Pointing up the slope in front of them, Chris said, "Keep going until it's too dark to see. Then we'll stop."

Mike wrapped gauze around Chris's hands and taped it down. They picked up and moved out.

It started to rain. Brandon led them uphill into slick mud and treacherous rocks. By the time it was getting too dark to see they still had not crested the hill and the rain still poured. Little streams formed in the dirt and rushed downhill.

They camped under a concentration of palm trees where the rain was not so heavy. Chris tied Boing's litter to a tree. Each man leaned against a trunk and clutched their ponchos about them to keep their body heat from rising up through the neck holes. Rain water ran off low hanging palm fronds in huge rivulets and spattered on the ground with the sound of a front-yard spigot in summertime. In the dark they reached out with their canteens open like blind beggars until rainwater splashed over their hands and ran into their canteens.

Before starting that night's shifts, Mike did a once-over of Brandon's chest tube. Then told him to get some sleep.

Brandon pulled his poncho hood tight around his face and pulled his knees to his chest. Resting his head on his arms and listening to the sound of the rain on his poncho hood going *pock... pock,* Brandon fell asleep.

Jaran was waiting.

The rain must have stopped in the night, but when Chris woke him in the morning the world was still soaking wet. Brandon stretched his stiff and aching legs.

"Any new dreams?" Mike asked.

"No," Brandon said. "More of the same. I'm trying to count the number of men stationed there. But there might be more when we get there. I don't want to put too much faith in the number I come up with."

Chris handed out rations and they ate in silence. When they were almost finished Chris said, "What happens if John reaches this place before us? Or what if the NVA zaps him before we can stop him?"

"Then..." Brandon stirred his spoon around in the syrup of his near-empty fruit cup. "I suppose Erlik Khan will have a brand-new body. He'll know our exact location, and he'll most likely alert the entire North Vietnamese Army of our whereabouts. We'll be captured, tortured, and killed."

"Mmm." Chris pointed at Brandon's fruit cup. "You gonna drink that?"

Brandon shook his head and handed it to him.

Chris sucked down the syrup. Smacking his lips, he said, "I don't know about you, but I'm ready to get going."

They walked through the day and stopped when it got dark. Brandon dreamed the same dream. Having found the communications buildings, he focused on counting the men and the logistics of the compound. When he dreamed he always saw the same things. Some trucks coming in before nightfall and the soldiers sitting around their tables. There was nothing that might suggest the schedule that was kept in the compound. And in any case, the commander of the compound might have rotated. Everything in the compound might be different by the time New York reached it.

Their path led them up one side of a ridge and down the other. They walked down sideways, digging their feet into the hillside. At the bottom, through the trees before them there was a green so bright it was almost white. So bright it hurt to look at through the foliage. They stood at the edge of the jungle with their hands shielding their eyes like a salute.

Before them was a very wide, very *open* valley.

Brandon looked left and right. Left again. Squinted at that gleaming sea of grass. And then he peeked out from beneath the foliage to look up into the sky. Because that was where he had been when he had first seen this place. It looked bigger from the ground.

A cloud's shadow, a giant black mass maybe ten miles wide slid across the grass before them.

"We can't cross this," Mike said. "We'll be exposed for hours."

Chris took out his binoculars and scanned the valley.

He took out his compass and looked at Brandon. "Straight across? That's where we're going?"

"Yeah."

Chris looked out at the valley. Palm and coconut trees still grew on a long spur running out from the hill they just came down. Extended long into the valley. "We'll stick to that flanking treeline. That should minimize our time in the open."

Brandon looked to where Chris had pointed. "How much time will that waste?"

"Probably an hour to reach the trees. Then an hour to get back on track once we make it across." He looked over his shoulder. "Unless you want to cut straight across."

Peeking out from the foliage, eyes adjusting to the brightness, Brandon scanned the open spaces in the grass. The bald spots on the hillsides. Dozens of NVA troops darted from hidden positions. But in the next moment they weren't NVA at all. Just shadows of waving jungle canopy. Clouds casting shadows against the hills.

Brandon sighed. "We make for the flanking treeline."

Chris's estimate about how long it would take to get back on track was accurate, and they were across the valley as the sun was at its highest.

Within the jungle's concealment they took a short rest to eat. While they ate they watched the valley they had crossed. If there was ever a time to see if they were being followed, that was probably it. But in that big openness, only a few white birds hung lazily in the air like kites. No one came.

Brandon took this opportunity to tell the men about the things that were bothering him.

"The guys stationed at the outpost..." Brandon said.

"What about them?" Mike asked.

Brandon shook his head. "Most of them are teenagers. Or, they were. That's what I saw in the dream. Kids, man."

"I think most of the U.S. soldiers are teenagers," Mike said.

"I know," Brandon said. "I just..."

The men looked down at their food. Chris nodded.

Brandon watched them. When no one spoke, he said, "Nobody feels bad about..." He searched for the words to put it delicately. To make what he wanted to say sound less ugly. Finding none, he said, "You don't feel bad about killing these kids?"

Chris shrugged as he chewed. "Depends."

"On what?"

"On if they shoot at me first."

Brandon scoffed. Looked at Mike for some help.

Mike saw him looking. He chewed slow. Circled his spoon around in a little circle, taking in the men gathered there. "You three are what I'm worried about. If someone tries to make it difficult for us to make it home, well..."

Boing watched them.

"Boing," Brandon said. "Maybe Boing can talk to them. Maybe they'll listen to one of their own."

Boing's eyes narrowed. "One of their own?"

Brandon leaned back. "That's not what I meant. I meant—"

Boing held out a hand. "I know what you meant. These *kids* you're talking about are *soldiers*. They're soldiers in an army trying to overthrow *my* government." The anger in his voice made Brandon uneasy. "Just because I share a country with them doesn't mean anything. They won't hesitate to kill me and my family. I won't hesitate to kill them. So, to answer your question, sir; no, I will not feel bad about killing them. I will not feel bad if *you* kill them."

Brandon raised his hands in surrender. "I'm sorry. It's... I don't know."

"You're nervous," Chris said.

"No—"

"*Yes*. I ain't asking you, I'm *telling* you." Chris munched on a cracker. "You talk a lot when you're nervous."

"Do I?"

"Yes," All three of them said.

"You can be nervous," Chris said. "Just try not to think about *why* you're nervous. When you start to enjoy killing it's probably time to walk away from this job. We'll make it through this. But we're gonna have to do some things we won't be proud of. Remember what we talked about earlier? Just leave that shit in the jungle, man."

Do what we must.

After eating they stood to get ready to leave. Brandon stopped Chris before he could pick up the litter. "You should probably take point from here. I think we're close."

Chris's eyes hardened. The slight grin that always seemed to be tugging at the corners of his mouth faded to a grim scowl. Chris nodded. "Stay close."

Seeing Chris turn his switch pumped adrenaline into Brandon's veins. Chris's immaturity and sarcastic mouth used to piss Brandon off to no end. Recently, though, there was something soothing about it—like Chris's attitude about everything made their situation less real.

But watching Chris put on his killer's face was a harsh reminder of what they were about to get into.

Mike was hesitant to let Brandon carry the litter.

"I know my weaknesses," Brandon said. "Chris is better suited to lead here."

Chris took it slow. Almost frustratingly slow. Brandon had to remind himself that covering as much ground as fast they could wasn't the goal anymore. Now it was a recon. Just like Laos.

Chris occasionally halted them to listen and to look. Brandon recognized the landmark of the valley from the dream, but he didn't know the distance to their target.

As Chris led them Brandon tried not to think about the young NVA soldiers he saw in his dream. Tried not to think of their plans after the war. Their joyful return to their families. Tried not to think about the children they had. Or wanted to have. Tried not to think about their wives.

But it was useless. He was thinking about *all* of those

things when Mike stopped abruptly and Brandon nearly dropped Boing's litter.

"What's up?" Brandon asked.

Mike's head turned slow. Very slow. He whispered over his shoulder, barely a breath to the words, "Chris stopped."

Everything around Brandon became bright. The quiet jungle sounds got loud. He smelled something. Tasted it. Something... something *mechanical*.

They set the litter down. Brandon moved up through the foliage until he came upon Chris. And Brandon stopped. Froze. Adrenaline spurted in his chest. Chris was lying prone behind his rifle, his non-firing hand raised just slightly in a fist.

Brandon sank down and dropped his rucksack and low-crawled to Chris.

Chris looked at him. He put a finger to his lips. Then that finger slowly rotated outward.

Brandon followed it with his eyes. He listened.

Beyond the foliage. Beyond a low, gray mist, he heard the rumbling of an engine. A truck? Brandon searched through the sharp grass and green blotches of undergrowth for a long time. He gasped as the tan, angled shapes of bamboo and wood huts materialized through the brush.

Chris's eyes flicked to Brandon. "We're here."

CHAPTER FORTY-THREE

Brandon hurried back through the foliage to Mike and Boing and told them about the compound. He told them to stay put and he grabbed a pair of binoculars from a rucksack and returned to Chris.

There was a slight incline concealed in the jungle and Brandon and Chris slithered up through the grass and undergrowth for a better vantage. They laid there for a long time. Watching.

Brandon handed the binoculars to Chris and whispered, "There's hardly any security."

"Why would there be?" Chris put the binoculars to his eyes. "They probably think no American would be stupid enough to attack this far north with no hope of EVAC or resupply."

"But that's what *I'm* doing."

"Did I say stupid?" Chris slid an eye sideways from the binos and winked at him. "I probably meant to say brave."

They watched.

It was hard for Brandon to grapple with the conflicting emotions fighting inside him. New York had been alone in the jungle for so long. They had been tired, wet, hungry, and scared for nearly a week. And there——right there across a dusty clay road lay civilization.

But it was the *wrong* civilization.

He felt like a marooned sailor, desperately hoping for a ship to appear on the horizon. Salvation. But when a ship finally appeared, it was a plague ship. Bringing with it only death.

Chris pointed at a square stack of green sandbags near the far side of the compound. "That's the generator."

Brandon nodded. The rumbling he had mistaken for a truck was a gas-powered generator. Next to it, near the rear of the compound were—

Brandon pointed. "There."

"What?"

"The three huts in the back there."

Chris shifted the binoculars. "Mmm. What about 'em?"

"Commo huts."

"You sure?"

"Yeah. I've seen them before."

Thick wires strung between them. The third hut was nestled in the back of the compound, up against a slate-gray escarpment. Three tall antennae jutted out through the roof.

"Yep," Chris said. "That's where the radios are." Handing the binos to Brandon, Chris asked, "Any idea how many people are stationed here?"

Brandon tried to remember the faces. To count them. But in the daylight hours they all seemed to blend into one face. One voice. "No."

They watched.

The compound looked like it had been there for a while. The jungle grew wild on the outside of the lashed bamboo fence. Foliage spilled over the top. But inside the fence the ground was bare. Reddish-brown clay with uncut patches of pointy grass sprouting from beneath the stilted huts.

The front gate, big enough for two trucks to enter side

by side, was wide open. A machinegun nest encased in sandbags sat just inside with two sentries inside. Deep, uniform tire tracks imprinted in the clay ran alongside the machinegun nest and curved in a long horseshoe. Came back around the nest's opposite side to exit the gate onto the roadway.

All over the compound NVA soldiers in black linen clothes and sandals went about their duties. Most of them carried AK-47s. Just outside the gate, a single sentry squatted on his haunches smoking a cigarette.

Chris pointed to the commo hut. "If I can get in there I can get ahold of some friendlies. We can wait until dark. Might not even have to fire a shot—"

"No," Brandon said.

Chris looked at him. "Why?"

Brandon watched the compound. Watched the NVA soldiers moving amongst the buildings and bunkers. "If any of these men get a shot at John, we're finished."

Chris's eyes lingered on him a moment. He turned his head to the men below. He drew in a deep breath. "Your call."

Do what you must.

Brandon didn't want to hear it said out loud. Didn't want to give the order. But the burden of command was his. And it was especially cumbersome here. Brandon nodded. "Sweep and clear."

Chris nodded. Then he watched. Three words from Brandon and he had turned Chris's thoughts to murder.

"Their clothes look nice and clean," Chris said. "They got some bellies on 'em, too. These aren't hardened infantry. Clerks most likely. Logistics folks. Or maybe their daddies had some clout and got them stationed way up here away from the fighting."

"How soon do you think they could be reinforced if they sent out a call out for help?"

Chris scratched the week's-worth of hair on his chin. "In Laos they spaced out their depots. I don't have the intel on this place to know for sure, but I'd say if they're reinforced by foot, it might take a day to get help from the nearest base." He flicked his finger toward the road. "These roads are good. Not like the washouts and camouflaged paths we see down south. If reinforcements are mechanized, trucks could be here in a few hours. Maybe less if there's a base closer than I think."

So many unknowns. New York was blind and deaf here. "We need to get this underway soon," Brandon said. "I know John is around here somewhere."

"You still feel him?"

Brandon ran his hand across the gashes in his stomach. "Kind of. It's weak."

"Doesn't that mean he's far away?"

Shaking his head, Brandon said, "I don't know. Hasn't been the same since Jaran…"

Chris sighed. "We really need to wait for a supply truck or two to come through and leave. See how long the pickups take. If they're spaced out at normal intervals we can at least plan on hitting them with less chance of being interrupted."

From what Brandon had heard, when the SOG Teams switched roles and played offense, the standard procedure was to insert, observe the target for as long as necessary and, once the target's defenses were significantly detailed, they'd move in and get to work.

But New York didn't have the time to properly acquaint themselves with their new friends and how they did things.

This compound had all the pieces of a good security layout. But judging by the soldiers' relaxed demeanor, there was an air of complacency that only came from never being attacked. Brandon trusted Chris's opinion about these soldiers' inexperience. Maybe—and Brandon was putting perhaps too much faith in the idea—if John *did* come here, he would have to give these men a good reason to kill him. Looking at them down there, so young, they might hesitate. They might try and take John prisoner. The bounty on an American Recon man paid double if he was taken alive—

No. Brandon couldn't go down that line of thought. If John had a gun, all he had to do was point it at someone. Those troops would open up with everything they had and John would be ground into hamburger before his body hit the ground.

Sweep and clear. That was the way it had to be. They couldn't let John get within spitting distance of this place while any of these soldiers were still alive. But New York didn't have enough time to wait and properly recon this place. They were running out of time, Brandon could feel it. If New York hit the compound lightning-fast with suppressed pistols, they might have a chance. The generator would drown out most of the noise...

"How many of these guys do you count?" Brandon asked. "I see twenty-five. Maybe thirty. But I haven't seen anyone come or go from those commo huts."

Chris scanned the compound. "I count about the same. We're gonna have our work cut out for us. We need to find their radio operators and neutralize them first. If not first, then at least fast. Then we mop up the rest." Chris blew out a stream of air. "This'll be tough. If we slow down for even a second, we're gonna get chewed up. We can't let them see us coming."

Brandon blurted a nervous laugh.

"What?"

"Everyone says John's team makes miracles happen."

Chris snorted. "Well they weren't lying. I didn't say we couldn't do it. I said it'll be tough."

"I trust you," Brandon said.

"Good," Chris glanced at him and that grin appeared on his face. "Because it's your team now. Just give me a few more minutes to plan this out." And he turned back to the compound. Lying motionless. A snake watching prey.

Something flashed white like lightning and Brandon's

arms gave out. He dropped to his chest. Arms and legs convulsing. Chest muscles tightening like concrete. Sucking sounds as his lungs tried to remember how to draw air.

Chris rolled him onto his back and shoved his hand over Brandon's mouth. "What the fuck, man?" Then Chris's eyes went wide. He must have seen the terror Brandon knew was painted on his face. "Is John here?"

Brandon's hands were clutched against his stomach. His throat tight, choking his voice out. All he could do was nod.

Chris grabbed Brandon's hands in his own and said, "Breathe." Sucking in air, Chris said, "Breathe, Brandon…" And he blew air out.

Brandon in—

—haled

In… haled.

Exhaled…

"Good…" Chris said.

Brandon's muscles, as if one by one, unlocked. His breathing slowed.

"Good," Chris whispered. "Where's John?"

"*Dung Lai!*"

Chris froze. Brandon lay trembling beneath him. Chris's eyes darted toward the voice.

"*Dung Lai!*" the voice called again. The Vietnamese accent ringing clear through the trees.

Shadows of waving foliage twisted on Chris's face. "Halt," Chris whispered. "He's saying 'halt.'"

The tremors in Brandon's limbs subsided and he pulled Chris's hand away from his mouth. "What do we do?"

"*Dung Lai!*" The voice called, but it sounded muffled. Softer. As though the speaker were facing away from them.

"I need to confirm it's John," Chris said.

"Are you fucking crazy? The whole camp probably heard that shouting."

Before Brandon could protest further, Chris floated to the ground like smoke and snaked back to the perch over the roadway.

Brandon, his heart sledgehammering his chest, rolled over with the grace of a dropped duffel bag and followed Chris on jerky hands and knees. Adrenaline exaggerating every movement, crawling like a newborn calf.

"*Shit!*" Chris hissed, unslinging his rifle from his back. "Shit!" *Click* as his rifle went to semi.

Scrambling to where Chris lay, Brandon looked out over the red clay, "*Shit!*"

The young sentry who had been smoking at the gate now held his rifle at the ready and was approaching a solitary man stumbling drunkenly right down the middle of the road. Straight toward the front gate as if he belonged there.

That man was John.

Other voices from within the compound called out in Vietnamese.

The plan. Everything they had planned fell apart in front of Brandon's eyes.

"FRAGO," Chris said. "That kid is gonna kill him."

"Use your pistol," Brandon whispered. "The suppressor."

"Too far."

"Chris!" Brandon slapped the ground like an excited child. "What the fuck do we do?"

Chris pulled his rifle's buttstock into his shoulder and put his eye to the sight. "Run back and get Mike. Tell him what's going on. The assault plan stays the same. I'll have to hold them here until you get back."

"What the fuck do you mean hold them…"

BANG!

Chris's rifle barked a single shot and Brandon sprang to his feet.

"No!" Brandon yelled.

But when he looked out, John stood there. His face

spattered with red. Caked with chunks.

The Vietnamese soldier lay folded over and twitching at John's feet.

John knelt and picked up the dead man's rifle. He didn't even bother wiping the blood and brain and chunks of skull—

Chris scanned with his rifle. "I'm guessing someone heard that."

"Yeah, no shit."

Another soldier came running toward the road from the compound. AK-47 swinging in his pumping arms. Chris' shoulders shifted, rifle muzzle traversing.

BANG.

The soldier winced, clutching his belly as he fell and tumbled and came up sitting. Face clenched. Teeth showing white in a grimace. Half a heartbeat later, Chris fired again and the soldier's hair flicked as if from a breeze and he stiffened and lay down.

Chris pressed himself flat into the earth and sighted another target. He glanced over his shoulder and saw Brandon and shouted, "What the fuck are you still doing here?"

CHAPTER FORTY-FOUR

Slapping away foliage, Brandon sprinted back to Mike and Boing. A hand reached out from the jungle and snatched Brandon's shirt so tight and hard that Brandon's feet lifted in the air. The hand shoved Brandon down to the earth, blowing the wind out of him with an "*Oof!*"

He opened his eyes to see who had grabbed him, but couldn't see anything beyond the matte-black suppressor hovering in front of his face.

"You scared the shit out of us," Mike said. He lowered the pistol and hauled Brandon to his feet. "What the hell is happening out there?"

Bent over, hands on his knees, Brandon said, "John. He's here. Chris killed some guys already. It's fucked, Mike. It's all fucked."

Another rifle shot snapped behind them.

Brandon straightened and looked back toward the sound. "Chris needs us. We can't let John get himself killed."

"I'll get the sixty," Mike said.

"No," Brandon turned back to him. "I'll get it. Just go. You're a better shot than me. Chris needs extra guns—"

Another shot rang out. And another.

Then the jungle quaked with staccato barks. NVA returning fire. Had they found Chris?

Brandon pushed Mike down the path. "Go! He needs you!"

Mike took off toward the gunfire and Brandon turned and ran to where they had left Boing.

When Brandon pushed through the green, Boing's eyes were wide. He lay by the rucksacks, rifle in hand. "What's going on?"

Brandon told him everything as he upended rucksacks and grabbed the M60 ammo cans and popped them open. Tore out belts of ammunition and slung them over his shoulders.

Ammo. Guns.

Boing said something.

"What?"

Ammo. Need more ammo. All the guns we have.

Boing said something again.

"Goddamnit, Boing I don't have—"

"*Sir!*" Boing shouted.

Brandon paused, heavy belts of ammo swaying in his hand. He looked up at Boing.

Boing said, "Take me with you."

"What..." He looked at where Boing's legs used to be. "What can you do?"

"I don't need legs to run the sixty."

Brandon was about to protest.

Ammo. Guns.

New York was vastly outnumbered.

Every gun we have.

Bullet tips clinking together, Brandon knelt next to Boing. "This might hurt." Grunting at the pain in his back Brandon hefted Boing and slung him across his shoulder in a fireman's carry. Without his legs Boing was surprisingly light.

The M60 sat on its bipods and Brandon bent and

grabbed it up by the carrying handle.

Gunfire popped in the near distance.

Brandon blew out. Stared into the jungle. Stared into the sound of gunfire. Whispered to himself, "Come on." Willing his legs to move.

Boing bounced atop Brandon's shoulders as they made their way toward the noise. The gunfire growing in intensity the closer they went. Friendly rifle reports indistinguishable from the enemy's. Mike or Chris could be dead for all he knew. Both of them could be. The NVA could just be shooting for the sake of it.

But he went on. Weighed down by ammo and Boing and the M60, Brandon jogged as fast as he could. Sweating, panting, heart pounding out of his chest, they came upon Chris's last position. The grass sparkled gold from expended brass casings. Two empty magazines lay on the ground.

Brandon knelt and rolled Boing onto the ground. Placed the M60 on the ground overlooking the road and planted the bipods in the dirt.

The gunfire had stopped. The jungle went quiet. Brandon shared a concerned look with Boing. Gunfights didn't just stop for no reason.

Pulling the foliage aside, Brandon stood to look out over the compound. People on the ground. Most of them dead. Some of them not. The dead were crumpled in heaps or sprawled out on their backs. Blood pooled beneath them in shiny puddles. The clay earth refusing to drink. Small mounds of yellow and pink gore spilled from heads and throats. Wounded men clawed at the earth, pulling their broken bodies away from their attackers. Their blood filling the gashes in the clay. Some men groaned like wailing ghosts. Others stared at their shaking hands covered in blood. Some panicked and cried out. No one came to help any of them.

Then Brandon saw his men. A knee-high ditch lined either side of the road and flattened out near the compound's front entrance for trucks to pass through.

Chris lay prone on the right side of the gate, pulling a rifle mag from a pouch and reloading. Mike lay on the left, aiming his rifle. They looked uninjured.

But of John, there was no sign.

"I…" Brandon turned to Boing. Searched his face. "I don't know how this is going to end."

Chewing his lip, Boing surveyed the compound. "We'll get through it, sir." He said it like he believed it.

Brandon could only nod and hope he was right.

"And if not…" Boing reached into his shirt pocket and pulled out the little pill bottle. Shook it. The single capsule rattled inside.

Cyanide.

Boing placed the pill bottle on the ground between the M60's bipods. He tried to smile. "Hopefully it won't come to that."

Brandon looked around. Checked behind them. "John disappeared again, Boing." He spoke quietly. Hoped that saying the name out loud didn't draw John's attention. "You keep that pill handy. If he comes for you—"

The jungle shook with rifle fire. Brandon jerked at the noise. Took the belts of ammunition off his shoulder and dropped them on the ground. Reached for the M60 to load it.

Boing waved him off and took the ammunition. "I got it, sir. Get out there with your team."

Brandon's mind was a cluster of all the things he thought he should say to Boing. This might be the last time Brandon saw this man alive. This might be—

No.

Brandon stood and shook his head. They'd get through this. They *would!* He drew his 1911 and racked the slide. Holstered it. Unslung his rifle. Pulled the charging handle back. Gold flashed as a round chambered. He took a long deep breath. "Good luck, Boing." He turned and ran down the hill to his men.

And in moments Brandon burst from the tree line into the road and sprinted toward Chris.

Chris rolled on his back and dropped a mag to reload. He saw Brandon crossing the road and his eyes went wide. "Get down!"

Light flashed. A roar blasted from the machinegun nest inside the gate. The ground at Brandon's feet churned and he yelped and kicked his feet high in the air. Screaming, he dove into the ditch beside Chris.

Pulling Brandon tight to him, Chris patted Brandon's arms and legs and back and belly.

"I'm fine!" he slapped Chris's hands away and rolled onto his back. "I'm fine!"

"You dumb motherfucker!" Chris slapped Brandon on the head. "You didn"t see the machinegun nest?"

"I thought you dealt with it."

"No, you asshole!" Chris slapped him again. "We're getting *ready* to deal with it!"

"Stop hitting me!" Brandon lifted his head to look at the machinegun, but Chris grabbed his neck and shoved his face in the dirt as the machinegun barked and dirt popped around them.

Chris's hand still on his neck, Brandon shouted through a mouthful of dirt, "Where's John?"

"Jungle somewhere. Limped off when I zapped the guys that came out to see what was going on."

Chris waved a series of hand signals at Mike.

Brandon rolled his head in the dirt. "What are we doing?"

"*You* are keeping your fuckin' head down." Chris let go of Brandon and pulled himself up to the top of the ditch. "If I get hit, I need you to put suppressive fire on the nest. Mike's going in."

Brandon rolled his head to Mike in time to see him get up to one knee and pull a grenade from the pouch on his LCE. Mike nodded at them.

Pushing through the dirt, Brandon got an eye just

enough over the ditch to see the space between them and the gun nest. "That's too much open ground. They'll rip him up."

"Yeah, that's what I'm trying to avoid."

Chris rose and fired an automatic burst. The machinegun barrel swiveled to aim at Chris and he sprawled out just as the clay erupted in the road.

Mike rose to a knee, rifle muzzle steadied on his forearm. The grenade gripped tight in his non-firing hand. He fired two shots. Two more.

The machinegun swung back toward Mike and he dropped, swinging his rifle around onto his back on its sling.

Chris rose. Fired. The machinegun swiveled. But Chris didn't drop. He fired controlled pairs as Mike jumped up and sprinted inside the gate. He had his 1911 in one hand. Grenade in the other.

As if startled, the machinegun barrel twitched between Chris and Mike. Like it was making up its mind which target to engage. And then it made up its mind. It swung toward Mike.

"Over here you motherfuckers!" Chris screamed. His rounds impacted around the slit in the gun nest. Making pockmarks. The dirt inside the sandbags ejected in puffs. He walked the rounds up the sandbags until they were hitting the slit where the machinegun's barrel was poking out. The silhouette inside dropped. Maybe dead. Maybe hiding.

Regardless, the machinegun went quiet.

Mike sprinted.

"Reloading!" Chris shouted, clicking out the magazine.

Movement in the nest. A head popped up in the slit.

"*Shit!*" Brandon leveled his rifle on the road, trying to steady his sights on the head inside.

Mike raised his 1911 and put two suppressed rounds into the slot. The head dropped again. He was still some twenty paces from the nest when something small went spinning from his hand. The grenade spoon.

So far away. The countdown started in Brandon's head.

Five.

Four.

An NVA soldier appeared from behind a hut directly in front of Mike and raised an AK-47.

Mike put two silent rounds in the man's chest. Black jets shot out from the soldier's back and he twitched and dropped his rifle. Mike didn't slow down. He booted the man in his bullet holes and the soldier fell and writhed on the ground. Chris transitioned and shot him in the face and the soldier's hands curled up into jerking claws.

Three.

Brandon and Chris could no longer provide covering fire without the risk of hitting Mike. He was on his own in that no-man's-land.

The machine gunner's head reappeared; Mike fired two shots that threw up clouds of dust from the sand bags. The 1911's slide locked back. Out of ammo. The machinegunner stood his ground. The barrel swiveled.

Two.

Sprinting at full speed Mike slammed the sandbag wall. A plume of dust shot out around him. He reached his grenade-hand in the slot and yanked it right back out like he had just stuck his hand into a hot oven. He turned his back to the machinegun and slumped against the sandbags. Palmed one ear with the now-empty grenade hand and shoved the other ear into his shoulder. He held his mouth open. Clicked out the empty mag from his pistol.

One.

Two distinct and terrified voices shouted from inside the nest. Probably realizing what it was that Mike had just delivered to them.

There was a flash of neon green and white and—

BOOM.

The nest popped with the concussion. A sphere of dust burst around the machinegun nest and hung white in the sunlight like God had punched through from Heaven. In the following, heavy silence the dust ball lost its shape and swirled away into nothing.

Mike slammed a pistol mag home and let the slide go forward. He holstered his pistol and brought up his rifle.

Chris grabbed Brandon by the back of the shirt. "That's our beachhead! Move!"

They scrambled up and sprinted through the gate, converging on Mike.

"Keep up the momentum!" Chris shouted. "Go! Go!" They darted out from behind the gun nest. Three abreast, spaced out wide, and pushed into the compound.

"Target!" Mike called, and he fired. Someone groaned in the shadows.

Movement in a bamboo hut. Brandon and Chris shot through the walls. The man inside stood up in the window, screaming through wet gurgles and clutching his chest. Chris shot him in the head and the man dropped.

New York fanned out. Bounding. Covering each other's movements.

Men ran out of huts, holding their rifles at their hips, screaming and wildly spraying rifle fire. New York cut them down. When they reached the commo hut at the back end of the compound, Brandon turned back to look out over the carnage in their wake.

Brandon and Chris had counted at least twenty-five men on their initial recon. Now at least thirty lay dead or dying in the dirt.

A voice shouted in Vietnamese beyond the commo hut's wooden door.

Holding up a hand for quiet, Mike listened at the door. "He's calling for help."

Chris reached for a grenade around his waist.

Brandon grabbed Chris's hand. "Don't frag it. We need the radios."

Chris pouted and buttoned his grenade pouch. He slung his rifle and drew his 1911. "On me."

They stacked against the sandbag wall beside the door.

Chris waved Mike away. "Hang back. I might need your services."

Pressing himself up against Chris's back, muscles trembling with adrenaline, Brandon whispered, "Ready."

Sharp splinters burst from the door as the man inside full-auto blasted his rifle through the wood. Brandon and Chris shied away as the bullets chewed through the bamboo.

Silence.

Chris blinked away the sawdust and shook his head. He looked up in the air and tick-ticked his head. Nodded. "Sounded like thirty rounds to me." And he spun and front-kicked the ruined door, punched out his pistol and fired one shot before he was even through the doorframe.

Brandon was right behind him, crossing the threshold when he saw the lone occupant of the room collapse, head banging hard on a table. Rifle clattering to the floor. Dark mist hung where he had once stood. An echo of a man.

They scanned the room. Boxy radios and microphones sat on dusty tables. Tiny frantic voices called out from three or four different radios.

Chris holstered his pistol and called Mike in. When he stepped into the room, Chris said, "Any idea what they're saying?"

Mike listened. "I hope you know how to make these radios talk to the spooks." He looked at Chris. The nervousness in his eyes terrified Brandon. "A lot of people are coming."

"Great." Chris packed his can of chewing tobacco. "More NVA?"

"Yeah," Mike said. "And they're bringing Counter Recon."

CHAPTER FORTY-FIVE

Chris took the notebook from his shirt pocket and twisted dials on a radio.

"Will anyone be able to hear you?" Brandon asked.

"If no one is monitoring the spook frequencies, someone will be monitoring SOG emergency freqs." He picked up the hand mic and nodded toward the door. "Secure that courtyard. Search the huts and make sure we didn't miss anyone. I'll let you know when I get us a ride."

Rifles at the low-ready, Brandon and Mike ducked out from the commo hut. Side by side, they made their way slow, counterclockwise around the compound's inner perimeter. At each hut they listened at the doorway. Then kicked in the door and went in, rifles raised.

Most huts were empty. In some there were bodies. Sitting up against walls. Lying on the floor.

After clearing the huts, Mike and Brandon made their way to the center of the courtyard and stood behind the machinegun nest. They listened. They watched.

The generator rumbled.

All around there were young, calm faces staring up from where they lay on ground.

Brandon wanted to say something to Mike. To congratulate him, maybe. He was proud of Mike's and Chris's bravery and of what they had accomplished. But he was also ashamed of what they had done here. What Brandon had commanded them to do. New York's assault on this compound, it hadn't really been a *fight*. It had been a slaughter. All because John decided to come here.

Brandon felt like puking.

Eyes drifting from one set of dead eyes to another, Brandon couldn't help but think that he could have prevented this. If he had been honest with Jaran when she asked about his connection to John. If he had helped her find him instead of running away. Then maybe these men, these *kids*, they could have lived. Could have gone back to their lives after this war was over.

Scratching his thumb against his rifle's safety, Brandon asked, "You see where John went?"

Mike nodded to somewhere beyond the bamboo fence. "Limped off into the jungle when I came to help Chris. Can you still sense him?"

"A little. It's weak."

"Does that mean he's getting weaker?"

"I don't know."

"Hey!" Chris called. And he came running, skidding to a halt. "I got ahold of the spooks. Gave them our grid and told them we had their precious cargo."

"Precious cargo?" Brandon asked. "We don't—"

"Yeah, yeah." Chris waved him off. "I thought it would motivate them if we told them we had precious cargo. But it worked. They dispatched some choppers."

Mike slapped him on the shoulder. "That's great news."

"Yeah, but I have some not-so-great news."

Seeing the look on Chris's face made Brandon go cold. "Oh shit, what?"

"That chatter we heard, it's worse than we thought. Every swingin' dick within twenty miles is on their way here."

"Where's the extraction site?" Mike asked.

"About ten kliks south along the road. Big clearing."

"*Ten?*" Brandon's heart sank. "How the hell are we supposed to get there without anyone seeing us?"

"We'll figure something out. We still might have some time before…" Chris's eyes drifted over Brandon's shoulder. "Fuck."

Mike and Brandon turned. And brought their rifles up.

John came limping toward them from the road. Stepping hard and dragging his foot. Clutching his gut. Despite the pain he appeared to be in, he was smiling below those dead white eyes.

"You stay right there!" Mike shouted.

"Oh," John said. "I intend to."

"The fuck is that supposed to mean?" Chris whispered.

"Why don't you ask him?" Brandon said.

But then John cocked his head. Put his hand to his ear.

Chris stepped forward. "What's he…" And then Chris cocked his head. "Everyone in the gun nest. Now!"

"What?" Brandon said. "Why?" But then Brandon heard it, too. Growing loud over the generator. The rumbling. The unmistakable *glug-glug* of a diesel engine.

They ducked inside, stepping over the two men Mike had killed with the grenade. Dried burgundy fluid caked with dust streaked from their ears down their necks and into their shirt collars.

The nest had a panoramic view of the front gate and the jungle beyond. Chris squatted down behind the RPD and fingered the trigger. "Check the lot number on that ammo."

Mike ran his fingers over the belt of ammunition hanging from the NVA's machinegun. Scanned the individual rounds. "They're good."

"How are we on rifle ammo?" Chris asked.

Brandon patted the mag pouches on his LCE. Two mags left. Plus the one in his rifle. "Sixty rounds."

"Two mags," Mike said.

Chris shook his head. "Make 'em count."

Their fight to take the compound had left them extremely low on ammo. The fight to get out would most likely deplete what they had left.

"Come out!" John lingered in that no-man's land between the machinegun and the road. He leaned toward the sound of the approaching truck and called mockingly, "More friends are here! Come out and welcome them!"

Mike and Chris said nothing. What was there to say? An overwhelming enemy force was at New York's door. They both aimed their weapons. Mike behind his CAR-15 and Chris's finger caressing the RPD's trigger. Mike and Chris were seasoned enough to know that their lives were going to end in the coming moments. But they didn't have to say a word for Brandon to know that they would die fighting.

The jungle waved in a light breeze. The truck engine yowled in the near distance. Brandon inhaled deep. Blew out. Inhaled. Chest tingling with nervous energy. Head going light. Heart punching his ribs. This was it. This was really how Brandon's life was going to end. Those NVA were going to rip John to pieces. And after that, they'd do the same to New York.

"*Motherfucker!*" Brandon hissed at John. Eyes stinging and going blurry.

The engine roared at his despair.

This whole nightmare was about to end for New York. But as soon as those NVA wasted John, it would just start over for someone else. Erlik Khan would go on terrorizing people. Ruining lives. Killing.

Those bodies lying out there in the courtyard, Erlik Khan caused that. All this death. Brandon had never wanted to kill anyone, but that devil had forced him.

Brandon's chest heaved with quick, hyperventilating breaths.

"It's alright." Mike put his hand on Brandon's shoulder. "We're with you."

"Mother," Brandon wheezed. "Fucker!" He squeezed his eyes shut.

Brandon was going to die. His men were going to die. He opened his eyes. He looked at John. He fingered the bottle in his shirt pocket. They were going to die. But this nightmare didn't have to go on.

Brandon unsnapped his magazine pouches and pulled out his last two mags and laid them on the sandbags.

Chris looked at him. "What are you doing?"

But Brandon couldn't say what he was about to do. Saying it out loud would make it real. If he said it his men would try and stop him. And Brandon would probably let them.

So Brandon sucked in air. Held it. He put his rifle on the floor and leaned it against the sandbags. He blew out the breath he was holding, long and slow. Heart slowing. Slowing. He whispered, "Cover me."

"Hey," Mike reached out. "Don't—"

Brandon darted from the machinegun nest and sprinted straight at John. Voices called from behind, but they were drowned out beneath Brandon's animal scream.

John turned. Stood there with that big fucking smile on his face. That smile was the last thing Brandon saw before he bent low and plowed his shoulder into John's belly. They slammed the clay in a twisted heap of arms and legs.

They rolled. A putrid cloud assaulted Brandon. The stink of infection. Rotting flesh. And then he came face to face with John.

John lay on the ground, head laid back as if he were tanning in the sun. He looked at Brandon and smiled. In that smile Brandon saw his own suffering. His pain.

It should have been you...

His fear.

You'll never be one of the good ones.

His anger.

That smile. Brandon grabbed John's shirt collar and smashed his fist right into the center of that smile.

John's head slammed against the clay. Brandon tugged John's shirt, yanking his head up. And he punched him again.

Choking laughter spurted from John's bleeding mouth. Somewhere beyond Brandon's rage, beyond that demon laughter, there was a squealing sound.

Brandon pulled the bottle from his shirt pocket. Twisted off the cap and shook the little pill out into his mouth. Tongued it into his cheek. "Keep laughing, asshole."

Still chuckling, John opened his eyes. Looked at the empty pill bottle in Brandon's hand. Brandon threw the bottle and it *ticked* off John's forehead and went tumbling away. John's laughter died.

Brandon drew his 1911 and thumbed off the safety. "You lost." And he tongued the pill into his teeth.

John's hand shot up and grabbed Brandon's wrist, wrenched it to the side. Brandon jerked the trigger and blasted a round into the clay.

"Swallow it!" John roared. And he smacked Brandon's face with his bandaged stump. He swung again. The blunt wrist bone pounded Brandon's throat.

Brandon gagged and coughed, tucking his chin against his chest. He tried to aim the pistol, but John's hand was like concrete on his wrist. Brandon pulled his arm, bicep trembling against John's strength. The pistol shook. He punched at John's elbow, trying to get his arm to bend. But John's strength held.

John swung his wrist again and Brandon's vision exploded black.

Don't let go, a soft voice said.

His vision cleared. The side of his head throbbed, ballooning out.

John's arm pulled back for a punch, then it came. Brandon tried to duck, but John's wrist caught him in the jaw—

I'm with you. Jaran said. *Don't let go.*

—and through the blurriness Brandon looked up at a giant puke green shape. Boxy. Big black circles. His mind clawed back from the fuzzed edges of near-unconsciousness and arranged the shapes into something he recognized.

A truck. An M35-looking troop carrier. A faded red star stenciled on the door. The tall truck bed bristling with stunted porcupine quills. No, they were rifles. AK-47s. A bunch of black-haired heads.

Now clearly seeing the twenty or thirty Vietnamese soldiers standing in the back of the deuce and a half. Adrenaline surged in Brandon's blood. The NVA screamed at him with words he didn't understand.

Beneath him, John's head titled all the way back to regard the soldiers there. The men aiming rifles at these two Americans lying on the ground. The definition of sitting ducks.

John rolled his head casually back to Brandon. His smile was full of blood and broken teeth. John's rumbling voice stunk of rot when he said, "The coward's bravery just before the end. Were you hoping to survive this?"

"No," Brandon grunted, and spat out the cyanide capsule on John's face. "I just need to keep you from getting killed."

Whatever was going to happen next, Brandon wasn't going to let John have a weapon. He thumbed the pistol's magazine release. The mag fell and thumped on the ground. He pulled the trigger and spat the last shot into the ground over John's head. He let the pistol fall from his hand.

John held Brandon tight. "Those men came here to kill us, Brandon. Do you have some power over fate?"

"No," Brandon gasped. His muscles were failing. He couldn't hold up against John's inhuman strength. "I have faith."

"*God?*" John howled with laughter. "You're putting your faith in *God* to stop those men?"

"Not God." The top of Brandon's head, his shoulders, they tingled with the anticipation of impending gunfire. Gritting his teeth, Brandon buried his face in John's chest and said, "Boing."

The laughter pumping from John's chest died. A vacuum of silence. In half a heartbeat, that silence was shattered by the roar of gunfire.

And beneath that terrible noise, something grunted. A steady rhythm. Like a heartbeat. Like a beating drum.

But it was no drum.

It was a pig.

John roared. Tensed. Arms pulled. Legs kicked. John flopped on the ground. Rolled. Brandon snaked his arms behind John's back and clasped his wrists. Got his heels behind John's knees. Squeezed. Squeezed so there would be no way John could sit up into the gunfire. From both sides John beat his elbows against Brandon's head. Screaming, "I'll kill you! *I'll kill you!*"

Zips and cracks rang out overhead. John bucked his hips and nearly flung Brandon off, but he hung on. A brief glimpse of the machinegun nest. Flashes of light as Mike and Chris fired over John and Brandon. In the clay, through John's chest, in Brandon's head there was a deep and constant *thump-thump-thumping*. The M60. The pig. Boing keeping time in this symphony of chaos. And through it, John and Brandon rolled.

Chunks of clay burst from the ground and sprayed Brandon's face. Accompanied by a *ping!* Or *zip!* But he hung on. It was all he could do, but he was tiring. His muscles were failing.

John rolled to the side. Brandon rolled with him. With his ear against John's chest, Brandon caught a glimpse of the truck. Heads ping-ponged against each other as men tried to roll over the walls of the truck bed. But the men jumping over the side facing the machinegun nest were peppered with Mike and Chris's rifle and RPD fire. They were hamburger before they hit the ground. The poor bastards jumping over the side facing Boing must have gone through the same grinder.

The din of war howled in Brandon's ears. Rifle and machinegun fire. Screaming. Pinging. Wrenching and twisting metal.

Chris's RPD and Boing's M60 popped holes through the truck's thin metal walls like they were paper.

John puffed out his chest and wiggled his hand free. Then he dug his fingers in Brandon's eyes.

Screaming, Brandon grabbed at John's fingers. Wrenched them away from his face. John's other arm went to work, the bandaged stump came across and slammed Brandon in the temple and again the world went fuzzy. John hit him again. And again.

Fingers wormed into Brandon's shirt collar and twisted, tangled themselves in the fabric. Tightened around Brandon's neck, shoving blood and pressure up into his head. Holding him there, John pounded Brandon's face.

"Fucking filth!" John screamed. "I am a *God!*" John punched him. "You think you've won? You think you've defeated me? *Me?*"

Brandon couldn't respond. His mouth wouldn't work. Dark pressed in on him from the sides. He hung on. Blood poured from Brandon's mouth and splattered across John's bared and broken teeth.

John bucked his hips. Dazed and weak, Brandon clung to John with his failing grip. He went limp and flopped on the ground. John rolled on top of him, straddled him. John wrapped his fingers in Brandon's hair and held his head down against the clay. Snarling, John threw his head down, slammed his forehead into Brandon's nose.

Deep in Brandon's head, something crunched. He reached out with limp arms to grab ahold of John, but his fingers wouldn't obey.

The world was losing focus. It was silent but for the sound of John's breath. Or maybe Brandon's. He looked up into squinting white eyes. Flat and dead. Filled with hate. John's head came down again. One final time. And when their heads collided, all went black.

You've done so well. Jaran whispered to him. *You can let go. It's alright. Let go.*

And he did. Sinking into the black comfort of oblivion, Brandon let go.

CHAPTER FORTY-SIX

"I'm here."

"Jaran..." Brandon mumbled into the dark.

"Can you open your eyes?"

Brandon tried. All the hurt throbbing in his head made opening his eyes a miserable experience. The muscles in his forehead pulled and his eyelids were slow to obey. Like they were plastered together. But they cracked open. Sharp edges of dark green and black stabbed into a bright blue above.

Mike's face shimmered in and out of focus. "I'm here."

Brandon groaned. "I thought you were someone else."

"I'm not surprised. You took a hell of a beating." He held out his hand in front of Brandon's nose. "Try and follow my finger."

He tried. Blinking at the smearing blur that was Mike's finger. "Which one am I supposed to follow?"

Mike chuckled.

"Boing!" Chris yelled somewhere far off. "I'm coming up, Don't fucking shoot me."

Brandon exhaled with relief. "You guys okay?"

"We're fine."

Rolling his head left and right, Brandon looked for

John. When he didn't see him Brandon sat up. And almost collapsed. Mike grabbed him, telling him to take it easy and steadying him so he could sit.

"Where's John?" Brandon asked.

"Gone."

"Gone?" Brandon's shoulders sank as he sighed. "How the hell did he get away this time?"

"He ran. When he saw his reinforcements were dwindling he took off. We, erm…"

Brandon looked up at him. "What?"

Mike shook his head. "We hesitated. We didn't know how to stop him. There were still some NVA left when he ran. We had to take care of them first before we could get after him. We lost him. I'm sorry."

Disappointed, Brandon nodded. "It's fine. If you guys are okay I'd call that a win."

"Not out of the woods yet. We still need to link up for extraction. Come on." Mike helped Brandon to his feet and gave him back his rifle. "Good news is that we have a ride."

On his feet now, the trees and the huts and the truck all spun around in a sliding wave. Clicked back into place and spun again. Brandon squinted and watched the ground, steadying himself with a hand on Mike's arm.

"Alright?" Mike asked.

"Dizzy."

"Probably a concussion. Let's try to walk a little."

Mike steadied him as they walked toward the compound's front gate. Brandon rubbed his eyes. The walking helped with the dizziness, but not much.

The metal walls around the truck bed were a twisted mess of gnarled metal. So many holes. Little sharp points curved out from where Boing's rounds had punched through. Smooth holes curving inward from Chris's RPD. Tiny dents and scrapes, probably from Mike's smaller caliber rifle.

But on the ground…

On the ground the carnage was overwhelming. However long Brandon lived, he was sure that image would haunt his dreams.

Contorted bodies lay everywhere in disgusting, unnatural positions where they fell from the truck. Feet curled over heads. Heads turned around. So many staring eyes.

The blood.

Blood poured, it *poured* from the little gap between the truck bed and the back hatch as if from a spigot. Spattering in thick, oily puddles in the red-brown clay.

Reaching up, Mike pulled the release and let the heavy metal hatch fall. It swung down and banged open.

They looked into the mouth of Hell.

The radio operator's distress call...

The NVA, in their haste to respond to the call for help, they must have shoved in as many men that would fit in the truck. When Boing hit them with the M60 they didn't have enough room to move. Didn't have enough room to escape. They trapped each other. As each man died, he became a bar in a prison cell. And he kept the next man trapped just long enough to become a bar himself and trap the next man. And so on.

Chris came out from the jungle with Boing over his shoulder. He put Boing in the truck's cab and came to check on Mike and Brandon. He looked in the back of the truck. Shook his head. "Let's make some room." He and Mike climbed up in the truck bed.

There was no ceremony for the enemy dead. There was no time. Mike grabbed a man by his forearms and Chris grabbed the legs and they pitched him out and he thumped on the ground. A puff of air blew out from his mouth. Then the blood trickled from his nose. They pitched the next man. And the next. They threw out men until Mike and Brandon would have enough room to hide in the truck bed.

Chris hopped down and grabbed a few fistfuls of clay

and smeared them on his face and in his hair.

Reaching down, Mike grabbed Brandon's hand and hauled him up into the truck.

Chris looked up at them. "Keep outta sight. If I blow the horn, start shooting." Then he closed the hatch.

The truck started up and Chris backed in through the gate and pulled out onto the road, heading south. Fast. The engine roared. The truck bounced and the metal bed shuddered and banged. Low-hanging palm fronds hissed overhead as they slapped the cargo area's gnarled metal.

Brandon and Mike sat with their backs against the hatch.

It was impossible to get away from the blood. From beneath the pile of dead men, thin rivulets of it ran in long parallel streams in the corrugated metal. With each bounce the blood rippled and splashed. The dead men watched their blood soak into Mike and Brandon's clothing.

The truck's mechanical sounds seemed so alien. So loud. For days there had only been the sounds of the jungle. The sounds of men breathing. All those quiet sounds. It was hard to believe he was in a vehicle. Leaving this place. Going home.

Home.

Days ago that was all he wanted. Hell, even *hours* ago he could think of nothing he wanted more than to get back to an American base. So why were his thoughts nagging him now? Why did he feel like he was cheating? Why did he feel like he was quitting? Like he was leaving something undone? He had survived. Mike, Chris, and Boing; they had survived.

Mike's eyes were closed. Hand draped over his knee. Mike had definitely earned his rest, and Brandon felt a little guilty for bothering him. But Brandon asked, "What do we do about John?"

Mike kept his eyes closed. He shook his head, rolling it back and forth against the hatch. Flicking out his hand dismissively, he said, "Fuck him, cap."

Brandon stared. He didn't know what to say.

Mike must have sensed him staring. He turned his head to Brandon. Cracked open an eye. Frowned with concern. "What? You want to go *back* for him?"

Brandon thought about that. Thought about what they would be risking. He shook his head. "I don't know."

Mike looked down at his LCE. He patted his empty ammo pouches and let out a sad laugh. "What else can we do? We're spent. We threw everything we had at him. And you…" Mike's hand moved up and down, taking in Brandon's body. "*Look* at you! You can barely walk. You can't go up against John like that."

"So what do we do?"

Mike leaned his head back against the hatch. He sighed. "We turn in our report. We give everything we learned to the people who need it. To the people who can do something about it. And if they want to go out looking for Erlik Khan and whatever body he happens to occupy, then more power to them. What do *we* do? We *survive*."

Survive.

Brandon picked at the dirt and dried blood under his nails. Survive. Tell people what happened. It made sense. No one else on the planet knew what New York knew. The knowledge they carried was important. Surviving now meant that any damage Erlik Khan could do in the future could be mitigated. Maybe someone could even capture him. Someday.

Mike was right. They needed to survive. New York's mission had evolved seemingly by the minute since they jumped into this place. Maybe after all that happened it had *devolved* into simply surviving. Mike and Chris and Boing lost a lot of their friends. But they would survive. Brandon nodded to himself. Their survival was a victory. Maybe it was a small victory in a sea of failures. But given the circumstances, Brandon would take it.

Still. The nagging thought that he was abandoning something troubled him.

The breaks squeaked and the truck slowed. Chris pulled the truck into a patch of jungle where the undergrowth was relatively thin. Plowed forward until the truck would go no further. The hatch still stuck out a bit. With luck, no one would spot it for the next hour or so.

They dismounted and moved into the jungle. Mike carried Boing on his back. They marched until they came upon a clearing. *The* clearing. But they knelt there in the jungle's concealment. Such an odd feeling to fear sunlight.

They sat in a loose three-sixty and waited in silence.

And soon there was a sound in the air. A sound that forced a surge of emotion up from somewhere deep in Brandon's soul. Their heads turned skyward. Mike and Chris and Boing, some of the toughest men Brandon had ever met, they had tears in their eyes.

Chris threw a smoke grenade. With a *puff*, violet smoke billowed into the sky. The silhouettes of three Hueys came in low above the treetops. Circled the LZ. Two helicopters remained in orbit, M60 machine-gunners scanning the area for threats. One Huey descended. Flat gray paint job. Oversized fuel tanks protruding along the side. In a few moments, it landed.

Chris stood and was about to step out into the clearing. Chris had told him once that this moment, right before extraction, it was one of the most dangerous.

Brandon grabbed Chris's shoulder. "I got it." And he stepped out into the sun. Squinting in the light, he ducked below the rotor wash and hurried to the aircraft. Rifle at the low ready, he stood alongside the skids. Looked out into the jungle. He saw nothing. He waved to his men.

The crew chief played out a long cord and handed a headset to Brandon and pointed at the pilot. Put his pinky and thumb to his ear and mouth. Brandon slipped the headset on over his ears.

The high-pitched engine whine screeched beneath the pilot's voice. "You the commander?"

"Yeah."

"Where's the precious cargo?"

New York came out of the treeline. "They're coming."

Mike came with Boing. Chris followed.

"You leave anyone behind?" The pilot said.

They loaded Boing first. A crew chief grabbed him around the waist and put him in a seat.

"No one alive," Brandon said. "We've got grids for everyone else. Why?"

"We picked up a radio transmission a few klicks out. New York one-one, requesting evac. He's still talking."

One-one?

Mike climbed aboard.

Watching the treeline, Brandon said, "Put me through."

There was a click as the pilot patched the radio traffic over the headset. Static. A voice. Weak. "This is New York one-one, requesting immediate extraction at the following grid…"

It was him. John. Repeating his transmission over and over again.

He's gonna get pinpointed.

Chris came last. Smiling and clapping Brandon on the shoulder.

"I almost aborted," the pilot said. "He keeps repeating our extraction grid."

Brandon went cold. "He's repeating *this* grid?"

"Yeah," the pilot said. "You're lucky we got here before someone else."

Over the sound of the engine there was a quiet popping. In the air, the hovering gunship's door gunner was going full auto.

"No…"

The door-gunner next to Brandon tensed in his chair, his black and bug-like face-shield swiveled, looking out over Brandon and Chris. He swung his M60 and waved Brandon out of the way.

Brandon went cold. He grabbed Chris's shirt, grabbed flesh, tensed to shove Chris aboard.

The M60 beside him barked loud, belching flame.

Brandon shoved. Chris jerked. Wet sprayed on Brandon's face and suddenly he held all of Chris's weight in his hand. Falling.

Brandon wrapped both arms around Chris's belly, like a wrestler he shoved with his legs and heaved and threw them both onto the Huey's floor. Brass casings clinked on the floor, dropped hot on his head. Brandon lay on Chris, shielding him. Wrapped his hands around his head. Fingers slid across something coarse and jagged. Pressed against something soft and spongy.

All around was noise and Brandon's gut dropped from the wrenching pull as the Huey shot hard and fast into the sky. The Huey banked. Brandon grabbed a crossbar under a seat and glanced down, the grass and jungle falling away beneath his feet. And he saw them.

"No!"

Shirtless men emerged from the jungle. Raised their AK-47s to the climbing Huey. Yellow sparked from their muzzles. Green straps slung across their chests. Satchell charges.

The door-gunner churned the earth. Walked rounds toward the men. The pounding, echoing machinegun fire inside the Huey rattled Brandon's teeth.

Men on all sides of the landing zone. Surrounded.

The Huey climbed.

Brandon put his hand to his face, pressed his wet and sticky fingers against his eyelids, eyes throbbing against his fingertips. He breathed deep. Exhaled hard.

The Huey screamed over the jungle. The guns went silent. The door-gunner swiveled his silent and smoking M60, scanning.

They gained altitude. Brandon rolled over. Got to his knees. Chris. *Oh, God.*

Blood.

Blood covered Brandon from chest to knees. Fingers black with it. Brandon tried to pull a bandage from the pouch at his shoulder, but his slick and frantic fingers kept slipping on the brass button. Chris's eyes were rolled up into his head and white. His face sunken and pale. The side of his head blown out. A soft pile of twisted yellow and gray flopped on the floor.

"Medic!" Brandon screamed. "Mike!" But Mike had been on the floor with him all along. Mike held out a gigantic white bandage and wrapped Chris's head.

"Plug him up, goddamnit!" Brandon screamed. His words lost amidst the whining rotors. Even as the words left his lips he knew it was useless, but he couldn't give up on Chris. He couldn't fucking give up on him!

Mike ignored him. He worked. Deft hands cocooning Chris's head in padding and cloth. Chris's mouth hung open beneath the giant bandage. The aircraft's rotors rattled the fuselage. The blood pooling beneath Chris's pale face rippled in shivering waves.

Brandon slumped, leaned back against the seat. Energy poured from him like he had been cut open.

In his headset, John's voice repeated, "This New York one-one, requesting immediate extraction at the following grid…"

Brandon's hands trembled. But it was not fear that made them shake. He curled his hands into fists and squeezed them until they shook. Shook with boiling fury. The fury of knowing that what everyone said about him was true. No matter how hard Brandon tried, the only thing he could do was get better men killed.

Still shaking, Brandon laid his hand on Chris's chest. Warm. Shirt damp from sweat. His hand searched, pressed. Tried to feel something beneath the skin. To feel life. To feel the beating of a heart. But there was only the vibration of rotors.

It should've been you…

Brandon's neck throbbed. A sting shot up behind his eyes. "Yes, sir," Brandon whispered to the past. "It should've been me."

He left his hand on Chris's chest. As if by touch he could somehow tell Chris he was sorry. Or thank him for pulling Brandon through this mess.

Then Brandon's fingers bumped something hard in Chris's shirt pocket. He traced the outline of it. Round. He undid the buttons and took out the pill bottle. Stared at it. Squeezed it in his hand. When he closed his eyes, he saw two white orbs.

When he opened his eyes he saw Boing and Mike. They were looking out the door. Not watching him. They knew that this was his minute. Brandon slipped the pill bottle into his own shirt pocket.

The anger inside him grew hot. The rage.

He drew Chris's 1911. Unscrewed the suppressor and threw it out into the sky. He wouldn't need it. Not where he was going.

He pushed through the seats to the small opening to the cockpit. "Turn around!" Brandon yelled into the headset.

"What?" the pilot said.

"I said turn around! I'm going back!"

"Like hell—"

Brandon reached through the opening and aimed the pistol between the pilot's legs. Pulled the trigger. Blasted a hole through the clear plastic floor at his feet.

The pilot jerked, legs going wide. "What the fuck!"

Jamming the muzzle in the pilot's crotch, Brandon screamed, "I swear to God I'll blow off your fucking balls! Take me back!"

The pilot held up a hand. "Alright, alright! Where do you want to go?"

"The compound. Ten kliks north of where you picked us up."

"You're out of your fucking mind!" The pilot turned around to look at him. Whether it was Brandon's destroyed face, or the look in his eyes, Brandon didn't know. All the same, the pilot shook his head. "You got some kind of death wish?"

Brandon kept the pistol aimed between the pilot's legs. He said nothing. He watched the horizon shift as the pilot turned them north.

CHAPTER FORTY-SEVEN

Mike had been so busy wrapping up Chris's wound that he hadn't bothered to put on a headset. He must not have heard anything Brandon had said. He didn't even really seem to suspect anything was amiss. Not until the Hueys were circling the compound.

Mike grabbed Brandon and spun him around. Yelled over the thumping rotors, "What the hell are we doing back here?"

Brandon took of his headset and yelled back, "I have to go back for him!"

Mike shook his head. "We'll come back with more men."

"They'll just try to capture him again! You know they will!"

Mikes eyes flitted back and forth between Brandon's. Maybe trying to think of the right thing to say to stop Brandon from going. The Huey descended and Mike looked out at the ground coming up to meet them. When he looked back his eyes were wet and his voice was lost in the rotor wash. He mouthed the words, *I'm coming with you.*

Brandon took Mike by the shoulders. "You need to

live. If I can't…" Brandon shook his head. "People need to know what's coming! You've seen! You need to tell them!"

Mike closed his eyes. The wind tore at his rough beard. Reaching down, he slipped his last magazine out of a pouch and stuffed it in one of Brandon's.

There wasn't enough open space in the compound to set down, so the pilot hovered over a hut's thatched roof. A crew chief waved his arm, signaling Brandon to jump.

But before he could, Mike grabbed him. Pulled him close in a tight embrace. "Give him hell!" And he let go.

Slinging his rifle, Brandon took one last look at Mike and Boing. His men. His friends. And he jumped.

He hit the roof. Like landing on a sponge, he sunk a bit and tumbled once and slid. Dropped down to the ground. He ran through that courtyard of death to the front gate and crossed the road and slipped back into the jungle. Before long the thumping of rotors faded into silence. And he was alone.

He knelt in the underbrush. Inhaled the humid air. Blew it out. Closed his eyes. Put his hand on his belly. "Where are you?"

Nothing.

"Come on, Jaran," he whispered. Breathed in deep. Let it out. "Where is he?"

Inhale… inhale… exhale… He searched for that feeling. The feeling that had pulled him to the compound.

Thoughts of Jaran came. Her face. Her voice.

Thoughts of John. His eyes.

A feeling in his stomach. An anticipation. Like Christmas morning to a child.

Somewhere he thought he heard…

I'm with you.

He opened his eyes. "Gotcha." He rose and pressed on into the jungle.

***

After a time Brandon discovered that reaching out for that connection with John wasn't entirely necessary. Erlik Khan, it seemed, had gotten sloppy.

Depressed vegetation. Obvious boot prints.

Blood on leaves. Thick yellow vomit in the grass.

Maybe John's body was finally giving out. Maybe he was just too weak to care about stealth.

This is New York one-one...

Brandon stopped dead.

John had been calling out on his radio. He had broadcasted New York's extraction grid and a Counter Recon team had intercepted them. Erlik Khan wanted Brandon and his team to be killed. But he also wanted the NVA to find him.

Brandon's heart quickened. Would another Counter Recon team be sent to intercept John?

The thought of Counter Recon crawling around was almost more frightening than dealing with John. Brandon could sense John. He knew approximately where he was. But those guys, they just materialized out of the jungle.

Brandon fingered the pill bottle in his shirt pocket. All he had to do was be the first one to John. He just needed to take the first shot. He took one last look around. Listened. Heard nothing. Then he went on. Pushing through tall grass. Birds called in the distance. Sweat ran down into his eyes. He followed the feeling in his gut. Focused on the present moment. Focused on each step. He ran until he heard the sound of babbling water. The canopy above thinned and the bright blue afternoon sky showed through as Brandon stepped to the edge of a steep hill.

He leaned out through the vegetation to get a better view of the river below. It was wide, but shallow. The water ran slow over brown and gray stones. He had seen this place before...

A cool drink was a small pleasure, but he was glad for

it. He wouldn't even need to purify it. If everything went right he wouldn't be alive long enough for dysentery to set in.

And if everything went *wrong*, well, he wouldn't be alive long enough for dysentery to set in.

Something sloshed loud in the water below and Brandon shrank back into the green and shadow. Watching. Pressing aside some vegetation to see—

John waded out into the water. Shirtless. When he bent to scoop up water in his hand, thick yellow puss oozed from his stomach wound. He slurped the water from his hand. His rucksack and rifle sat on the riverbank nearby.

Heart thundering, Brandon brought up his rifle. Clenched his teeth to keep from making a noise. He blew out his breath and reached for his shirt pocket.

A voice called out. John lurched up in the water and spun around. Brandon's hand froze on his rifle. He followed John's eyes.

Four short, shirtless men appeared on the riverbank below. AK-47s leveled at John. Green canvass satchel charges hung on their shoulders.

No!

John stared at them. And the son of a bitch smiled. He'd planned this.

Counter Recon and Erlik Khan stood mere meters below. The leaves hissed as Brandon shook with such an absolute fear. He pulled his hand off the foliage to quiet the noise. He got down on his belly and squeezed the rifle's plastic handgrips so hard he thought they'd shatter. After a few deep, deep breaths the shaking in his hands slowed, but did not stop. He clicked his rifle to semi.

A Counter Recon man waded out into the water. Rifle held at his hip, cautiously approaching John. He looked at the festering wound in John's abdomen. Poked at it with his rifle muzzle. John winced.

The Counter Recon man called over his shoulder to the men on the shore. Someone called back.

Brandon had to do it now. Right now. He clawed at the pill bottle in his shirt. Thumbed off the cap and shook the capsule into his mouth.

The man in the water smiled as he turned back to John. Then he slammed the butt of his rifle into John's face. John's lip came apart like unzipping a jacket. Blood spilled down his chin. His head went slack and he collapsed in the water. Vanished in a white splash.

No, no, no!

Brandon kept his eyes on the man standing over John. If John died Brandon could still take the shot. He just needed to wait for the change. He tongued the pill between his teeth. But how would he know Erlik Khan had taken the Counter Recon man? He'd never see it happen before.

The man knelt in the water and straddled John. Put his hands around John's throat and held his head under the water. John flailed, grabbed at the man's shoulders, clawed at his arm. His bandaged wrist flailed.

It was an act, and Erlik Khan played the part well. It looked like John was really fighting for survival.

John's arms went limp. The life finally choked from him.

The three other men waded into the water. They laughed with the man who just murdered John. The soon-to-be-Erlik Khan. They had no idea what kind of horror awaiting them.

Brandon aimed. He didn't know how long he would have before the cyanide killed him. He might only have a single shot, maybe two. But with the men huddled together, Brandon couldn't get a clear shot. A 5.56 didn't have the reliable penetrating power to go through another man to hit his intended target. And as soon as Brandon fired, those men would react with speed and terrible violence.

The new Erlik Khan stood calf-deep in the water. He looked around for a moment as if admiring the scenery.

Then he fell over backward and splashed in the water.

Brandon followed him with his rifle. How long would he be out? It had taken a few hours for John. But in Jaran's story everyone was different.

The men laughed at their friend and watched him for a moment. When he didn't get up, their laughter cut off. They grabbed him up and carried him dripping to shore and out of Brandon's line of sight. Words were exchanged. Probably confused as to what had just happened to their friend.

But Brandon knew the story well enough. He almost felt sorry for the Counter Recon men. As soon as that man regained consciousness those men were dead.

John's lifeless body bobbed to the surface. Nose and lips poking from the water. He floated lazily down the river. Brandon's hopes of finishing this floated away with him.

That was Brandon's one shot and he'd blown it. And now he was stuck. There was no going back. No calling for a ride out of there.

He listened to the Counter Recon men dragging their team member, the new Erlik Khan, into the jungle. He spat the capsule back into the bottle.

He'd have to track a Counter Recon team on their own turf. That wasn't going to be easy.

John's floating body caught in some reeds. His split-open face floating above the water. The white in his eyes had vanished.

The water...

He thought immediately of Conway.

CHAPTER FORTY-EIGHT

The gut-wrenching feeling of falling. A roar somewhere below him. So dark.

Things. There were things in the dark. The whipping rush of giant things flying by at unbelievable speed. Snapping, like flags in a wind storm.

He fell deeper into that dark.

Noise all around. Reverberations of rending metal. Hawks screeching underwater...

Water.

He remembered water.

But the freight-train slam of screaming tore the memory from him.

"*John!*"

He tumbled down as the voice rose above the cacophony. The anguish in that voice so clear.

SMACK

John's entire being erupted in searing pain.

Burning. Burning all over. He tried to scream but something stuck in his mouth. The burn bubbled up around his ears. Sinking. He was sinking into heat. So dense. The pressure pushed against him. His arms, he couldn't move them. His legs were stuck together.

Help! He tried to scream. *Please!*

But his voice was lost in that terrible roar. A roar, he realized with growing terror that was made up of voices. Of screams.

The boiling liquid sucked his head under. The acrid smell of petroleum. The horrible bite of tar on his tongue, thrusting into his throat.

When his ears dipped below the surface he heard everything so clear. As if the liquid amplified the screams.

And in that absolute darkness, he felt them. He felt his friends.

Not with hands or any other sense he had ever used before. He felt them in his soul. A noose of despair around his neck constricting each time they wailed his name.

John! Dan wailed.

John! Howard roared.

John, John, John John JohnJohnJohnJohn! Pilots, crew chiefs, George, and Terry.

All of their emotions. The weight of their fear and their anger pushed him deeper down. Crushing pressure and heat. Charring his soul. He wanted to weep. Wanted to be rid of that hurt, but it would not go. Always it pressed. And pressed. Heavier.

Visions flashed white in the dark each time his name echoed in his head.

Clapping his hands against a clacker.

Helicopters bursting in oily red fireballs.

A man ripped in half.

A man exploding.

Brains blowing out into the night.

Your fault! they all screamed as one.

Cried out, *You killed us all!*

Wailed, *you said you'd protect us!*

Stop, John screamed through the tar gagging him. Bubbling as his words tried to escape.

Stop, stop, stop! The pain. The burning. The weight.

Maddening. *It wasn't me!*

The tar wormed into his lungs. His belly. Cooked him from the inside.

I'm, John tried to say through the sticky, boiling pain. *I'm sorry!*

A freezing light pierced the black. Everywhere it touched it soothed his burns. Drowned out the screaming.

But the light revealed the insane world around him. His friends. Their thin faces contorted in snarls and drawn with sorrow and eyes wide with confusion.

And beyond them...

Oh, God.

Millions upon millions of faces. People he did not know, but somehow knew their despair. Somehow he shared it.

The light spread. Penetrating the darkness. Widening to reveal the walls of whatever prison held him and all those people. Like looking through clear tropical waters that went on forever. Penetrating the darkness. Deeper, ever deeper, but never losing its radiance.

The light grabbed him.

Jolted him.

Lightning struck him. Again and again and again. Coalescing in a blinding sphere around him.

Lifting him. Pulling.

He broke the surface of that foul liquid with amazing force and the tar erupted from his nose and mouth. The blackness clung to his face like there was life to it. But the light proved stronger and the slimy black fell away.

He sailed higher and higher until he saw the edges of the lake of tar. The boundaries of the place where all those screaming people boiled. And in the ambience of this holy light, he saw that it was no lake.

It was a cauldron.

And beside the cauldron, looking down on those tortured people, were dark shapes shying away from the light. Hiding their eyes from it. Forms like people, that seemed somehow *wrong*. Perverted. Impossibly big. Bigger than worlds. And their eyes glowed with malice.

One of those figures laughed as John sailed higher into that celestial abyss. It called out to him in a sensual feminine voice. But she spoke a foul language, dripping with filth. Horrible and foreign, but instantly understandable. He could feel the meaning of the words deep in his soul.

We await your return.

John had so many questions. *What are you?* John thought at the thing. *What is this place?*

It never answered him. But it didn't need to. Deep in his soul, he already knew.

CHAPTER FORTY-NINE

John's glossy blue eyes stared up at the sky.
"Twenty-nine," Brandon panted. "Thirty."
Pinching John's destroyed upper lip, Brandon lowered his mouth to John's. Blew. Took a breath. Blew again.

Water spewed from John's mouth in a jet. He coughed. Rolled to his side and curled up. Hacking. Heaving out frothy river water into the grass.

Brandon fell back on his ass. Pure joy sprang up from his belly. "Holy shit!"

It worked. John was alive.

Events of the last days slammed Brandon's mind and he jerked his pistol from its holster. John was alive...

He fished out the cyanide capsule from his shirt pocket and stuck it between his teeth. Yanking John's arm, Brandon pulled him onto his back and sprawled on John's chest, holding him down. He shoved the pistol under John's chin and grabbed a fistful of hair. Pulled John's face toward his own.

"Open your eyes," Brandon said, grinding the 1911's muzzle into John's fleshy neck. "Let me see 'em."

John ignored him. His fingers searched around his belly

and found the festering, stinking bullet wound from days ago. When John's fingertips brushed against it, he winced.

"Open them!" Brandon hissed, keeping his voice low lest the Counter Recon team was still within earshot.

Bloodshot eyes, wet with a layer of coughing-fit tears, peaked out from beneath John's eyelids.

That milky white was gone.

Brandon's finger relaxed off the trigger. "John?"

John recoiled violently, his eyes wild and searching for things Brandon could not see. Focusing and refocusing. They finally settled on Brandon's. John's voice was raspy when he whispered, "Brandon?"

"Yeah, John. It's me." Brandon couldn't fight the grin spreading across his face. "Good to see you."

A weak smile found its way onto John's face. His head dropped, thumping in the grass. "Jesus," he laughed weakly. "I thought it was real. He covered his eyes with his hand. "God, what a nightmare."

Brandon winced. He didn't have time to ease into what had to be said. "John..."

John's hand slid off his face and fell in the dirt. He brought up his other arm. Looked at where his hand should be. So many different expressions passed over John's face. The look of a man caught between belief and disbelief.

"No..." John whimpered.

"What do you remember?"

John's eyes went hard as he stared at his bandaged wrist. Jaw muscles quivered beneath a week's worth of beard growth. He shook his head back and forth. His torn lip trembled. A rush of air, a heavy, despairing sigh escaped his mouth.

"John," Brandon said. "What do you remember?"

It was like there was a dam holding back John's tears. The word he spoke next was the demolition charge that destroyed it. "Everything."

Brandon took John's hand. The cold of John's palm

seeping into his own. "Can you sense him?" Brandon tapped John's shoulder. "John, can you sense him? He jumped bodies when you... he's in a Counter Recon man. I need to know if you can sense him."

"They're all in Hell," John mumbled. Lips wet with tears and spit. "All of them."

"Can you sense him? I lost him."

"It's my fault."

Brandon was losing him. Just like Conway. Irritation grew tight in Brandon's guts. He slapped John hard across the mouth. "There's time to mourn later, sergeant. Tell me if you know where Erlik Khan is."

John quieted. In his eyes something was working. Slowly, John pulled himself back from hysteria and his cool, calm face returned.

When John's eyes refocused, he said, "Who?"

Brandon sat down hard beside John and blew out a frustrated breath. "I guess we have a lot to talk about."

***

With John's arm around his shoulder, Brandon helped him along as he stumbled away from the river. Brandon set him down in the jungle some fifty meters from where the Counter Recon team had emerged. He went back for John's radios and his rifle. He set these things down in the grass and let John lean back against the ruck sack. The sound of the river bubbled beyond the heavy foliage. Brandon reached in the pack and clicked off the radio in case the Counter Recon team was still tracking it. In case they came looking for it.

The jungle was quiet as Brandon sat and looked over John's wounds. He didn't mention them, but he could tell it was a miracle John had survived as long as he had. Erlik Khan pushing John's body so hard for so long clearly took its toll.

"Just assume," Brandon said. "That what I'm about to

tell you is true. It'll save time. Just listen."

Staring off into the jungle, John nodded absently. Brandon told him everything that had happened after he had shot that cripple. John's eyes wandered as he listened, settling on a spot in the dirt. By the time Brandon had finished, John's head hung limp and he stared at his filthy hand in his lap.

What John had done, or rather, what Erlik Khan had forced John to do, Brandon couldn't begin to imagine what that had done to John's mind. Or his soul if there was such a thing.

"You need my help to find him?" John asked. "You can't sense him?"

"Yeah. I guess I was somehow linked to him—you…" Brandon threw up his hands. "I don't fucking understand a lot of this, John. I'm just telling you what happened."

John's heavy, bloodshot eyes drifted up to Brandon's shirt pocket. He pointed. "You're gonna swallow that after you shoot him?"

Brandon fingered the pill bottle. Cleared his throat. "Before, actually. I need to do it *before* I shoot him. Otherwise I won't be able to control my actions. You know about that part."

John nodded. "You don't want to do that, Brandon. You don't want to go where you're going. I've been there. I've *seen*. I know what's waiting for you." John rubbed his hand along his arm, as if rubbing cold from his bones. "I had these notions. The priests always had these descriptions of Hell. I thought I'd lived a good enough life. Thought I'd been a good enough man that I'd never have to worry about Hell." He dropped his hand in his lap. "Apparently that's not the case."

Brandon chuckled because he didn't know what else to do. "Well," and he patted John's leg. "At least we can keep each other company. It's only for eternity."

Dark eyes looked up at Brandon. The sarcasm obviously not sitting well with John.

Of course it wouldn't. John came back from Hell just to learn he was moments away from going back.

John sighed and looked around. "You got Mike and Boing out of this?"

Brandon nodded. Then shrugged. "To be honest, they got themselves out. I just kind of walked in front of them to show them where to go."

The un-split side of John's mouth turned up in a grin. "Led from the front, did you?"

"If you like. Like I said, these guys—"

John held up a protesting hand. "That's all these guys need. A leader who sees himself as one of them. They can handle the mission. It's the bureaucracy they don't want or need to deal with." John dropped his hand. "So, you got them out?"

Brandon grinned. "They got out."

John grinned too. "But you came back."

"I came back."

"Why?"

John didn't look good. And with such little time of John's life remaining, Brandon suspected he wouldn't have time to explain that he was carrying around the spirit of a shaman girl inside him. "Somebody needs to stop him," was all Brandon said about it. He fished around in his shirt pocket until his fingers touched the tiny piece of metal and chain. He pulled it out and handed it across to John. "I hope you don't mind that I borrowed it."

John smiled at seeing his cross. He took it gently. He held up his stump for Brandon to see. "You mind?"

Brandon untangled the gold chain and draped it around John's neck and clasped it. John looked down at it. "You came back to kill me."

"Things changed a bit."

With thumb and finger rubbing the tiny gold metal, John said, "Mike would have come back with you."

Brandon nodded. "He tried."

"You didn't let him."

"I didn't let him."

John nodded.

A series of pops rattled off somewhere in the jungle. Somewhere not too far away. Like being a few blocks over from kids playing with firecrackers.

Brandon and John turned their heads toward the sound.

"He's awake," Brandon said.

"Yeah."

"Can you sense him?"

John nodded. "I can *now*."

"All I need is a distance and direction."

John shook his head. "Don't go, Brandon. He's powerful. I can feel it. The outcome is bad no matter how you spin it. Just listen to me for once in your fucking life and get out of here."

"The outcome if I do nothing is worse. Show me."

John closed his eyes. He looked so weak. All his vitality. All his strength. Gone. The toughest son-of-a-bitch Brandon had ever met reduced to this. John lifted his hand. Languidly swung it back and forth in an arc. Then his fingers struck out, pointing rigid. "That way. Not too far."

Brandon stood and unslung his rifle.

"Wait," John winced as he leaned over and reached into his pack. He dug in it and pulled out an AK-47 banana mag. He held it out to Brandon.

"What's this?" Brandon asked as he took it.

"First two rounds in there are Eldest Son ammo."

Brandon turned the mag over in his hand. "Mike and Chris mentioned something about this. What am I supposed to do with it?"

Flicking a finger at the magazine, John said, "Those rounds are designed to malfunction. Catastrophically. The spooks manufacture defective mortars and 7.62 rounds that SOG teams leave in NVA ammo caches. Don't be fooled by the size. One of those rounds turns an AK-47 into a grenade."

Brandon hefted the magazine.

"Listen, Brandon. Listen good. Find a way to get that into his hands. Then you run. Let him die by his own hand. If you ever feel like he's got the upper hand, you pull out that pistol of yours and you eat it." John's eyes went dark. "I'm sure God will forgive you. That place. Being there…" John looked up at the sky. "It's like knowing God exists. And knowing He hates you."

Brandon slipped the AK magazine into his cargo pocket. "Good luck, John."

John leaned his head back against his pack. "Good luck, sir."

Brandon grinned. Then turned and ran into the jungle.

CHAPTER FIFTY

Grimacing at a tugging pain in his stomach, John lifted the wadded-up T-shirt pressed against his stomach wound. Slick and wriggling bodies gathered there. Leeches.

He used to fear these things. Now he sighed in simple annoyance and plucked the slimy black things off with thumb and forefinger and flicked them into the grass.

"I suppose I should just let you eat," he said to a leech pinched in his fingers. He flung it and reached for another.

When he had tugged them all off, he pulled out his pistol. Turned it in his hand.

He was dying. He could feel it. He felt so *old*. He clicked off the pistol's safety.

Was there a difference between waiting to die and doing it yourself? Would he just be swapping out one Hell for another? Did the Hell he thought he knew even exist? Did his God?

From what Brandon had told him about that shaman girl, what she knew about that boiling place, there didn't seem to be much he could do besides wait to go back.

Erlik Khan takes souls, Brandon had said.

"Fuck."

John slid his pistol back into its holster.

Spending eternity listening to his friends accuse him of sending them to Hell. Hearing them suffer. What fate was worse than that?

Jesus, help me.

He touched his cross. Thumb rubbing the smooth gold. So little time left. He didn't know what to do. So little time to try and alter his fate. Before all this he had never considered the possibility of going to Hell. Now...

What could he do to fix this? Was there even a way?

His head dropped and he let out a heavy sigh. Sun glinted on the gold around his neck. He took his cross tight in his fist.

"I know there's something I can do to make this right." He winced at the sharp pain in his side. "I know I can do something with this little time I have left. You had Brandon bring me back for something more than pointing him in the right direction. I can do more. I can do *more*..."

Sadness throbbed in his throat. He said through gritted teeth, "Just tell me what I can *do!*" He squeezed his eyes shut. "*Show me!*"

John rocked his head. "What did you bring me back for?"

Mike and Boing got out. They're safe.

Nobody alive was left behind...

But that was when the numbing calm settled in his belly.

"Nobody except Brandon."

Leaning his head back on his ruck, he opened his eyes. Stared at the slashes of blue sky through the canopy.

This was the way God had always spoke to him. When all that confusion and emotion clouded his mind, these little moments of pure calm descended on him.

He understood.

But when he tried to stand, the pain grabbed his belly and floored him. Head smacking in the dirt.

Groaning like he'd been kicked, blowing a tiny cloud of dust into the air, he squeezed his eyes shut. He saw them.

Their faces. The men he had left behind in Hell.

"Dan," he hissed, shoving his hand onto the ground. He braced himself. "George." He grunted. He pushed. "Terry!" The pain took hold and his muscles trembled, trying to keep him up. "Howard!" he screamed. He shoved. *Shoved…*

He was nearly up.

Bracing himself against a tree, straightening through the burning, gut wrenching pain, he stood. To his friends' faces screaming out there in that blinding pain, he said, "I won't leave you behind."

He reached out: reached out for Erlik Khan.

If John was destined for Hell, he wasn't going to wait for someone to drag him there. He was going to kick in the fucking door.

CHAPTER FIFTY-ONE

The heavy banana magazine in his cargo pocket beat against Brandon's knee as he crashed through the jungle. Every instinct pleading with him to slow down. *Don't make so much noise.*

Pushing through some underbrush, a sharp gunpowder odor hit his nostrils. Brandon stopped, knelt down in the foliage. Rifle muzzle shifting with his eyes. Nothing.

Trying to listen, his own panting was loud in his head. He forced himself to take slow, deep breaths through his nose. Hold... then exhale slow through his mouth.

He listened.

Silence.

He smelled the air. Tasted it.

Gunpowder. Body odor. But something else beneath that.

Blood.

This must have been where Erlik Khan executed the Counter Recon team. Brandon scanned the area. Where were the bodies?

Creeping forward in the familiar slow, methodical movements of the recon team, it wasn't long before he found them.

A small man on his knees, ass in the air. Shot in the top of the head. As if he had died while listening to something on the ground.

New York had laid John out to treat whatever injury they thought he had. Maybe this man had been kneeling next to his buddy when Erlik Khan finally took control. Maybe listening to his friend's heart. The last thing he would ever do.

Further on, a pair of dirty, calloused bare feet stuck out from the foliage, like the jungle was consuming a man.

"Number two," Brandon whispered. He turned. Looked. And there was number three. The third man lay opposite the barefoot man on the other side of a worn game trail.

Kneeling down, Brandon searched their bodies. He found what he was looking for and picked it up. An old, but serviceable AK-47. Tiny spots of rust speckled the barrel. But inspecting the rifle's action and chamber, the guts looked clean and dry and gray. It maybe could have used a little lubricant, but looked like it would function properly.

All it has to do is fire once.

He dropped the magazine from the AK and threw it into the jungle. Racked the charging handle a few times to make sure the weapon was clear.

Pulling out the magazine that John had given him, he rocked it into the mag well. He was about to rack the charging handle, but his hand froze. Chambering that round was essentially the same thing as arming a bomb. He looked and made sure his finger was nowhere near the trigger.

He racked the charging handle and the bolt slid home, chambering an Eldest Son round with a meaty *click*. Clicking the safety lever on, he slung the AK over his back. Brandon stood, examined the track, got his bearings, and went on.

***

John doubled over in agony. The pain in his stomach worming its way around his waist and sinking its teeth into him.

How long had he gone without food? Heaving, his gut forced up thick, sour liquid into his mouth. He spat yellow-green foam on the ground.

After a time the pain abated and John straightened himself and searched for Brandon's track.

It was easy to find. The kid had bulldozed his way through the jungle. Something John would have previously chewed his ass for. But now an enormous pride filled John's chest. Brandon had absolutely nothing to gain in this fight, and everything to lose. Brandon, the man John was sure only looked out for himself was not running away. He was running toward certain death. Toward an eternity in Hell. *And why?* Simply to spare anyone else that same fate.

If he weren't in so much pain, John would have laughed. Phil had beat up a guy for refusing to believe John had *saved Christmas*. What would he do if someone refused to believe Brandon had saved the world?

He hasn't saved it yet.

Staggering on, John wished he could have been there to watch Brandon become the man he was now. Wished he'd have more time to fight alongside him.

He'd make a good leader now.

Nearly puking, John followed Brandon's bull-trail. Reciting the names of his friends.

***

A sound. Brandon knelt and slipped the rigged AK from his back. He listened.

Someone was close. The swish and zip of fabric against elephant grass. The slap of sandals.

Adrenaline pumped through Brandon. Head going light. He looked for the source of the sound. The colors of the jungle, hyper real. Too green. Too vivid. How predators must see prey.

He crept low along the trail the way Chris had taught him. Avoiding foliage. Making no sound. When he poked his head out from behind the tree, he saw him. Brandon froze. Head throbbing with blood.

The man was shorter than Brandon. Shirtless and skinny. Tight muscles twitched and rippled beneath his deeply tanned skin.

Slung across Erlik Khan's back, an AK-47.

It was dangerous to get close to such a powerful rifle. A good burst from that and Brandon would be dead in seconds. But for John's plan to work, for Brandon to survive this, getting close was exactly what he needed to do.

And the penalty for any fuck-up was a ticket straight to Hell. The cyanide was still an option. His original plan. He wouldn't have to get too close. He could take the shot from here. With the cyanide, maybe Brandon would already be dead by the time Erlik Khan swapped bodies. Maybe.

So many unknowns. Too many 'what-ifs'.

Still, Brandon wanted to live...

Alright, John. We'll try it your way.

Brandon scanned the trail, looking for the best way to get ahead of Erlik Khan.

***

"Fuck..." John leaned his shoulder against a tree and looked down at the blood he had just vomited. Wiped his lips with the back of his hand.

He was running out of time.

"Almost there."

He could hardly feel the pistol in his hand. He fingered

the trigger guard with numb fingers. A far-away feeling. Like his hand was asleep.

He spat out bloody slime in the grass and shoved himself off the tree.

"Almost there," he said. And stumbled forward.

***

Brandon cut a wide arc around Erlik Khan, paralleling the most obvious direction of travel. At one point he saw Erlik Khan a short distance away. When Brandon was sure he had gained a significant lead, he cut over, completing the arc and finding the game trail again.

He found a cluster of brush and tore out some fronds. Hollowed out a little alcove. Crouching inside, he covered his legs and boots with the torn-out fronds.

He gripped the AK-47. Wiped his sweating hands on his pants. Breathed long and deep. Felt his heart slow. The blood quieted in his ears.

He thought of success. Only success. Clung to every image the word conjured. Defeating Erlik Khan. Going home. Winning the war. Medals. Tickertape parades.

He imagined success until he heard the slapping of sandals on clay.

"Breathe," he whispered to himself.

Flip... flop...

Breathe... But it wasn't his voice.

Jaran?

Shh... Breathe.

Flop...

Brandon breathed.

When the slap of sandals sounded beside the tree, Brandon shot out with the AK's butt stock and smashed the man in the eye socket. Blood poured from his split-open face.

Not giving him a chance to recover, Brandon sprang, grabbed Erlik Khan's AK and yanked, tore at the sling around Erlik Khan's shoulder. It slipped off. Brandon ejected the mag and flung it. Racked the charging handle, the ejected round went spinning and landed somewhere in the grass. Then Brandon swung the rifle itself like a baseball bat and let go. It went spinning off into the jungle.

With his palm slapped over his eye, Erlik Khan laughed. "Brandon?" Voice now heavy with his victim's Vietnamese accent. "I thought you and your friends ran away."

Crouching, he retrieved the rigged AK from the grass and stood. "We came back for you."

"*We?*"

Brandon tapped his temple. "You know exactly who I have in here."

Erlik Khan's white eyes shifted back and forth. Then a look of realization. "My little whore?" Khan smiled with the sound of bone crunching beneath bruised-purple skin. "Her power to protect you died with her. Unfortunate for you."

Erlik Khan sprang forward. Brandon swung the buttstock, but missed. Khan struck out a hand and grabbed hold of the rifle.

Brandon struggled to keep it.

That's right you fucker. Grab it! Take it!

Pulling and twisting the rifle, Brandon tried to feign resistance. He jabbed a fist at Erlik Khan's broken eye socket.

But Erlik Khan slammed his forehead into Brandon's face, vision exploding in stars. He stumbled back. Brandon wasn't feigning that.

That hurt.

Vision clearing, Brandon found himself on his ass, looking up at Erlik Khan. Looking down the barrel of an AK-47.

"So weak." Erlik Khan said, thumbing the safety lever to *auto*. "So stupid."

Warm blood leaked from Brandon's nose. He wiped it

away and stared defiant into Erlik Khan's cataract eyes.

Erlik Khan's finger caressed the trigger. Then he lowered the rifle a hair's breadth. Erlik Khan studied Brandon. "Just having the girl in there wouldn't make you so brave…"

Brandon said nothing.

Erlik Khan closed his eyes. Head elevating as though he were sniffing the air.

***

John howled as something assaulted his mind. Doubled over, arm trembling, John gripped a thorny tree to keep himself on his feet.

This wasn't coming from the stomach wound. This was something different.

It tore through his mind. The pressure in his head, he felt his eyes popping out.

Screaming, he tried to pull himself upright. Tried to keep hold of the pistol. Tried to pull himself up.

And suddenly the ache in his head was gone.

But though the pain vanished, a terrible fear still slithered through his mind. Slipped down his spine and spread out through his chest.

A word formed in John's mind. But it was like someone else put it there. Through bloody lips John whispered, "Clever…"

An image flashed, just a flash, but it was enough to see what happened.

With hot breath ripping through his blood-covered teeth, John pushed off the tree and staggered as fast as he could.

"Run, kid!" He limped through the jungle. "Goddamnit, *run!*"

***

Erlik Khan's white eyes opened and burned into

Brandon. Mouth turned down in a grimace. "You brought John back…"

"Fuck you, Khan!"

"Shh…" Erlik Khan put a finger to his lips.

And then that finger slid down from his lips. Slid down to the AK-47's barrel. Down the wooden foregrips. In a flash, Erlik Khan racked the charging handle. Spinning gold flung from the ejection port.

Erlik Khan snatched the round from the air. Brought it close to his face. Looked at where the primer would be.

Check the lot number, Chris had said.

Shit.

Throwing the rifle into the grass, Erlik Khan's mouth spread in a shark's smile. "Clever."

And the word was punctuated by grinding steel as Erlik Khan drew the AK-47's long, thin bayonet from the scabbard on his hip.

Scrambling to his feet, Brandon drew his 1911. Aimed it at Khan's chest. So close. Would the cyanide work in time? He fumbled with his shirt pocket.

Khan shrugged his shoulders chuckled. "We've been through this, Brandon. You won't shoot."

Just need a little time.

Brandon dipped the pistol and fired. Khan shuddered and howled as his knee exploded.

But the howl soon turned to cackling laughter as the skin—

Oh my God…

—the skin and bone put itself back together.

Brandon pulled the pill bottle from his pocket. Nervous fingers trembling, he dropped it in the grass.

Khan's face turned down in mock sadness. "Little Shaman girl didn't tell you about my parlor tricks?" Erlik Khan stepped closer. "They get better." He turned the bayonet blade-down in his hand, for stabbing. "Now then. I remember promising to do something special with your guts. Have you brought your gloves?"

Brandon took a step back and put another round in Khan's leg. It barely even bled before stitching back together.

Annoyance spread on Erlik Khan's face. "I don't intend to spend this man's life energy healing his knees."

Brandon shot him again.

Erlik Khan rolled his eyes. The skin slowly stitched back together.

Run...

Whether it was Jaran or his own panicking mind, Brandon didn't know. But he listened. He turned and ran.

Ran as hard as he could. Jumped over bushes. Sucked in air. Pumped his arms. Blew out air. He ran and ran.

And all the while, Erlik Khan followed. Cooing taunts to Brandon through evil laughter.

Air filled Brandon's belly. His gut protested. There was no way to keep up this sprinter's pace.

He'd vomit soon.

And when he puked that would be the last thing he'd ever do in this world. He couldn't stop. No matter what.

But he had to stop.

He glanced behind him. The Counter Recon man must have been a sprinter. Or Erlik Khan was using some unnatural ability to run faster. He was gaining.

Brandon leaned forward, slapped through foliage in the path. He had to go *faster!*

Turning and firing was out of the question. Brandon would have to knee-cap him again to slow him down. *Would it even slow him down?* Hitting such a small target after sprinting for so long was one-in-a-million. He wasn't a good enough marksman. He'd have to stop and aim. If he missed completely it would just give Erlik Khan time to gain more ground.

Just keep running just keep running just keep—

"Ah, fuck!" Brandon gasped, words nothing but dry rushes of air.

Then the vomit came. Hot and sour.

He tried to keep running, but his abdomen clenched and he couldn't keep up the pace. He went sprawling in the dirt. Stinging sweat poured into his eyes and as he retched he turned to see Erlik Khan slow to a leisurely walk. Chest barely rising and falling. Unfazed by the run.

Closer now, Erlik Khan raised the bayonet. As Brandon gasped for air he did the only thing he could think of. He did what John had told him. He put the barrel of the 1911 in his mouth and pulled the trigger.

But Erlik Khan's hand shot out impossibly fast and there was a dull, fleshy *click* as the 1911's hammer fell and pinched the meat between Erlik Khan's thumb. Khan yanked the pistol and the front sight ripped a gash in Brandon's tongue. C*lacked* his front bottom tooth and it shattered, the shard of tooth spinning bloody from his mouth.

"No no no." Erlik Khan twisted the pistol, catching Brandon's finger in the trigger guard. "I *earned* your soul. You won't deny me that." Erlik Khan twisted. Brandon's finger popped and cracked and the skin rippled from his knuckle to wrist as things beneath the skin snapped and broke.

Brandon screamed between panting breaths and grabbed at his ruined finger.

Dropping the pistol at his feet, Erlik Khan straddled Brandon. "Time to boil with your friends." He yanked Brandon's shirt up. Pressed the bayonet into Brandon's bellybutton.

Brandon slapped the blade away. It sliced his stomach. Rubbery yellow fat puffed out. Blood poured into his pants.

Erlik Khan laughed—

BANG.

—then his face jerked. His eye bulged wide from its socket. He sat there for a moment, jaw slack. Bayonet dangling.

Twin streams of blood poured like a river from Erlik

Khan's nose and he fell over backward, thudding in the dirt. Writhing and twitching.

Brandon snatched up the 1911 and racked the slide with his good hand and slipped his middle finger onto the trigger. Pointed the pistol out into the jungle. "Who's there?"

He waited. No answer came.

Erlik Khan shook on the ground. Orange chunks of brain peeked out from a hole over his ear.

Brandon searched in the jungle from where the shot had come. He stood. Crept into the jungle. But he didn't have to go far. He had gone maybe ten paces when he found a man slumped over in the grass. A 1911 on the ground next to his hand.

John.

Barely breathing.

Brandon danced around, grabbing his hair. Not knowing what to do. He knelt beside him. "You dumb son of a bitch, John!" He looked back to Erlik Khan. Back to John. This wasn't the way it was supposed to go. "I don't know what to do for you."

"You've—" John hacked. A frothy yellow slime dribbled from his mouth. Stinking of rot. Head on the ground, John said. "You've done enough. Go home."

Brandon looked back toward Erlik Khan. He was still sprawled in the grass. "We can figure something out." He turned back to John. "Maybe I can—"

But John's eyes were dark. Focused on something far away.

Brandon knelt there for a moment with his hand on John's shoulder. This wasn't fair. To take away his men like this. Before he could ever thank them. Before he could do anything to repay the debts he owed them for saving his life. Behind him, in the silence came a weak bubbling. Turning his head to the sound, he picked up John's pistol.

He walked back and stood over the dying man. Erlik Khan twitched and hiccupped on the ground. A wound like that should've killed him instantly.

Brandon aimed John's pistol at Erlik Khan's face. "Taking you a while to die." And Brandon put the other pistol to his own head. "It ends here. One way or the other."

Erlik Khan reached a trembling hand out to Brandon. He kicked the hand away.

"It was John who shot you," Brandon said. He nodded to where John lay. "And he's dead."

Face contorting in pure hate, a deep groan spilled from Erlik Khan's chewing mouth. "I h-h-have yo-your f-f-f-f-friends."

"I know," Brandon said. "But I'm guessing you haven't heard the stories about the guy you just let into your house. Good luck keeping them."

For the briefest of moments, a look of fear appeared on Erlik Khan's face.

A light breeze blew and the jungle canopy parted. A ray of sunlight lit Erlik Khan's face. His eyes shifted and shimmered. "Muh… muh…"

Brandon knelt next to him. Looked into those white eyes. "It's really annoying when you talk like that."

The milky-white faded from the Counter Recon man's eyes. There was nothing flashy. Nothing biblical. No lightning crashed in the sky. The ground did not open up. There in the dirt, in some patch of jungle in Vietnam, Erlik Khan died.

Brandon knelt there for a long time in the silence and the peace.

Then he took Erlik Khan's bayonet and stuck it in his pistol belt and went back over to John. He holstered John's 1911 and tossed his own into the jungle. Hefting John in a fireman's carry, he said, "Not every day you find a weapon that killed the Devil, John." He walked back along the game trail. "I hope you don't mind me hanging onto it."

It was a long time before he reached the river and

John's rucksack. Brandon took a poncho from the pack and wrapped John's body. He lay down next to John and looked up at the sky. Rolling his head, he looked at John's pack. He reached in and clicked on the radio. He wasn't expecting to hear anything, but there was someone talking.

Hearing a voice was almost annoying. He didn't want to talk. He just wanted to sleep. But he shook the thought away and grabbed the handset and listened.

"New York element," said the voice. "This is Air America Zero-Two, over."

"Zero-Two, this is New York One-Zero, over."

There was a pause, like the radio operator wasn't expecting to hear anyone.

"One-Zero, glad you're alright, break. Friendlies are on the way to come get you, break. A lot of 'em. I don't know who the hell you are, but they're sending the biggest formation of aircraft I've ever seen to come get you. Break. Sit tight. Rescue element will be landing soon. Over."

"Roger, I'll walk them in. What's their call-sign? Over."

"One-Zero, rescue element's call-sign is going to be *Icarus*. Over."

Brandon shook his head. Those boys were going to be disappointed when they learned their HVT was wasted. But Brandon wasn't going to kill their motivation by letting them know. He smiled. "Roger, Zero-Two. Copy all."

"Roger," the voice said. "Out."

EPILOGUE

The heads of the various Venus and Mercury operations sat at a glossy, wooden table in an air-conditioned conference room.

When the man at the head of the table asked for a report on the Vietnam operation, a thin man in a suit and glasses laid an orange and white manila folder on the table and opened it and said, "The commander of the operation was not immediately forthcoming. He was resistant to enhanced interrogation methods, retreating into some sort of extreme meditative state."

"Did you ever convince him to talk?"

"Eventually, sir. Yes. Although we had to agree to some, ah, requests."

"*Requests.*"

"Yes, sir. The interpreter and his family, we are expediting their immigration and citizenship paperwork. We are also providing a housing allowance and seed capital for a small business when they arrive in Seattle."

"Fine. Anything else?"

"A retroactive battlefield promotion for the medic to Master Sergeant and immediate retirement with one-hundred percent service-connected disability."

"Fine. And what did the commander ask for?"

"Nothing, sir."

"Nothing."

"No, sir. When we provided confirmation to the commander that his requests would be honored, he agreed to talk. The information he provided was fascinating…"

When the briefing was concluded, the man at the head of the table turned to the other men. "Those of you with dry holes, start looking elsewhere. Immediately."

Then he pointed and listed off men according to their areas of operation. "Honduras, Iraq, and Nepal, get with Vietnam and see if our new asset can shed some light on your discoveries.

Made in the USA
Middletown, DE
23 February 2021